AL~~EX~~

Sidney Knight

www.sidneyknight.com

For Tina
Never change.

ACKNOWLEDGEMENTS

My thanks go out to Helen Falner for granting me clearance (many a time) into her place of work in order to gain insight into the catering business for the purposes of this book. If there are any errors in this regard, she is not to blame. Her ability to put up with my many questions was truly remarkable.

Thanks to my family and friends for their support, my father in particular for listening as always, my proof readers, Gillian, Cathy and Maureen, my editor, Kate, for her brutal honesty, my wife for her patience (and brutal honesty, likewise), and to Steve who worked his magic wonderfully, managing to design the perfect cover from a few terrible sketches I provided.

And finally, to the monster I allowed to come forward from the back row. Without him, this book would not have been possible.

CONTENTS

PROLOGUE

Wednesday, 9 June 2010

Every day was filled with pain now. It was relentless. Constant. Killing him.

Death was what Ed Dorne wanted. But what then? What *then?* Where would he find himself? Hell? Was *that* what waited? He had never been religious – but something had flooded in since the killings. Maybe it was God? *Who knew?*

But if this God, this entity, did exist – and the devil likewise – then Ed himself was certainly a ticket holder for damnation. Of this he was sure. Because he was a man who had done worse than murder. He was a man who had said nothing. And that silence had caused death. Death to many. Men. Women. Mothers. Fathers.

Of course, the police must have already known. And his arrest was probably just hours away now, wasn't it? They'd surely be coming for him, banging at the door before the day was through.

The house was empty. Silent. But there was no peace in the kitchen where he sat. Though he was alone, it didn't feel that way. He felt company – the company of other Ed Dornes forever staring.

His hands found the six-day-old newspaper and slid it beneath the unfocused vision of his helplessly glazed eyes. When clarity returned, they saw the tabloid was still open at the same double-page feature of its headlined article.

He forced himself to read it. Again.

HAMPSHIRE'S CHIEF OF POLICE: "HE MUST'VE WANTED THEM ALL DEAD."

DECEASED killer Alex Merton has ensured even more deaths continue.

Yesterday afternoon, The King's Royal Hospital was inundated with hundreds of people from the Safe Insurance call centre in Vulnham.

Investigators have strongly urged all staff who consumed anything on Tuesday 1st June to undergo full examination and toxicology testing, even if they *didn't* purchase their food or drink from the building's lunch hall.

Hampshire Constabulary has issued a statement warning of the EXTREME seriousness of the situation.

"Members of Safe Insurance staff who consumed anything on the day in question, whether solid or liquid, cannot afford to take any unnecessary risks. Even something as simple as the water dispensing machine could have been infected."

The King's Royal Hospital itself has been criticised for banning family and friends from visiting potential new victims of sadistic killer, Merton.

A hospital spokesperson stated: "Staff are already under increasing pressure, having to respond to this critical incident involving all of the emergency services in a co-ordinated response. As the number of people needing clinical tests increases, the risk of fatalities is apparent and real. It is with regret and compassionate understanding that the hospital is obliged to turn away visitors of those involved in the tragedy.

"We must remind the public that we have an ongoing responsibility to those other patients who remain in our care during this intense period."

Evidence

Monster Merton, 25 – who ended his life just days ago by slashing his wrists after murdering presumed girlfriend, Layna, 24 – has been confirmed as the perpetrator due to new evidence found on Wednesday 2nd June.

It was a large—

But Ed had to stop, his eyes closing for a brief moment. He always stopped at that point. At that very word.

He flicked weakly through a half-dozen more pages, but soon found himself holding the phone to his ear about to call up the paper's *CASH FOR YOUR STORIES* number. After one ring, he heard a young man's voice say: 'Daily Reporter, what's your story please?'

'Yes, h-hello,' Ed answered, his words beaten, broken. He wiped away the sadness as it began to pour from his eyes again. 'I...I have a story. For you.'

'Great, what is it please and who's calling?'

'Surname...Dorne.'

'And the story?'

But Ed couldn't speak anymore. His throat was constricted. Lungs breathless.

His grip on the phone gradually weakened, and seconds later it fell to the table with a thud, the voice on the other end of the line still talking. Ed closed his eyes, feeling lost in more than just the darkness behind them. He was alone. So alone. Now living in an empty place, a deserted town in ruins, its welcome signpost devoid of a name.

So terrifyingly blank.

PART 1

From Josephine Lexington's *Merton: Discovering the Invisible Man*:

Within the last two weeks of Alex's life, there are notable differences throughout his journal entries. Though his perceived enemies were still conveyed as an indiscernible mass (*Them*), the mention of two individuals in particular – who were to be his final victims – also suddenly begin to appear:

"And after the others choke on the bile they've been spewing over my kind for years, I'll be coming after you, Sam. Oh how I'll enjoy watching the life bleed from your eyes as your soul drops like a rock to hell. And then I'll be coming after you, Layna. You'll be the last on my list. I want to enjoy you the most. And I will. But I still wonder: will my knife be sharp enough to puncture the layers of filth and decay that encase your heart? Oh I hope it will be. I really do."

1

The ten storey office block was buried beneath the dark cloak of early January, yet to be relieved by the morning's awakening sun. At its roof level the bold letters of SAFE INSURANCE stood proudly.

The gun metal four-by-four raced through the car park below, finally swinging into space 257. Sam Henderson stepped out, pressed the button on his key and two intermittent beeps followed. He was soon walking along the pathway to the reception entrance, looking briefly up at the building, the place he belonged and felt best. He was still feeling the hangover which was strangely lingering and quite a bitch even into the second day. But even though it drained on his mood a little, he was nonetheless fully able to make the transition from Party Animal to Head Chef before entering the building.

The entire Ground Floor past Reception had existed as a massive food court to serve the company's many mouths ever since the building had been constructed for the Safe Insurance workforce. The original up-and-coming catering company, Refiul, which originally had the honours a few years back, had buckled under the pressure of such a high number of customers based throughout the ten storeys. After just six months, the many customers who'd once flooded the food court at breakfast and lunch times had diminished to but a few, with the majority opting to either make their own lunches or find them elsewhere. And it was at the time of Refiul's collapse that Sestern had stepped in confidently and secured the lucrative contract, having fought off the other catering companies hoping to prosper from the Vulnham City site on England's south coast.

Sestern had already been an established catering company with its various facilities planted in many an office complex across the country, and had even begun to spread worldwide. It had been critically acclaimed for its quality of service and ability to cope with the heavy populations in which it operated. It targeted mainly medium to large-sized institutions like Safe Insurance, and since setting up there six years ago had completely rejuvenated the ground floor, accumulating an average of two thousand five hundred transactions per day. Its many food stations provided hot food and self-service, live action, and the ever-popular retail and Rocsi coffee hubs.

Sam now strode through the main corridor with a *don't fuck with me* look on his face, the look which always appeared when walking alone – though he hadn't noticed it in years. After reaching the double doors and making his way through into the food court, he glanced around at a few of the minions, each busy in their allocated tasks. One was cleaning behind the hot food service counter, one was stocking the sandwich bar, one was opening a small box of sugar sachets in the Rocsi station, and another was pushing a trolley with saucers and ramekins on it, headed in Sam's direction. As this one got closer, it greeted him with a smile and said 'Hey, chef.' Sam looked at it with disgust, and muttered a sarcastic '*Hey*' back before pushing the door open into the kitchen.

He could tell within seconds what the state of play was inside, almost smelling, feeling the aura of the place, how it was running. Everything.

'Hel-lo people!' he bellowed theatrically. '*Hello, hel-lo!* Guess who's here? *It is I!*'

They all, except for one, greeted him back.

He then turned to *that* one, Alex Merton, the kitchen porter minion in the corner who hadn't said a word, and shouted over at him: '*And you can shut up an' all!*'

The other chefs laughed.

Alex, as Sam expected, didn't reply or even flinch, carrying on washing up amongst the piles of dirty pots as if not having heard him. But Sam knew he had.

Stupid minion, he thought. *A little more…? Yes.*

And of course, he did give some more, asking him the same question he always did each morning: 'Still not talking, faggot?'

A little more.

'What are you like, eh? *What-are-you-like?*'

He then noticed something different about Alex, though – something he hadn't seen before. What was it? He was the *same old* faggot, *same old* minion. And the guy still hadn't said a thing as always, had he? But there *was* something.

Wait. Hang on. Was he...was he angry? He *was*, wasn't he? *Real pissed even!*

Well done faggot! he thought. *Well done indeed!*

A little more...?

No   Sam knew his fun time was up and that he had to move his arse about the place now. It was going to be a busy old bitch today, what with being a chef down and all. There would be lots going on in the kitchen, the office, and not to mention attending to the big dogs when they came down later, who would want to surely flap their robotically-hinged tongues some more, never content with the current menu, prices, layout of the food court and general processes of the business – basically any bloody thing or system they could destroy with their own moronic *suit-side-of-the-line* ideas.

He just loved those guys.

Sam started himself up and got to work quickly, satisfied enough from knowing the kitchen mouse in the corner had been played with. In his mind's eye, he could see the sparkling lights which awaited him. Vegas wasn't far away now. And soon after his flight took off tomorrow morning his long weekend vacation would begin.

He glanced back at the mouse again, finding it hard to resist the urge.

A little more?

Just one more...?

No. Later.

***

It had just gone 2:00pm. Alex Merton was on his break, sitting facing the wall in the corner of the food court, eating his lunch. Behind him, the many once-occupied tables were almost deserted, with only a handful of customers remaining. The place could've looked ever so close to being clinical had it not been for the thin lines of the well-known strong Sestern colours of orange and red which ran across its walls.

He was adding the final touches to the sketch he'd been working on for the past couple of days, and was about to slip into one of his dream-like visions to gain him access into the scene his pencil was creating. And to do this, he would have to recite the words from his—

'Hey there,' spoke a soft voice from behind.

Shit! He knew who it was, and as he felt the presence of the woman, he instinctively shut his sketch book, slamming his hand down on the cover, a twisting torment soon ripping through his insides. He'd already seen her once last week, but it didn't matter – she was one of *Them*, part of the same group as everyone else. He wanted to show all of *Them* his sketches, shove them right in their faces, plaster them all over the walls of the place.

(*But you can't can you? You're just going to sit there like a good boy. Go on, eat your lunch now. Good boy. Good, good boy…*)

And as he felt his inner voice beating at him from within, patronising through its hideous, rancorous malice, one side of his jaw locked, his teeth jamming, grinding together.

He knew the woman had just been sent over again as part of a joke, so he didn't even bother turning around, just as he hadn't done last week. And he wouldn't have acknowledged anyone else for that matter either – no matter who they were. He didn't need to speak to anyone. And what was the point in trying to communicate with these people? What was the point? Why waste breath on *Them*? Why waste *anything* on *Them*? He knew she'd been told to come over and talk to him, anyway, and that it was just part of a prank, another *one*, another *wind-up*, *piss take*, and that some people or *someone* was fucking with him, *again*, and he didn't know why and it didn't matter and he wasn't going to turn around and acknowledge her and give them all the satisfaction of seeing him fall for it. They were all going to whisper and laugh and have a *good-old-good-old* time on him, weren't they? *But fuck them, fuck them all!* They can burn in the flames of hell, can't they? *Fuck* whoever had planned it…the kitchen, customers, food court staff – *whoever it was.*

It wouldn't be like this forever, though, he told himself.

Not much longer.

(*don't have the balls to do anything about it though do y—*)

14

Again the woman's words cut in against his thoughts, causing his frustration to boil over even more.

What does she want? Can't you see I'm busy! I'M BUSY! ME! LEAVE ME ALONE! I KNOW IT'S A PRANK OR WHATEVER – SO JUST-LEAVE-ME-ALONE!

***

'Do you mind if I sit here with you again...that is, if there's enough room?' Layna asked jokingly, knowing that apart from the chair the guy was sat on, all the seven others at the table were empty. She smiled at the back of his head, standing with her lunch tray, telling clearly from the silence that ice-breakers weren't going to make a lot of difference here. 'Hope you don't mind,' she said, and sat down opposite.

She looked across at him briefly, watching as he continued to ignore her presence and keep a firm hand upon the sketchpad. *Nobody's getting a look at that thing are they?* she thought, as her eyes cast over the thick black cover with interest.

But Layna badly wanted to see it. She'd caught a glimpse of one of the sketches while looking over his shoulder last week in a scene which had unfolded just as this one was now. Back then, she'd sat with him because she'd been the new girl working in the food court. The staff she'd already met hadn't been on the same lunch break time as her, and so after searching the room, she'd found this guy right in the corner (in the very same place) and joined him, sharing the same *in-depth conversation*. And had it not have been for the talent she'd seen flowing through his artist's hand, illustrating those gorgeous lines upon the page, she probably wouldn't be back sitting there again now.

Layna knew that was the main reason. But apart from that...why else was she sat there, exactly? The guy hadn't even spoken to her *once* for Pete's sake!

She tried breaking the silence with: 'I still don't have a clue what I'm doing in this place yet! When I was serving people earlier, they kept asking me so many questions about the food and things, and I had to just keep asking the kitchen. I felt so stupid! I'm all over the place, I'm telling you!'

But only silence answered her.

Why was she *still* sat there? Anyone else would've moved on, told him how rude he was and left, got out of there, pointed a finger – or even held one up. So why? Why was she there?

She just didn't know. And only knew there was something about him that she could *see* or *feel*. Something had made her come back, and it wasn't just the damn drawings – those...*beautiful drawings*.

Still the silence prevailed, and as she studied his face, she noticed it was different from last week. He didn't seem nervous at all now. There was...nothing. Just nothing. But...then again, there was possibly anger, or something more blunt along those lines in his eyes. Something was hurting him, perhaps?

'So you draw a lot, then? I can tell you do. I actually do some drawing myself. Well...more painting, really. Photography's my main thing, though. But I...can't draw anything like *that*. You have talent there. I got a glimpse just now when I came over. Maybe I could have a little look?' His hand pushed down harder on the sketchpad. 'So...' she went on smiling, '...I think you're gonna have to tell me your name soon if we're gonna carry on having these conversations...'

There was a further silence, but then something happened: the guy finally spoke his first word to her.

'Alex,' he breathed, still staring at his plate that had been empty for a while. The voice which had spoken the word was almost rigid, mechanical, but at the same time somehow full of the darkest depths of human emotion, of gnarled discomfort and pain.

Layna smiled inside, feeling pleased with her progress, but soon wondered why the word *progress* had even entered her mind – as if she were a shrink trying to make progress with her patient.

She knew it wasn't like that at all, though. It was *something* else.

The two of them sat in silence till 2:30pm, with Layna never coming any closer to seeing the sketches she knew without a doubt would overwhelm her senses.

'Right, better make my way back I guess,' she said, getting up from the table. 'See ya later, Alex. Maybe you can show me some of those drawings some other time.'

She expected to hear nothing back in return. But as she started to walk away, her ears then picked up on the mumbled words of perhaps a 'see ya' from behind.

Alex was back in the room commonly known as The Wash Up. He was filling to the brim with hatred because yet again that bastard customer, whoever it was (who was going straight to fucking hell), had positioned their plate deliberately in that *specific oh so purposeful way* on the plate tray trolley just so it had been hanging *just a little too much over the edge*, so that when Alex had wheeled it away from the wall in the food court, the plate had fallen off and smashed into *lots of lovely little fucking pieces – again –* and then, of course, everyone had stared at him *– again –* and then they'd all laughed *– again.*

Thank you everyone, he now thought. *Thank you all so much – you fucking disgusting scum!*

Here in The Wash Up, in this separate room, he was away from the kitchen and food court. And this was how he liked it. Isolation. On his own. Alone.

He thought for a moment about the woman who'd sat with him at lunch, wondering why she'd come over a second time. He tried to remember her name, but soon realised he didn't care, and didn't want to remember *anyone's* name anymore. For why bother? *They* were *Them. Them* were *They.* All the same. They didn't have names to him, and they all looked the same now too, all merging into a poisoned congealed mass, all coming from the same stuff, spawning from the birth pool of assimilation, every one of them a product of the same sickening bile.

The industrial dishwasher was a huge piece of machinery that covered the wall's length in front of him. As he pushed the plates along the conveyor belt, sending them through the gaping metal mouth and into a fifteen-foot tunnelling belly of steaming high-pressured water jets, the machine made a thunderous roar. Some of the staff called it The Dragon for this very reason. Alex often imagined pushing each and every occupant of the building through it, wondering if their filth would get removed, but usually found himself wondering more whether any of them could actually make it to the other side – alive – or, how badly burnt and disfigured they would have become. The screaming would be unbelievable, wouldn't it? It would be deafening as they incessantly scrambled through the long shaft, manoeuvring over the various moving rods and pipes, getting stuck and caught up along the way, their skin scalding and blistering from the blasting water and relentless heat of The Dragon's breath, their hands shaking, maddened, desperately reaching ahead for the tunnel's end...

The high temperature and moisture from the machine filled the room's air to the usual thirty-two centigrade, an almost unbearable heat most people could not endure. The possibility of the doors ever being allowed open (which the Health & Safety bitch upstairs wouldn't budge on), or of an extractor fan or air conditioning being installed, didn't matter to Alex anymore. He was used to it. The physical didn't bother him. Not now. Pain was pain. Any physical discomfort felt would soon fade away once he'd left the room, as it would in any other situation. Physical pain was easy. It would always pass. All it needed was time – a ticking clock – and all you had to do was wait. Time always loses in the end. It never lasts.

Beside the dishwasher, across from the deep sinks which were part of the same unit, was the waste disposal, or in chef tongue, The Food Muncher – another great one, Alex always felt, for the wonderings of *what if?* in relation to a human's head being inserted into its merciless flesh-tearing teeth. On the opposite wall ran a stainless steel table, followed by shelving units and cupboards holding the various culinary implements for service of food and drinks, ranging from families of different sized china saucers, bowls, plates and cups, to silver jugs, heavy trays of cutlery, and coffee canisters. An ankle-high trolley sat facing the far end of the dishwasher, stacked with three tall piles of clean plates, missing one pile which soon would be built up. By its side sat another pile of clean lunch trays which had too passed through the machine.

Alex continued scraping the leftover food and rubbish into the bin from the stacked plate tray trolley he'd just wheeled in. He soon cringed, grinding his teeth as another piece of cutlery fell from the edge of a tray he'd pulled out. The fork bounced across the floor, *and of course*, into a place right beneath the dishwasher. As he was about to bend down to pick it up, he noticed in the corner of his eye another note on the trolley. It was folded and addressed with the words: *To Wash Boy*. There had been variations in the past that had addressed him as *Washer Boy*, *Dish Monkey*, *Wash Monkey*, and *Cock Washer*. The contents of the notes usually contained messages along the lines of: *If you want some extra work, you can wash my cock…in your mouth*, or *Hurry up…those dishes aren't going to clean themselves!* One time, a customer had even put on their tray a folded piece of used toilet paper.

Alex didn't bother reading today's note, just as he hadn't bothered with the others previous for many weeks – but seeing them nearly every day still sent a torrid blast of fury shooting through every vein in his body.

After picking up the fork, he returned to his feet, took a moment to breathe, and prepared to enter one of his dream-like visions again to lose himself. But before he did, he thought about the woman from lunchtime once more, even though the recollection of the scene lacked any real vividness, feeling like just another shadowy imprint in his mind. Why had she come over and stayed when he'd still said nothing? What did she really want?

And why was he even giving it a thought – *her* a thought?

He couldn't even remember her name, could he? Had she even told him her name, or had she given it last week?

A few questions. But none of them were worth thinking about, he concluded. They didn't matter. Her name didn't matter. And neither did she.

No one did.

He carried on with his work, soon starting to run on autopilot as his mind began to drift, getting lost in his imagination, ready to knock upon its door. When he entered, the picture of the scene he'd been sketching at lunch was brought to the foreground, and then in the background his mind's eye flew around his home, finding his desk, looking upon the single sheet of paper laid upon its surface, and finally its recently typed words which lifted off the page. The sketch and typed words merged together and he was living the scene, reciting the page's words exactly from the bank of lucidly recorded memories deep within:

The Long Road,
It's all dark like midnight – everywhere blackness is surrounding the lonely road. And they're all here, all in their cars, all waiting to drive home to their wonderful sickening lives. But they can't get there. The road on either end leads into darkness, no place. They are stuck, have nowhere to go. And

then I appear, all dressed in white at the front of the traffic. I face the first car, staring at the driver. She is scared, but this is just the start and she doesn't even know it. I glance up and over the line of traffic that runs way back for a quarter mile. It contains all the staff from Safe, Sestern, my family, and anyone else I've ever known who deserves to be here. And then I raise my weapons of choice in both hands, two pump-action shotguns, and they feel like a part of me, and they communicate, agreeing to do their job as painfully as possible. The first scream from the car in front begins it. The woman, the laughing one who's always fucking laughing, is screaming, pleading for her life, but I don't hear her or understand her poisoned mouth, all I see is bile and desperation oozing from the gaping hole in her face, and this is when I step up onto the bonnet and point both of my friends directly at her through the windscreen. She isn't laughing anymore. But I don't pull the trigger right away. I leave it for a moment while she struggles, trying to get out. But she can't. None of them can. They're all locked in their cars, sealed in their fate. By this time everyone's screams fill the whole road because they all know what's happening and are far beyond terrified, knowing what I'm going to do to them. 'Oh I'm here all right, and it's too late for your screams now,' I tell them. 'Now you'll see me. Now you'll see me. NOW YOU'LL SEE ME!' And I shout it and it travels down the whole road and their eardrums explode and blood pours down the sides of their faces. I pull the trigger on both weapons and the woman erupts, separating near enough in two, splitting vertically, and now the windscreen is just red. Gloriously red. Then I step down and continue walking along the pavement, moving up to the next car and see it's the glasses man, and I don't even stop to look at him while he wriggles around trying to escape. I just point one barrel in his side window and blow his head to fucking pieces. Then I carry on to the next car, and then the next, and then the next, blowing them all away, one by one, killing them, no mercy, just blood, and it flows from the car doors, filling the street in a rising red sea, and I just continue my work, never stopping and—

The scene was cut short by Sam who stuck his head in through The Wash Up door yelling '*DELIVERY FAGGOT!*', forcing Alex to return, to come back into reality. Alex chucked his wet gloves on the side and proceeded to the back door, mouthing the final words of the scene before they faded to nothing:

and I never stop. Never. Never. Never.

***

Alex stood in the Goods In corridor looking at the two heavy duty cage trolleys crammed with the dry and retail goods. His ever increasingly distracted and distant mind had forgotten all about the delivery and that it hadn't turned up earlier in the morning as it usually did. And now it finally had arrived – *fucking late* – and just in time to make *him* late, and of course, he would be leaving even later than usual because of it. It was going to put him back – *way back*.

He knew it would take a solid hour or maybe even longer to unload all their shit, and as he thought about it, a tsunami of rage flooded into him out of nowhere, crashing violently at the walls of his heart. He then felt breathless as if his lungs were freezing within a constricted rib cage about to cave inwards and shatter at any moment. It was a familiar feeling to him, a feeling he'd recently been experiencing even more, with shocking intensity.

The delivery was going to make him so late and nobody was going to help him and—

(*What are you going to do about it? Nothing. You're not going to complain are you? No balls have you? So just be a good little boy and get on with it…*)

For a few seconds his fists clenched, locking hard, his eyes closing.

After just over an hour later, he'd finished taking down the retail goods and was back in the dry store on his knees, unpacking the last remaining boxes of the various foodstuffs to be placed on the heavily loaded shelves in front. When he ripped viciously into the next one, he was startled, his limbs jerking like an electrical bolt had shot through them as Sam shouted '*HAVEN'T YOU DONE THAT YET?*' from behind.

Alex didn't answer and just remained on the floor looking at the half-opened box. And the head chef had expected this – but the silence from the kitchen porter wasn't from fear or intimidation this time. It was from something entirely different.

'I mean, anyone would think it was your first day on the job, *wouldn't they*?' Sam went on.

Still Alex's lips didn't move.

'Is it your first-fucking-day on the job? Mmm…?'

Alex had been filling with the slow building of an inferno for a few weeks up to this point, except no one had noticed. It had started with just a crackling light of kindling. But that very once small flame was no more. It had changed. Grown out of control. It was peaking. Sweltering.

And now his eyes were beginning to bulge, his body about to tremble.

He'd had enough of that man, enough of the chefs, the kitchen, the customers, the building – *the whole fucking place* – and his eyes just burned there as he remained mute, still on his knees, and he wanted to scream at the man, scream into his face and tell him what he was thinking, what he wanted to do to him and all of them. But he couldn't. And he knew he couldn't and wouldn't be able to, and so just stayed down there, the raging fire scalding in his chest and engulfing his heart, and soon he could almost feel it blazing in a circling ring all around him. His vision was nearly shaking as the man behind carried on spewing his eternal words of abuse, and he just wanted to hit Sam now, over and over and over, beat him to death with one of the heavy bean tins from up there on the shelf that could crush his handsome fucking face, smash his nose, knock his fucking teeth out, pummel his face into the floor, and just keep on hitting him until it was nothing, and just keep hitting him over and over and over and over and over and—

But he couldn't do any of that.

He couldn't do anything; instead not moving, unable to act, taking it all, taking everything, absorbing it, having every word injected like some noxious poison. And he was permitting it, allowing every word, and he knew it was the truth that he would do nothing and that he was simply paralysed there. His hands again turned to fists – fists wasted with nothing to destroy.

The man behind still persisted with his vicious, vindictive rants and gibes, and as he did, Alex just stared at the shelves in front, his

22

body still shaking, almost hallucinating as his vision became blurred, distorted.

'...and when you're done down there on your knees, grab a mop cos George has spilt a load of the old fryer oil tryin to get rid of it – tryin to do *your-job*. And how come you haven't done it already? I mean, what *exactly* have you been doing? You're-such-a-fuck-ing-burden. *You know that?* You're a burden on every one of us.'

After Sam then finally stopped, turned and left the dry store doorway to return to the kitchen, Alex exploded. He exploded like some kind of crazed, frenzied animal, his rage having nowhere else to go, having to get out, be released, and so he punched with all his weight at the shelf, and as he stared at the floor, he felt like he could burn a hole through it with the flaming torches that had become his eyes, and then it was all beginning to happen on the top shelf above as the violent force from his fist had caused movement around the large bean tins stacked three high, and then one of them was tipping over the edge, falling down from the great height, all three and a half kilos cracking hard onto the back of his head with the bottom of its metal rim, and as it cut deep into his scalp, the pain tore in with it, a thousand deafening screams of insanity erupting inside him, and then he knew that he had to smash the place up and destroy it and scream into the faces of everyone and go fucking crazy in there and—

But he couldn't.

He couldn't do any of that.

He couldn't...do...anything.

The blood slowly began to trickle through his hair, soon finding a moist brow of sweat, and before long, his tongue could taste it as a thick line of the warm liquid coursed to his lips, rolling into a dry corner of his mouth.

And then he knew.

He knew he had to do something, had to *really do something* this time, *destroy something* – something small, yes – something small he could start with, something that was...that was not human, but something *definitely loved*...and *fucking beautiful* as well. And that weekend, first thing Saturday, he would go to the place which flashed in front of his eyes, and then he *would* destroy it, destroy that something beautiful beyond recognition. He breathed in deeply, his eyes swollen with madness, and he knew it would feel good – *GOD,*

IT WOULD! – like a fucking drug, and he knew now that he had the balls to do it, to finally do something, to *take action*. And then once he had done it, he knew it would change him, make him rise to a new height, give him something, take him somewhere, and give him what he needed to finally *take things further*.

He continued to kneel there, thinking about all of this for the next ten minutes. The pain was there all right, but only in the physical sense, and he enjoyed the sensation, the erratic sharp bursts, like a serrated knife was playing the cut at the crown of his head like a violin. He was pleased, knowing anyone else could not endure such pain the way he was.

As Alex slowly got to his feet, an amusing thought then entered his mind, almost making him laugh. The thought was about reporting the injury. But it *wasn't* an injury, was it? His *real* injuries couldn't be written into some fucking accident log book, could they!

He made his way to the toilet to tend to his blood-streaked face and the slow steady drip of blood that was pattering at the back of his neck. But before he cleaned himself up, he stopped motionless. He stopped because he liked what he saw in the mirror. He liked the sight of his bloodied features.

It was like war paint – an indication of progress to the next level.

***

Up on the eighth floor of the building, the sullen eyes of Ed Dorne stared out the window. To say he was bored would be an understatement. And to say he was looking for nothing would almost be a lie. He was maybe looking for answers, a meaning, a message perhaps – that there *was* a point to it all.

But he'd received no answers as of yet and wasn't about to waste any more time doing so, and now, instead, decided to spend his time more productively – by thinking about absolutely nothing.

Dead brain time.

Maybe do a little daydreaming, perhaps?

No – that was always something he struggled with. He lacked the imagination for it, he always figured. Trances were better, however. They were his thing. And it was what he fell into next.

After ten minutes of hypnotic staring passed, he came back to when he noticed the rain gently spattering against the ceiling-height window by his side. The rain seemed lethargic to him, almost as if it too did not have the energy to release anything meaningful or of real substance, lacking the motivation even to cause a light shower. His eyes searched for something outside of interest – anything would do. *Anything* to take his mind off the never-ending, mind-numbing work that sat inside the computer screen upon his desk. It was waiting for him in there. All of it. Mocking him, saying; *that's it, clean my shit up, do your shitty work in your shitty little job…Ed.*

God he hated that two-letter word others had reduced his name to since childhood.

He glanced back at the screen, not even showing the usual contemptuous look this time, and blasted a thought right at it, saying it would have to fucking wait because he was busy doing nothing which was far more satisfying.

Then something outside did catch his eye – something boring, yes – but it *was* something, all the same, and an event of sorts. It was that four-by-four leaving the car park below. It was *that guy*, the head chef, the hot shot, the one who shagged around – and an awful lot, too (according to the building's loose tongue). Ed liked to believe rumours and, since first seeing the guy in the flesh years ago, had decided they were true about him – all of them, in fact.

His dreary eyes followed the vehicle as it sped through the car park. He pictured himself as a giant about to crush the tiny-looking vehicle into nothing, and was pleased with this peculiar train of creativity, knowing all he could usually envision was logic, stark reality and, well, numbers – *goddamn numbers*. And the useless things had gotten him nowhere. Why wasn't *he* shagging around like *Mr Four-By-Four* down there?

Again the thought came of his giant foot falling through the air and crushing the tiny car as it neared the exit. He even envisioned a little blood pooling out from the bottom of the wreck, surprising himself another time with what must have actually been imagination.

But the fantasy scene was of course meaningless, pointless, and seconds later, forgotten after disappearing into a smoky backstage room of his mind.

As the head chef neared the boom gate, his onlooker in the dark tower above looked down on him, scorning, thinking: *Aww, such a tough wittle life isn't it? How horrible that you can only manage a four-day trip to Vegas tomorrow. Aww, never mind. You have my sympathies...*

2

The thought tried to break in, gain access – find a way into Sam Henderson's mind. But it was short-lived, cut off, unregistered, and as always, unwelcome. Sam quickly poured more booze down his throat from the bottle of the strong stuff. The name across the label didn't ring any bells through his partially pissed vision, but it didn't matter – as long as it stopped the thoughts coming through, who cared? The only reason they had even started on their journey was because he'd sat alone for too long and not kept his mind active enough, therefore allowing himself *time to think*.

His subconscious told him to move, get up quickly and go do something. So he rose from the corner of the bed onto his feet. Back straight, shoulders set.

Mind wiped clean. Blank.

He glanced out the hotel window: Friday night, bright lights, Vegas.

Behind in the room, the sound of the running shower came back to him. It then stopped and Gaz could be heard stepping out the tub in the bathroom.

Sam turned around and called out: 'What are you *doing* in there?'

'Still trying to wash out the crabs your missus gave me...' answered the muffled voice through the wall.

'How can that be? You know you only fuck arse!'

'Well that's how she normally likes—'

'*Come on!*' Sam cut in. 'Get ready, we gotta meet them in twenty minutes! Gonna take fifteen to get there. You've got *five minutes!*'

'*All right, shit bag!* Be ready in five.'

Sam knew the guy couldn't be ready in five minutes, or even ten. Fifteen was a lot more likely.

'None of us are forgettin' tonight, birthday boy…but *you* might just wanna!' Gaz yelled, followed by a deranged animal noise.

Sam chuckled lightly to himself, then lay back on the bed, being mindful of his carefully wax-styled hair, and pulled out his mobile from his black stonewashed jeans as it began to buzz.

'ERE' E IS! IT'S THE BIRTHDAY BOYYYYY!'

The screeching voice on the other end of the line belonged to David Matersby, a.k.a. Winger, and its sheer tone made Sam wonder for a moment why he himself wasn't already *that* drunk. But hey, he knew there was plenty of time left to alter his own state of consciousness with drink, and if need be, the hard shit was still on the table – and that stuff could mess anyone's head up quick.

'WINGER, IT IS I!' Sam responded, looking up curiously at the cream ceiling, surprised to discover the whirly swirls of artex in such a modern-styled room.

'Where are you, Sam? Hotel still?'

'We are indeed.'

'Well get your arse down here! We got the mother of all tables, and we tipped off the door monkey – he's bringing anything that looks like hot meat straight to us. *So come on!'*

'Nice touch,' Sam said with an impressed delivery, though having already, again, more than half-expected the occurrence of his friend's ingenious idea.

Winger couldn't hear him over the bass of the club anymore, so ended the call with *'Just hurry up, I've got two huge tits sittin here beside me with two big' ol nipples with your name on' em, so get down here now!'* and after a short thinking pause, *'…and get Gaz out the fuckin bathroom or just leave the little princess there!'*

***

Sam looked at Gaz who was sat next to him in the rear of the limo. He was positioned like some rock star, his feet up, cigar in mouth, champagne bottle in one hand, and dick in the other as he began pissing into the ice tray which ran along the wall of the black leather upholstery.

'Jesus, Gaz!' Sam said, failing to convey his intended seriousness, his words rolling off his tongue with a heavy coating of amusement.

'Just piss in a glass! How obvious you wanna be? We can't be doin with gettin kicked out tonight.'

Gaz spluttered out a brief childish laugh that soon simmered to a chuckle before he explained: 'Dude, when you gotta go…'

Sam's attention then shifted as he caught a glimpse from his friend's window, realising just how little progress they'd made on their journey. '*Hey limo man!*' he shouted through the sixteen seat shaft to the back of the driver's head. 'It should take *ten minutes* to get to the hotel – we don't want a fuckin tour of Vegas, yeah?'

'This is the quickest way,' the driver explained, seemingly calm, but feeling offended by his passenger's tone all the same. 'The traffic's slowing us down.'

'*How long then, eh?*' Sam quickly stabbed back.

But the driver decided to say nothing.

Still pissing, Gaz joined in. '*Hey he's talk-ing-to-you! How long—*'

'TEN MINUTES OKAY!' the driver let out, his voice nearly breaking at the last word like a pubescent teenager no closer to being a man than a boy. His heart was thumping hard and his stomach was building into an uncomfortable frustration as he now, only four days into starting his new job – and life in the big city – felt a little afraid of, or at least intimidated, by the two passengers behind.

'*Wooooooohhh!*' followed from the back in a duet.

'Sod this, I'm not stayin here with this prick,' Sam said as if it were a public announcement. 'We're not even movin are we? *It's me birthday fa' cripes sake after all, me mateys!* He looked over to his friend. 'Come on, Gaz, we're goin'. We'll walk. Man can't drive for shit, anyways…'

'Come on guys – the traffic, *please,*' the driver tried his best to reason. 'Hey…*what are you doing? YOU CAN'T JUS—*'

'You had your chance,' Gaz said following Sam out the door. 'There's just a bit of a smell in here, you understand…'

Sam and Gaz both knew from experience the guy wouldn't chase them for the fare. Apart from the fact this particular driver had been unusual, and a wet pathetic pussy, it basically just wasn't worth his time. A driver would never leave the limo. The roads were too busy. The whole damn place was. It was Vegas – and besides, the night would be filled with endless fares to come for that prick.

Fifteen minutes later, they were both strolling through the casino looking for the entrance to the club, and as they did, their senses weren't overwhelmed by it all anymore; now used to the room, used to the clashing sound effects and light fest of thousands of blinking machines, the sounds of eager hands pulling down moneymaking arms, the desensitized faces of the dealers, the pacing legs of smiling skirts with trays of colourful drinks, the windowless walls without the time for a ticking clock, and the bewildering maze of isles that would lose a Vegas virgin carelessly.

Once the club was located, they walked straight to the front of the queue, gave their names, said who they were meeting, confirmed their admission had been paid, and when still told to join the back of the line like everyone else, both shook the door monkey's hand with a fifty.

Heavy shades of blue and purple lights danced with a menacing rhythm around the lengthy floor and high ceilings of the club, racing across the nearly bare white flesh straddling the dance poles on the high platforms. Beneath them, the writhing, perspiring bodies of the club-goers fused seemingly as one on the dance floor, their limbs tingling from the boom of the giant speakers while their lungs drank in the humid lust-filled air. Amongst the crowd, the eyes of Will Burston, a.k.a. Lobby, were staring at his meat, his chosen one – fuck for the night – and he wanted it, wanted that whore who massaged his stiff cock, pressing hard against it with her filthy arse. He looked at the back of his prize, its curvaceous body snaking from side-to-side. He bit and sucked at her fingers as she caressed his neck, and thought about how she was going to be his, and how the dirty cock-tease would later get everything she deserved, hard and fast in her throat, and then he grabbed her arm and pulled her around and—

'Excuse me, would you please leave this lovely young lady alone?' Sam asked comically from behind, clasping a hand upon his friend's shoulder.

Will turned around quickly, still possessing animal in his eyes, having not heard the voice or its intentions clearly, and was ready to fight, argue, or do whatever was necessary. The drink made it hard to focus on Sam for a second, but when clear, he threw out an arm and pulled him in close. *'If it isn't the one and only!'* he shouted through a grin. *'Sam, this is Vanessa.'*

Before shaking her hand gently, Sam deliberately acted surprised by Will's roughness, knowing that there was potential meat in the form of Vanessa; but something told him this wasn't actually her name – although he knew Will's chances of a fuck would've been far from impossible, even after a blunder like that.

'*Happy birthday ol' boy!*' Will's slurred words continued. He looked back over his shoulder at the tits of his meat and up to her face without her noticing. 'Today's his thirty-fifth!' he told her.

'*Wow, is it?*' the meat said, displaying a rehearsed in-front-of-mirror-smile, showing as many of her gleaming white-capped teeth as possible.

'Why don't you leave this young lady alone, and come have a drink with us?' Sam said steadily to his friend. 'This girl is far too young…and pretty, to be dancing with the likes of you, I'm sure.' He gave a quick glance over to the meat who looked back, her eyes giving off a bashful innocence. 'I mean, how old are you…twenty-one, twenty-two?' he asked, knowing she was a minimum of twenty-eight and nothing less.

'Ha, come on…!' she giggled, not being able to hold back a natural big smile this time. 'A lady cannot reveal such things!' She was loving the man's well-spoken words (and of course, his English accent) and his pretty-boy-yet-marginally-rough features. He could have anyone in the place and she knew it. Realising her eyes were still staring at him, she then quickly turned them back to Will who was now looking with fixated intrigue at her teeth.

Sam smirked. 'Right, come on friend, we're over th—'

'I'm going to the little boy's room, I'll be right over,' Will told him about to walk off. Before he did, he glanced back at the meat and said: 'Nice teeth, but…I could've done better.'

After he was gone, Sam apologised. 'Sorry, he's a dentist. He means no offence.'

'Oh,' she happily shrugged off, seemingly unfazed. 'No problem at all!'

'It was nice to meet you, anyway,' Sam said before turning to find the others. 'Take care.'

'No – *keep me company!*' the meat quickly pleaded. 'Why don't you have a dance with me before you go see your friends?'

Sam looked away, his face turning coy. 'Oh, I would love to, really, but I can't. My friends – I have to get back, you see. Maybe later. Enjoy your evening.'

She gently touched his arm as he was about to turn away again, and said: '*Please*...just one dance.' She put on her best salacious big-eyed stare with an additional bite of lip, bringing both hands up to his shoulders. 'My friends haven't arrived yet,' she made up. 'Just till they get here, maybe?' And then she reeled off another lie: 'My friends bet me I couldn't find a cute well-spoken English guy and dance with him...'

'But you already did,' Sam assured her. '*Will*. He's English.'

'But not well-spoken,' she said slowly. 'Or cute...'

'Listen, um,' Sam started, letting out a long breath while gently removing her hands which were now making their way down toward the top of his chest, her lengthy false nails gently making tiny circles on his shirt. 'I really can't stay any longer, I'm sorry. But my friend, Will – he'll be back later, I promise. And he *is* well-spoken. Trust me. One or two drinks have just added an extra little something to his diction, that's all. But you're in good hands. He's a good guy. And I can tell he likes you.'

He walked away, leaving the meat alone, a new body rubbing itself up against her within seconds. When she again started to dance, she was left thinking: *But I don't want Will. I want* you *Sam. You're a nice guy. I can tell...you're* genuine. *Come back. Oh please come back...*

Sam walked away thinking: *Easy. She would've been so ee-zy.*

He made his way back through the crowd toward Winger and Gaz who were seated at the table, its surface shiny with tall misty bottles of expensive vodka surrounded by short stumpy glasses and a bucket of ice. Soon, all four friends were sat together, their laps all straddled by their own piece of meat.

***

As they partied on into the early hours of Saturday morning, back in England Alex Merton was already awake, already at the very place where he hoped to find himself his something loved and beautiful.

3

At 10:00am, the overweight centre attendant Malcolm said to the silent man: 'He's actually a lucky little fella, ya know.' He pulled a baby face at the puppy stood on its hind legs in the paddock beside him. Its heart was pounding, eyes glowing with hope. 'Yeah, came to us just under a week ago, comin from a nice little family livin not far from here, in fact. Had him for just over a month and then, *you know* – we get a lot of that, believe me. They brought him here unscathed, nice little life, just not the right time for the family. And that's that. That's how you got here, isn't it, cutie!'

He looked back at the man to his side for some kind of response, but his expression still hadn't changed. That hard-locked face had been consistent ever since he'd arrived an hour ago, fixed throughout every viewing of cell-after-cell of stacked canine. Malcolm was usually able to spark life into the best of those who visited the Vulnham City Canine Rescue Centre, but knew his bubbly words just weren't cracking *this one*. And in realising this and feeling a little uncomfortable in the man's presence, he looked submissively away back to the puppy. 'So, er, you interested at all…mister?' he tried.

No response. The two men remained standing in the gangway, the barking of every long-serving inmate filling the damp air.

But then the man moved over, looking down deep into the eyes of the small furry creature. And while he did, Malcolm took a moment looking into the eyes of the man, quickly doubting there was little in the amount of thoughts passing through the mind behind that blank canvas.

'*Mister…?*'

The man slowly reached out a hand, and Malcolm, though it wasn't reaching in his direction, shuffled a little to the side, feeling slight unease. The hand went into the cage and reached down, touching the head of the tiny puppy, its eyes instantly lighting up in a fire of excitement, changing from hope to a warm pleasure. The fingers began to scratch its crown gently, drawing out a wide hot tongue which pressed against the cold metal woven bars.

The puppy had become a lonely, saddened creature from living in the old rundown building. It had felt scared in the bitterly cold noisy nights, curled up and afraid in a corner of its steel-barred enclosure, missing with desperation its previous owner and, though short, pampered life. And now, it did not care that the man's face failed to show any of the warmth or emotion of the ones it had once known. Because *now*, it only cared about the possibility of freedom, the outdoors – a better place.

'He seems to like you,' Malcolm said, carrying traces of angst. 'That's always a good—'

'Was this animal loved?' the man's quiet voice interrupted.

An awkward expression hit Malcolm's face. It was an unusual question; not so much the question itself, but in the way in which it was asked, asked in a strange kind of way he couldn't quite understand. 'Yes, I believe so. As I said, it was—'

'How do you...know?' the man said cutting him off again. There was still little volume, but the words were direct, seemingly forced out as if speech itself was painful.

'Well...' Malcolm struggled, '...the family was very—'

'Were they...*upset*...to see it go?'

'Yeah, I mean...yes, they were definitely sad to see the little guy leave. They really didn't want to let' im go, and I think...even the little girl cried a little.' He stopped talking. He was confused, not knowing quite what to say or how to act in front of this person.

But then something happened: the man finally made eye contact, and as his face almost lit up with a small grin, he asked 'And *you* love him, too?'

Malcolm's fat face changed back to its old chirpy way as a reassuring amount of relief entered. The man before him was wearing an identifiable human emotion, and though not in abundance, Malcolm felt comfort; enough to reach the decision that the man no longer posed a threat to him or his friends, the dogs.

'Oh yes, of course!' Malcolm replied joyfully, his yellowing black-rooted teeth showing through a smile. 'We *all* do here! How could you not love that little guy? I mean, look at that face. How could you say no to that *little face?* And ain't he a *handsome little thing?*' He raised a hand to his mouth as if to conceal his words from the other dogs present and whispered: 'He's a little easier on the eye than some of the other mutts we got in here, too, don't ya think? He's a pure bred – don't tell the others I said so, though, will ya?' A wink finished the joke, but he soon felt guilty about his hurtful words toward his canine friends. 'No, but seriously – we love all the dogs here. No one's more special than the next!'

The man barely nodded in response, his eyes trailing back to the floor. His face was devoid of emotion again. Blank. Numb.

But it didn't bother Malcolm anymore, because he was only thinking good things now, thinking that sure this guy was more than a tad weird and had given him the creeps a bit, but so had a lot of the people who'd walked through the centre's doors in the past. And they'd all turned out to love their dogs more than anything, which he'd found out later when he'd called in on them at their homes (it wasn't something the centre permitted as routine exactly, but was something he liked to do himself all the same). He only had to reflect on his own lonely life and home, which was overrun with his own *dog friends* – all human substitutes of course – and this thought alone, as always, was enough to make him decide that he had no right to judge *this man*, or any other. *Some dog people*, he always thought, *can just be a little weird...*

'So you ain't gonna tell me you ain't interested now, right?'

'I'm interested,' the man replied, his eye contact long gone.

'Great! *That's great news!* I love it when the little guys only have to spend a little time in here, and then before they know it...they're outta' here!'

The two talked for a while longer against the background barking, discussing what was needed, though the man barely spoke any words, still mostly just nodding. They filled in forms and followed procedure, and not long after, Malcolm was waving goodbye from the entrance to the man and his new happy companion as they both drove away together.

***

'That's it, enjoy it while you can, cos you aren't gonna be here much longer,' the puppy's new owner said, feeling the sharp tugs on the lead. The little dog scampered along through the freshly cut grass of the park, its curious wet snout running in all directions.

It was excited. Very excited.

So desperate to explore, it was now willing to temporarily choke itself against the collar, and when it felt the sweet release from the lead, its short stubby legs managed to spring forward in an explosive movement, the small furry creature not knowing where it was or going, but knowing at least that it had one thing: Freedom. The two played together in the fast-fading light of the January afternoon, owner chasing, dog running, owner throwing ball, dog fetching, owner assuring the dog it was safe. Safe with him.

And the puppy did feel safe, and, saved now, back in good times, running free through the magnificent bristly green stuff it hadn't seen for so long. It had someone to take it out, to care for it. And whoever it was didn't matter – because that person had granted *freedom*.

The man eventually had to come to a halt, panting. He'd chased the dog and thrown the ball again and again for close to two-and-a-half hours. Something important had been achieved, though: the dog seemed to feel happy, secure, and most of all, Loved.

The darkness was beginning to takeover, but the remaining light, with help from the lampposts' amber bulbs running along the footpath, allowed yet another park-strolling couple to stop and admire the furry ball of fun. Now back on the lead, the puppy had reached a standstill, finally resting with tired, aching limbs. Its tail persisted to show a keen sprightliness, however, from being petted by the new admirers making the familiar sounds of '*awwwwww!*' and '*look at you!*' and '*ooohhhh, what a beautiful dog!*'

The man welcomed the attention it was getting, making him feel certain he'd picked the right one; one that was loved by others – a lot, by *all* it seemed – and one that people spilled with affection over, without judgement, and would certainly love if it were their own.

Once the gleeful couple had moved on, he knelt down, stroked the dog's head, and said it was time. Time to leave. Time to go home.

The flat was without any trace of light. And even if it were at an hour of day when the sun had been present, any external rays would've struggled to have made their way in through the thick curtains. Even though the flat would be empty for another ten minutes before the man and his dog returned, the place, behind the blanket of darkness, was not without life. In the lounge there were many things breathing. They lived within the many different sized square and rectangular-shaped glass tanks which were stacked upon every wall of the lounge, shelf-upon-shelf, level-after-level up to the ceiling, almost covering the room's entire perimeter. The inhabitants of the moist humid tanks were still, motionless – except for the fangs of one that were drinking, extracting the fluid from an unfortunate locust which had walked straight into the path of the bristly dinner-plate-sized creature. It was the owner's favourite, named Laura. Other neighbours above and below, and on each wall, were mostly cold-blooded, scaled and un-scaled, either possessing four legs or none at all, the latter of which relying on a coiling motion and or a slimy underbelly to travel over the earthy ground of their enclosures.

Soon, outside in the second floor hallway, Alex's tense hand turned the key in the door. As he pushed it open, the smell of the place hit the puppy's snout, awakening its tired eyes in an instant.

The feeling had flooded back. And it had come on strong, heavy, with a great, great power, like a ram-rod banging incessantly at the door of his mind. Something was wrong. Very wrong.

Even though he felt the ability to butcher the damn thing and send it into a frenzied drawn-out execution, it was as if something had also drained away, gotten lost, faded out.

The little dog looked up at him with its confused eyes while he held it down on the kitchen worktop. In the air above, the knife continued to shake in his other hand. His breathing was laboured, body wet with perspiration. The clock's sharp echoing second hand continued to slice through every thought.

His feet remained planted, his eyes repeating the never-ending process of looking back-and-forth between the knife and the face of the creature that frequently let out soft baby-like cries while its limbs pawed at his veining arm. His vision was blurring, mind swirling in a tornado of twisting incomprehensible whispers and screams. But there was one clear thing about them which he was more than aware of: they had so far managed to stop him from killing the animal.

Maybe he'd waited too long? Maybe the visit to the park he'd made, in order to earn the affection of the dog before killing it, had taken too much time?

With every minute he let melt away, he knew weakness was creeping in. He was losing the higher strength, the very thing he had acquired. And it was losing out to another part of him he thought had left, been killed in the past unequivocally from a time that seemed so long ago. It was plaguing this new power, stabbing, causing it to recoil into its armoured shell, and it wouldn't let his hand come down with the knife and do it – just fucking do it! – and bring about the puppy's demise.

Another half-hour passed, the salty taste of sweat now infinite in his dehydrated mouth. There were constant screams inside an ongoing war of voices which bounced off the walls of the room, and he was being told to do it, do it, do it, *do it now*! But the quieter voices were controlling the waves and calming the building of the tsunami, and they were winning, then they weren't, then they were, then they weren't, then they were. The headache came next, and he was hardly blinking at all, just staring with bloodshot eyes at the dog and then the knife, then the dog, then the knife again, and everything else had become blurred around the edges, and he was stuck in that moment, but then he screamed, breaking away his locked stare, screaming into the kitchen that harboured only an empty loneliness and the tick-tocking of the pale-faced clock. He threw the knife across the room, freeing the frantically squirming animal, and yanked open the cupboards, sending their contents flying and smashing against the floor. The dog cowered in a corner, its whimpers growing even higher in pitch as it watched its owner search for something else to destroy.

But there was nothing left.

Nothing left now to be smashed or broken.

He'd already destroyed the few plates, bowls and cups that had fed and watered him for the past seven years – the implements that kept the heart of his lonely, unfulfilled single life beating. And he felt so helpless, standing there sweating, panting, so unable to act, and he just couldn't do it, kill the dog, do the very thing he felt would help him gain so much *back* from the world.

He breathed in deeply, pressing his palms against the worktop, and then collapsed on the floor as the tears began to break out. He knew the feeling was coming back, pushing its way into his skull. It was as if the rage had never been there – like some kind of switch had seamlessly taken place.

And then he was on his knees, bent over, head buried in his hands. The voices were firing, ricocheting off the walls of his mind. It was now that he blamed himself. For everything. He knew he was useless, weak, and not just because he'd failed to end the dog's life. It was all him. He was the one who should have never been, and everyone else was right. *They* were right. It was him who was the mistake, the square wheel, the alien, the one…*the burden* on the world.

But he had a little fight left to challenge these thoughts, and so a conflicting chaos ensued. The exploding fireworks soon took their toll, turning his throbbing headache into a migraine. He tried desperately to defend himself against the thousand-voice army and disappointed faces in the room taunting him time and time again.

He couldn't do it, though. Not anymore. Because his strength was dying, being swallowed into a bottomless sinkhole within. He would never make anything of himself, he knew. Never could his talents gain any success, never could his art achieve anything or be looked upon with praise. It would always be his, and everything he ever made would be a product of him, a product that *They* would loathe and push aside with disgusted faces. *They* could never love anything he did, or ever look at him in the way they would at *normal* people – in that way…that *special way*. He would always be ignored, living in the shadows, dying alone without understanding.

And did he even *deserve* understanding? Did he deserve *anything*? What could he offer a world that could never listen to or notice him? *Their* voices were right.

Every one of them.

His family were now in the room, and so was everyone from work, school, and all the rest – and they were *all* right about him.

He was nothing.

Not welcome.

Should never have been.

4

Alex hadn't made it into work that day. He'd tried to – but he just couldn't do it anymore.

He sat in the middle of the lounge at his desk, with only the screen of his laptop boring a square white hole through the darkness. Shiny surfaces that contained the creatures he loved so dearly surrounded him. He didn't want to move. Didn't want to open his eyes to reality – to anything. He wished he could just live inside his dreams, in another place beyond this life, never having to face the world. He craved another existence, a place that had to exist. Somehow. Somewhere. He wanted nothing more than the sweet release of his own end, demise, termination. His own death.

He'd spent two days without sleep, battling through in his head his menial existence, the only one he would ever participate in, cleaning pots, running trolleys, and cleaning the filth from *Their* plates; an alien born on earth, born to act as the minion and slave to the earthling human creatures. It was his destiny, and he couldn't fight it anymore.

He looked at the blank page displayed on the laptop screen, but still couldn't think of anything to type into his final memoir to the world. Nothing he could write would mean anything to them, anyway, would it?

He'd been thinking about how he could do it all week, but there was only one way that it could all go down, the other methods being too hard to put into action. He just couldn't inflict that kind of pain on himself, even though he knew he *could* deal with large quantities of the stuff every time he picked up the big knife and held it against his wrist. But he just couldn't do it. He couldn't push down hard and slice through the artery the way he wished he could. It was amazing how something seemingly so simple, which only consisted of such a temporary pain, could be so hard to do. And what would happen after? How long would it take for him to die – to slowly bleed to death? How great would the pain *actually be*? Would he be screaming? Would he faint? Would he even die at all? Maybe he would do it wrong? *Yes* was probably the answer to that. He just couldn't rely on himself anymore. And the same went for dangling from the rope. There was too much to think about and get right – and quite frankly, it was just too hard to do any of that stuff. He thought he wouldn't care *that* much at this stage; he wanted it, wanted to end it, but couldn't make the cut, jump off something, or hang from the ceiling.

Luckily there *was* an easier way out. And it lay in the grasp of his hand now. He'd bought three packets of painkillers on his way back before he'd returned home earlier that morning after realising he couldn't face work – or anything else – anymore. When he'd walked through the convenience store everything had seemed different. The sounds of chatter had been clearer, the quiet humming of the chilled section louder. Everything had somehow sounded, looked, and smelt different. And it was strange knowing that tomorrow he would not be here anymore. It was the oddest, strangest thing to think about – because it caused him to think about not just his ceasing to exist in this world, but also the other thing: Where would he be going? What did all this mean? – *this life?* What was it for?

As he'd gone through the checkout, he'd picked up a newspaper to accompany the three packets of painkillers in hope that it would remove any suspicious attention toward the fact that he was buying thirty-six pills in one hit. He'd even remembered hearing something once about a rule of how many could be bought in a single purchase. But they went through fine, for it had seemed the plump checkout girl had been far too busy in her own daydreams to have paid any real attention to what she put under the scanner and into the bag. The trip home had seemed neither long nor short, though he had felt it should've seemed at least like one or the other. Everything had seemed to have just been out of balance.

Alex looked at one of the packets in his hand. The other two packets were sat side by side next to the two glasses of water on the desk. All he had to do now, he thought, was drink them all down. He opened all the packets and made a pile of all thirty-six in front of him. He grabbed a load in one hand and took hold of one of the glasses of water in the other, ready. His lips opened slightly, slowly, but then closed. *All I have to do is drink them down*, he thought again. *Just put the pills in, then drink the water.* His hand began to rise to his mouth a second time, but returned to the desk. He did this a few more times, always with a long pause in between. *I'm not going to be here anymore.* He didn't know whether it bothered him or not – but all the same, the feeling of not being here was a strong one. And he thought about it for a moment. Not being here anymore. He would be dead and not...*here*.

Another attempt at drinking them down was about to come.

But it had to wait while he still wondered about the strange notion: *I won't be here...anymore. Not in this place, this Earth. I will be gone. Not here...*

He knew it did bother him in some horrible, unexplainable way. There was, he had to admit, a part of him that wanted to stay. But he just knew he wanted so much more to leave than to carry on living. The other part was just survival talking – but its reasons were flawed. It just wanted to live, that's all. For *him* to live. And who could blame it? That's what it was built for. But he couldn't, could he? *Live* – that was an odd word, wasn't it? He hadn't known what it meant for a long time.

He knew he was making the right choice, anyway.

And then he was giving himself a countdown, telling himself to just do it after the numbers had run out. But when they did, he still found himself not moving.

After another ten minutes passed, he was looking at the pills, at the glass, at the pills, at the glass, counting down, counting down again. And then somehow – *somehow* – after the numbers had run out, he just starting doing it, and it scared him as he felt and saw himself scooping up the pills and pouring them in, swallowing mouthfuls of them in a violent action, gulping down the water, more pills, more water, more pills, more water, more pills, more water, more, more, more, more, more! And as he did, his heart was racing and his eyes were wide and afraid for he knew what was happening and what was going to happen within the seconds that followed...!

And then it was over.

He dropped his palms to the desk and waited.

Waited. Waited. Waited.

43

But…he felt *fine*.

He looked around and saw nothing had changed, knowing he felt no different. But he was still scared, waiting for the lights to suddenly dim into darkness like at the end of a film before the credits rolled.

But they didn't.

A minute flashed by. Perhaps he was feeling a little dizzy or light headed now? But maybe he wasn't – maybe he was just expecting that feeling?

He sat back, realising life was totally out of his control. And so he continued to wait.

Wait for something to happen.

Wait for death to arrive.

***

It was only a few minutes after 8:00pm when Malcolm noticed it. He'd just stepped outside and was locking the outer door of the rescue centre, cutting off in an instant the barking of his many friends. At that moment, as with every night, he felt sorry for them and bad about leaving. But he'd already stayed on for an extra hour as it was – and he couldn't really do anymore than that now, could he?

And it was then as he began to walk down into the empty car park that he noticed it: the barking noise. But in the darkness of the night he couldn't see where it was coming from. He stopped moving, deciding his loud plodding feet were not helping the situation much, and then, when he still found it hard to tune in to the quiet yapping sound, also stopped chewing on the remains of his microwave cheeseburger. *Where's it coming from?* he thought hard. *Where are you fella? Where are you, eh?*

Once he'd swallowed the last mouthful of his second dinner, he started to walk around the perimeter of the car park, looking, listening, trying to move without a sound – trying to make his overgrown imposing feet tread as softly as they could.

He needed to find that dog. And he knew he was looking for a *little dog* for sure. It was obvious because of the sound it was making.

Soon, Malcolm was close. Real close. And as he reached the back of the car park near the bushes, he knew he was about to find it.

He could make out its small form, seeing that it was tied to the lamppost. But the post's dead bulb overhead wasn't exactly helpful, having not shone any light into the place for over a year now.

On his knees, he smiled and greeted the lost soul. '*Hello, little one.* What are you doing out here, eh?' He scratched its head and instantly felt hot breath as a wide tongue fell from its mouth. But he couldn't see a thing out here still. It was too dark, especially with the overgrown bushes blocking out even the light from the moon. His sausage fingers felt their way over the cold damp fur, and after finding a lead, soon managed to untie it. The newly released dog was then scooped up into a pair of big arms and carried over to the light back at the centre's entrance doorway.

It was then, as Malcolm stepped under the bulb, that he realised who it was, and he immediately gasped '*Oh my*…what are *you* doing out here?! *What happened?*' He'd recognised the dog instantly because of its purebred features and handsome little face, making him realise he'd known the little cutie before, having cared for it himself at the centre – and having only found it a home literally days ago. He thought about the strange man he'd given it to, feeling tempted to almost blame himself, feeling bad about giving it to a person about whom he'd had such doubts.

Back on his knees, he put the puppy to the ground. His hands and eyes carefully inspected it, searching for any signs of mistreatment to its body, and soon he was relieved to find it was actually in very good shape – if not a tad hungry. But it was OK. Unharmed.

Maybe he *had* made a mistake by giving it to that man back then, and maybe he *had* done the wrong thing, Malcolm thought. But he wasn't to know *this* would happen, was he? No – not at all.

Whatever had happened, it was all over now. And the most important thing was that the little guy was safe, back at the centre, and in his own kind, capable, and caring hands.

And that was enough to make Malcolm smile.

***

When Alex had rung work earlier that day and told them he wouldn't be coming in for the rest of the week due to illness, Sam had been angry with him. He'd had no one to cover for the little faggot and had

had to force a couple of the minions from the food court to cover for him. Those minions had been terrible at doing his job, and though the head chef hated to admit it, it was true that they had shown no method in what they were doing and had no sense of timing, and therefore had been unable to perform the role anywhere near as well as Alex did.

Sam started to really wish that he *had* employed another kitchen porter to work along with him – as he should've really done to start with. He and the management knew Alex needed another kitchen porter working by his side in order to finish each day at a respectable time. But the management had agreed with Sam's original idea that they could get away with making Alex finish each day entirely on his own, and back when he'd made this suggestion years ago, he'd received a good pat on the back for his forward thinking.

But never the less, everywhere was of course clean by the end of that day, for Sam made damn sure the food court minions had done a good enough job for him – and that they'd done a good enough job for *his* kitchen.

5

Layna was feeling pleased with herself. She'd clocked in at 12:00 noon on the dot, which was a first since she'd started working at Sestern.

She'd driven there on red again for the second day running, having refused to fill up with petrol. She would fill up when *she* wanted to, wouldn't she? End of. To have filled up with petrol at this stage would've meant giving in to her mother's anxious voice which kept on telling her that one of these days she was going to break down. Sometimes Layna even thought that the two brightly coloured petrol stations she'd begun to drive past every day to get to work, and all the others for that matter, resembled her mother. For sure the woman was petrol crazy – along with a number of other things – but all the same, Layna still loved that silly old woman to death.

She'd played the petrol game many a time since passing her test and peeling those square plates from both ends of her car. It was the only area of her life where she experienced and was aware of this relaxed, lazy attitude – and sometimes she even surprised *herself* by how she could not worry that much at all about breaking down.

The car itself had never slugged to a halt from a dry tank, and strangely enough, even with its old age, had never broken down for any other reason. It hadn't even had any real problems in the time in which she'd owned it, apart from the hole in the exhaust, and, the slashed tyre – well, four actually. But the tyre, or a similar type of vandalism to a vehicle, was not exactly uncommon in her area of residence these days in Kilnsea, Vulnham. What should've been more common was to have run out of fuel before reaching the station for all those years.

However, her luck was set to expire later that evening, when after firing up the engine, the car would go on to barely reach the end of the car park before shuddering in protest.

***

As it neared 2:00pm, she welcomed the thought of sitting herself down with the roast dinner featured on the menu, though from where she was standing behind the deli station, she couldn't actually see what items were likely to be left for her. But all the same, a free lunch was never a bad thing. If it came to it, she would just toss on a load of the healthy stuff from the salad bar – though this really was a last option.

Layna was a slender girl who'd always managed to somehow keep a good shape even though her eating habits never held any consistency, and although fruit was usually gorged on, foods of the sweeter kind managed to creep into her hands more than often. Cooking a proper meal herself was a rare thing at home, and she'd decided this was a good reason to take full advantage of the free lunches at work.

Have a *free* lunch and a *free* pudding.

And custard. Yep.

The good thing was that usually by the time she helped herself to the lunch from the hot food counter, it had already closed for business, so within reason she could take from it whatever she liked – *within* reason. And it was within reason because the kitchen liked to take as much back as possible, salvaging all they could get away with to reuse or mix into another dish for another day. Waste was a big issue in this business, and each day records were kept of exactly how much food, and profit, had been lost.

As Layna soon sat down with her lunch tray, which held a piling mass of vegetables and the day's last piece of beef lonely on top, she couldn't help but wonder where that Alex guy was. He hadn't been at work for the last couple of weeks and none of the staff seemed to know anything about his situation. Nothing could be concluded from most of their responses, and only speculation was there to be ignited. She hadn't worried about it too much at first, until she'd asked Sam (who she'd already learnt from the food court staff was known by a number of other names also) where he was. His reply had been: 'I told him he could fly if he jumped off the edge of a cliff. Maybe you should check the bottom. *How the hell should I know where he is?!*' And then he'd gone on to say (typically): 'Anything else, Layna? No? *Good*

– *I'm busy.*' She hadn't been surprised by that dickhead's predictable response, because she'd more than half-expected it. The thing, however, that had lodged itself in the back of her brain was the first couple of sentences he'd said. It was stupid to think it, though, and silly. But was it? Was it so strange to think that *that* could've happened? She'd heard the way Alex was spoken to in the kitchen, and had seen something in his eyes. Maybe he'd... *done something?* Not jumped off a cliff exactly – but maybe something else? She was being stupid thinking like that, though, wasn't she? She didn't even know the guy. But she knew he was troubled, at least. Just like she'd been once.

Layna spent little time devouring the food in front of her, and rated it as one of the better meals served there. After she'd finished flicking through the tabloid newspaper she'd salvaged from another empty table, she sat motionless for a moment as she started to feel that unwelcome feeling return. It didn't come back strong, and was in fact fairly weak – but still powerful enough to stop her from getting up.

A thoughtlessly written article from the paper had triggered it, reminded her of what had happened all those years ago. Not that she could ever truly forget – that was impossible. For what had happened could never leave her.

She then cleared her thoughts, got up, and placed her tray on the trolley at the nearest wall. But as she did, something caught her eye at the end of the food court behind The Wash Up room's long glass-panelled double doors. Obviously she knew it was one of the staff who must've been covering the kitchen porter job in there. But as she looked at the counters, at the tills, and at the retail shop, she could see that they were all working out here. So who was in The Wash Up, then? Someone from another site?

She *had* to know out of deep curiosity now. She had to know Alex – if it was him – was

(*not dead*)

all right. She wanted to know he was OK. Maybe she'd just not noticed him about the place today, and maybe he'd just not come out for lunch like he usually did?

That was a lot of maybes, though, she thought. And so then she made her move. She walked over toward The Wash Up doors and

49

could see, as she approached, the flashes through the glass panels of somebody moving on the other side. And when she finally got there, peering in, she could see who it was.

It *was* who she'd hoped to see.

It was him.

***

That evening was a pain in the arse for her. Not only had she broken down shortly after pulling away, but had also found she'd almost had to do something even worse: call her mother. But luckily it hadn't come to that. Yet. She knew the reason she'd broken down, and to ring her mother and ask for her assistance in driving up with some petrol would've been too much that day...*or any other.* Her mother was great, caring, everything – the best in fact. But having to listen to her rants about filling up and how she'd always told her to and blah, blah, blah, would be too much. And she would also have started complaining that she didn't visit enough, and then more questions would be loaded and fired at her.

Layna had tried all her friends beforehand of course, trying to get them to come up and help, but none of them could make it. Maybe they were being paid off by her mother who'd been anticipating this day for a long time coming? And as for breakdown service, she had none, and so wouldn't have been able to afford the outrageous charges demanded for one-off incidents.

So she just sat there in the car for half an hour, her mobile in her lap, her thumb hovering over the button that would connect her with her last resort: The Petrol Preacher. And she nearly pressed the button, but before she did, she noticed in her rear-view mirror that someone was leaving work. A few more people had left before, but their faces had not seemed like those who would be inclined to help her. They'd also, for some reason, all been women, and from Safe Insurance. She'd been aware that most of them would've probably turned her down, not wanting to help someone they didn't know and who wasn't from within their own company, and so had decided to not ask for help.

But now after noticing the familiar face, she got out the car and started walking towards the guy who'd just left the reception entrance.

50

As she looked at him, she saw he was still the same as when she'd seen him earlier, looking like death, a walking corpse.

'Hey, excuse me!' she called out, the gap between them closing. '*Alex, hi!* I'm Layna, Layna...' She paused for a moment. 'Layna Davis – from lunch, *remember?* Listen, you're not gonna believe this – but I've run out of petrol.'

He stopped and just looked at her, not saying a thing.

'I, er...know I don't know you very well...but I know there's a petrol station not far from here – maybe five to ten minutes by car. I was wondering if you wouldn't mind driving over and bringing me back some petrol? Just enough for me to get moving, anyway. I have a can here in my boot and I'll pay you for your travelling...and the petrol, of course.'

He remained silent and still.

He's going to say no isn't he?! she thought. *He's not going to do it! Phone your mother!*

No – she couldn't do that!

Then offer more money!

She was feeling so stupid. The situation was stupid, and of course, so was the reason for it ever happening in the first place. She had crafted a great problem. A real peach to go up on the wall.

'You know, it's okay – I can fill up myself. Sorry, it was silly of me to ask. I'm just gonna walk, it's...not far really. Thanks anyway.'

It is *far – and maybe you should've listened to your mother...*

But as she turned away she heard: 'No. Wait. I can help you if...you want.'

She turned back and smiled at Alex, and couldn't help but notice his hurting eyes. Something had clearly changed about him within the last week.

'Really? *Honestly* I really appreciate it, Alex. That's such a big help!' She nearly went on to tell him how she'd almost had to make a dreaded phone call...but decided that was best just kept to herself.

When they got to Layna's car, she lifted up the boot, took out the empty fuel canister and passed it over.

She could tell he was uncomfortable being involved in conversation, and that being alone in the car park with her had probably made it even worse for the guy. He said only one other thing before leaving: 'All right, I'll be back in...ten minutes.' She knew he'd found it hard to not turn his eyes away from hers. She could sense it – like she could read his mind and see right in through to his pain somehow.

She thought about saying to him what she'd wanted to earlier, but before she could utter a word, he'd already turned and started to walk toward his car.

I'll say it when he gets back, she told herself. *I must. And I will.*

***

When Alex returned fifteen minutes later, besides feeling paralysed under the unrelenting constraints of his tortured, weakened mind, he felt strange, as he always did when someone had spoken to him; not in a way in which was mandatory in giving orders or disgust, but out of what seemed to be genuine conversing or something of a pure nature. And maybe he had changed his opinion of this person – though he hadn't logged her name – and did feel she was different from the others?

No, wait...he didn't know that, did he? He didn't know anything. Never had done. Never will. He'd been brought back from the dead to walk the earth as *the dead* – as he'd been before. Dead inside. Dead to Them...unless maybe they needed help, like plates or pots washing – then he could be their pathetic slave, couldn't he?

Alex sat there for a moment before getting out the car, sensing his bloated stomach and its hardness. He felt uncomfortable and wanted to just go home. But he had to finish what was going on first, didn't he? So he drew air deep into his lungs, let it free, and got out.

'Thanks, that's really great of you to do that for me, Alex,' Layna said smiling. She handed him the money. 'At least I don't have to sleep *over here* tonight!'

But he was only half-listening, just wanting to leave. He went to the boot, pulled out the fuel canister, placed it on the ground and went straight back to the driver's-side door.

'Alex, wait…' he heard suddenly. 'There's something I wanted to say to you.'

He looked back at her and saw her pause for a moment, her eyes thoughtful like she was building herself up to say something important.

52

'Tonight I'm going out for a drink with a friend. And I was wondering…if you wanted to join us? It's at The Rabbit's Tail. I know you're going to say no and you probably don't want to. But my friend – she's a good person. Trust me.'

'I can't,' he said slowly, his eyes falling south.

'It's just a drink. That's all, I promise. You should come.'

He looked at his dirty wet trainers. 'I'm sorry, I…can't make it. I'm…busy.'

'Actually, no. Listen, Alex. Don't take this the wrong way…but I'm not asking you. I'm *telling you* to meet us there.'

***

The time had gone quickly for Alex since getting in from work – really quickly. He knew it didn't usually go *that* fast. Nowhere near.

He'd been walking around the flat for a while, thinking, thinking, thinking about the pub, and could now feel the wetness of his armpits and the sweat dripping down over his cheeks.

He sat down at his desk to try and calm down, telling himself not to think about anything at all – but *still* he could see silhouettes and humiliation and panicking and sweating and hotness and more sweating and panic and heavy breathing and people, people everywhere all looking at him, and he was disorientated and he couldn't even speak to tell them he was unwell and had to leave and then when he would leave they would all be laughing at him and talking about him and—

He managed to discontinue his thoughts and rest his forearms against the desk, bowing his head over. As he did, he realised his breathlessness and sucked in a big gulp of air. But he was by no means having a panic attack. He had enough control and probably wasn't going to go out tonight at all, anyway. Why would he want to? Why would he want to be out there amongst *Them*?

(*Layna? Is her name Layna? Layny? Laura? Lanya?*)

Salty droplets appeared on the desk's surface, and then he was saying to himself out loud: '*Just don't go. Don't-go.*' He knew he wasn't going to, but it was the fact that he'd actually been asked by her – *a person* – to go out, to meet her, to meet her and her friend. It was confusing. Beyond weird for him. And he didn't like the sudden change from depression to this bizarre feeling of panic in such a short space of time. No – he *did* still want to die even at that moment, but this thought of going out, and this contact, this *friendly contact* with another *human being*, had unsettled him greatly.

But then Alex was giving tonight second thoughts...like he didn't even know if he *was* going to stay in or not. *But why?* Why was he thinking about changing his mind? Walking into a pub would kill him. He could see it – their eyes watching him. They would judge him in a second, sensing his difference. *HE'S NOT ONE OF US! HE'S NOT WELCOME! NOT ONE OF US! BAR HIM! GET HIM OUT OF HERE!*

He didn't know what he was feeling exactly at that moment. It felt like it could've been lots of things. Nothing had even happened yet, though, had it? It seemed like he was maybe experiencing the product of a never-ending culmination of vivid thoughts. Some were created from memories of the past, but were mostly from the creation of his own mind – his own horrid preconceptions.

The fireworks continued inside his head, each thought going out with a bang, getting lost in the other's bold colours, never sticking around long enough to be examined. Too much was going on in there – but he *was* in control, wasn't he? Because he *was* at home. He *was* safe. And the sweat meant *nothing*. It just...happened sometimes. It was just part of him and a regular occurrence, *that's all...*

Alex looked at his mobile.

19:45.

He was running out of time.

(*Out of time? There's* no problem! *You're going to just sit here and do nothing. And no – I don't know why you're still alive either. You fucked up with the pills didn't you? Of course you did...you couldn't even get that right. But you haven't the balls to do it any other way now have you? Unless you're braver now? Are you?* No – *I didn't think so. So you're just going to lie on the bed and do nothing*)

His inner voice stopped for a moment, but came back at him even stronger as he still sat there not moving.

(*STOP THINKING ABOUT GOING OUT COS WE BOTH KNOW IT'S NOT GOING TO HAPPEN SO GO AND LIE DOWN AND REST YOUR STOMACH! YOU CAN'T DO ANYTHING BECAUSE YOU'RE DEPRESSED! YES! YOU ARE FUCKED!*

FUCKED UP MY FRIEND! LOOK AT YOU! JUST LOOK AT YOU!)

He got up and headed for the bedroom. He had no more tears left. He was dry, empty, as close as he could be to dead while still breathing. He caught his reflection in the mirror of the bathroom on the way, seeing exactly what he'd failed to achieve looking back at him: Death. He was *fucked, done, killed, dead, hollow*, all the things he told himself he was – courtesy of the other guy living inside him.

The pills had nearly killed Alex. The problem was that he just hadn't taken enough. He'd had a few minutes, back then on the day of taking them, where he'd just sat there, waiting, waiting. But nothing had happened except for what had later followed: inexorable nausea and vomiting for hours and hours on end, day after day for a whole week. And he'd needed those two weeks off work if only to recover physically. He'd been alone, not knowing whether he would live or die, scared, wanting only the sweet release of death, that painless escape. But it was taken from him. He'd gone on to live, to exist in the same world of people who didn't give a shit about him, who still would look at him in the same way, with none of them knowing that he'd tried to take his own life. Nothing had changed. He didn't live now as a ghost...but in many ways it was the same thing. He was still invisible walking among the *seen*, never listened to or welcomed. His body had fought for its life, not letting him die, forcing him to carry on living. But it had also been injured and given him something extra – a severely bloated stomach. He didn't know when it would go away or even if it would. The only thing he knew was that it was extremely uncomfortable, and meant he could barely eat half an apple these days.

Alex stood in front of the bathroom mirror, staring at himself in the same way he always did every day, still surprised to see he was actually there. He opened his mouth and examined his face with his hands, feeling his features. He even punched himself on the side of the jaw, just hard enough to feel the impact, and looked for a reaction, sparks of pain, proof that the mirror reflected what was really before it. He asked the man in the mirror the same two questions he always did. 'Who are you?' And then: 'What *happened* to you?'

***

55

It wasn't until he began to walk down the street that it really started to bother him. He was hot, sweating, burning up, even in the cold chill of the night air. He scratched at his hands, the soft wind picking up the falling flakes of dried skin.

It must've been sheer curiosity that was taking him out here to meet Layna. And it was dangerous, for this *sheer curiosity* was bound to hurt him even deeper than he already was, causing more damage, more pain – more humiliation at the hands of *Them*...

Once turning out onto the main street of Moulden Road, Alex found himself walking amongst the nightlife of bands of young teenagers yelling and laughing (probably at him, he thought), some drinking from soft drink bottles filled with booze. There were adults too, but he daren't look at them. He'd looked at one when he'd first moved into town, and that one had said: '*Fuckin problem, mate?! Pretty, am I? Do you like me, do ya?*' At the time, Alex had just looked away immediately, wishing for the moment to pass, and after the guy had spat to the ground and walked on, it eventually had.

But this was one of the many thoughts his mind held onto. It reminded him that although bad things needed time to happen, that also time *would* run out, and that it was just a matter of waiting. Time would *always* lose in the end.

The pub was now in sight, and even its very name, The Rabbit's Tail, looked daunting, like it was almost watching him, inviting him into the uncontrollable situation that would commence within. Once he set foot inside that pub, he would be out of control, out of his depth, in the place where they all assembled; in *Their* place of congregation.

Alex had to stop. Stop right there. He tried to casually lean up against the brick wall of a shop, trying to make it look as natural as possible. The shop itself, Disc-Connect, like many others in the street, was tired, beaten looking, inside and out. Earlier during the day, it had been alive with the monotonous clicking sounds of hopeful fingers flicking through a hundred horizontal racks, flicking through a never-ending jumbled alphabet of second hand CDs, DVDs and video games, while crackling speakers had played out a collection of early-nineties rock in the background.

A runner with deeply focused eyes moved swiftly on past. Then there were bangs and a smash, all of which could be heard from somewhere up the shop-lined street in the distance. The traffic, which had lessened by more than half since the daylight hours, still created its own cacophony in Alex's ears, always declaring that the city was still alive and breathing.

And to him, the city *was* breathing. Breathing heavily.

The pelican crossing traffic lights burned a deep burgundy red, staring back at him, almost as if possessing eyes of their own. He then saw a black boy-racer hatchback filled with booming music drive straight through them.

The air was now biting cold and he had to move, if only to create some body heat. But what direction was he going in? Back home? Or to the pub? Back home to his flat, where he felt calm, without all this anxiety, perspiration and fear? Or to the pub to meet the woman? – who just herself maybe he could deal with. But her *extra friend?* He didn't know. Wait – what if there were *others? More friends?* What if other people were to arrive too? Who would they be? How many would be there? What would they think of him? They would all give him *The Look*, wouldn't they? They would be kicking Layna or Layney, or Laura – or whatever her name was – under the table. And they would be whispering: *Where did you find this guy? – he's weird! Look at him sweating and shaking over there. Don't ask him anymore questions, guys – he hasn't even answered my question from two minutes ago yet! What is your name, then? Hello...?!*

That was it, wasn't it? – he wouldn't even be able to speak and tell them his name! And even the other congregators in the pub would all sit around him, sniggering and laughing and sniggering and pointing and—

But then Alex simply moved. He began walking again and with every step he took he could feel himself getting closer and closer. The traffic seemed to die down, like it somehow wanted him to reach the other side quickly, his dreaded destination only yards away. As he stepped onto the road, he started to watch his feet, watching to see how fast they were moving. Each step seemed like a mile. The sweat was building again and his chest was burning through his coat, the pub seemingly inches away. He was then startled, stopping dead in his tracks, jumping back, his upper body rotating away from the whizzing sound of the cyclist who sped past in front.

He wasn't going to make it, was he? He knew it. He decided he had to leave it, walk away – cross the road, follow the breadcrumbs back. And as he turned around, he almost felt dazed, his vision foggy like the lens of an unfocused camera overwhelmed with objects that constantly moved in and out of the foreground. He then clutched at his bloated stomach as he started to feel sick. It was hard, its aching relentless as ever.

But then he turned back to his side as he heard a voice call to him: '*Hey Alex!* Looks like we got here just as you did!'

It was Layna and her friend crossing the road towards him.

(*Shit!*)

They hadn't even been in the damn pub, had they? Now he was fucked. He couldn't say no now, could he? He couldn't—

(*YES YOU CAN! YES YOU CAN! IT'S A WASTE OF TIME! A WASTE OF TIME! IT'S GOING TO END BADLY! BADLY!*)

'Come on, Alex, you're buying the first round.'

(*SAY NO! SAY NO! SAY NO SAY NO SAY NO!*)

Alex touched his forehead, its surface moist. He had to say something. Had to say *something*. 'Hey,' he tried through a forced, rigid smile. And then he was suddenly doing it. He hated it, but he was. It was the *truth*. He was following them in – into the lair...the lair of *Them*.

***

It was quite dark inside. Gloomy almost.

He felt like his heart was going to explode there and then, like it was beating out of control, banging against his ribcage.

Not many people took much notice of him as he walked in – but he noticed the ones who did. Two men glanced over from the bar – who Alex knew were obviously talking about him – making his eyes shy away, causing them to look over to a nearby table filled with people, but then he had to look in another direction quickly, not wanting to wait for them to gaze over at him also, but it was hard to look anywhere else now, because people were everywhere – *They* were everywhere! – and so he just had to stare down at the carpet and soon he felt dizzy being amongst *Them* in that place amongst the unsettling chatter and laughter of them all and it was making him feel ill – so ill! – and his stomach was churning and hurting and his mind was racing and—

'Alex!' Layna called over from a table close to the bar. 'We're over here, okay!'

He walked over to the table and sat down facing the two women, unable to make eye contact.

'Alex, this is Patricia,' the familiar voice said.

'Uh...please, Layna!' her friend said. 'No Alex, don't listen to her. Just call me Pat, okay?'

But Alex had almost missed her name because he was still thinking: *Her name's Layna, Lay-na.* He could barely look at either of them, but knew they'd smiled when they spoke. After a brief moment, he managed to lift his head up high enough, fighting against a neck that didn't want to allow it, and looked over the top of his glasses at Pat. 'Hi,' he said. 'Nice to meet you.'

'So you work with Layna, right?'

'...Yes.'

The questions, the presence of contact and conversing – all at once – was hurting him. He wanted to leave! *Leave right now!*

'Right, ok-ay...' Pat continued, struggling for words herself. She remembered something. 'So how about those drinks, then?'

'Oh...yes, *sorry*,' Alex said with guilt, realising he'd completely forgotten. He felt terrible, his body beginning to perspire even more, his clothes now becoming closer to wet than damp.

Thinking her friend's comment had sounded a little malicious, Layna quickly nudged her hard with her knee in protest.

'*What...?*' Pat hissed through a whisper.

'That's all right, Alex,' Layna assured him. She pointed her thumb in the direction of Pat. 'The longer this one's without a drink the better. We'll have two jack and cokes, please.'

He half-smiled awkwardly at their necks, losing eye contact again before he went off to the bar.

'Who *is* this Alex guy?' Pat soon asked, more with concern than curiosity.

'*Keep your voice down…*' Layna snapped. After she looked to her side and checked he hadn't heard, she calmly said: 'Alex is fine. As I told you, I've seen him around at work, and I can see he's…troubled.'

'Layna, I love you…but what exactly does that mean?'

'Don't worry yourself. I feel like I can almost see inside him. That's all. Like I've been him once – kinda.'

'Right…'

'I recognise…*that look* in his eyes.'

'Honey…Layna – what are you talking about?' Pat said with a hint of laughter, putting a delicate hand on her shoulder.

'It's all right. Back then when – before you knew me – I was alone in just the way I think *he is*. And I…' But she couldn't find the words.

'Go on…' Pat encouraged, her expression turning supportive.

'This makes more sense in my head than in my words – clearly – but what I'm trying to say is: I don't want him to have to wait for help. *I* was lucky. *I* had friends. Good friends who stuck by me and wouldn't quit even after I'd told them to leave me the hell alone a million times. But Alex – I feel like he has no one.'

'Layna…are you okay? What—'

'*I'm fine.* Listen, I just think that *I* am that person who should help him. I think he's trapped like I was. But maybe he won't get out of the…*bubble*…and realise he needs to go looking for help. Maybe—'

'Yeah, but wait. *Wait.* You don't even know the guy at all. Do you? Honestly…?'

'No, but that's the thing. I do. Well…it's *like* I do…'

'What do you mean? You've obviously barely spoken to—'

'*I know I haven't.* I know, I know. But I know him, I swear. *I feel him.* I realise it sounds strange, but…I feel like I know him *already*.'

'And you want to help him in what way?'

Layna noticed a familiar look in Pat's eyes. 'It's not like *that!*' she said, letting out a small momentary smile. 'I just wanna get him out of himself. That's what helped me – in the end. I can just…feel his pain, I think.'

Pat looked at the friend she'd thought she knew, but now felt almost like she was sat next to a stranger, sat next to someone who she didn't really know that well at all. Of course, she knew Layna had had some major problems in the past, but she hadn't known her long enough to have heard anything about those hard times or the stuff she was coming out with now. She didn't have a clue what to say next, but still came out with: 'I wish I'd known you back then. But I didn't. I only know you now, Layna – and you're *fine*.'

'But something's telling me to help him,' Layna said with conviction.

'You need to concentrate on *your* life now. That's what you need to do.'

'I know…but all I want to do is get him out of that dark cave I see him living in.'

'And you're not…*you know?*'

Layna understood Pat's expression again. '*No* – it's not like *that*…'

They both then stopped talking as they noticed him coming back over.

Alex set down the drinks and took a seat, and both women nodded in thanks. He felt a slight ease in anxiety now, even though he was still very much inside the lair of *Them*. He didn't know whether having seen himself in the bar's mirror had been comforting or not, but one thing he did know, was that he was there, in the pub, outside.

He was *outside*. With *people*. Amongst *Them*. And a nightmare though it was – he *was* there.

'So what do you do when you're not at work, Alex?' Pat asked.

'I…like to paint. And draw. Sometimes.'

'I've seen some of his stuff at work, and it's…*unbelievable*,' Layna said, her eyes confirming every word. 'You should see it, Pat.'

'He draws at work?'

'Sometimes…' Alex quickly added. 'In my breaks. At lunch.'

'Oh,' she said turning back to him.

'You're too protective of it, though, aren't you?' Layna said laughing a little, his troubled face not putting her off. 'You never know – you could be an artist, work in design or something?' There was a brief silence and then she carried on with: 'I'm into photography myself. I've done my studies and now I'm trying to get my own career to take off, doing shoots at my flat and stuff like that whenever I can. In between I have to fill my days of course with random jobs – well…bills are bills, aren't they? But soon I want to be moving on to weddings, then eventually go as a pro freelancing full time. It's my dream. I—'

'The best photos…' Alex started, '…are the ones…you don't know have been taken.'

Silence followed.

'What?' Pat asked, her face turning to confusion. 'What do you mean?'

He lost eye contact and slowly went on: 'Smiles are…' But he stopped.

'Smiles are *what*?' Pat quickly questioned again.

He suddenly realised he'd been in some kind of a trance and hadn't really known he'd spoken any of the words at all. 'I'm sorry…' he said shamefully. 'It doesn't matter.'

But Layna was interested, wanting an answer too. 'The best ones are the…*unplanned ones*, do you mean?'

'Don't worry,' Alex said, lowering his head some more. 'I don't know what I mean.'

'How long have you lived here, then?' Pat quickly asked trying to change the subject, feeling frustrated with him.

'Um…about seven years.'

'You like it round here? – in this part of the city?'

'No, wait,' Layna said. 'I can see from his face – you hate it, don't you?' Some laughter escaped. 'Come on, be honest!'

He then couldn't help but smile a little on one side of his face as he heard her amusement. It felt strange to him – to have even this broken, not even half-smile on his face. 'No, I guess not.'

'Me neither!' Layna laughed.

'I'll second that,' Pat said. 'This place is – excuse my french – a shit hole! *Good old Vulgar Vulnham*. But I guess it's home, isn't it? For now at least, anyway…'

Layna laughed at her, but her face turned more serious as she said to Alex: 'You know, some of the people around here – I see it in their faces – I think they're trapped. Lost. Their faces…I wish I could take photos of them.' She laughed as the memory of what she was about to say flashed before her eyes. 'I tried once, to take a picture from a distance…but I nearly cried after the abuse I got from some lady! That was when I first moved to the city, though – before I got tough.'

'Before you met *me*,' Pat said pulling a macho face. 'And you ain't that tough, missy…'

'It's…maybe good for pictures around here, I guess,' Alex said. 'I think it's actually…black and white, really.'

'I know what you mean,' Layna agreed.

Pat's eyes looked back and forth between them as she wondered what the hell they were talking about.

Alex didn't know where the strength had came from, but he was now able to straighten his neck and look up at both of them again, this time making genuine eye contact. And though it lasted only a short while, he managed to settle long enough to ask Pat: 'Are you a photographer, too?'

She told him how she and Layna were both in fact very different people, going on to explain a detailed story of how she was studying and working as a nurse. But he didn't really care about what she did for a living. He'd just wanted to throw a question of his own into the conversational mix to allow himself to feel slightly better from knowing that, if nothing else that night, he'd at least made some kind of a *social contribution*.

***

Earlier that day, straight after work as usual, Sam had gone to the gym. He wasn't interested in the benefits of exercise or the *good feeling* the gym freaks told him he could supposedly get, and wasn't interested in building muscle or becoming fit (although he *had* got into great shape due to the extreme amounts of cardio he always subjected himself to). In terms of diet, he knew he must have been pretty healthy, mainly because his wife Merissa always had a nutritious meal waiting in the fridge for when he returned from his workout.

Usually Will, who was his best friend and closest ally, would be with him most evenings. But not today. He would usually join him much later around 6:00pm, and by this time Sam would've already been on the treadmill for an hour and a half.

The gym was in fact where they'd first met, and since then he'd formed relationships with both Gaz and Winger, though tonight they'd not been there either, as they both, working for the same advertising company, had been unable to attend because they were away up north presenting to a new frozen food company. Sam had made acquaintances from work amongst a few others he'd met at the gym, and sometimes they would join him for a drink one or two nights a week, as would some of Will's friends. But on the whole, Sam and Will stuck together closely, often going out places together, and if appropriate, took their other halves along too.

Sam had been at the gym for seven hours, remaining on the treadmill for over four. He'd done so because he'd known that neither Will, Gaz or Winger would be joining him. And also, as typical of a Monday night, all four of them would have gone out for an early week drink, but all of this had of course been off the cards too, and he hadn't wanted to drink alone in a club. When at the nightspot after, he would generally drink just a few beers, and that, combined with the excessive exercise, would get him to fall straight asleep as soon as his head hit the pillow at home later. His worst fear was to spend any time awake in bed, as it would allow his mind too much control. It would make him think. Laying there in the dark, in silence, was just too much for him. Because that was when The Beast would always try to find him. And if he couldn't sleep, he would take just the one sleeping pill, though he usually found he didn't need it.

Just after 10:00pm, Sam collapsed on the treadmill. In the final seconds before, where his eyes had rolled and his legs turned to rubber, his neighbouring runner, who'd been peering over (anxiously wanting to say something for a while), had stepped across, jolting her arms out, clumsily grabbing at the sleeve and chest of his t-shirt as he'd fallen.

'Jesus Christ!' the woman breathed with shock, kneeling behind the machine which remained in motion. She dragged Sam's feet till they were away from the convey belt, and looked up and around, desperately trying to locate a member of staff near closing time in the now empty gym.

'Can somebody help me?!' she shouted, raising and waving her hand in the air.

But there was no reply. She couldn't make out the sight or sound of anyone.

She tried again. But still got nothing.

And then, as she looked back down at the lifeless body once more, she knew she would have to really shout it this time. '*SOMEBODY HELP ME!*'

6

At 12:00 noon, Sam was talking on the kitchen phone in his favourite sarcastic *you're a stupid fuck and I'm going to make sure you know it* tone.

'Yes, I know you're sorry. *Yes, yes, yes, yes* – let's move things forward, shall we? You being sorry isn't helping anything, is it? Cos your company doesn't give a shit about whether half the order's missing or not, clearly. A credit won't help and adding it to the next order won't help either.'

There was a brief moment where he almost let the woman on the other end speak, but soon cut her off when he realised what her next line would be.

'*Of course I need it today!* Why do you guys always say that? Why the hell would I order it if I didn't need it today?! You know what? – put my sales manager on the phone, will you? I would absolutely *loooove* to know what he's going to say...'

The woman told him to hold and that the man he was after would be along shortly. Sam showed his appreciation by saying 'Thank you *so* much...' He waited, his thumb and index finger as impatience as he was, swivelling the lid of his pen, flicking it on and off.

'Mr Henderson?'

'*Yes...*'

'Hi, Christian Landers speaking. How are you d—'

'I'm doing dandy, just dandy, thank you. You're fine and I'm fine. *We're all fine.* The problem is this: order's arrived, more missing yet again. Yesterday it was the meat missing. And today it seems your packers can't count six mushroom boxes. I understand you can't guarantee availability of stock, but this is just ridiculous, *surely*? So—'

From the background of the kitchen a voice shouted out: 'And the mixed peppers!'

'Did you get that?' Sam said to Landers. 'It's just so much trouble dealing with you guys. I don't know what to—'

Sam paused as Landers finally managed to get some of his own words in, and as he did, Sam began to pace about the kitchen as far as the phone's cord would allow. But his silence didn't last long. 'Short staffed doesn't help me, though, does it? If they can't pack a simple order, then I'm wondering *what else* they can't do...' He listened to the response but didn't like it. '*No!* Today. I need it *to-day.* Six mushroom. Two mixed peppers.' But Landers couldn't tell him what he wanted to hear, still speaking of no miracle deliveries. 'Then I'm telling you, it better all be there with tomorrow's order,' Sam fired. 'And tomorrow's meat – the topside, chicken breasts – better be there too. All by twelve. No later. Nothing missing.'

Landers started with apologies, but Sam wasn't interested in them or calming down. 'Look – I don't want to hear sorrys, credits...or whatever. It's not gonna help me today in *any way...*' He thought about saying goodbye next, but rejected the idea, instead just putting the phone straight back into the cradle. A moment was needed for him to breathe, but once he'd settled, he thought of something that would cheer him up. His eyes looked over to the kitchen porter who was silent and scrubbing away in the corner. 'And *you* can shut up an' all!'

And as he said it, the other chefs who were moving busily about the kitchen laughed.

Sam finished by calling him a 'Fuckin faggot' and then, after noticing the sandwich lorry arrive, proceeded outside. He walked up to the driver's door and knocked on the window. 'Sandwiches. Eight o'clock. You're late. *Why?*'

He realised, once the largely built guy had climbed down from the cabin, that this delivery driver wasn't going to buckle as easily as he would've liked. He figured the guy probably wasn't even scared of him – but still, he showed no fear himself in return.

'Calm down, mate, you're wastin your breath,' the driver said, his ears seemingly having heard it all before. 'It's what's on the computer. The computer organised today's drops. I am *not* the computer.'

'No shit...' Sam said. '*Well done!* What's your name, please?'

The driver tilted his head, his eyes narrowing. 'Simon.'

'*Simon, nice to meet you!* Don't worry, Simon, I'll make sure when I ring up later, that your employers are made aware of how remarkably *clever* you are...'

The driver stepped closer into the head chef's face. 'And who do you think *you are*, eh? You think this is some *plush hotel or somethin*, don't ya...?'

'Just get the delivery in, all right sweetheart?' Sam said. He then turned and kicked over the brick to keep the Goods In backdoor open. 'And I want them credited,' he went on, his back now turned as he went inside. 'What's the fucking point in bringing the sandwiches this late? *They're useless now!* We'll just sell every one of them at lunch time, shall we? I mean, who needs the morning, after all? *Fuck-ing-hell...!*

He made his way past the walk-in fridge and freezer and staff lockers and headed down the corridor. When he got into the kitchen, he heard a voice from outside behind the hot food counter call in through the serving hole for more chips. As it was said, a rushing body, which already happened to be moving past the fryers, dropped the basket down, submerging the semi-defrosted chips into the oil. A shrill hissing filled the room.

Through the wall on the hot food counter, the number of battered cod had already halved, and soon the second tray that was being kept heated in the cupboard underneath would be brought up. More fillets were already being coated with batter inside the kitchen, ready to be dunked into two hundred and fifty degrees of oil.

'How's that breakfast prep doing?' Sam called out. 'How much you done?'

'Just bacon and beans left,' Joseph answered. '*I'm on top, baby!*'

'That's ma' boy!'

Joseph was young and relatively new in the kitchen, but he caught on quick and had so far seemed invincible to the stress the job brought with it.

This was what Sam, in fact, disliked – and mainly hated about him. But all the same, he did find Joseph to be a likeable character. Of course, Sam always assigned him the donkey work such as the breakfast prep – or as much as he could get away with, anyway. And hopefully it was taking its toll on the man's self-esteem.

Sam was now at one of the six-foot steamer ovens, calling 'Sausage rolls are on their way out!' Sebastian acknowledged the head chef and then bent down in front of the fridge, taking out a tin container of tuna and mayonnaise, along with some additional containers of salad to bring out to the panini counter on the other side of the door to his left in the food court. A long queue of customers awaited his return.

Further to the side of the fridge were a small and managed pile of dirty trays, plastic tubs, a mixing bowl and colander, and a dirtied sink of water with large silver slotted spoons and other cooking utensils partially visible at its surface. In front of this area was a half-full trolley containing various washed items ready to be taken through into The Wash Up for their final deep cleanse. The sink itself was without its attendant, who had left the kitchen to go out to *The Bin Pen* (as the chefs called it) to get rid of a mass of cardboard boxes and two black bags filled with rubbish from the morning's waste.

Sam was at the serving hole with a long deep tray, alerting the hot counter servers that the 'Jackets!' were behind them. As he placed them down, he heard in the distance his mobile notifying him of a message being received. He went over quickly to inspect it, reading:

Is it true you nearly died at the gym last night? I heard that you fought off the gym monkeys who tried to save you! What the hell happened...?!!!

He quickly went outside, called its sender and said while laughing: 'What are you talking about, old friend?'

'*Hey, he's alive!*' Will exclaimed humorously.

'Yes, of course I am. Now can you be quick? – some people have to work...'

'It's just something Jeff said...'

'*Who?*'

'Never mind. His wife said she saw you faint or something.'

'*Faint?*'

'At the gym. Last night. Said there was a big scene – but apparently you resisted. Said you pushed one monkey away and then verbally abused all the rest as you left...on somewhat *uneasy* legs. But it wasn't you old boy, you say?'

'*Ha!* William, William, William! This woman's obviously stupid...*and blind.* I wasn't even at the gym last night. I was at home with the wife.'

'Merissa?'

'Yeah – that's my wife last time I checked, shithead.'

'But she was with Sarah and Sue last night...'

There was a pause from Sam. 'Look...' he then started. 'You want me to tell you where I really was?'

'Shoot.'

'Okay, I was—'

'Hang on, Sammy. Hang on...'

'What?'

'Just *one second...*'

'What...?'

'*I know what's going on here...*'

A silence came.

'You know *what*?!'

'*You dirty dog!* Will finally let out. 'You were with old *Lick Your Balls Liz* again, weren't you?! Who, as with many of your liaisons, I am yet to meet...'

'Why would you ever meet her?'

'You've met mine...'

'Because *you* are a dog.'

'*We're both dogs!* Will laughed.

'Whatever. It looks like my confession isn't needed now. You figured me out, William, I—'

'Please – say no more, old boy! I have to go.'

The line went dead.

***

At 3:00pm, apart from the kitchen porter who was in The Wash Up, all the chefs were at their lockers getting changed, readying themselves to leave for the day. Inside the office near reception, Sam's fingers tapped away at the keyboard while his eyes scrolled through the order he was placing. There were two others in the office, Matthew Cullman, the assistant manager, and the manager himself, Gordon Slayne. At that moment, they were hearing more of Sam's rants about the deliveries, mainly that of Statons. But then Gordon, who was already a little on edge as it was, couldn't help but cut in sharply with: 'So what do you want to do about it? We don't have power over who we choose as suppliers. *Sestern do.* You want to phone them up...?' Sam was staggered by the comments from his boss (a man who never put any kind of real emotion or passion into any sentence – probably not even his own wedding vows), and thought the words *fat cock* in his head while he carried on talking as if not bothered at all, casually going on with: 'What's the point, eh? What's-the-point?'

He leaned forward to look at the screen closer, and when Gordon noticed him squinting, he asked: 'Why don't you just wear them?'

'Um...nah, I'm okay,' Sam said.

'They're right there on the desk,' Gordon advised him. 'Come on. I'm wearing mine.'

Sam thought that this was almost a childish thing for any man, let alone a manager to say, and thought *So bloody what!* But all the same, he had to admit his eyes *were* struggling, and if the other two hadn't been in there, he would've been wearing them. The only reason he was experiencing this visual struggle was because Merissa had forgot to pick up his contact lenses at the weekend.

He looked at the glasses hesitantly and then back to his left, looking through the glass panel on the door. He hurried himself with the order after putting them on, eager to be able to take them off immediately. But when Joseph and Sebastian pushed the door open to say their cheerios before leaving, Sam quickly whipped the visual aids off and said as naturally as he could: '*Take it easy, boys!*'

His eyes focused back on the screen once the two chefs had made their way down to reception. He felt angered with the glasses problem, and that he'd definitely just made a fool of himself as he'd more or less thrown them across the desk.

A few minutes break was maybe needed from staring at the monitor, wasn't it?

But no – he couldn't take a break. Not now. Because now, even in that moment where his mind had casted away from work to consider that break, he could feel it – *The Beast.* He could feel it trying to make his mind think again.

But then the distraction he needed from himself was immediately delivered. As he heard the phone make its first ring, he yanked off the receiver and fired out the words '*Sestern Vulnham site Sam speaking.*'

***

At 5:00pm he was heading out through reception. He swiped his I.D. badge, walked through the turn-style, and grunted as the security guard said goodbye to him.

The night would go the same as any other Tuesday, he hoped. Tuesday was always a night where he was in, and Merissa and his son Jake were out. It was a night of recreation – a *man* night. Porn. Curry. Wank.

As the key turned in the ignition, he was not shocked by the volume of the deafening rock playing from the CD in the stereo; it was always set to that level when he was driving alone. Before the four-by-four approached the boom gate he was already singing, and when he looked across at the camera, he screamed into its tiny lens as the vocals on the song reached a high-pitched climactic screech.

After a twenty minute drive, he officially crossed the borderline into Meadling. He then turned into the Maple Forest estate on the country village's outskirts and soon located the small new build end-of-terrace. As he pulled up on the driveway and yanked up the handbrake, he felt a small yet very noticeable amount of relief, feeling more like things inside him were getting easier, as if returning to normal.

Before stepping out the car he smiled at his reflection in the rear-view mirror. 'It's all good, baby,' he said. 'It's all, all good.'

7

Wednesday, 10 – Saturday, 27 February 2010

It had only taken a couple of days for Alex to forget about his encounter with Layna, Pat and the outside world; the conversations, discomfort, awkwardness – and all the rest of it. He didn't want to hold onto the memories. He wanted it to never happen again, instead wanting nothing more than to continue in his depressing life; his life where he would stay up all night watching TV into the early hours of the morning, trying to avoid sleep because he knew that if his eyelids did close then he would be subjected to the experience of waking up the next day – experiencing that moment where he would realise he was still alive and would have to go on living...

But he would be shit out of luck again, as just before the month ended he found himself pacing around his lounge, knowing that for some reason he again wouldn't be able to *just say no* and stay where it was safe. He'd been asked by Layna to join her and some friends at a theme park tomorrow, and not only that, he'd also been asked to drive. He would have to talk and converse with her friends. Friends he'd never met. And also the others – *Them* at the theme park. And they would look at him with *The Look* and it would all go wrong, wouldn't it? They'd all hate him. And then Layna would say as he dropped her off: *Actually...Alex, do you mind if you don't come out with us, anymore? – it's just...you know, I don't think you can be part of this group. Maybe I'll see you around...one day in the future...*

8

Alex held the keys tight in his fist and could hear the clock ticking away, echoing throughout the silence. He scratched at his hands again.

Just stay! the voice inside him cried out. *Why leave? I don't understand your thinking.* You *don't either! – so what are you doing? You're going to kill us!*

After locking the door behind him, the clicking sound only made it clearer the day had started – that its gears were now beginning to turn.

Then came the stairs. The walk to the car. The starting of the engine.

And now it was time to drive to Layna's. But before he did, he looked at the text she'd sent earlier during the week:

117 compaine street :) x

As he pulled away from the curb, physical discomfort set into his body.

(*Look at you sweating already! You don't have to do this! It's going to end badly! Badly! BADLY!*)

The weather on February's last day had Vulnham's residents walking the streets wearing an extra layer or two. But still, Alex wound down his window all the way in an effort to cool himself.

For some reason, even the traffic seemed to be against him. It was particularly light, making it easy to pull his old hatchback out onto Moulden Road straight away – something which never usually happened. Soon he could see the sign on the left getting closer, closer, closer. And then it was clear. Horribly clear.

Compaine Street.

He made the turn and drove slowly down the centre of the road between the parked vehicles on both sides.

(*You won't find it! You won't even be able to see the number! It's not even here probably! She didn't give you the right address! Why would she? It's not here! It's not here!*)

But he kept on looking.

(*She won't come out! It's pointless! Just turn around and go back!*)

He saw it and stopped the car, hoping she would come out immediately, as soon a car would most likely turn into the opposite end of the road wanting to get past him.

(*You're blocking the road! You can't stop here! They'll all be beeping you! — shouting at you soon! Forget it! Let's go home! You're not feeling well! Let's just go!*)

There was movement through what looked like the lounge window.

(*Go! She hasn't seen you yet! You can still leave! Just drive on now!*)

But he argued back under his breath 'Of course she's seen me! I can't go. *Not now!* I'm fucking staying! *I'm staying all right?!*'

A smiling Layna was running out from the house, and then within seconds she was in the car next to him saying 'Hey Alex!' He forced himself to look back at her and say 'Hey Layna. How are you?'

'I'm doin real good, thanks. So excited about today!'

Alex smiled involuntarily a little, and it felt strange. The happiness in her now had a hold of him. He hadn't seen a happy face up close like that for a long, long time. And it was in *his* company.

'So you ever been to this theme park before, then?' she asked.

But now he couldn't talk. He didn't know what words to send to his lips.

'To Sowchester, I mean...?' she added.

(*can't even speak can't even speak can't even speak — look at you!*)

And then he tried. 'Um...'

(*What are you doing Alex? What are you trying to talk to her for? It will end up ruined won't it? What are you trying for? WHAT'S WRONG WITH YOU?!*)

He got a hold of himself briefly. 'As a kid, maybe. Long time ago.'

(*WHY?! WHY?! DON'T YOU KNOW WHO SHE IS?!*)

'Well I think it's changed a bit since then,' Layna said. 'Last time I was there was last year. Me and my friends have been for the past two years running. Turning into a bit of a tradition now, I think!'

Alex wondered what he could say to that.

(THERE'S NOTHING TO SAY! SHE'S ONE OF THEM! DON'T YOU KNOW WHAT THAT MEANS...?!)

He desperately tried to think of something, but in the end all he could get out was: 'Oh.'

(Oh? Oh? My god! – is that the best you can do? What's that supposed to mean? See?! – you CAN'T do this!

He quickly added: 'That's good.'

(That's good? Quite the wordsmith aren't you! THIS IS GOING TO END BADLY!)

He argued back with himself again, yelling through his thoughts: *I don't know what to say all right! Fuck you! If you know – then you say it!*

'Right,' Layna said. 'We should probably make a move now. We need to go to Hardling Road first, then Stapleton Crescent.'

Luckily, all the pickups were in the city, the only place he really knew. He'd lived there from the age of seventeen, ever since moving out from his parent's place and getting the job at Sestern.

The first of Layna's friends to get in were Brian and Jayne. They spoke to Alex, greeting him, and somehow he'd managed to respond as casually as he could, but had known he must've sounded abnormal to them. Brian had even patted him on the shoulder, and as he'd said 'Good to meet you, mate,' Alex had actually thought he'd seemed kind of, well...*nice*. And so had Jayne. They'd been nice to him. And he hadn't even made much conversation back either. He'd just said the kind of things he'd said to Layna. They'd probably just been trying to be polite, he now supposed, having only acknowledged him in a friendly way because he was driving.

(BINGO! You're just a taxi! They are using you! That's all...so don't get all excited now will you? Nobody is nice – REMEMBER THAT!)

He knew the second pick up had to obviously be just a single person, as there was only one seat remaining in the back. This made him feel marginally pleased, in spite of the day ahead. He guessed he could maybe deal with all the thousands of strangers who'd be at Sowchester Adventures – *this* was possible. But how was he going to deal with trying to talk and act like a normal human being around the people in the car all day? Was it even possible? Could he pull it off?

Not likely at all.

(it's going to end badly...)

When the next person got in, Alex saw in the rear-view mirror it was another girl. And he liked that fact. Girls, at least, seemed less threatening to him. Stacey too greeted him and asked how he was, but also went on to ask more like 'I haven't seen you before, have I?' and 'How do you know Layna?' It was hard work to answer and make conversation in return, and when she seemed interested and was making eye contact with him (which he almost thought was genuine) in the mirror, it felt strange. A *good* strange? Did he feel good? Did he feel *good* about having a conversation? He felt under pressure, for sure. But he was hardly getting a headache. And the conversing, the talking, felt easier than at the pub – *not much* easier, but easier somehow all the same.

Alex had been sweating, but since starting to focus on communicating – as far as he could manage – it seemed to have stopped. He was more than aware, though, that he was certainly in the deep end. But...on the other hand, he *had* met everyone now, hadn't he? There were no more pickups. No more people coming. That was it.

As he drove away from the curb of the last person's house (the name of whom he now couldn't remember), he wondered whether it was the weight of her that had caused the car to work noticeably harder. But it wasn't just because she was fat, he thought. It was the weight of everyone. He couldn't even remember the last time he'd had anyone else in his car, or if he'd *ever* had any passengers before at all...

As he listened to their voices chatting and exchanging stories, through what he thought *light bantered conversation* must've been, his ears suddenly tuned in, picking out some selectively heard words: something about *more people meeting them there*.

Oh god... he thought.
Shit.

***

The car park was a large field packed with numerous rows of organized vehicles, all being directed by fluorescent-jacketed men.

Once Alex had taken note of the time on the dashboard, he pulled the keys from the ignition. 10:53am. As he shut the door behind him and stood there trying to calm himself, he took in his surroundings, seeing hundreds of people all walking in the direction of the theme park entrance. His concentration returned to the car when he heard Layna's voice to his side, and also movement from the backseats. He turned to her, seeing she was holding her seat forward to let everyone out, and then instantly felt stupid as he thought about how he'd done the complete opposite by closing his door on them. It was *his* car, after all, wasn't it? So did that mean *he* should be the one to let all the passengers out?

(*Why do you care? Why are you worrying? Fuck THEM!*)

Or was that stupid? Or...should he have at least let a couple out his side – from politeness, good nature, helpfulness?

(*They can find their own way out! Don't worry! They will soon turn on you. FUCK-THEM. What are you doing here Alex? Look how bad you're feeling! You feel sick don't you?*)

Alex looked over as he heard Brian make a caveman-like noise, which at first almost sounded threatening. But he realised the man was just stretching his back out, adjusting his limbs from the long journey, and letting out a groaning yawn.

'Right,' Brian said, pointing toward the herds of people travelling into the distance. 'Let's follow the masses.'

They joined the trail and soon found themselves amongst the clusters of families, teenagers and young adults. Two separate fields, divided by a line of tall thick brush with small chopped back pathways in between, had to be crossed. Alex wasn't surprised to hear Stacey complain when the ground started to incline into a semi-steep hill as the entrance drew closer, though he felt bad about thinking she was fat and needed to deal with all that weight she was carrying. And then, out of nowhere, just as they were all about to make it over the brow of the hill, that very woman was grabbing at his arm, laughing the words 'Sorry, Alex, I just need a little pull! I can't make it!'

Layna called back '*Stacey...?*'

'*What?*' she questioned with an exhausted laugh. 'This hill's stupidly crazy!'

And then everyone was laughing – except Alex. He didn't know what to think of the situation; of someone touching him, talking to him, and seemingly enjoying what looked like a form of...*fun* – all at the same time!

77

He smiled a little, though with unease, thinking it was probably the right thing to do.

'Lighten up, Alex!' Stacey said.

'*Sorry...*' He felt embarrassed, his eyes sinking to the ground.

'Don't be sorry – it's just us fat people need a little help sometimes. But, we're great for cuddles – so I've heard anyway!'

'*Stacey...!*' Layna called back again.

'*What?* I'm not asking him for a cuddle! – I'm just saying us fatt'uns are better for cuddles than *you skinny bitches.*'

'Come on!' Brian and Jayne called, both of whom were now walking towards one of the five lengthy queues leading into each gate at the park's entrance.

The rest of the group started moving again, joining up behind the impatient couple.

Alex felt uncomfortable knowing the queue could take some time to get through – enough time for him to have to start having a conversation. And he wouldn't be able to get away with just standing there in silence looking away from them, would he? No, because they would ask him questions. *They* would start it all. And he would *have* to answer.

A minute later, it began, just after they'd joined the queue.

'So, Alex,' Brian started. 'How long you been working at Sestern, then?'

Alex didn't want to say his *whole life* – he couldn't say he'd spent over seven years as a pot washer, could he? He thought quickly of what to say and a couple of words came out: 'Too long.'

And then the craziest thing happened: Brian laughed. It was only a light one – but he had laughed. He, Alex Merton, had made a joke. And Brian had laughed

(*he was laughing at YOU...*)

at it. He hadn't even intended it to be funny exactly, either. But that didn't matter.

'I know what you mean. I've been a carpenter for the past...six years it is now.'

'Oh.'

Alex immediately then thought *Stop saying Oh!*

'I moan about it a lot to people, but truth is...I love it. I don't know how or why. But I *do*.'

There was a short silence as Alex again didn't know how to reply.

'Anyway,' Brian went on. 'I know this is just standard menial run-of-the-mill small talk, so listen – you know me, I know you, right? *Well*, you know what I mean, anyway. You're just another guy.'

Alex smiled and said 'Yes', but was thinking: *What? No...what are you talking about?*

'Tell you what. There's a ride here called Dr Flamer. It's a big mother, goes every which way, makes most people sick for *a week*. Anyway, me and you – we're goin' on it.'

'What? I don't know. Let me...see it first.'

'Alex, I'm the only one here who can ride that thing, and...' he chuckled for a moment, '...you'll be a *real man* like me if you can do the same!'

For some reason, even though he'd never really done in the first place, Alex didn't trust him based on his choice of words, and after a pause said again: 'I don't know...'

'Don't look so worried! It's your choice, anyway – I'm only messing...'

But this next lot of words Brian had said changed Alex's view of him slightly. It was strange how his feelings could suddenly alter like that, and this made him wonder how he could ever possibly understand *other* people. They were complicated. So abstract.

He then became aware that he'd completely forgotten where the conversation had got up to. Was it his turn to now say something?

(*Who cares?! There's nothing to think about! Sounds like he's TRICKING you into something. Maybe he's going to—*)

'You'll enjoy yourself,' Brian continued, slapping his hand on the back of Alex's shoulder.

'Thanks,' Alex uttered.

'You'll be able to say *that* again, soon,' Brian said. He smiled and chuckled once more. 'After you've tamed old Dr Flamer...'

***

He had actually thought he would somehow have managed to walk around the park and just wait for everybody after they got off the rides – basically avoiding really doing anything. But he would soon find himself in an awkward situation.

The group were well into the park now. Hordes of people were everywhere, walking past in every direction, a mixture of emotions on the many thousands of faces. Brian, who was walking next to Alex, then announced: 'Flamer is close!' Alex had so hoped that somehow, for whatever reason possible, the man would've forgotten and simply not mentioned it. And so Alex did the only thing he could do: pretended he hadn't heard him.

'Come on, mate,' Brian encouraged.

(*Mate? Ha!* MATE! *Yeah you're right to have doubts about* that one! *Oh my god! – he doesn't even like you! How could he already be your friend?! It's so—*)

In the background, amongst the chatter of the others, Alex thought he could hear at least a couple of them jeering him on. *Fuck off* he thought. *Fuck-off!* It wasn't helping his escape from going on the bastard ride at all, was it?!

'Come on, what was the last ride you went on?' Brian asked.

'I don't know, the…' But he couldn't even make up a ride, because there wasn't any he'd ever been on or heard of. 'I've never really…been on any,' he said, his eyes to the ground again, expecting Brian, or maybe all of them to laugh.

They didn't, though.

All that happened was Brian said: '*Really?* Never as a kid?'

'I never really liked them…'

'Then you're coming on with me, cowboy!'

'I don't know, maybe…later. Something smaller first. I don't—'

'Look, you tackle this beast and *the rest'll be easy.*'

'But I've never been on…anything like—'

'*Ahhhh shat' up and get over here!*' Brian said playfully, pulling under his arm. 'Follow me. I'll make a man of you yet!'

Alex felt it again as he heard those words – the feeling that maybe this Brian person actually wasn't that bad. Something still made him unsure, though.

The rest of the group laughed in the background, apart from Jayne who raised her hand to her forehead and called out to Alex as he walked away with Brian: '*I'm so sorry about this!*'

Stacey leaned over to Jayne and said under her breath: 'God, your Brian's just terrible. Poor guy's only just met him – and already he's trying to kill him!'

'Yeah, but you gotta love him, haven't you?' Jayne said smiling fondly, looking ahead to her man Brian.

'Why's that?'

'It's sexy, isn't it?'

'Jeez – control yourself, would ya?' Stacey joked. 'Kids around here, you know...?'

Jayne attacked her friend playfully with her handbag as she told her to shut her trap. When the mini fight was over, she glanced away to her side and said loudly. 'Looks like someone around here has a crush...'

'What?' Stacey questioned, her smile almost leaving her face.

Jayne sent her an *I'm not stupid* look and said: 'Alex...'

'*No way!* He's cute, but...'

'But what?' Layna asked.

'Well, he is cute...but that's all I'm saying! Nobody even knows him yet. You don't even know him yet, Layna.'

'I know, but I think he's doing okay, right?'

'Yeah,' Jayne said. 'I think it's...I don't know the word. I think that you're beyond human sometimes.'

Layna looked at her confused.

'No, seriously,' Jayne went on. 'You helping this guy is like...well, I thought it was gonna be weird and that he was gonna be a complete psycho or something!'

They all laughed.

'But he's...he seems okay to me,' she continued. 'I would never randomly ask someone I didn't know to come out with my friends. Well, it wasn't *random* – but you know what I mean.'

'I just feel like I know him every time I see him, that's all,' Layna said. 'And there's no harm done, is there?' But then a speck of doubt crept inside her. 'Or...is it weird? Is it weird me doing this? *Honestly?*'

'No, no, no!' Jayne assured her. 'Listen, Layna – you're weird and that's why we love you. It's okay. *Really*. And he seems *fine*.' She let out a little chuckle. 'I'm not sure whether throwing him to *The Brian* was the best idea, but hey...'

Layna looked to the faces of her friends. 'I love you guys.'

'Oh God, is she gonna cry?' Stacey joked, playing an imaginary violin.

'No, come on!' Layna said. 'I haven't cried since…' Her eyes fell to the floor, as did her emotions while she took a moment lost in her thoughts. 'Shall we…go and find a ride or something while they're queuing? What you think?'

The others agreed and they started making their way. Soon after, Stacey was at Layna's side saying: 'Hey, look…sorry about what I just said. You okay?'

'Yeah, I'm fine, it's just weird. I don't think I've actually cried since…back then. About five years ago. It's so strange, you know?'

'Oh shit!' Jayne said suddenly coming to a halt. 'What about Vicky and Peter? They meeting up with us or are we finding them?'

'Hang on,' Stacey said, soon with her mobile against her ear. '*Peter?* Hi. Sorry, we're at the sci-fi zone-y bit with the Flamer – right outside the Nice Space to Eat cafe. Okay…see you in a minute.' She dropped her mobile back into her bag. 'They're gonna be here in about ten,' she then told everyone. 'Now, can anybody see a good place to take a seat? My legs are killin me…'

***

The queue seemed to be moving far too quickly. It wasn't exactly a short one, either. The worst part was that the thing he was queuing up for wasn't even something he wanted to experience.

So far, he hadn't had to talk much with Brian, but had said enough to get by. Brian was certainly a man who liked to talk for long periods of time.

The images in Alex's mind and the ones right before his eyes of the rollercoaster – a monstrous train which roared above over his head every fifteen minutes – had helped his social anxiety subside enough for it to be partly replaced with a different kind of fear.

'Don't worry,' Brian said. '*Seriously.*'

'I'm not.'

'No, I mean, if you want to go back you can. I know I'm being pushy – just like my brother. Sometimes I don't realise it, but me and him are the same. It's disgusting.'

But then, even though Alex hated to do it, he knew he had to as the reality of what he'd soon be doing became too great. 'Actually…you know what? I…think I…*will* head back. I'm not—'

'No worries! My fault really, anyway. Well, *kinda...*'

'Yes, um...thanks,' Alex said ashamedly, wondering why the man was being so nice about it all. He turned and started to make his way back through the queue, beginning to brush his way past all the people facing him, knowing they were judging him, thinking what a coward he was. And they were probably right.

With every time he had to then speak up and say 'excuse me' and 'sorry, can I get past?' he felt even worse. He didn't know whether it was because of the failure felt in walking backwards against the *forwards people*, or simply because of the anxiety from looking into the faces of so many strangers – who of course were giving him *The Look*. And it was the first time he'd noticed *The Look* from anyone today.

After what seemed like an eternity, Alex knew he was getting much closer to the start of the queue. But he began to slow down, suddenly feeling terrible. What was hurting him, though? It was probably obvious what the answer should've been. But was it really just *that*? Or was it something else? Maybe that ride? But why? Why would that ride he dreaded so much make him feel this way – this *terrible way*? Why did he even care about it?

He was out, back on the other side again at the entrance of the queue. In the distance, he could see a lunch bench where Layna, Stacey and Jayne were sitting. As he walked closer to them, he found with every step the terrible feelings were getting worse, stronger. But he didn't know why.

When he got to the table he knew they were going to start asking questions. And of course, they did.

'Where's Brian?' Layna asked. 'You been on already?'

'That was quick!' Stacey said.

And then he had to tell them, though he was confused as to why he felt so bad about speaking the words aloud, as if it mattered that he hadn't been on the ride which had meant nothing to him. Why did he care so much? Why was it so hard to tell them? 'I couldn't...

(*do it because you were a pussy a wimp a fucking coward a—*)

do it in the end. I was just...feeling that—'

All of a sudden something strange happened inside him. Something had entered him, shooting around his limbs like electricity. It was overwhelming. And he didn't know what it was. Alex felt like he wanted to...to do something. But what? He wanted to do *what*? A second later it was suddenly there. Clear. He knew what it was, and it made no sense at all, but for a reason unknown it felt right. He was thinking about going *back*.

(*You're being so stupid! You're being stupid Alex! You can't do it. You can't. Stay* here! *It makes no difference. You don't have it. Oh* courage! *– is that what you think you have? You don't know what you are do you? You—*)

'I'm just gonna...' But he didn't finish the sentence, because something had carried him off back in the direction of the queue.

(*They won't even let you back in the queue now anyway. So just go back*)

He brushed past the people in line, only this time he was moving in the same direction as they were, and he was saying 'excuse me' and 'I need to get through' again – but this time it felt different.

(*What's the point?! You are so stupid! You can't make it all the way to the front anyway. Brian will have been on by now! You won't make it. Just watch! JUST WATCH!*)

Alex kept moving forward, looking for Brian, hoping he'd not already boarded the ride. And before long he could see him in the distance, and as he sped up, awkwardly manoeuvring around everyone, he desperately wanted to be able to reach him in time.

(*you'll never reach him look at all these people the way they are looking at you they're going to turn on you any second now look at them look into their eyes LOOK!*)

But he did make it. Though he thought it would've been impossible, he was up there standing by Brian's side just as he was about to board the ride, with the train only seconds from arriving.

'*Holy shit!*' Brian gasped as he noticed Alex standing there panting, his brow dripping. 'Alex. Change your mind, eh?'

'Yes...' Alex said catching his breath.

'Here we go, then...'

They stepped off the platform and entered the carriage, now empty of its previous passengers. When they were seated, Brian turned to Alex who he thought resembled a statue, a statue with a vice grip for hands clinging to the safety bar. 'You can swear if you want to now, you know? It's okay.'

'I can't even...speak.'

Brian let his amusement be known. 'Love it! *I love it!*'

Alex liked the way Brian had looked at him and laughed. But it was far from important in his mind now. Because he was thinking more

84

about that loud hissing noise, which must've been some kind of air pressure being released in the background somewhere, and the safety harness wrapped over his shoulders and lower stomach that had been pushed down even tighter by the passing ride attendant. It was more than a little disconcerting looking at the very young staff walking about the platform, yelling indecipherable things across to one another. They didn't even seem to care at all that they were just about to send a whole bunch of people off to their doom, instead chewing gum and making lethargic hand signals to someone who must have been in a control room somewhere.

As he felt the carriage jolt forward, his buttocks, thighs and calves tightened.

'You know,' Brian joked, 'you're gonna break that handrail if you grip it any tighter? Other people are gonna need to use it later...'

But Alex didn't laugh.

Nothing could be funny at that moment.

***

'And...?' Stacey asked.

'In one word – fucking brilliant!' Brian said.

'I didn't mean *you*,' Stacey said, and then looked back to Brian's victim who she thought looked to be in a form of mild shock. Everyone laughed when he answered straight faced with: 'I...don't think I like it.'

But Alex himself was just stunned by their amusement, not understanding what was so funny. He was still shaking a little from the ride, but also had a surreal feeling within – a buzz even – from knowing he'd gone on that thing which had been just *so awful*. It didn't make sense to feel good from doing something he'd hated so much. But it *did* feel good.

There was something else that he felt, though. *A gain* of some kind. He couldn't see anything he had won from riding that thing with Brian (who was now patting him on the shoulder saying: 'You didn't die, man, I told ya.') – so what was it, then? He tried to organise his complicated wiring that seemed to be knotted, interwoven, impossible to make sense of. There were sparks flying everywhere, pressure valves which had been released, and a carriage of his own inside that had started rolling. He felt like he had...*what?* Like he'd *achieved* something?

The rest of the group then began to move forward, as did Alex and his confusion.

And what about these people? Were they just people? Or friends? He knew their names, didn't he? So did that make them *friends?* He'd spoken for a while with one of them – did that mean anything? Was *Brian* a friend? He certainly seemed to look at him differently now that he'd been on that ride with him.

What was going on?!

He needed to sit down, and soon, luckily the others all decided to once having found a lunch bench. But there was a bad part to this also: there'd been two extra people who'd been waiting at the table to meet them.

And one of those new people now leaned across the table and stuck out his hand toward him, saying: 'Hey, I'm Peter and this is Vicky. How you doin?'

Alex looked at the hand for a moment, and then shook it and said: 'Alex. Nice to meet you...*both.* Both of you.'

(God you sound so fucking stupid...)

While he remained quiet amongst everyone as they chatted, it gradually dawned on him where he was and that he was outside the flat, in a theme park, with people, surrounded by thousands more, had been talking, had been on a rollercoaster, was out in the open – *was outside, outside, outside, outside...!*

For the rest of the day Alex managed to avoid going on any of the bigger rides, but did agree to go on the smaller ones, even getting talked into going on the log flume. But he'd found everything confusing. The whole day was. He hadn't had an actual conversation with a person in years. It had been so long. And he'd been in a group photo today! He'd actually been told to get into a group photo with them. The roller coaster had done something to him – he knew *that much.* And at least, by riding it, it had got Brian off his back about going on any of the other more intense rides. It was all so baffling. Were these people *really* his friends? Or was it too early to tell? Yes, probably too soon for that – but he knew he'd made a dent, an impression on them. Had he shown some normality? *Some humanity, even?* Yes, maybe a few times they'd identified with him, seen him as a real human being...*maybe*. The oddest thing had been when those moments had come, where the people in the group had looked at him and it had been as if they could *actually* physically see him. And when they'd spoken to him and he'd spoken back, he'd had to think: *Is this real?* and *Am I really talking to you?*

Alex used to think he was invisible to other people. But that day people had seen and even touched him. It was so much to take in, but it created an indescribable feeling. He didn't even know what it was – whether it was good or bad.

At 3:00pm, the group were walking around the Rustic Valley region of the park. Both Brian and Peter suggested their next move should be in the direction of Doom Drop, and after receiving no objections led the way, soon joining the back of the ride's queue.

'Actually guys, I'm gonna wonder off and find the zoo,' Layna said. 'I'm gonna sit this one out.'

'Some people can't handle the pace...we understand,' Peter said, his head nodding and eyes squinting comically.

'Well I would rather my lunch stay where it's *currently at*. So when you guys are done, give me a ring.' She turned and looked to Alex. 'Wanna keep a girl company?'

'*Me?*' he asked surprised.

'Yeah. Come on.'

***

They both made their way to the animal enclosure, Wild Kingdom, along the way discovering how bad one another's map reading skills were. When they got there, Layna immediately started taking photos. She'd taken quite a number throughout the day already, but had been looking forward to the zoo most of all as, though people fascinated her the most, she felt solace and calm when photographing the behaviour, ways, and beauty of animals.

'Do you like wildlife?' she asked, while snapping at the flamingos with her black chunky camera.

'Yes, I guess so.'

'You wanna elaborate on that a little?'

He looked away for a moment, embarrassed. 'I have pets,' he added. But as he said it he thought straight away: *No – don't mention them!*

'Pets?' she asked, moving to the other side of the path to snap away at the warthogs.

'Yes,' he said quietly, praying she would leave it at that.

'What kinda pets?'

'Um. Well…'

(*Look at you! You're so pathetic! Don't you think she already knows you're a freak? Don't y—*)

'Not cats and dogs,' he managed.

'*Right…*' she said, turning back to him. 'You *are* a little strange, aren't you?'

(*she's actually going to start telling you the truth* – see!)

'Yes…' he said.

She giggled to herself.

A curious '*What…?*' then came out of his mouth, and he hadn't expected it to.

'Nothing,' she smiled. 'Come on. Take some pictures.' She handed him the camera.

As he took hold of it a click sounded. 'Oh…I didn't mean to—'

'Don't worry! It's digital, it can be deleted. Look, pass me it here a sec.' Once she'd brought the accidental photo up to the LCD screen she then said: 'Nice picture – you've really captured the roundness of that *warthog's arse!*' Her eyes showed her amusement. 'I think I'll keep that one,' she said. 'Come on, Alex, let's see what other species of arse there are around here…'

Within the next half hour, they'd made their way through most of the small zoo. She had often given him the camera, encouraging him to take a few snaps, though he had usually shown his reluctance. But her feet gradually began to slow down as they passed through the aviary enclosures, and soon she said: 'Do you know why I asked you to come with us today?'

'No,' Alex answered, feeling that even *he* could sense it was a serious moment.

'When I was a little girl…I was attacked,' she said. 'I was only a toddler – nearly three years old – and my mum had taken me round to her friend's house. They'd both been in the garden. It was a hot summer's day and they were having a few drinks and we were all having so much fun. I was playing on the grass. Chasing butterflies and…things like that.'

Alex felt uncomfortable just listening to her, and had noticed she'd not made any eye contact for a while, her camera completely redundant, just hanging around her neck as they slowly walked.

'And then I thought: *Where's my hat?* It was a big summer hat and it was on the lounge table…inside. And so I…went back to go and get it. It took a while…the back lawn was long, and I think I even stumbled over a couple of times. I climbed up the patio steps…and the kitchen door was ajar, so I pushed it open, let myself in. I went through into the lounge, but…I couldn't see the hat on the table. I couldn't see it anywhere. And then I saw it with…Russy.' She paused, her eyes closing for a moment while she took in a deep breath. 'Russy was my mum's friend's dog. It was a…well, I – I just remember it being big. It was lying down…but then I could see that my hat was in between its front paws…and then I…' She paused again, breathing in deeply as if all air had left her lungs in an instant. 'I went to go and get it, and then…and…' Her feet suddenly stopped and she turned to Alex. She held her hand to the right side of her face, her eyes looking deep into his. 'It's how I got these scars…'

Alex didn't know what to say or do in that moment which seemed to last an eternity. Something was going on inside him. *This* he knew. *This* he was sure of. And then, before he knew it, they were both walking again.

She talked. He listened.

'It didn't actually…go straight for my face. I fell forward as I reached for the hat…and it…bit into my ribs…right arm…shoulder. Everything above the waist on my right side. Then it got me in the neck, and…the right side of my jaw. And then…that's when my mum came in. Some of the memories are…well, I don't know if my mind made them up because I was so young…but I feel like…like I remember *everything*.' She cleared her throat.

Alex thought he would've seen her cry, but he hadn't yet. She seemed to be only emotional talking about it, her eyes dry, free of tears.

He wondered about the situation unfolding before him. What was he supposed to do? Feel? Say? How was he supposed to feel about

89

other people? Maybe he couldn't? Maybe he didn't know how to feel for them?

'Anyway,' Layna said, her voice now in a lighter tone. 'The only good thing that came out of it – which apparently the doctor said should've been seen as a miracle – was that it didn't go for my eyes. And they *both* still work today, and, at least don't have any scars. But…I didn't exactly see it that way when I was growing up. I didn't feel *lucky* or like any *miracle* had played its part. As you can imagine, I had a *pret-ty-tough time* at school and growing up with it. And up until five years ago, I wasn't…' She let out a big breath this time. 'Well…I'd basically locked myself away in my room. I wouldn't talk to anyone. I'd even tried…*you know*. But everything changed when I started University. I met Stacey and a lot of other good people. She actually came to stay with me in my room. Forced herself in, I should say. In the end, all my new friends helped me, though. But *she* was the one with the balls, I guess, to get out of her comfort zone and put herself through the hell I gave her for not leaving me alone.' She stopped talking for a few seconds, her eyes alive with memories. 'Anyway. My other friends had always tried, called, and done what they could. But in the end, it was Stacey who got me out and back into the world. She saved my life, really. When I got out, my other friends were still there waiting for me, though. And they all nursed me back, supported me – did everything. And I'll never forget that.'

Alex tried to think of something – anything – to say.

'So what I want to tell you is…I brought you here, because I think you're hurting. I think you're hurting bad and…I think you are alone. I think you live alone…and I think I can see inside you somehow…like you're hurting inside and you're just…*alone*.' She quietly laughed to herself a little. 'Sorry, I'm…not making much sense, am I!'

Alex still couldn't speak and just looked at her.

'I was lucky enough to have found friends to pull me out of my problems – my illness. But I don't think you have anybody. Do you…?'

A few seconds went by. Alex looked to the ground, his mouth opening hesitantly. 'No. I have…no one.'

'I can't watch you drown, knowing I can offer you a life jacket. Especially when I can see that you are talented…and gifted. I think you're stuck within yourself. In your job. In your thoughts – inside your *head*. I don't know. Call me crazy – and I do *feel crazy*! – but...I just feel like I wanna help you. I think I—'

'I think you *are*,' Alex said.

'*Really?*'

'...Yes.' He then made eye contact, and this time there was no discomfort. No pain. No hurting.

No wanting to look away anymore.

***

As Alex entered his flat, the sound of the door banging shut behind suddenly sent a shockwave of those same feelings from earlier back into him; the same feelings he'd felt after his seats had become empty, leaving his car light once again after dropping everyone off.

But what *was* that feeling? What was it?! He was glad to be back, wasn't he? Back home with his *real friends*? Back where he was safe?

He was, right?

Alex went into the bathroom and looked in the mirror to see if anything had changed. He didn't look different. Or did he?

He began to talk to his reflection. 'What is it?' he asked. 'Tell me! What is it? *What is it?!*' He then went into the lounge, not feeling angry – but bewildered. He took a good look around, realising where he was: centred lonely in a room with a desk and painting trestle; a room filled with strange creatures nobody liked, wanted, or loved, with hundreds of paintings rolled up and stacked inside his bedroom through the wall behind him.

As Alex sat down at his desk, the reality and clarity of the day started to fade. His usual descent into the murky waters within was slowly happening. But as everything inside his head began to sink into the depths below, there was just one thing he could hold onto that his mind couldn't destroy. He knew – although it was most likely Brian, Peter, Stacey, Jayne and Vicky had all been pretending to like him – that Layna was different. She seemed real and there was vividness about his memories, the moments they'd shared together. Her face wasn't drowning like the others were. He could see her, feel her. She was real. She got him.

She did...?

Yes! She did, didn't she?! She had understood him. She *did* understand him! And she was the only person who had never given him *The Look*.

He sat back in his chair thinking about this. He didn't smile. But he did feel a kind of positivity creeping into him, because he knew, felt that maybe, just maybe, things were going to change – change for the better.

Alex Merton had found a friend. Found someone who got him.

PART 2

From Josephine Lexington's *Merton: Discovering the Invisible Man*

The tapes from the CCTV cameras, which showed Edward Dorne running through the corridors, screaming at employees and finally setting off the Food Court's fire alarm, were more than enough. This was all the evidence the police needed to strongly suspect him of withholding vital information which could have saved the lives of twenty nine people. However, the case was about to take another unexpected turn, as Sgt Paul Blandfield recalls:

"Upon arriving at the house it was apparent something was very wrong. Many of the neighbours were crowded outside and there was a continuous blaring sound resonating from within the Dorne residence. When I then realised exhaust fumes were seeping from beneath the garage door, I immediately expected the worst. Edward Dorne was later found inside slumped over the steering wheel of his car, his chest pressed against the horn."

Further investigation into Edward's connection with Alex's June 1st killing spree proved unsuccessful. His wife, who wasn't at home on the evening of his suicide, had little insight to offer:

"We were...like strangers in the end. Even though I tried to tell him I'd been seeing someone else for some time, he didn't listen. He was so self-absorbed like that...that he didn't listen to anyone. He could never be happy. He had no real friends and refused to speak to family. But he liked it that way. Ed was my husband, yes...but that didn't mean I knew him."

9

Ed Dorne was sitting at his desk, as usual watching, staring down into the car park at the last few people either running or speedily walking toward reception. There were always those kinds of people in the mornings: those with bad timing – and probably bad organisational skills – always *almost late* for their 9:00am start. He looked down on them, his face disgusted, trying to imagine what their excuses would be if he were to line them all up and question them. And if he could, he would've said 'Not good enough...' and '*Well that's no excuse!*', and even if the smart-arse-comment-king on the line's end came up with a good one, he'd have told him '*There's just no excuse for lateness! – end of!*'

Ed changed the focus of his attention, drawing back to his reflection on the inside of the window again. He now realised why he despised them all so much: their Freedom, the freedom to be late. And the only reason he knew they were always *almost late* was because – *yes* – he was always there *too early*. 'Without organisation, a man cannot take control of his life and accomplish anything,' his father had told him (*a million damn' times!*) as a teenager. And he was right, wasn't he? He must've been – because Ed had accomplished *so much*, hadn't he? He had an *organised* desk with all its stationary in exactly the right fucking place, worked in a *cracking* job at the call centre, had a clean, tidy and *organised* house, and his life was *so controlled* that it was like it was goddamn automated, robot-like – all of which his wife had pleasantly confirmed to him last night through a one-way argument in front of their *go-to-couple friends* (whom he was continually forced to spend time with) while out for a meal.

And had it not have been for her outburst, her *high perceptiveness and awareness*, then he would've never realised that his life was stuck inside a revolving door, without point or meaning, would he? No – because up until then, he thought he'd been cursing God through his office window for all these years because Harry Longheart had stolen his custard cream back in the school playground...!

Even the pot wash guy from the kitchen downstairs, who he'd seen walking in earlier, looked happier than Ed himself had this morning – and that really was saying something. The pot wash guy hadn't been smiling...but hadn't been frowning or miserable, either. And it had pissed Ed right off. That guy was always supposed to be more miserable than he was. It was the law – one of the only things which made him feel good each day.

Later that night Ed was going to have to go home to his wife and try to patch things up. And he'd decided, though he didn't want to and hated admitting being in the wrong, that he would have to completely take the blame for the whole thing. Because he *had* been a – *yes* – royal shit last night. He'd already decided also, as he'd driven into work this morning, that he was going to get her some flowers. He was pretty sure he loved the woman, after all. And it was terribly clear to him that he'd done a lot more than just step over the line a tad.

His life was the problem. That's what was killing him. And sometimes it shone right through and onto other people. His words would pour out over them, burning. *And was it so wrong that it felt so good trying to argue with others?* Sometimes he would deliberately attempt to get under their skin, just as he'd done with his wife last night at the Aurelio's restaurant at the port. All four of them had been there, all talking about the time he and his wife had been to Greece three years ago. It had been then that his words had started attacking her on an almost unconscious level. They just came out. And it wasn't the volume or tone which did the damage – just the deliberateness of his interruptions. She originally began by talking about the complications with the flights and how they had to change planes, and as she spoke, he kept cutting in, correcting her about the times. Of course, his brain had always had a thing for numbers, hadn't it? Even to this day, he could still remember the school bus timetable from when he was a kid.

After she'd stopped a couple of times to allow for his corrections, she moved on to discuss the weather and the temperature of the one day of freakish heat they'd experienced. And of course, he hadn't been able to let that one go either. He hadn't even noticed that across the table Claire and Scott had grown uncomfortable watching, knowing any second the woman, the once dormant volcano, was about to explode. And after his next correction, she did.

Ed felt shocked, embarrassed even, never having thought his wife could've erupted like that; not having shouted exactly, but having spoken in a horrible slicing tone, saying things which hurt him – really hurt him. She continued to eyeball him as if she hated every aspect of his existence, and was about to say every damn thing she disliked about him there and then. Whether he liked it or not. It was only when Claire and Scott managed to cut her malevolent stare, trying to diffuse the situation, that she controlled herself, cupped her face in her hands, looked back at them, pulled an unconvincing smile from somewhere, and after a moment said: 'Sorry – I'm *so sorry* about that, guys.' Ed himself was still pale, sunk into the back of his chair tensely. He remained that way for a while. Pretty soon he started questioning himself, wondering why he was so persistent in always doing *that thing he did* to her. He leaned forward and apologised to Claire and Scott – who looked like they were experiencing the worst, most awkward dinner evening of all time – and then turned to look, though it was petrifying, at the side of his wife's face. 'I'm sorry,' he said, his voice like that of a regretful schoolboy who had found himself in trouble for the first time. And after no response came he tried: 'Darling…I *am* sorry, all right?' The rest of his words that night, even after arriving home, had received no reply either. Only silence.

Ed's thoughts were interrupted as a customer call now came through. He pushed the microphone on his headset closer to his mouth, and then answered as sarcastically as he could allow himself to with: 'Safe Insurance, Edward speaking. *How can I help you?*

10

Saturday, 6 March 2010

There had not been much different about Layna's Saturday. She'd spent it inside her bedroom, which had been turned into a semi-professional photography studio – well, the best she could afford at present, anyway. All three shoots, which had taken her up to 3:00pm, were now complete.

First of all, she'd photographed a teenage wannabe-model who'd insisted upon doing poses Layna had advised wouldn't come across well on camera. But, in the end, the little prima donna had gotten her way and struck the poses which, apparently, were in all the magazines. Layna hadn't really minded, though. It was only her great sense for what looked best on camera that had made her want to help. The main thing was that, like this client, although none of them were being charged yet, it was all good solid experience Layna could happily strap to her work belt; pictures she could put into her mind's photo bank, her portfolio, website, and most importantly, her confidence. It was also very handy to have intimate settings and an environment like this that allowed her to get used to directing people.

The other two bookings had been from a mother living locally, who had obviously known better than to pass on a free photo shoot opportunity, and so had also decided to take her two children – and then, toward the end of the shoot, her *husband* had even turned up! Layna had not been happy about this. But...another shoot was another shoot, wasn't it?

The next booking had been from a man who ran what she'd gathered was a martial arts class or a gym (or something along those lines), wanting to make some flyers. His torso had looked great on camera, she'd thought, when suddenly he'd just thrown his t-shirt off and started demonstrating some high kicks he'd wanted to try out for the shots. Layna wanted to warn him many a time about how close he'd been getting to the light stand of the umbrella (and especially her new 26-inch soft box which she'd only just unpacked and set up earlier that morning). The size of the room hardly helped either in creating the ample space he needed. But the guy was just a little eccentric if anything, she'd thought, and it had amused her as she'd watched him admiring himself, going on to cause no serious damage to anything but his own modesty.

At the end of the day, as with most Saturdays, she hadn't been too short of pocket. This was because she'd almost, though she felt it foolish, come to expect most people to now pay for their shoots (even though she advertised them on her website as free) simply because many already *had* done in the past. Like that day, some of them had commented on how friendly, attentive, and professional (and that part had felt good – *boy, had it*) she'd been, and had then said they couldn't possibly leave without contributing something. They'd paid up what they thought was a fair amount for the hour, and this amount hadn't been a silly figure, either – from anyone. Even the family who'd expected to get something for absolutely *diddly-squat* had coughed up some dough in the end, after the mother developed somewhat of a conscience as she'd reached for the door handle. She'd come back, breathing through her thirty-a-day lungs the words: 'Take this, babes – *photos' amazin.*' It made Layna feel good seeing happy customers, and was always comforting to know she was on the right track.

She would usually advise clients it would take two or three days before they would receive the two photo CDs promised, one with a selection of shots she touched up with her ProEdit software (giving them that extra quality and professional finish), and the other being a master copy with every shot she'd taken during the shoot. As they left, she would also give them her business card, telling them to ring her if, once they'd seen the CDs, they wanted any large printouts or canvases made. These Layna had to charge a fixed price for, as getting prints made was far from cheap. She didn't usually get many requests back, but did receive a few emails and phone calls every now and then from people saying they were interested; generally those who were pursuing a modelling career or teenagers who just wanted a modelling style portfolio. Even still, producing the canvas prints was expensive, and though the client's money *did* pay for them, the time and effort needed to go all the way to the printers felt sometimes wasted for such a small number on each occasion. She couldn't blame the customers, though, because there was in fact a more local printing company she could've visited. It was just the pride and perfectionism in her work that always made her go further afield to Spectrum, the more prestigious printing company.

'How you doin over there?' Layna called to her assistant for the day. 'They lookin okay?'

'Yes,' Alex replied from the corner of the room, squashed tightly behind the desk and computer screen, his comfort sacrificed to allow for ample studio space.

'Good. I'm just gonna make a brew, you want one?'

'Yes, please.'

'Cool,' she said, and then did a little skip before leaving the room to make her way down to the kitchen.

Alex's eyes looked around, still fascinated by how the place could also double up as a bedroom when its alter ego, *The Studio*, wasn't in full swing. The wardrobe and chest of drawers had been pushed right up against the back wall, along with the bed which was on its side horizontally. He turned his focus back to the screen where he'd been in the process of uploading photos and writing them to CDs.

Like every other encounter he'd had with Layna recently, he of course did feel nervous, and before making his way there that morning, had worried about helping her out. What made it worse was that he'd had *responsibility* that day. The clients – the people who he didn't know and were complete strangers – might've wanted to talk to him, he'd thought, and when they actually had done, he'd received *The Look* on more than one occasion.

As Alex felt the unsettling anxiety inside again, he remembered what Brian had said to him after he'd got off that ride: *'You didn't die, man, I told ya.'* And it was…*comforting*? Yes. *Yes* it was. Even though today *had* made him uncomfortable – he *hadn't* died. Nope. He was still here, and Layna had told him he'd been doing all right, and he thought, though the initial job was easy, that he hadn't actually done anything wrong. No disasters had happened. And as for getting *The Look* – well, that was just expected, wasn't it?

'I put one sugar in your tea,' Layna said as she came back in. 'You look like a one sugar guy, am I right? I usually have a feeling for people and tea. *And sugar.*'

'Yes, perfect,' he lied. He didn't really care much for tea, and hadn't had one since he was fifteen.

She handed the red mug to him, and after hovering her own yellow mug around trying to find a suitable space, set it down on the cluttered desk. She then did another light skip out the room while saying 'I'm getting some biscuits I forgot! They're mandatory around here if you have a cup of tea, you know?' As her voice travelled with her down the stairs she then added 'And then we're going over to your place. I wanna see where you live!'

Alex's heart dropped to his stomach.

***

As Layna locked the front door behind her, Alex realised why it had been safe enough to store all that expensive photography equipment in her bedroom (which perhaps wasn't even that expensive). The property itself was in fact a three storey house, consisting of a lounge and kitchen on the ground floor, two bedrooms and a bathroom on the first, and another two bedrooms and a bathroom on the second. Her friend Stacey lived in one of the rooms upstairs apparently, and the other two rooms were also both occupied, all rented out by the couple living on the first floor with their names on the lease. Having this many people living there would probably mean that at least one person would always be in. And that fact surely meant the place had a good enough security blanket most of the time.

As they walked out of the cul-de-sac, making a shortcut through the alley to Moulden Road, three kids on their bikes cycled past and then abruptly stopped behind. They stared. But they weren't staring at Alex. The tallest boy was jeered on by the two others, and suddenly called out '*What happened to ya face??*'

Alex suddenly filled with a jet black anger. It hit fast. Out of nowhere. Just like that. And this time, for a reason he didn't understand, it had shocked him deeply. He hadn't felt anything like this for a while, but could sense the sheer power of it clouding his vision.

They both carried on walking, with Layna soon saying to him, seemingly not fazed: 'Don't worry, ignore those pricks.' But when he heard them all laughing, sniggering in the background again, the anger turned into a scarlet rage. A few seconds later he couldn't even feel the social angst from being outside anymore. All he could think about was what he wanted to do to them back there. And he was ready – *so fucking ready* to go back and do something. He felt like he could, like if someone handed him a long steel bar he could smash their heads till busted bone showed at their temples. Whatever was going on inside him, it had manifested alarmingly fast. And of course he recognised it. Of course he recognised that feeling of *wanting to destroy something*.

But then it started slowly draining away. Because he...couldn't do it, could he?

Not because of himself. But because of *Layna*. Things were starting to change in his life now. And that meant he had to control his emotions – do things *differently* now.

But the hatred was fierce for the kids who were still mocking her. It would feel *so good* to grab them by the throat, wouldn't it? To watch the blood vessels surface around their pupils at bursting point? And to—

Alex shut his eyes firmly, and forced his fingers out from the tight fists they formed. This mood was dangerous. He had to get out of it. Had to get out now.

Luckily, once he and Layna made it out the alley and turned the corner, the waves of scarlet and tar blacks crashing together inside began calming. It was gradual. But it was happening. Things also got easier when Layna started talking again. She didn't mention the kids or anything that had just happened, though – it was as if she didn't even care.

And he admired that a lot.

Her strength.

Five minutes later they were nearing his home, with Alex feeling total and utter dread for what was about to come. He also felt absolutely helpless. Helpless because he couldn't stop it from happening. They were drawing so close now, and he couldn't just say *no*, could he? He might lose his only friend if he did.

He tried to stop the record in his head that was playing a thousand incomprehensible sounds but—

Wait...

He then examined that last thought – that last word which had been clear in his mind.

Friend

What is that? he thought. *Is this what a friend is? Is* she *a friend? Is this a genuine friendship? Do I...have a friend?*

Alex looked over to her face. But was it a friend's face?

He wasn't sure.

It seemed that way, though, didn't it?

He returned his vision ahead, and then looked back at her to clarify that she *was* really there. She seemed to be, didn't she? But how did he *know*? How could he *prove it*?

Alex thought about the drink he'd gone out for with her, and the day at the theme park too, wondering whether it all had been real. Were the people he'd met been real? Were the brief conversations he'd had been real? Had he really driven all that way to the park – there and back?

What was real?

Who was real?

Only a mirror could prove that. What was there. What wasn't. What existed.

And he'd never seen anyone but himself standing in front of one.

***

After the key turned inside the lock, then came the awful confirming sound of the door's hinges squealing open – and next, the horrible knowledge that they were both about to go in. Alex pushed it open, his eyes closing, knowing that if she hadn't already had enough of him, and *had* actually forced herself to be in his company up until now, then seeing the contents of his flat would definitely get her to that stage. And it would then be the last time she would ever associate herself with him, for sure. *Of course it would* – she'd freak after seeing a lounge filled wall to wall with reptiles, wouldn't she?! And she'd freak if she saw any of his art work, or saw any of the printouts, his writings (which had sometimes turned into booklets) of the dream fantasies where he'd written – not too long ago – about brutally murdering his colleagues, his family, and the kids from when he'd been at school...and also, sometimes, even just imaginary people!

Before he'd brought her there that day, he hadn't given a second thought to what it was to have any of this kind of stuff in his flat, but now that he had someone else with him, who he thought was more than likely to *be* real, he felt a heightened awareness of it, and questioned the *normalness and suitability* of his possessions.

Once inside, Alex was suddenly off. He quickly peered into the bedroom to the right, seeing it was fine, and then went further down to see what sights could hurt him in the lounge. As he went, he could envision Layna literally seconds from that moment walking in behind and being simply speechless, just thinking she wanted to run away – run away and never look back...

He scanned the room a couple of times, finally deciding it was just the small pile of *murder papers* (which he now named them in his mind) that had to be hidden. Well – it was the only thing he *could* hide, wasn't it? He couldn't exactly cover up every glass tank on every shelf of the walls now, could he?

Just before she came into the room he quickly stuck the pile of papers inside the top drawer of the desk. He then found he'd been wrong about her being speechless.

'Oh my God...' she said.

And there it was: that feeling in his stomach. The feeling that meant it was about to happen. The feeling that meant it was the beginning of the end.

'It's so...dark in here, Alex. I can hardly see *a thing.*'

He knew that any moment now she was going to start running. As soon as she saw what was in there, she would be gone. Out. Never to be seen again.

As Layna's eyes tried to adjust she said: 'Are these the pets you were talking about that...*aren't cats and dogs*?' She squinted her eyes some more. 'You know what? – I really can't see *anything* in here...' Her hand reached back through and around the doorway, flicking at the light switch, but nothing happened inside the bulb at the ceiling.

Alex was on edge with every step she made as she started to move about the lounge.

'Your light in here doesn't work. A little creepy, don't you think?'

He found *himself* being the one who was speechless – for the sole reason that she was still there. Maybe her vision just wasn't good enough yet to have given her brain the nod it was time to run off? Yes that was probably what it—

But then Alex saw something else happening, and he was screaming inside his head *NOOOOOOO!* while he watched her hands reach out as she said: 'I'm gonna open the curtains, okay?'

Open the curtains? he thought. *Open the curtains?! No! No! No! You can't do that! Then you will see the…the fucking mess…my life…my farm of unwanted aliens…my weirdness…my unacceptable life that…that nobody wants to see!*

It was all right, though, because she wasn't able to reach the curtains over the glass tanks at the far wall. And for a moment he thought it was over. But within seconds Layna was up on the chair which she'd carried over from the desk, and was standing on it, leaning over the top of the tanks' roofs. She yanked the curtains open, revealing the light, letting in the flooding brightness that seemed to be blinding, causing him to turn away in an instant.

'That's better,' she said looking out to the sky. 'Shame it's so dull out there, though, eh?'

But Alex didn't think it was dull at all! The day's light she'd let into the room carried a terrible intense glow with it, making everything look unfamiliar. Everything was too clear, too open to see – unconcealed! And it made him feel awful. Exposed and unprotected, like he was standing there naked.

He could hear her in the background step off the chair onto the carpet. With his back still turned, he waited and waited for the moment where, now that she could see the horrors before her, she would finally say: *Listen, Alex. I'm tired and…I think I'd better go. Maybe we'll see each other someday in the future…*

Seconds passed and yet Layna hadn't said a word, though. He couldn't hear anything – not even the sound of fleeing feet.

But then it was about to happen. He could make out the moment just before she was about to talk. Air was being drawn in.

'Alex…'

Here it comes… Here it comes…

'What is this?'

He turned, looking as she hunched over trying to see what was in one of the middle-shelved tanks, and then said through a quiet unsettled voice: '…What?'

'In *this one*?' she asked him. 'What kind is it? It's one of those giant tarantulas, right?'

'…Yes,' he answered, hesitantly approaching her side.

'Wow – it ever bite you?'

'…No.'

'Better call an ambulance if it does, though, right?' she joked, throwing a smile his way.

A little laughter almost escaped him, but he caught it before it could.

But hang on – *what was going on?!* He had just almost laughed for what was possibly one of the first times in his life – and that feeling alone had managed to start draining his anxiety in one hit, hadn't it? And more importantly: *Why was she still there?!* She didn't *mind* the creatures? They *weren't* disgusting or too weird for her?

No. *No, no, no.* Not possible. She must be acting. Hiding it. Just until she can escape later and start running. Or maybe there would be a moment where she'd simply walk away slowly, allowing him to watch her descend the stairs; to watch gradually, with every step, as his only friend would walk out of his life? And then at the bottom she would give an apathetic wave and say: *Goodbye, Alex. Have a nice life with your monsters. It's where you belon—*

But now Alex suddenly attacked his thoughts, shouting back with a strength not usually present. *No! Don't be so fucking negative!* His inner nemesis obliged with pleasure to argue back, though, saying: *Don't be so negative? My dear boy, your whole life has been negative! Why would it change now?!*

Alex managed to temporarily shut down his mind, resisting listening for as long as he possibly could, wanting instead to enjoy the moment with Layna. He started to talk to her about the inhabitant of the tank which had caught her interest, though he felt awkward and strange doing so, mostly with guilt and a sense of eccentricity for having such a vast collection as he did in that one room.

'It's a Goliath Bird Eater,' he then answered.

'Oh, cool! So…it eats birds?'

'Well…I feed it dead mice. And locusts. Food has to be large. But in the wild it would eat birds. But actually…' He stopped to take a breath, realising he was saying quite a long sentence. 'But actually…they only eat dead or injured chicks that fall from the nest onto the forest floor.'

'Well that sucks.'

'…Why?'

'Cos before, I thought it was this badass-bird-eating-machine – but now I'm educated enough to know that it's just a *lazy thing* that waits for chicks to fall into its mouth.' She looked into the tank at the tarantula and told it: 'You've been taken down a few notches there, my friend!'

Alex didn't laugh, and didn't really understand what she was talking about, but decided to show he agreed and said 'I guess so.' Then he had a thought. 'Do you want me to get it out for you?'

A burst of laughter forced its way out of her nose. 'If you're talking about the spider, then yes…'

After enduring a moment of embarrassment, in which blood had instantly filled the vessels of his cheeks, he removed the tank from the shelf. Layna smiled softly as she saw how gently he placed the heavy object down on the desk, appreciating how careful he was not to discomfort the creature. 'You care about them a lot, don't you?' she said.

'Well…I don't know. I—'

'Alex. It's okay. You can be honest with me. You think you're the *only* person on the planet with an obsession? You like reptiles and spiders, and…some other *unique pets*. But so what? See this thing round my neck? – my camera? I take it with me everywhere. I take snaps of everything. Once, I even took a picture of a public toilet I thought looked interesting. I've actually slept with my camera still round my neck before. *But so what?* It's an obsession. *Everyone has one.*'

Alex smiled inside, liking her reasoning, confirming to himself she was definitely smart.

After a short moment of silence between them, he looked back at the tank, took off the lid, and put both his hands in. Layna watched curiously as he effortlessly, yet so gently, picked up the eight-legged creature and cradled it in his hands, hardly causing it any distress whatsoever. When it was out, right in front of her, she said with absolute annunciation: 'Ho-ly-shit.'

She jumped a little as it moved all of a sudden, but Alex handled it with ease as if he'd known exactly where it would go, placing one hand under the other to stop his pet from falling.

'Don't worry,' he told Layna. 'It's just your breath.'

'My *breath*?' she exclaimed, surprised at what she thought must have been an unexpected joke.

'Try…not to breathe directly onto it, I mean. It doesn't like the pressure of the air much.'

'*Oh…*' she said, quickly realising just what he'd meant. 'Sorry!'

'That's all right. You wanna hold it?'

'*Now?* I don't know – I might drop it…'

'You'll be fine. Just…relax. It can feel you.'

'I don't think I can do that. The thing's as big as a dinner plate. It hardly fits on your hands, let alone mine…'

'Well…you can sit at the desk. Just in case you drop her.'

'It's a *her*?'

'Yes, it's a female. She's called Laura.'

She brought the chair back over from the window and placed it in front of the desk. After sitting down, her hands went out. 'This okay?'

'That's fine. You ready?'

'*Wait, wait, wait!*' she said as more doubt shot into her. 'I don't know…'

'Want a minute?'

But Layna knew there was only one way to do it. And it wasn't by waiting longer or by psyching herself up. 'Just do it,' she said with conviction. 'Do it now, Alex. *Gimme!*'

And then he did. She'd got a good couple of second's worth of cringing in before he'd placed it onto her hands. But now it was done. The hardest part was over.

Once settled, the tarantula didn't move. It appeared to be moving slightly, however, but this was only because of the tiny trembles Layna's hands were creating. She didn't want them shaking, of course. She wanted them to be *dead still*. That was easier said than done, though. She was afraid, yes – but somehow got a kick out of holding the thing. There'd never been one like this in her hands before. She had held one at some kind of children's educational show in a zoo once as a kid – but never like this. Not one *this* size.

The thin tips of its legs, which Layna supposed were kind of like the spider version of feet, were very close to the edges of her palms. She couldn't believe the thing even fitted on her hands at all! She focused mainly on keeping completely motionless, deciding not to say anything. The tarantula itself didn't feel heavy, in fact surprisingly light. It was simply the *not moving part* that was the hardest bit.

'You can rest your hands on the desk if you want,' Alex said. 'To stop the shaking.'

'I just don't wanna lose it. Won't it run away if I put my hands down?'

'No. She won't.'

Layna lowered her hands as slowly and smoothly as possible, imagining they were like a spider elevator. As the backs of her hands touched the wooden surface, one of its legs sprang up and then back down. She pulled a grimace as it happened, hoping she hadn't caught its *foot* between her hand and the desk.

'What now?' she asked, and then immediately after she did, a little scream echoed inside as all its many legs started to move, tapping lightly on and off her hands.

'*Alex!* What now? It's *escaping* I think!'

'No, she's all right,' Alex said, his voice a calm sea. 'Just curious. That's all.'

'Can you put it back now?' she said uneasily yet laughing also, somehow managing to see the funny side of the situation. 'I'm worried about it – *her...*'

She watched again as Alex picked it up in a scooping action and lowered it back into the tank.

'Wow – that was...*an experience*...I think...' she said, still buzzing with adrenaline. 'I must admit, I was actually scared, and it was kinda ugly looking...' She turned to look at the tarantula for a moment, which was now making its way back under the arched piece of bark, and said 'Sorry!' before turning back to Alex and continuing with 'But once I held it, it wasn't that monstrous. I felt it...its *grace*, in the way it moved. It was actually...beautiful, I guess.' She laughed lightly. 'I never thought I'd say that about *a spider.*'

Alex couldn't help but smile when he saw hers.

109

He then looked at her. Really looked. *She understands*, he thought. *She gets it.*

***

'So,' Layna said. 'Now that I've done something crazy…I want *you* to show me something.'

'…Something?'

'Yeah. Something I don't know about you.' She noticed his baffled face. 'Something easy, then, like…*your artwork.*'

Just having heard the request took his breath away. 'I…I don't know. I'm not—'

'What are you afraid of?'

'…Nothing.'

'*So…?*'

'I've never shown anyone before.'

'And you think it might be…bad? *Terrible even?*'

'…I know it's not good.'

'If no one's ever seen it, how do you know?'

He knew where she was going with this, and that she was doing *that thing* again. She was trying to get him to do something he really didn't want to do at all – and he didn't like it one bit. It was even worse knowing that what she said actually made sense somehow. Horrible sense. 'I don't think it's a…good idea right now.'

'Won't get any easier.' Her eyes now filled with sincerity. 'Come on, I'm interested. I've wanted to see your work for a long time.'

'…Really?'

'*Of course.*'

Alex then realised she was referring to the brutal dream sketches she'd seen him doing at work, one of which had been of himself shoving Sam Henderson's head down the Food Muncher, complete with overflowing chunks of skull and bloodied flesh. He couldn't show her those, of course. And not only that – he couldn't show her *anything else* either!

'*So…?*' Layna tried again.

'I'm sorry. I can't. I never show anyone my art. It's not…'

'It's not *what?*'

He opened his mouth, but no words came out.

'What are you afraid of?' she asked.

'I'm not *afraid*.'

Silence filled the room for a while, but soon Layna started to talk again. 'At the end of my first year in primary school...I remember me and my classmates all received a kind of end of term year book. Well, it was more like a paper booklet, really, printed in black and white. It was late afternoon when our teacher handed them out, and as she got round to me, she gave me a...a *funny* kind of look...and I didn't even think much of it at first. All the other kids were all looking at the small thumbnail photos and were all having fun and enjoying themselves. I noticed that about six of the people on my table, some of who were my friends, were all laughing and pointing at something. I laughed at first, wanting to join in, and soon got curious and said: *What?! What?! What is it?!* But then I realised what they were all laughing at. They were laughing at...*me*. They were laughing at my photo. My face was different to theirs and...so they laughed. I was different to them. I remember going home, and spending hours and hours looking at my face in the photo and then looking at theirs. It was the first time in my life that I'd noticed I was different. Before then, I'd just been a kid — the same, and I don't think even they'd really noticed. But I'd stood out in the booklet that day, and they'd recognised it. Become aware. Before that day, I'd always carried around the camera my dad had given me before he went away — *well*, abandoned us — and had always been taking photos with it. Everywhere. *Of everything*. But...I couldn't touch it again after that. Or any other camera.'

She stopped and tried to laugh a little, but the strength of the story's seriousness shone through. 'I didn't pick one up again until about five years ago. I'd decided after that day at school, that if a camera was capable of capturing such an ugly image, then I didn't want to ever be behind one again.'

'You're...not ugly, Layna,' Alex said.

She sent a smile his way, but he could sense she hadn't believed a word he'd said. 'Anyway. Long story short — I could never bring myself to actually pick up a camera for many years after that. Because when I did, it reminded me of *me*, the way I looked, the way that everyone stared at me and made me feel bad. But after one counsellor, two psychiatrists, and a whole load of time to deal with my problems,

I finally realised *I* wasn't the ugly one. *They* were. If people judge you without knowing you – then *fuck' em*!'

Half a smile appeared on Alex's face.

'*Seriously* – a lot of people have judged me, made me feel guilty, ashamed, paralysed. I spent a large portion of my life feeling paralysed. *And for what?* – because I didn't fit their *criteria*? I made new friends, and it was a miracle that I'd had the opportunity to meet these people, cos they saw me more clearly than many others had. I'd spent my whole life trying to please the others…and be like *them*. But it had all been a waste of time. It was *never* about what they'd thought. It was about me accepting *me* for who I was. And my friends – my true friends – saw me…with *true vision*. The others were blind. And now, when I hear people taunting me, staring at me – I don't care. I don't get upset and worry about what they think. I don't wanna waste another second of my life listening to anyone who wants to bring me down. I don't go backwards anymore.'

Alex was amazed by her words – in awe of them. She was so…different.

Different as in *the same*?

No. She was not like him. But she was not like *Them* either.

'Anyway, so you have something unusual about you. Your art is unusual, controversial, pornographic, *whatever*. Maybe you've painted Jesus fucking Hitler – I don't know, I haven't seen it yet! But my point is: don't be ashamed of it. Don't hide what you have just because people tell you it's not normal. I have known normal people…and guess what? They are as boring *as hell…*'

Alex's modest smile returned to his face again.

'So when you're ready to show me…' she said, '…I'll be here waiting.'

Alex still didn't want to do it, though. He didn't want to show her his artwork. But something about the way this woman spoke – the things she said, the way she said them – also made him want to, if only to see if there really was a way she could be right, that there really was a way it could be a good thing to do. Maybe he wasn't right about everything? Maybe he had to listen to *other people* sometimes? And maybe it had been too long – too many damn years – since he had? Because this person, at least, seemed worth listening to.

112

Alex got up, his heart beating faster straight away, and headed towards the bedroom. But that slightly better feeling he'd had about showing his work vanished as he was swamped with one much more familiar; one which weakened his spirit by the time he reached the doorway. It told him, cried out to him disgustedly, that what he was doing was wrong. It was wrong to show her. *So very wrong of him!*

The room itself looked more like a storage facility than a bedroom, with almost two hundred canvases and tubes of rolled paintings stacked against the walls, on top of and inside the wardrobe, and under the bed. Alex, standing on the threshold looked around, his feet firmly planted. Before long, his eyes dropped to the floor, his focus coming and going. He could feel *Them* all around him. Closing in. Whispering.

His father was telling him his art was *garbage*, a *waste of time and energy*, and that *nothing good could ever come from it*. His primary school art teacher hanging up a drawing on the wall and saying: *The whole class is drawing witches, Alex. What you have drawn is unacceptable. It doesn't even look like anything. It makes no sense. I'm leaving it up on the board as an example of how not to behave in class.* His secondary school principal talking to his parents quietly. *Before you go, listen – he's not fitting in well in his classes. Some of his ideas...the things he writes in his stories for English, are...how do I put this? – a little challenging. It causes trouble. And so we are having...trouble, um...moulding him.*

Alex could feel them all. Hundreds of eyes leering and staring. Gossiping mouths and pointing fingers. Disapproving heads shaking from side to side.

But then he was over the threshold and on his knees, grabbing at a canvas, pulling it out from under the bed. He felt that he still needed a moment to think about what he was doing – a moment just to *breathe*. That couldn't be done, though. It couldn't, because he knew he had to carry on. He had to stop thinking! Had to ignore the voices, the people in the room.

He had to ignore *Them*!

***

Five minutes later, Alex slowly walked into the lounge. He leaned the four canvases he had selected against the desk and took a seat.

'Crikey—' Layna said with surprise. '*They're big...*' She moved in closer to them. 'May I?'

Emotionally drained, Alex looked down at his hands, and only after a few seconds breathed out: 'Yes.' Heavy doubts about his actions – and fear – played in his mind. But it was too late now. It was going to happen. And of course, then it was. For the first time it was really happening...

Just the sound itself of her unwrapping them was terrifying. It was the waiting, the apprehension, the exposure of his art – of him! *He* was being exposed! And she was going to see it in the paintings; his thoughts, his world, his life – *everything!* She would see the truth. Then that would be it. She would go running. Gone for good.

Alex held his hands tightly, his gaze glued to them while he waited for *those words* – or some kind of ghastly sound – to come from her.

How long would the quiet last before he heard something like: *Say, Alex, I'm feeling tired, so...I think I should get going. I think it's probably for the best that we...just don't see each anymore, you know?*

There was still nothing, though. Nothing at all. What was happening? What was she thinking?

What was she thinking of *him*?!

***

Layna had seen the canvases – all four of the paintings which were a mixture of acrylic and oil. As she'd uncovered them one by one, she'd had to sit back on the floor to allow herself to take it all in. Each image had been unutterably powerful, overwhelming her. The pain they conveyed left her helpless, bereft of speech; made her feel every emotion that every brushstroke signified. The art had injected itself into her soul. It had meant something to her. And she'd remained there for ten minutes not saying a word, her eyes and mind lost within.

When Alex turned toward her, he saw she was crying. She then looked back; looked back into his eyes, deep into something beyond anything she had ever known. 'Alex...' she said, her voice breathless, bare with raw emotion. '...They're beautiful.'

11

'How was it?' Sam asked.

'I stayed as long as I had to,' Will said as he got in the back of the taxi next to his friend. 'Same old story, I'm afraid. Same as last year and the one before. Same meal. Same donation. Same—' He reached for his seatbelt as the car pulled away. '—people. Same smiles. Same—'

'*Tie*,' Sam filled in.

'…Yes. You noticed?'

'Jesus, Will – it's a *Paul Chenco*. You've worn it for the past two years each time we come up here to London for the dinner ball.'

'Whenever *I* come up for the ball,' Will corrected. 'You are not a dentist or a BDA member, Sam. You just…tag along.'

Sam pretended not to have heard the man's response.

'That's very observant of you, though,' Will said. 'I am impressed.'

'Good set of eyes I have, don't you know? I see things *clearly*.'

Will turned and looked ahead. 'My cousin's joining us later, by the way, Sam. And if he is *still* challenged with the ladies, then I am going to need your help.'

'Oh really…?'

'*Of course*. You have *meat game* just like me – well, obviously not at my level…but you have it.'

'*Very ouch*, but what's the point? Sarah and the wife are meeting us there, anyway…'

'I may have already created a diversion. They are staying in the hotel, you see? Eating there, too.'

'*Just like that…?*' Sam questioned disbelievingly.

'I told Sarah she could marry me next year. Right now I can get her to do anything. I said we needed a boy's night out – so she agreed to let us fly alone. Simple. Done. *Perfect.*'

'And Merissa?'

'The sheep always goes where the dog tells it to, Sam.'

'*Dog?* You're calling your future wife a dog, now?'

'Yes – in a figure of speech.'

Sam chuckled to himself briefly. 'Well tonight is sorted, then. And I'm yet to see the talents of your *game* you speak of…and this – what was it you called it? – *higher level…*'

'*Ha!* Look, don't hate me because it seems to happen so easily for me. And I don't just make it look easy. It just…*is.*'

'Right, right…' Sam uttered beneath a laugh.

'My cousin – he's going to be like a chrysalis. Then by the morning, he will be a *man.*'

'Well I'm here, aren't I? You can count on me.'

'Right-hand man,' Will said, letting his head fall back to the headrest. 'Right-hand man.'

***

They arrived at The Blue Suite at 10:30pm. Soon after, as Sam was sipping his imported Italian beer, he saw Will turn from the bar with a big smile on his face and hug a man who'd appeared through the crowd.

'Hey!' Will shouted over the pounding dance music. 'This is Adam, my cousin!'

Sam sent out an open hand. 'How are we doing tonight, Adam? Sam Henderson.'

'Just fine,' Adam replied, his apprehensive eyes wandering around the club. 'I'm good.'

'So…' Sam began, '…you—'

'Get the man a drink already!' shot from Will.

'*He's right* – what you drinking?' Sam said, his hand dropping into his pocket. He knew his wallet was empty before even pulling it out, but was confident enough to do so because of the way it felt to be crammed – though in the currency of receipts – with money. He was relieved when he heard '*No, no* – I'm getting these,' from Will, but still

116

insisted paying, playing along in the game where he'd eventually have to give in to his friend. It was a safe game. And so of course, he was soon saying '*Okay*, have it your way, William...'

His next thoughts were *Cash. I need to get more cash.* He stepped off the stool. 'I need to get to the ATM, be back in a minute.' As he walked through the doors and out onto the street, he made sure he got the door monkey's attention, ensuring the guy got a good look at his face. Since it wasn't exactly the kind of venue that put a stamp on your hand for re-entry, this was well worth doing as it could save you from forking out another costly admission fee later.

The night air was biting, but luckily the cash machine was without a queue. As he inserted his card and punched in his number, the feelings then started to come back, though. *The Beast.*

But why was using the cash machine bringing it on? Why was it reminding him of—

He shut his eyes tightly and flared out his fingers, stopping the thoughts.

Sam's balance showed as £32.17. He knew he would have to go overdrawn; his two credit cards were already at the max, and so he had no choice but to bite into the red of his debit account. It would be in the red area because he had to get £100 – no more, no less. That would be OK for the night, wouldn't it? Plus, if he spread the notes out enough in his hand at the bar, it would look like there was even more. He was good at doing that.

Sam took the four twenties and two tens and held them in place in his hand, pulling out and adjusting their positions like a professional card player. He walked back inside without trouble from the door monkey, the notes fixed and ready. As soon as Will turned to acknowledge his presence, Sam then held them out at chest height before slowly sliding them into his wallet. 'That should do it,' he said approaching both men at the bar, speaking loudly enough especially for Will to hear.

'What about the strip club after?' Will questioned.

'What do you mean?' Sam asked.

'Well...that's only one hundred you got there, Sammy.'

'It's a hundred and fifty.'

'No, it's two tens, four twenties.'

Adam sat there, his face bored, still not having touched his drink.

'I *always* get a hundred and fifty out – what is this?' Sam said, shrugging both hands up to his ears comically.

'Let me show you,' Will said, his voice weighted with granite confidence. 'Give me your wallet.'

Sam laughed again. '*It's a hundred-fifty.* I counted it myself...'

'Look, give me your wallet,' Will said, his eyes rolling upwards. 'I will bet-you-*anything.*'

'It's one-fifty.' Sam's heart was beating faster now, his party face starting to fade.

'Fifty,' Will said through a grin. 'I'll-bet-*you*...fifty notes.'

'*Jesus...*' Sam fought on with, casting a look over to Adam that said: *can you believe this guy?!*

'All right, if you're so sure...then why not make it a hundred?'

'So,' Adam cut in, wanting to break the conversation, 'this place – it's, er...it's owned by Stanley Young, right?'

'I'll bet you one-fifty it's *a hundred* you got there,' Will went on.

'It's one-fifty,' Sam fired back. 'I don't need to bet. I know it's there.'

'If you *know* it's there – take the bet. I've got two-fifty in my wallet. I've nothing to lose.'

'Guys, please,' Adam said, almost pleading. 'So...how's the practice been going?'

And that was enough to get Will's attention, his head turning to his cousin almost immediately. It also bought Sam some time now to change the amount in his wallet. As Will and Adam started talking, he then turned and made his move. 'Where you going?' he heard from behind. 'To get an extra fifty, *right?* I've got my eye on you, Henderson!' It was followed by a trail of laughter, which Sam knew had escaped through that smirking grin. 'I'm goin for a bloody piss!' Sam sent back over his shoulder. 'If it's okay with you, *your fucking highness!*'

As he made his way through the packed dance floor he was thinking: *Shit! Shit! Shit! How am I gonna get another fifty without going outside? Maybe Will'll forget? No – he'll look over at me every time I get my wallet out to pay for drinks, won't he? Need more money. Just fifty. One more fifty. BUT I CAN'T TAKE ANYMORE OUT! – what about the CAR, the damn HOUSE?! I'm gonna just have to wait now. Pay day isn't that far away. Leave it. But think for a second.* Think. *You know why this is all happening* don't you? *Don't you* know *why you keep on having—*

But Sam told those last invading thoughts out loud to fuck off. They were wrong. He needed the money and *now*.

He slowed his pace and cautiously looked back, focusing through the crowd to the bar. Will wasn't looking his way, instead still deeply in conversation with Adam. *I can make it. If I go now, I can make it.* If he could make it to the entrance, get to the cash machine and be straight back in, then he could soon be back at the bar, couldn't he? He could be stood there, his head cool, saying: *Okay, okay – fine! Take a look in my wallet. Go on, Will…be my guest.*

Sam was on the move, sidestepping to his right, turning to face the door, moving forward, forward, then turning his head slightly to the left. He heard a shout that sounded familiar in the background and it made his heart beat even faster, but he realised with relief that it had not been Will. He was outside next, his brisk walk changing to a run at once. There was a queue of at least six people at the cash machine, but he joined the back anyway – what *else* could he do? They were all laughing and chatting and he wanted them gone. The bimbo at the front wasn't even pressing anything, just talking to her bimbo friend beside her, giggling away continuously. He looked at his watch, wondering how much it was worth, but his attention was taken away as the queue shortened slightly. After what had seemed like fifteen minutes, he was finally at the front, punching in the number, punching it in wrong, but getting in the second time, the fifty quid note frustratingly coming out at its own leisurely pace. He then ran straight back to the club and strolled up to the bar.

'*I do believe it's the one and only!*' Will announced behind a pointing finger.

'*It is I!*' Sam said with equal enthusiasm. Though his brow now glistened with sweat, an expression of confidence remained in service below.

'What took you so long? Thinking about that *bet*, were we…?'

'I'll take that bet,' Sam said, trying to sound as calm and composed as possible.

'*Oooooo!*'

Adam's tired eyes gazed around the club once again.

119

'Go ahead,' Sam tried to persuade, offering his wallet. 'One hundred and fifty, right?'

'Keep a hold of it,' Will said. 'I don't wanna take your money.'

'*What?* No listen, I—'

'Forget it, Sam. I was taking you for a ride, is all.'

'But I insist you take a look.' Sam's voice was beginning to lose its calm, starting to clearly press for what he wanted.

'Nah...let it go, friend.'

'No – *take a look*. If you're so sure, *take a look!*'

'Sam, I'm trying to have a good night with my cousin here...and, yourself also, of course. *You all right?*'

'I'm fine!' Sam said grabbing his drink from the bar, a splutter of agitated laughter spilling.

'You're sweating,' Will said.

'It's hot in here, isn't it? You guys not hot, *no?*'

Both men shook their heads and a short silence followed.

'Anyway...' Will said turning to his cousin. 'Let's get you some meat.'

'Meat?' Adam asked confused. 'Are we eating?'

Will's jaw dropped and released loud amusement. 'Oh my!' he said pushing at Adam's shoulder. '*No-no!* I'm talking about a little bitch for you to stick later.'

'...Oh. Well, that's—'

'Don't thank me now. But *do* thank me later.' He turned to Sam. 'Adam *will* be thanking me later, won't he?'

Sam looked at his friend, feeling another sweat coming back on. The Beast was still trying to play with him, barely letting his attention remain with the two men in front. He decided it would be wise to start drinking more – and fast. 'You're right,' he said trying to look as relaxed as he could, and then turned to Adam. 'He *is* right, my friend.'

'I've got somebody...actually,' Adam said. 'A girlfriend.'

'*Great* – me too,' Will said. 'She here?'

'Well...no.'

'Mine neither. So there's no problem, right? The—'

'Even so...I'm not interested. Thanks, anyway. Actually I, um, think I should probably get going, so—'

'*Woh, woh, woh there, cous!*' Will exclaimed, his grin becoming more prominent still as he necked another brandy. '*Get ya butt back-on-that-*

120

stool, boy.' He put one foot down to the floor and reached over to the man's shoulder, pulling him back lightly. 'Now that's all mighty high and...*righteous* of you. But you're a Burston. And *Burston's* are the shit, quite frankly – if I may say so myself? So it's time to *man up.* To step up to the plate.' He waved his hand blindly over the bar to the side, his clicking fingers signalling for another brandy while his eyes remained on his cousin. 'You'll thank me tomorrow.'

'No, I'm okay. *Really.'* The polite appreciation on Adam's face carried an unmistakable awkwardness lurking beneath. As he tried to leave the stool again, Will said *'Listen.* You should take advantage of every moment you have with me tonight. I can show you the way. Do you know that *me,* and *I*...could shag...' and then he looked about the place, '...most of the girls in here? *Tonight.'* He scanned around again. 'I could get the numbers of every girl. This I could.'

Adam's eyes filled with slight interest, the most they'd done all evening. 'Wait. You could get the number of every girl in this room?'

'Well...*every* number would take some time, now, wouldn't it? But in theory, I could get *any* number I wish, yes. But they're just numbers, remember? And...even *I* can't guarantee sex after. I admit that part. Hands up.' He knocked back the rest of his drink. 'Sam on the other hand, can. I guess it's that *damn*-fucking-handsome mug of his, isn't it? But...I could—'

'Okay,' Adam cut in with. 'That girl over there.'

'Where?' Will asked gazing over.

'The one at the table,' Adam said now pointing. 'Ten feet away. To the right.'

'Oh, I see...'

'The one with the guy.' Adam deliberately left a moment of silence before he carried on. 'Can't get *that one,* though, I suppose?' He felt like he was starting to enjoy himself, knowing he must have just put a dent in Will's armour, punching right into the heart of his ego. He smiled in the silence that followed.

'Hmm,' Will then replied. 'Piece of cake.'

'What...?'

'Yep.'

'Piece of *cake?'*

'Yep.'

'You're kidding, right? Her boyfriend's right there...'

121

'Sure is.'

'He has his arm around her...'

'We're definitely looking at the same one, cous', yeah.'

'The guy could lift you with *one arm*!'

'Well, actually I've put on a few pounds recently, so I'm not too sure about that. Anyway. Shall we perform the experiment now?'

'What, you're going to—'

'Yes. And if I get the number, you will let me get you *la-la-laid* tonight. Yes?'

'I don't know about...' But Adam stopped and thought about it, deciding in an instant to just lie and agree to the terms and conditions – to just sign the thing. It would be worth it to see Will get humiliated, wouldn't it? To see the look of failure, of losing on the man's face...now that would be something to treasure dearly. 'I'll do it – *if* you get the number.'

Will said nothing. He simply grinned, and then looked to his right-hand man who grinned right back.

12

Sunday, 4 April 2010

'You're leaving?' Alex asked, holding his mobile closer to his ear.

'Yeah,' Layna said.

'Why? You haven't been there…even that long.'

'I've got too many reasons to leave, I guess.'

'But the recession, it…will be hard for you to find something else.'

'I've enough savings to get me by for a while. I know it's careless, but…what the hell.'

'Well, that's…not too bad then, I suppose.'

'It's just that, that place is all right if you don't mind being overworked, underpaid and undervalued – but I can find somewhere else with the same pay that *gives a shit*, you know? So I just think fuck it. It's just another job till I get myself going. And I know everyone's telling me to get into a secure job in graphic design or something, but I'm just crazy, I guess…and I wanna hold out for my photography – it means *everything* to me. Besides, I got my first gig – *a real shoot* – coming up this Saturday! *Woo-hoo!*'

'That's *really good*, Layna.'

'I actually have three bookings this month! *Proper bookings, I mean – advertised with a charge.* Not for *free* anymore!'

'That's great…'

'It really is quite something. For *me*, anyway. It means an actual definite exchange of cash! Maybe my hard work has finally paid off in that portfolio of mine? I dunno – but all the same, I'm excited about it!

'You should be. You deserve it.'

'Thanks!' She took a pause. 'Listen, Alex. Those paintings, the sketch books you showed me, and…well, I was thinking, you should definitely pursue a career in art.'

'...Like what?'

'I'm thinking like...a proper artist or something. Those paintings actually made me feel...I don't know the word exactly. But I've never felt like that. Every time I think of you wasting your life at Sestern, I can't help but think you could be really making something of yourself.'

'...In what?'

'*Art!* You love Art, Alex! You're a fucking genius!'

'I don't think I...*love it*. And I could never earn a living selling—'

'Alex, *don't* think about it, okay? I think you should just...*yeah* – I think you should just do it!'

'I don't know, it's...not a good time and—'

'*Sure it is!* And you should change your job for now. Leave Sestern and try something different. Something low stress and what not – but something different. How long you been at that place?'

'Since…I don't know. Nearly eight years, maybe?'

'*Eight years?!* Jesus, Alex – we've gotta get you outta there! I see you there in that place all the time, surrounded by those morons in the kitchen. It's not good for you. So for God's sake, leave! Try something new!'

'The recession, I don't think—'

'Just start looking at least, yeah?'

There was a long pause, but then Alex softly said 'Yes.'

'*Excellent.* A fresh start for both of us.' When she didn't hear anything back for a few seconds she said 'Alex? You all right? You sound like I've just ripped out your guts. You okay?'

The silence continued.

'…And your vocal cords,' Layna added.

'Sorry, um…I've just worked there a long time.'

'Change is all this is. And you deserve it. You just need to let go a little. You're holding on too tight, that's all.'

Alex didn't know what to say.

'*Oh!* – I've just thought of what I was gonna tell you earlier!' Layna said.

'...What is it?' he asked, worried of her next idea.

'My old friend Richard from Uni – he's an agent.'

'An agent…?'

'An *Art* agent. Can you believe it?! Anyway, he works in London, and the last I heard he was a multi-millionaire – and is probably plotting world domination next like he always said he would. I used to know him quite well and, I think I can *maybe* spin a favour out of him. So what you think?' Alex didn't say anything, but Layna thought it sounded like he was thinking, and after a moment she added: 'When do you want me to call him?'

What...?! screamed through Alex's head. 'I don't know, really. Um...'

'You know what? I don't even have his number yet. I'm just searching on the net for him now. Shouldn't be hard to find – the guy's a bit of an egocentric. So I've read anyway. I've seen him in a few magazines.'

She then stopped talking and all Alex could hear was the faint sound of mouse clicks and keyboard taps.

'Here we go. I've got him up on the screen now. Richard Dowsteene. His other partner is Colin Goadman – obviously both of them making up the name of the agency *Dowsteene and Goadman*. He's supposedly the absolute of hard-headed business types, but...he's also gotta be the guy to go with, if you know what I mean? He'll most likely be *the* one to take an artist places.'

Alex listened to the sound of her voice, the sound of enthusiasm and positivity. He wondered what it must feel like to want to speak through emotions of that kind. He even wondered if *he* might be feeling some of that positivity stuff himself – maybe some kind of low-grade happiness at least? But he still, ultimately, found it hard to know what the emotion was – *if it was indeed there* – as with all the other new ones he'd been experiencing lately. 'So when are you leaving?' he asked, trying, if anything, to change the subject.

'Gonna tell them tomorrow. Give them my two weeks. Then after that, I'll probably find another shitty job, *ha*! Depends – maybe I'll be a professional overbooked photographer by then? Oh, don't I wish!'

***

After the conversation ended, Alex couldn't help but feel even more anxious. But he also couldn't help but notice more of that positive feeling, of something strangely good stirring inside. He didn't want to leave his job. He didn't want Layna to leave her job. And he definitely didn't want to show his art to an agent. It was hard enough showing it to her, let alone anyone else – particularly to someone who knew art, and could judge and *value* it. He didn't feel any better in knowing the guy was some millionaire type, either. His art was nothing special and he knew it. It wouldn't sell. It was worthless. He didn't want the hassle, the stress of it all. And it would all be pointless, anyway.

But as Alex sat at his desk, looking out at the Sunday evening sunshine which still poured in through the lounge window, that optimistic feeling came back and started to overcome some of the negativity. With no strings or commitment attached, he soon told himself it wouldn't hurt to search the internet for this Richard guy.

Just as he fired up his laptop, Layna then called again. The conversation was horribly brief, with barely ten words able to escape his mouth. She'd told him she was coming over to the flat. Coming over now.

***

Before long she was there sitting next to him at the desk. He listened to her, wishing he could've had longer, longer to have put off getting her ideas into action – wishing to have had at least a week to pretend he didn't have to change a goddamn thing at all! But it wasn't going to be that way, was it? No – not with the things she was saying now. Because she was saying that tonight they were going to check out some of the clients and galleries which Richard Dowsteene represented and owned, so that when she got Alex to call on Tuesday, he would have a good idea of the kind of things to say to get the agent hooked. *Yes!* – she wanted him to actually call the guy at lunchtime on Tuesday (obviously permitting she could first get him interested in doing a favour for her after calling him, and, provided he had the time to talk to Alex).

It was *crazy*, and Alex just didn't want to do it for so many reasons. But he knew he'd end up making the call because...well, he *just would*, wouldn't he? She would do her bit, getting him the opportunity, getting him *the* opportunity to speak to the tycoon. And then he wouldn't be able to say no to her.

And he didn't know if he would ever truly understand why that was.

He hated that!

***

The night had soon passed for him. A night which had seen the both of them at his desk browsing, searching, printing, circling, discussing the guy with whom there was surely a microscopic chance of getting representation. And yes, she'd also managed to call the guy. And even worse, he had agreed to talk to Alex and hear about his work over the phone tomorrow.

But, although Alex had despised the idea and felt that being around this woman was causing his life to move at an excruciatingly painful speed, he'd had to admit to himself that – on some bizarre level – he *had* taken an interest in researching into Richard Dowsteene and the agency.

13

Tuesday, 6 April 2010

It was somehow just minutes away from lunchtime already! *Had a morning at work ever gone this quickly before?* It was time – it had gone faster, hadn't it? His whole life had dripped on by for years, but now there was something terrifying waiting around the corner, the first and second hands were spinning mercilessly against him.

Alex was in the toilet, pacing up and down as much as the small room would allow. He'd wondered whether to make the call outdoors or inside the food court, but had decided it was best to do it alone, in a confined space. If it was made outside, he would be amongst the people from Safe Insurance who'd walk by all the time, along with those enjoying a cigarette in the smoking shelter. Maybe they would all be listening, laughing at his conversation, because they would somehow know he actually thought there was a chance of selling his artwork? And if he'd sat in the food court, then maybe everyone else nearby would be thinking the same thing?

God he didn't want to ring that number – *make that damn call.* And for sure, the man would pick up the phone, wouldn't he? – with his rich voice travelling through the line. *They* always picked up when it was a call Alex didn't want to make. And Richard Dowsteene would probably do just that after one ring.

His legs stopped pacing and his thumb hovered over the ring button.

Could he press it? Should he press it? Was he ready? Was it too soon?

He had to, though, didn't he? If he didn't, then when Layna spoke to him later she'd be disappointed in him, wouldn't she?

In the corner of the screen a little bit of hope flashed, though, and—

No! – it wasn't hope! He shouldn't be thinking like that! The mobile was just indicating the battery life was low.

Ring before it runs out then! Ring now! Quick!

But then he thought: *And say what?* Because he couldn't even think straight about what he would say now. The memories of what he and Layna had planned to say last night were barely distinguishable at all. They couldn't be made sense of – put in any kind of coherent order whatsoever. The thought of Richard laughing hysterically down the line was too distracting.

So what are you going to do?! echoed through his mind. *What are you going to do? What are you going to do? What are you going to do?!*

***

Fifteen minutes later, his mobile was back in his locker. Layna had said a couple of days ago he should come and find her to relay what Richard had said. But now he couldn't see her anywhere. She wasn't on the food court floor, in the stores, the kitchen – any place. He plated his lunch and sat down, facing into the food court, looking out across the room waiting to see the woman.

But she never showed.

Alex wanted to tell her about the call. It had been – in a strange, almost unbelievable way – actually good news. Richard Dowsteene had said he was interested. Well – he'd said he would take a look, anyway. Apparently he was meeting up with one of his clients next Monday who lived not far from the Vulnham area, and so was going to stop by to briefly view some of Alex's work after. None of this made any sense to Alex, though. How could it? Why would he, Richard Dowsteene, be personally coming down from London to see his work, to talk to *Alex Merton*, an unknown who'd proven no merit in his work to anybody whatsoever?

All he'd done was make a phone call.

But...he had to admit, it did feel good. Maybe the guy had liked his words, the things he'd heard – though Alex couldn't even really remember quite what those words had been. He knew he'd made the call, but the call itself, the conversation, was somehow fogged in his mind now. Maybe it was adrenaline, the remains of the nerves still in his body, which was preventing recall?

Nothing would come of the whole art thing, anyway, would it? Not in the end. He still wanted to tell Layna, though, tell her he hadn't failed and had made the call at least.

Things were...moving. Moving towards nothing for sure, probably – but they were *moving* somewhere.

As Alex got up and started to walk towards The Wash Up with his empty plate on the tray, he looked around for a final time before going inside, still hopeful. But there was nothing. She just wasn't there.

***

He tried to call her twice that night, but got nothing except voicemail. The decision was made not to leave a message because he would probably make a mess of it by saying something stupid or by muddling his words. A text message was sent instead, expressing how he hoped she was all right and that Richard had seemed interested and was coming down to see his work next week.

It was strange typing the first part. Did Alex *really* hope she was OK? It felt like he did – but maybe he'd just typed what he thought other people would? Text messaging in itself was a whole new experience for him. Of course, he knew of texting and how to text and of its communicative reason to exist, but before knowing Layna, he'd never texted anyone before. He hadn't needed to. There'd been no one to text. And now he was texting someone, a friend who he...*what?* Cared about? He did care, didn't he? *No* – it was for certain. And it was strange to care about another human being and wonder how that person was, why that person wasn't at work, what had happened to them, whether they were ill, had had an accident, had died or had the flu or had been run over or a hundred other things...

What was going on? He was suddenly finding himself wondering about *someone else*. Her face could be seen in his mind's eye. She was so clear. *So vivid.* And the other thing was that...he couldn't see the third person view of himself much, any longer. It had moved to the side more than a little, its lens nebulous, hazy, experiencing an interference of some kind.

What was going on?!

Alex continued to sit at his desk for hours until the light outside finally turned to dark. It then became clear he wasn't going to hear his mobile ring that night. He wanted to be able to do something else to take his mind off her, to draw, paint – do anything. But he just couldn't stop thinking: *Is Layna all right?*

14

Alex always felt a little stupid thinking: *The freezer's really cold.* And yes, of course, it *was* a freezer, after all — but some days it seemed colder than others. And that day was one of them. Maybe it was because the morning was a particularly cold one, even for the time of year when the weather had been recently warming up? Another strange thing this year was that the hot weather, sunshine, and longer days of light, hadn't seemed to be bothering him as much as in previous years. He used to hate that fiery ball in the sky, and would long for the winter, the season which brought forth short days with modest light. But things were feeling *different* this spring.

Alex stepped out of the walk-in freezer, clenching and unclenching fists, shooting out his fingers in an effort to warm his hands. In the Goods In corridor there were three stacks of boxes containing frozen goods from the delivery, and to the side of them, two boxed piles of chilled goods. The food had to be put away quickly, not only for hygiene reasons and the fact it would drop fast in temperature, but also because all the time there was anything covering the floor space, it would be causing an obstruction to the access of the fire exit — and by God did the facility management and health and safety team like to moan about it...

Soon, after the piles of the delivery had started to diminish, he tore into the next box, pulling open both its flaps and exposing the clear blue bags with cooked chicken strips inside. He made his way back into the freezer and leaned over the large stacked baguette boxes, trying to force the bags into a gap on the second shelf. Behind in the corridor he heard a passing voice say: 'Make sure you put that stuff away *right*, boy…' He didn't need to wonder who it had come from, but still, just the sound of the man's voice created an awful churning in his gut.

Alex didn't feel angry anymore, though, like he had done not so long ago. After his depression back then, he'd turned back to his normal ways, beginning to feel intimidated, threatened, and unable to talk back to the man.

He *did* think about him noticeably less these days, however, mainly because of the fact he'd instead been thinking about other things – other things *outside of work*. And now that things were happening on the other side of those walls, it was funny how everything happening *within* them seemed to have lost a number of their pointed spikes. Not much, and only really a few. But they *had* reduced.

Within the next twenty five minutes he'd cut into all the boxes from the delivery, removed their contents, and packed them all onto the shelves inside the walk-in fridge and freezer. He signed the delivery into the log book, stating the company, invoice number, temperature upon delivery, and initialled his name. He then heard a shout travel from the kitchen through the corridor: '*The pots are piling up in here! Get a move on, faggot!*'

Alex's feet moved swiftly back toward the kitchen, but as they did, he saw in the corner of his eye another lorry pulling up outside the backdoor. As he turned to look at it he heard another voice shout '*Delivery, faggot!*'

It felt like the anger was coming, but as usual of late, it didn't. He was worried less about washing up and putting orders away now. Because he was thinking about *Layna*. He still hadn't seen her, having not called or texted her since yesterday, not wanting to bother or harass her, feeling that if he did she may have felt pestered or smothered by him. He'd told himself a lot that she'd probably finally had enough of him. And he almost believed it – but there was enough of him, a tiny percentage, that said otherwise. And it was enough. But he still wanted to call her, text her again, go and knock on her door to see what was wrong so he could know where she'd been and what had happened.

It's you! the voice hissed inside him. *She's trying to avoid you! Can't you see that? She's had enough of your weirdness, your sanctuary of creatures, your pathetic art that she lied about liking – oh it's so beautiful, oh oh oh oh! – and now she can't even bring herself to come to work and she—*

133

Alex's eyes blinked hard, and then he made his way back to the sink in the kitchen. The worktop's surface now resembled a long row of metal and plastic, a chaotic sculpture, which went so far in length that it crossed over in front of the service hole. The sink itself could hardly be seen. He slowly started to move the various cooking implements blocking it, taking away bigger items such as the colanders, large pans and long trays, and put them back on the trolley behind. As he was about to wheel it on through to The Wash Up, he then realised the guy with the heavy gut, Jason (who was some kind of head chef of all the sites, he always supposed), was in the room. Alex noticed the guy was looking at him. Not with *The Look* – but with a different kind. He kept on moving, deciding not to make eye contact with this person who'd never once spoken to him in all the times he'd visited before.

'Wait there a second...*mate*,' Jason said.

Alex stopped by the man's side, waiting to hear about something he'd done wrong.

'The pots – does it usually take this long for you to wash them up?' Jason asked.

'It depends on...how busy it is.'

Jason turned his eyes to Sam who was moving past him with a tray of gammon. '*Hey chef...*'

Sam set the tray down by the service hole. 'Yep?'

'The pots. Everyone needs so much, and it's still all there...'

'I know,' Sam laughed, still not giving Jason his full attention. 'You cannot get the staff...especially with *him*.'

But the fat man didn't find anything funny. 'No, I don't mean that. You know what? I don't often come down here. But I've realised something today.'

'What's that?' Sam asked now in front of him.

'What time does your KP on *lates* come in?'

'You're looking at him.'

'Say again?'

'*Alex* – he works full time.'

'I've never seen a KP run round so much. The man's *sweating*, Sam. Why is he sweating?'

'He's a busy boy, I guess!'

134

'Right, let's cut to it, shall we?' Jason said, the hostility in his voice peaking. 'It's impossible for...' A gap then presented itself in his sentence.

'...*Alex?*' Sam prompted.

'*I-know* his name, Sam.'

'I guess you do...'

'Isn't it a little difficult for Alex to manage the deliveries and the washing up simultaneously? And what else? – *the plates?* He does the plates at lunch as well, I'm guessing?'

'He sure does.'

Jason looked back to Alex, who was still standing by his side, and said 'Sorry, you carry on,' and then turned back to Sam. 'Can I have a word with you a minute, chef? Outside?'

Alex passed between them, not knowing exactly what was happening, but having a good enough idea of what was *going* to happen. At the very least, he enjoyed knowing Sam was being spoken to like a piece of shit.

***

'What are you doing?' Jason asked, his anger and frustration really beginning to show.

'With what?'

'*The KP?!* Making him work two jobs?'

'It's not two jobs,' Sam said. 'It's maybe a little extra work – but he copes.'

'Copes...? *The man is exhausted.* How's all his overtime getting paid for? – cos he *must* be going past his hours. How much is he doing?'

'I dunno. Works till around six...six thirty. Something like that.'

'And he gets paid for it?'

'Till five.'

'*Five...?*'

'Yeah.'

'And how the hell are you getting away with that?'

'Well, Jason...*come on* – you've seen him, right?' Sam said smiling, his hands up talking too in an effort to win the man over. 'Guy's like a fuckin *door mouse*, you know? Just won't speak up!'

'So you thought, what? – you'd be the hero and save the company a bob or two? That it?'

'Well, yeah. Sure seems that way, don't it?'

Jason didn't say anything for a few seconds. But his eyes did. 'I think this is that moment, isn't it? This is that moment, the one where I need to remind you not to get *fucking smart with me*. Because *I* gave you this job, remember...?' He deliberately created a silence between them before carrying on, wanting to let his message sink into Sam and present itself on his face in the form of submission. And when it came, he was pleased. Just that little moment when Sam's eyes had looked to the side for a split second was enough for him. 'Look – I just can't believe you're treating this guy like some kind of fuckin' workhorse. *Believe me*, I'm always trying to cut corners and save every penny I can – cos God knows business is on its knees right now – and if I could get away with selling shit for food and piss for coffee at a good price, then I would. But Sam...have you *seen* this guy?'

'I've seen him.'

'Have you, *though*?'

'Yes...'

'*He's doin' two jobs!*' Jason said, throwing his hands out to the side like a boxing referee who'd just declared the fighter in front unable to continue. '*End of*. Every other site this size I go to has *two* KPs.' He then spoke to Sam as if he were a small child. 'One works an *early shift* – say nine to three. And the other works a *late shift* – like eleven thirty to five. *Make sense?*'

'I see where you're going with this, yeah,' Sam said with a dash of sarcasm, hating every moment he had to agree with his superior.

'Great. *Exc-ellent*. So what you're going to do is get another KP in. By the end of this month, shall we say?'

'Not possible,' Sam came straight back with.

'No, actually...you're right. The end of the month just won't do, will it? So what I want now...is another KP in by the end of the next *three weeks*.' He took a moment to enjoy the sight of the man's expression dropping again. 'That's more realistic for you, I think.'

Sam wanted to say many things at that point, but knew that under any kind of circumstance he could never do it. 'No problem.'

'I'll tell you what, Sam...I like you – even though you're a mean shit like me. *I'm* going to hell for sure – but do you not have a conscience when it comes to that kid, *man*?' He almost turned to leave, but stayed to ask another question. 'And what the hell happened to ya' damn lip?'

'Just some girl in a club playin hard to get...'

'A *girl* did that to you?'

'No,' Sam chuckled dryly, shaking his head. 'Her boyfriend.'

***

As Alex pushed another tray through the machine, he heard the familiar voice behind him at the door say: 'Looks like you're gonna have a little friend joining you soon. Oh, and it's not all good news. No...*afraid not*. You're hours are gonna get cut the fuck up, *faggot*.'

He didn't bother to turn and face the man. But when he heard the door shut, he smiled on the inside, knowing that soon the days of energy draining, never-ending work would be halved and *finally* made more reasonable for him. It was strange that Jason, the man who'd never spoken to him before, had in a way saved him.

He then felt the negative coming back, though, coming through, making him wonder whether he deserved to have help in his job. *YOU deserve to struggle! Why should YOU have help, Alex?*

But he knew he welcomed the opportunity of help, the help of another person's hands, and so he simply told the voice inside that everything was done now, and that there was nothing he could do to change it.

***

The two final jobs of mopping the floors and locking up were done. Alex now looked in his locker, hoping to find what he'd been wishing for all day: a text message – or even a missed call would be enough. And he soon smiled inside:

Hey Alex. Sorry I haven't spoken to you. Have been sick. Can you come over tonight?

That meant she was all right, didn't it? *It was good news.* She wasn't feeling one hundred percent, exactly – but she was all right! *Layna was all right!*

***

Sam hadn't turned back to drink for over a year. But tonight he was going to. He had to. Because things were getting bad again. And it was going to get even worse now that he couldn't go to the gym or out for a drink with Will during the week. Earlier that night, Will had rung and enquired about him, asking why he couldn't work out anymore, and why last night he hadn't been able to join him and the others in town after. Sam had then made up an excuse which he himself knew must've sounded like bullshit. Absolute-total-bullshit.

But it was the money. That was the truth. He just couldn't do it anymore. Spend it. His savings – that stash of money he'd always lied to himself about, believing it would never disappear and would enable him to hang out with Will forever – were gone. And he would have to spend a lot of nights at home because of it.

Time at home was going to be hell, though. *It* was going to eat him up – *The Beast* – ripping into his mind, trying to tell him things he didn't want to know. The thoughts would try to get him, wouldn't they? – but he would stop their lies with a powerful weapon: *Alcohol.* There'd been some times throughout the past year when he'd needed some of the consciousness-altering-liquid, but had chosen to just go out more instead, exhausting himself physically and mentally, rather than picking up the bottle again which he'd worried may have reminded him even more of The Beast.

Sam sat in his chair with the leg extension up, alone in the lounge watching another action film (which Will had previously recommended as good wanking material), getting the most out of cable TV before he'd have to ring tomorrow to cancel his subscription. The film's star, Claudia Harpe, was now in a fight scene where she battled numerous vampires who also wore blood-soaked lingerie.

'This is a great film,' he said out loud, taking a sip from the whisky bottle he'd bought on the way home. He lifted it into the air, nodding to the invisible presence. 'Great...*fuckin film.*'

***

He was standing outside Layna's house, but wasn't knocking the door or ringing the bell yet. He was thinking about her. What did she want? What was she going to tell him? Why face to face? Why tonight? Why couldn't she have just spoken to him about it over the phone?

(*maybe tonight is when she's finally going to tell you she doesn't want to see you anymore...?*)

He brought his hand up slowly to ring the bell, but when the door opened it wasn't Layna he saw. Instead it was Stacey's chubby face. She invited him in and told him the woman he was looking for was upstairs, but wasn't feeling well.

When he soon reached Layna's room he waited silently outside, listening for some kind of noise through the door. But it was deathly quiet. No music. No sound. Nothing.

He knocked, and a few seconds later heard a faint voice (which he thought surely couldn't have been Layna's) invite him in. But once stepping inside he saw it *was* her. Why had she sounded that way, though? Sounded so different? Sounded so...*sad?* How could she, this strong-minded woman, be sad? And why could she now barely look at him?

(*It's* you! *This is what you've reduced her to. Look what you did! Look what you did!*)

Alex stayed by the door, waiting for Layna, who sat on the edge of the bed, to say something, to make eye contact – to even move just a muscle. And a few seconds later she did, looking over at him with a horrible beaten look; a look he knew well from the reflection in his bathroom mirror, one which had been upon his *own* face not so long ago.

'Hey, Alex,' she said. Her voice was weak, lifelessly pale.

There was another silence, but then she patted her hand on the bed by her side. 'Come and sit next to me.' After he did, while staring at the carpet she said: 'I have to tell you something.'

'What is it? Are you *all right?*'

'I'm...' she took a breath, '...not who you think I am.'

He waited for her to continue, not knowing what kind of feeling was about to be raised inside him.

'I...lied to you about everything,' she began. 'I told you that I'd learned to live with myself, and...and that I was strong, and...'

He then saw her cry for the first time. And it made him feel terrible.

'But…' she went on, managing to speak through the tears, '…it was all bullshit. I'm not that person. *I'm not*. And I…just can't take it anymore. I lied to myself all through Uni – ditching my pill junkie diet – telling myself I could and that I didn't care what anybody thought about me. But the truth is…*I do*! It's always been there. I never know when it's gonna hit and I can't take it…' She looked at him. 'And lately at work…at Sestern…serving all those people…and seeing *every one of them* looking at me and…*judging me…turning away*…having to watch their eyes turn to…*that look*, and I…' She took a moment. 'And I just couldn't pretend I was fine with it – *Mighty Layna* who was above all those people's bullshit! So I…just had to leave.'

Her eyes returned back to the floor, and as they did, a tear rolled off her nose.

'And the only reason…' She took a breath and swallowed. 'The only reason I ever got the job was because…'

'Layna,' Alex said.

She looked back at him again, and he then took a deep breath of his own before telling her: 'I…think you're beautiful.'

'What?'

'I think you're beautiful. It's true.'

He watched as her reddened, tear-filled eyes gazed into his own. Even though something was very wrong in that room, he knew something was also very right.

But then something else was suddenly happening. She moved closer to him, her head was now just inches away, and he could feel her breath and then her lips were touching his, and they were wet, flavoured with the taste of salty tears, and they were moving more, and she was…she was *kissing him*…she was kissing him and he was unprepared, caught off guard, and he didn't know what was happening or why and so he pulled back and then she pulled away too and he said '*Um – I'm*…' but he couldn't speak and she said 'What? What's *wrong*?' and then that saddened fading look of hers got worse and she tried to kiss him again and he pulled back a second time and then rose to his feet and said '*I'm sorry* – I can't do this!'

He stepped backwards, seeing her sobbing and holding out a hand toward him. 'Alex…*wait*,' she said helplessly. '*Please wait*…' But he was turning around, leaving, making his way down the stairs with haste, and was then out the front door, his feelings and thoughts in a mess of confusion. What had happened? Why had she tried to do that? Why had she tried to kiss him? Did she...*what?*

Did she...*love him?*

Of course she didn't!

What did she *want*, then? *Sex?* And if so, why had he gone? Why had he refused her? Why had he left? *Why? Why? Why?*

Alex kept on walking away.

It almost felt normal outside, at least maybe a better place to be at that moment. And even with the life of the town buzzing around him, it seemed oddly quiet. But he knew back in that house something strange had happened – happened to him. It had happened to *him* and—

What about her, though? Was something...wrong with *her?* Yes – *something* was happening inside her, wasn't it? And he'd left her. *He'd left her hurting!*

The speed of Alex's walk increased, and as his mind filled with a mass of stabbing ambiguous thoughts, his fingers tried to sooth his temple. He tried to latch his attention onto something else, scanning his environment for the first thing he could see, managing to then focus on the silver car parked by the alleyway. He concentrated on the details, hoping to become absorbed, lost in a part of it.

But no! – that wasn't what he really wanted, was it?

What he wanted was *answers*. She'd tried to touch him and *kiss him* for God's sake! And why? What had happened back there? *What had happened?!*

***

He lay on his bed thinking about her, thinking about her smile, who she was, and whether it was all real. Had he *really* seen her?

It felt like he had.

She'd always seemed so happy behind that beautiful smile. But she hadn't been really, *had she?*

He wondered again about whether she was real, but casted aside any doubt as he assured himself of her existence. That moment at her place just minutes ago had been too real. He'd been so aware of it and had felt his emotions bursting, exploding in a way that *had to mean* she was real.

His mind fixated on the smile she'd worn in the past. The image was there. It was absolute. Lucid. But the image died not long after, being replaced by her wet glistening eyes, her depleted, hopeless expression.

Soon Alex's eyes closed, and his body became motionless as he wandered off into a daydream, a place filled with floating cameras, photographs and muffled conversations. Then he could see smiles, and as his mind's eye focused in, who they belonged to: his parents and brother. He could see that day back then, all those years ago as a kid, when they'd gone for the family photo shoot. He could hear his father's voice saying: *No – we have to have a professional family portrait, and a professional photo album. A photo taken by one of us isn't good enough. Any fool can take a picture. I want them to be perfect and to reflect how successful and strong this family of ours is. It will sit upon the wall in the hall, and as guests arrive and enter our home, they will see a glorious portrait of us. And then they will know that it is of a family to be highly spoken of, a family that is functional – a good example for society.*

In his half-conscious state the portrait came floating in, closer and closer into view, but quickly faded. All he could then see was the studio, the thin man giving direction, telling him and his family what to do. No one was smiling yet. His parents argued, his mother multitasking, checking the bruise on her neck was covered up. His brother was silent, doing as his father had told him. And the young Alex Merton himself stood there, staring into the eye of the camera before him, knowing in a moment's time it would catch the scene, the mouth of reality that would vomit dark truth.

But it wouldn't turn out that way.

The photographer's words echoed as he said 'Right, ready?' And then the strangest thing happened: his mother, father and brother changed, transforming completely. Their faces lit up with a thousand lies, and they seemed to get larger and larger. They smiled – every one of them. Just like that. And when the camera clicked and the room flashed with light, the moment was captured. Done. Over.

Alex felt the confusion he'd experienced on that day. He could feel his thoughts questioning, saying: *What? What was that? That wasn't real! That's not how it is?!* The photographer asked why he hadn't smiled in the shot, and then everyone was looking at the young Alex with disappointment. The boy said nothing back, though. Before he knew it, the photographer was again saying 'One, two, three…' and then Alex did it – *he smiled* – somehow forcing the lie upon his face.

The scene gradually faded and the large framed portrait came towards him again. He could see them all in the photograph looking so happy, so much like a family, his father having even placed a hand on his shoulder. The voices came next of his parents' friends as they walked into the hallway, astonished as they said 'Oh, look at that!' and 'A remarkable portrait – such a charming family you all make.' He could see his mother and father's approval, the way they welcomed the compliments. *But it was all lies! All of it!* And he could see the lie hanging there. He could see the—

Alex's thoughts were interrupted by the loud music from a car pulling up outside. It took a few moments for him to adjust to where he was in reality. And to his surprise, he found his mobile tightly held in his hand.

He thought again about what had happened earlier that night with her. *What am I going to do now?* he wondered. *What am I going to do about Layna?*

15

Thursday, 8 April 2010

As Ed Dorne ended yet another call, he realised again just how hideously monotone his voice had become.

But he didn't care. Not anymore. Not after last night.

Last night it had all happened, finished, ended – just like that. But it had been inevitable, hadn't it? And even though he'd tried to feel sorry for himself and pretend it was out of the blue, saying to her 'What are you talking about?' and 'Where has…how long have you been feeling like this?', he'd known all too well that it was him who'd ripped the relationship clean in half, though slowly, over many years. He'd tried to blame it on the child thing – but it wasn't because of that. It was him. *He* had killed the relationship, the marriage, shooting it within an inch of its life a long time ago. It had merely been breathing, occasionally convulsing in an unconscious state for all that time. But it was his own death, his meaningless existence, his bland life which had disabled him from pulling it out of its coma. Now, Edward Dorne – of 47 Finch Lane, Hilbrook, son of Lorraine and William Dorne, husband of Kerry Dorne, father of no children, cynic, realist, machine, straight shooter, slave to the clock upon Safe Insurance's wall – was getting divorced.

His eyes grew even more tired as he entered into a conversation with another one of them.

'Okay,' he spoke into the headset microphone, 'I'm now going to ask you, in your own words, to give me a description of the incident where the crash took place. As I've already told you, we may record this for our own records of the claim. Is this all right with you?'

'Yes, no problem,' said the young woman, Eve Sultan, on the end of the line.

'Okay, so in your own words, please.'

'Well, I was approaching the roundabout – on Cintron Road – and as I was slowing down, approaching slowly – like you would – as I approached the roundabout…'

Ed was thinking: *Come on for god's sake just tell me someone hit you already! You wanna tell me how you changed down the fucking gears as well?*

'…and then I suddenly felt a bang behind me, and at first I thought that I might've stalled and I panicked…'

I don't care about how you felt. My wife is leaving me and I'm going to be a lonely forty year old man with no friends except for a brother who only still sees me so he can tear me apart on the squash court…

'…I was scared and I didn't know what to do! I've never had a crash before. Well, it wasn't actually *me*, was it? Anyway, so I felt this big thud – well, it was a bang – and then I suddenly knew it must've been…'

A crash, *my dear?* Or maybe a firework in your head had gone off? An epiphany suddenly happened, perhaps? Maybe it was the point where you realised you're a total airhead? I bet you're blonde, get pissed a lot in town, have never voted, and think that the world is all innocent and fun with bubbles and teddy bears…

'…couldn't believe it. The guy behind me must've been looking to the left…'

The right.

'No, hang on…*no*, the right I mean!'

Congratulations, airhead – you've scored five points! Deh-dehhhh!

'He must've carried on accelerating and then he just went into the back of me and—'

'Okay, okay, that's all I need from you there,' Ed said cutting her off. 'Thank you so much. A very *detailed* and helpful description of the incident.'

'Thanks!'

'Can you tell me what damage your vehicle received – *briefly*?'

This should be interesting.

'Well, it's the back that has the damage.'

You're kidding me? No way…

'It's damaged on the bumper, and also the bit where the boot goes in to close up. Well, you can't shut it and there's a little light hanging out—'

'Okay, that's great. That's *really* great. Thank you.'

'No problem!'

'Can you describe the damage to the third party's vehicle? Just a very short, *brief* description.'

There won't be any, of course...

'Well, actually there wasn't any. Only a few—'

'That's great. Thank you. You know, an interesting fact is that in most cases the third party rarely receives any damage to their vehicle. It's quite an anomaly.'

You don't have a clue what an anomaly is though, do you, you stupid girl?

'Yes it is. That's...it's interesting, I guess.'

'Okay. Since you can't shut the boot, we deem the car too dangerous for you to drive. We'll need to get a courtesy car sent out to you. And also, as the accident wasn't your fault, we'll arrange for the repairs to be carried out at a body shop. All costs will be billed to the third party. I will now redirect you to Bartley Assistance, a contract company which Safe Insurance authorises to handle its claims. Is this okay with you?'

'Yeah, no problem.'

'They'll sort out an appropriated time to deliver a courtesy car, and also find a body shop that is local to you to arrange collection of your vehicle. I'm now going to put you through to them. Before I do, is there *any-thing-else* I can help you with?'

'No, that's great, thanks.'

'Okay. Thanks for calling, Miss Sultan. I'm now connecting you with Bartley Assistance. Have a brilliant day, won't you?'

Ed disconnected from the call and took a moment to think about his wife. He had loved her once – *truly* loved her all those years ago. He'd bought her flowers the first time they'd gone out. Fresh, vibrant, beautiful. Just like she was. That man was nothing but a stranger now, though. It had been hard even back then to show his feelings. But he'd done it, and they'd both been happy. He remembered how he'd smiled on the way home after dropping her off, and how that old piece-of-shit car (which he'd actually loved) had made every kind of disconcerting sound an unworthy road vehicle could've. But he hadn't cared at the time, because not everything had—

Ed stabbed his pencil into the desk as another call came in, his lungs filling to full capacity, ready to force out a controlled scream into the office.

But it stayed right there inside him, of course.

'Safe Insurance, Edward speaking. How can I help you today?'

***

Alex found himself outside her front door again – outside the door of the woman he knew he'd reduced to tears three days ago. He hadn't seen or heard from her since, and this had given him time to think, speculate about what had happened, and to his surprise, think about how to fix the problem. Fix *her* problems. He had *actually* spent time thinking of how to help *someone else*, and if anything, he'd felt relieved to have been freed from the constant awareness he had over himself.

'She's upstairs,' Stacey said after greeting him at the door, a sausage index finger pointing to the ceiling. 'I can't get a word out of her. Won't even get out of bed. Barely come out her room in days.'

'Well, hopefully everything will be...all right,' Alex said.

He made his way in and started up the stairs, wondering how old the staircase was (and the whole house itself) as each step creaked like it was in pain.

When he reached Layna's door it seemed to look different now. Bland. Pale. He felt like it was some kind of barrier, not only used to keep people out – but to keep that newly changed woman inside.

(*Let's just leave...what's the point? You wanna make her cry some more? Is that it? She hates you! Don't you get it? – don't you understand? She cried to make you leave her, leave her alone, get out of her life, to stop pestering her, to let her get on with her own existence without—*)

He knocked and moved his ear closer to the door, listening for a response. But nothing came. He tried again, this time letting his ear softly touch the wooden surface. Nothing could be heard, though.

'Layna,' he tried gently. 'It's Alex.'

Something was then caught, a rustle of slight movement. Someone was inside for sure. He waited for a response, waiting for that voice to return. But nothing came, the silence soon prevailing again.

Alex stared at the door, wondering what to do, and then tried to build up the courage to open it and go in.

(*Go in? And once you go in...what are you going to do* then? *Once you're done making her cry again that is...?*)

147

'I'm going to help her,' he said, breathing it quietly through his teeth.

(*Oh right. You, Alex Merton – pot washer extraordinaire – are going to help. The man who is totally fucked up himself wants to help other people now does he? Awwww. Well guess what? – you're not going to help anyone…least not her. You want her to end up like you? You want to make her worse? You want to make her really go over the edge?*)

'I don't even know what I'm going to do yet…'

(*Cos that's what's going to happen if you go in there. Why don't we just go home? – I'll even let you do some awful painting. We can do some painting before the agent gets here on Monday – yes? Do we have a deal? Do we?*)

He didn't answer.

(*Do we have a deal?! ALEX?!*)

But then he did speak. And out came the words: 'No deal.'

He turned the handle and pushed the door open slowly, and as he did, his eyes struggled to make out anything clearly in the room. Everything was lost, swamped inside the darkness – and darkness was something he'd never seen in this place before. He wondered for a moment where he was and whether this *was* all real, suddenly feeling a great awareness of the situation. He expected to hear Layna, wherever she was, protesting his intrusion after being startled. But still, there was nothing.

As Alex closed the door behind him, he said into the black: 'Layna, I hope you don't mind, but…I wanted to see if you were all right.'

Silence followed, but as his fingers ran along the wall to find the light switch, he heard a voice, though it now sounded unfamiliar in its lifeless tone. 'No, just…leave the light off,' it said.

He did, and then gradually began to make his way over to the bed, trying not to fall over anything. He knew just how dark it must've been in there upon realising his vision had not yet adjusted, still not able to make out any light or shapes. The place felt as if it was rotten, dying, hopeless, without life. He knew this kind of atmosphere well, but didn't welcome it like he once had.

His hand reached out for the side of the bed and patted the duvet gently at the nearest corner, trying to find an area to sit. When found, he knew it was then time to start talking. But he didn't want to. He didn't know *what* to say – only that he had to say something. He had to, didn't he? That was why he was there. *Or was he just lonely?* Would he rather be in the company of a silent depressed person than be on his own?

A couple of minutes passed, but nothing got easier. It only got worse, and with every time his mouth opened to speak and then closed with nerves, the worry about talking built more.

(*You'll be talking to yourself anyway! Just leave! Let's go home! You've done enough damage! Just leave it for a few days come on and then you can come back to see her I promise. What do you say? Huh? What do you think? ALEX?!*)

His first word came out: 'Layna...' He had to pause while he thought of the next ones, the awful quiet filling the air once more. 'I...' His hand rubbed his temple. 'I wanted to tell you something, I...' He just wasn't going to be any good at doing this, was he? And every time he had to pause, it sliced deeply as he wondered what she must've been thinking about him. 'No, I just wanted to see if you were all right. I'm sorry about Wednesday. It was...' Then he was thinking: *Was it my fault?* And immediately after: *I don't know! – just say something! Anything!* 'It was my fault. I shouldn't have just left like that. I'm sorry.' He stopped to allow himself to return back into a normal breathing pattern. 'I...'

(*Don't say it! She won't care! She doesn't even feel the same! She'll—*)

'...was worried about you, and I...'

(*Don't say it! Let's go! NOW!*)

'...I guess I care about you. I've never seen you like this.'

A few seconds passed and still there was no response from Layna.

(*SEE! – she can't even bring herself to talk to you! You've said what you wanted to say and it's all done! Finished! Now let's go lets—*)

'So...' he tried again, '...I've got the agent coming over tomorrow. Don't know whether to bother with it, though. I don't want to waste his time. Think I'm gonna call him up and...cancel, actually. I don't...want to bring him all the way down to see that stuff.'

When Alex continued to hear nothing but his own voice in the room, he decided to just sit there and stop talking completely. He started to think, think about Layna, and now that he'd just mentioned it, his art and the dreaded agent. The picture in his head of what the man would look like was an intimidating one. He was tall, wearing an expensive grey suit, his hairline receding (yet hardly noticeable because of his immaculate haircut and side parting), owned a top of the range saloon because his aching arse had grown tired of low-suspension

149

sports cars, and had a terrifying smile and laugh that Alex himself wouldn't be able to forget once his professional eyes had taken a look over his art.

It was simply going to be hell tomorrow when he came over. Absolute hell.

When Alex finally felt it best to leave, he thought about his visit, and how useless and unhelpful he'd been. As he reached for the door handle, he turned back toward the bed and said softly: 'Layna, I'm sorry I haven't made much of a difference being here. I'm not good at…*this*. I'll see you soon, I guess.'

(*maybe she* doesn't *want you to come over* another day *soon...*)

'Not tomorrow because I have the agent coming, but...maybe after he leaves, then, if he's not there too long. Which he probably won't be.'

(*Tomorrow? She's only just seen you* today! *Maybe she's lying there in bed thinking: No! – not tomorrow for christ's sake, just leave me alone Alex, leave me alone you fucking freak, leave me alone!*)

'So I'm gonna go now. I'll see you later, all right, Layna...'

He left the room, closing the door without hurry just in case in that last second she'd spoken out to him. To just hear her say *goodbye* would've been more than enough.

But nothing came.

16

After getting home from work, all he could think about was the man who would be turning up later that evening. He didn't want it to happen at all, but since he'd never picked up the phone to cancel the meeting – or whatever it was that was going to happen – he was just going to have to let it be. But at least, however the night would pan out, its events would need *time* to fuel it, right? And time would always run out. It would always lose.

Alex soon found himself sitting at his desk, surrounded not only by his pets, but also an entire body of artwork, the many canvases and rolled paintings now stacked and arranged neatly around the lounge. On the desk were three piles of sketch books almost as tall as he was.

He worried again about *Layna*, but the feelings of anxiety for the rest of the night to come took over, shoving her out the picture. He longed for the moment when he could close the door after the agent and go back to finding a way of helping her.

(you *can't help anyone...*)

He looked at the clock on the wall, listening to it ticking, ticking, ticking. Time was running out, burning, losing, wasting away, and it wouldn't be long before the game would be in the agent's hands – but as soon as it was, the agent's time would *then* be running out. Alex held on to this thought tightly.

The buzzer rang.

Its sound was deeply unwelcomed in his heart, and as he got up and pressed the button to allow his visitor into the building, he knew that this was going to be the only easy part of the evening. What wouldn't be easy would be when he had to allow him entrance into his flat, and then, entrance into his art; entrance into his *world*, his *visions*, his *insanity*, his *weirdness...*

A knock came at the door.

Alex still stood there ready, having heard through the thin walls every step of the man as he'd made his way up the stairs. He took a second to react, and then just went for it, removing the catch, turning the key.

'Hello, I'm Richard Dowsteene of the D & G agency,' the warmly smiling man said. His suit wasn't grey exactly like Alex had imagined beforehand, but was close enough. His hair wasn't a complete match either, it being combed back with merely the early signs of a receding hairline on show. In fact, the only true match was his height; the man was, without a doubt, tall. 'I'm here to take a look at the artwork of a Mr Merton.'

'Yes, h-hello,' Alex said, the pitch of his voice going off course for a moment. His finger then began to frantically tap away on the inside of the door frame as a silence fell between them.

'Can I come in?' Richard asked.

'Oh, yes...*sorry*,' Alex said flustered.

'Long day, huh?' Richard joked stepping in. 'I understand.'

'Well, um...I—'

'So I understand you have some work you'd like me to take a look at?'

'...Yes, that's right.' He turned away from him to shut the door.

'Great,' Richard said walking toward the lounge, leaving Alex behind. 'So how long have you been an artist?'

'Well, since...'

(*An* artist! *Ha! A fucking artist! Oh my god, that* is *a good one! Just wait until he sees all that shit in there!*)

'...since I was about fifteen, as in...when I *seriously* started. So about nine, ten years, maybe?'

'Excellent. And how would you describe your work?'

'Describe?' Alex asked, having almost caught up with the man, his face panicked and heart pumping fast, his eyes looking on ahead as Richard was about to step into the lounge.

'What's your style?'

'Um...I don't know. I just...*do*.'

(*Do?* Do? *What does that mean?*)

'I just paint and sketch and...'

(Oh my god…you're completely fucking this up aren't you? This is going to be a disaster. You do know that now don't you? Are you going to listen to me next time? – Hmm?)

'…and that's just what I do.'

'Fair enough,' Richard said positively. 'I like the sound of it already.'

(He likes the sound of it already! Oh this is funny isn't it?! Well I guess you can relax now then eh…?)

They both stood together side by side, now looking into the lounge.

'So this is all your work, I take it?' Richard said, motioning toward the piles of canvases, tube rolls and sketch books.

'Yes,' Alex answered while thinking: *Time will run out run out run out, it always does…*

'And *wow*…a lot of…I don't know – snakes, are they? In the tanks?'

Alex said nothing, already knowing the man must've then wanted to leave.

'You know,' Richard said looking around at the shelves, 'I have something even worse than this. *Truly worse*. It's called *cats*. A lot of them. Rebel Wave magazine interviewed me once at my house, saw them all, and obviously couldn't help but write about it. Apparently, according to them, I'm *the ruthless art world tycoon who finds his own peace in a house filled with feline kitties.* And just for the record – it's-not-true. I'm maybe ruthless at times, but I don't find peace being indoors. And as for the cats, they're my *sister's* – she lives with me, you see?' He paused for a moment and then his head tilted to the side slightly. 'But…in truth I don't mind, I guess. The article helped make my character come across as more *dynamic* possibly, I think.' He nodded his head a little, agreeing with himself, and then turned his eyes to Alex. 'So where shall I start?'

'Wherever you like…' Alex said, his mind bewildered, in disbelief that the guy wasn't running just as Layna hadn't either.

His heart sank as he saw the tall man bend down onto one knee and carefully pull away the protective plastic sheet from the first canvas on top of the pile nearest him.

Quiet fell in the room.

He watched as the man shuffled his lanky body over to the next pile, removing the sheet from its top canvas also, and then the next, and the next, and the next, and it seemed like it was lasting an eternity, with the agent still not saying a word at all.

But soon a voice could be heard, this time in a much softer, gentler tone say: 'Oh my – I don't know what…'

(*Now you're fucked! I told you it was a waste of time!*)

'…I don't know what to say,' Richard slowly went on.

(*That he wants to leave.* That's *what he wants to say!*)

'I don't think that I've ever – *me, personally* – seen anything like this in all my years in this business.' He got up, erecting himself to his great height, and took a moment staring at the piles of canvases again. 'I wasn't expecting this, Alex.' He turned back to their creator. 'Do you mind if I take a look at everything here? *I need to.* Tonight. I'm going to have to see everything.' He scanned the room's collection of work. 'I'm going to need to talk to you about all of this.'

'It's fine,' Alex told him, his mind spinning, trying to make sense of what was happening.

Another silence fell in the room as both their heads filled with thought.

'I think *this*…is going to be big,' Richard said. 'I can feel it.'

Alex said nothing. He felt strange. The feeling was flooding into him, but this time it was not of black oil-slicked waves, but of bright colours of yellows, oranges and reds, and the relief, shock, and surprise at the words he'd just heard, from the once supposedly *threatening* visitor, words he thought he would never have heard. Not from anyone. Ever. It felt like something had now started, like a fire had been ignited, and not just inside *him* – but on earth too.

Over the next three hours, the agent carefully surveyed every one of the paintings and sketch books, discussing various aspects of them with the artist, and as he did, pages of notes were made. Alex just stood there, taking it all in, not wanting to sit down, watching it all go on inside his very own lounge, the place which was supposed to be of loneliness, unproductiveness; his cage, prison that welcomed only him – *the unwelcomed* – to spend eternity within its cold metal bars.

But now it felt more than otherwise. There was a man in here, a man seriously looking over everything, genuinely interested and excited about his work. And, *him.* It was crazy, absurdly unusual – *unbelievable!* He blinked and allowed himself to become even more aware of the situation, seeing clearer the movements of the lanky figure moving about the room, listening to his voice and the scribbles of his fountain pen. And then he knew it *must* all be real.

It *was* real!

This was it, wasn't it?! He had been noticed, *noticed by him* – the agent. The agent had found his work. He had found him, and now Alex felt like his life was about to begin. His body felt like...almost like there was electricity tingling his flesh!

Suddenly a moment was needed alone. A moment where he could gather his thoughts and take it all in. And he needed a mirror. That was for sure. He needed to see himself in a mirror.

'I'm just...going to the toilet quickly. Do you—'

'No, no, go ahead,' Richard told him. 'I'm sorry to have been here so long. But you couldn't throw me out right now. *Believe me.*'

As Alex walked over to the bathroom he managed a real, genuine smile for the first time in years. It was a *real* smile. And he knew it was too. It felt fantastic. There was no mistaking what it was. It was *real*. And the moment was *real*. He felt something...a light, a bright light inside. How could everything have turned so different in such a short space of time? How could everything have suddenly changed within just a few hours?

He had absolutely no idea!

After shutting the door and looking into the mirror, he saw himself smiling back. But the smile left as he then decided he wanted to seriously understand and absorb just what was going on before he got too carried away. It felt bizarre knowing that just beyond the door, in his lounge, something was happening – possibly his whole life. And it was possibly all about to change. Maybe it was absurd to think it, but maybe he was finally going to be what he'd always wanted to be: *An Artist*. And just maybe it would happen. But the main thing was he had been noticed, and had been accepted by another human being. His art had been accepted. The agent had found him, and he had been accepted by him.

Alex looked hard at his reflection, deep into his eyes, and soon realised something.

It wasn't the agent who'd found and accepted him, was it? He hadn't just turned up unannounced, out of the blue. *No* – he'd been pointed there, guided there. It was someone else who'd accepted and helped him. It was *Layna*. She'd accepted him, helped him, and got

155

him to call the agent. *It was her.* She was the one who'd given him this feeling of being alive. *It was all her...*

He then knew what he had to do.

He had to help that woman.

17

Tuesday, 13 April 2010

Alex knocked on the door and said delicately, with just as much nerves inside as before: 'Layna...?'

There was no reply of course. But he'd expected this.

He pushed the door open gently, entering into the thick darkness, and proceeded to feel his way for the corner of the bed. He sat down, the silence continuing as he tried to think of something to say.

But thinking wasn't going to help, was it? So he just started talking, not knowing what was going to come out, forcing it, and it scared him as he said 'Layna, listen, I just wanted to let you know that the agent came round, it's...it's good news actually and he said he was really interested and...' He took a pause, knowing his words were coming out fast in a clumpy mess, and took a breath and carried on, again not knowing what his words were going to be. 'What I wanted to say was that...without you none of this would've happened, and maybe it'll go nowhere anyway...but without you none of this could've been. It's because of you that my art has been noticed so...I just had to say...*thank you.* It means a lot to me. *Everything you've done.*'

It was hard not receiving any answers like he usually would've gotten from the chatty girl – the one he had once known. And it was uncomfortable to be the only one talking, not knowing whether to carry on...or to shut up and go.

'Anyway, um. I know you're upset and I know you feel like you, er...'

(*oh god look at you...*)

But then Alex stopped.

He stopped because he suddenly knew – knew exactly what it was he had to do.

He got up and went straight over to the drawn thick curtains, feeling his hands over the fabric, and then pulled them apart fiercely, and as he did, the light of the evening sun poured in, painting the room with light. He squinted as it hit his eyes. But it felt good.

He went back to the corner of the bed and sat down, looking at Layna whose entire body and face were covered beneath the duvet. He shuffled along closer and hesitantly put his hand over a bump of what he thought must have been her arm. 'Layna…'

A muffled teary voice then spoke. 'I'm just so…*I'm so ugly, Alex! I'm so ugly!*'

He was shocked to hear such words coming from her, as he was also at how alive with emotion he felt at that moment. 'I don't think you're right. In fact…*you're wrong.* And anyone who thinks that is crazy. I…' He took a second. '*I think you're beautiful. I—*'

'My scars will never fade. They'll always be there. *Always.*'

'I don't see any scars. *Only you.* And you're beautiful.' Alex couldn't believe the words that were coming out of his mouth, and so looked around the room to become aware of his surroundings to confirm the validity of what was happening. He looked back to her bumpy outlined shape as movement was heard, and then soon she was out of the duvet with her arms around him, sobbing into his shoulder. He put his arms around her, feeling her wet tears against his neck, and began to have no idea of how long the moment was lasting, feeling like it could last forever. The act of hugging another human being was an alien experience. But it wasn't something he wanted to run from.

'You're not quitting on yourself, all right?' he said. 'Your photo shoots are next week and you're going to do them. Every one of them.'

Layna said nothing, but he knew his words had meant something to her. She lay back down on the bed, her face in the pillow. Her hand soon found his, though, holding it loosely. It was another strange feeling, and although he wanted to leave because there was little more he sensed could be done that night, he continued to sit there for a while longer, not wanting to break the connection between them.

But after a short time, she was the one who broke it. 'Alex, you should get going. You have work tomorrow.'

He knew it wasn't late at all, not even 8:00pm yet, but also sensed now would be a good time to leave. As he got up and walked to the door, almost without sound he heard her say 'Thanks, Alex.' And then out of nowhere he desperately wanted to do something else, help some more and say *just something else*, and then it came out: 'On Saturday...we're going to London Zoo.'

(*London Zoo?* London Zoo?! *What are you talking about? That sounds stupid! That sounds* crazy!)

Alex left the room, shutting the door behind, and as he did, he hoped again in those final seconds for a response. Nothing came, though. He felt like a fool. Ridiculous for making such an idiotic proposal. But as he made his way down the stairs, he realised he'd done something much better than just make a stupid suggestion – he'd helped her slightly that evening. And something *else* had happened too. She had hugged him. Did that mean there was affection between them? And that they understood each other? He wasn't sure. But there was no denying the connection that had taken place within those walls.

It was strange knowing he had *actually* helped another human being, knowing his concentration had not been entirely on himself for a change. As he thought about it more, he realised his over-awareness of himself had in fact been slipping lately, and that he'd been becoming less self-conscious overall. This couldn't possibly be true, though, could it? It couldn't be.

But – *somehow* – Alex knew it was.

And it was a good thing.

A magnificent thing.

18

Sam woke up on time as usual and completed his routine morning rituals, but with the addition of something that would become a regular occurrence: a chug of whisky.

As he looked into the mirror, he thought he could truly see *The Beast* looking over his shoulder, accompanying its voice that constantly whispered into his ear. He so desperately wanted rid of it, to kill the thing, to extract it like a surgeon would a growing cancer. He'd come to realise that this time it wasn't going to go away that easily, and maybe wasn't going to leave at all. Ever. It was actually beating him this time, and he didn't have the energy he'd once had to fight it with. Everything was falling apart in his life, and it was feasting on every aspect of his destruction, using it against him; his failed marriage, his alcohol abuse, his debts – his whole fucking life.

Sam looked ahead at his reflection and smiled, though the deep lines in his brow suggested another emotion. 'Everything is fine, man. *Everything*...is fine.'

He knew that once he got to work he would be able to lose himself – hopefully – and forget about The Beast for nine hours. But as he made his way down the stairs it reached inside, tearing into his mind again, causing his legs to descend slower, his eyes to close. He tried to go further but couldn't. He couldn't even make it down the stairs and out the front door.

(*You're fine goddamnit! Fine I tell you! This is all so stupid and ridiculous and you know it Sam. Now move!*)

Then The Beast was using another memory to hurt him. It was showing a film reel of Vegas from the time he'd gone back to the hotel with that woman, and how he'd sobered up and had known exactly what was happening and

(NO NO NO NO!)

the way that they'd kissed and then

(NONONONONONONO! I DON'T CARE IT DOESN'T MATTER IT DIDN'T HAPPEN!)

how she'd tried to get him hard but hadn't been able to, and then the way she'd tried to get him up by going down on him and the way that he suddenly hadn't been able to take it anymore and had told her he just couldn't do it and was married, and the way he'd left her room and—

Sam knew he had to do something! *And now!*

He had to talk to someone – there was no avoiding it any longer. He needed help. Alcohol wasn't working. He needed to deal with that demon, that weight, that wretched voice inside him, that *Beast*, that constant whispering in his ear. He knew he had to talk to someone. He didn't know what he would talk about, what he would say, confess, give, learn. Just that he needed to talk to her. His sister, Layna.

19

Alex waited, looking through the passenger-side window of the car. When Layna came out the front door, he suddenly realised he wasn't going to see that joyful smile and happy little walk he'd seen all those weeks ago when he'd first picked her up.

But this was enough – it had taken a lot to even get her to this stage where she could leave the house. For the past few nights he'd devoted his time to the woman, continuing to go over, sitting, talking, listening to her – trying to understand the best he could. And finally last night, as he'd gone into her room, he'd found something different, something amazing: the curtains hadn't been redrawn tightly to cover the room in darkness, but had been open of her own choice, allowing in the sun, letting in the light. And then he'd known things were going to get better. That *she* was getting better.

As Layna approached, everything about her movements seemed to have slowed down. She was different. Of course she was. The change was so noticeable, though, and so clear now that she was on her feet. She slipped from his mind for a moment while he experienced another bout of complete self-awareness, wondering about everything that was happening and why he was going to the zoo today. But just as he was about to be plagued with angst, he instead diverted his attention to Layna as he caught sight of her walking through the gate. She wasn't just walking, though. She was wearing a little smile now it seemed, too. How she had managed it or why it was happening, he didn't know. But it was. And it made him feel good, like something inside had been finally lifted. It was strange that a part of something else – of *somebody* else even – had managed to do this.

Not everything was bad with her, then, was it? It can't have been. He knew he must have at least helped her in some little way. His being there each day and talking and listening had helped, right? It must've done. After all, she *was* there now. She *was* walking towards him. And she *was* coming to the zoo with him!

After getting in the car, Layna said with loose eye contact: 'Hey...'

Alex looked at her, wishing again that she could appear in the very same way as when he'd first met her. He wanted to see that glow so badly. 'Hey,' he said back. But he couldn't think of anything else to say because he became distracted once more by the worries of the day ahead in London. He didn't want to go, wanting to just stay in town, in Vulnham, the place he knew. The *only* place.

But Alex couldn't do what *he* wanted! – he'd told her they were going to London Zoo and that was what was going to happen. He would just have to get by with the maps, directions and notes he'd printed off. He couldn't disappoint her and back down and look stupid and be...what?

Selfish?

Yes, that was it. He couldn't be *selfish*.

Not anymore.

Not when it came to Layna.

***

As he stepped up into the doorway of the train, his discomfort immediately increased. But of course, it didn't surprise him. He made a right turn into the carriage and sat down after locating two free seats, with Layna following behind and soon joining him. She seemed to be in better shape than earlier that week, but still held the look which hurt him every time he saw it. She turned her gaze from the floor up to him. 'Thanks for taking me out today, Alex,' she said. 'It's really kind. I...think I needed it. The *tough love* as they say.' He told her it was no problem and watched as she managed another little smile, though he was unsure of its legitimacy.

Seconds later his stomach went cold as the train started to move. It was happening now. They were leaving his comfort zone, the place he was familiar with. It was all going to go badly today, wasn't it? And he knew it was true. He could only remember being in London once from when he was a kid, and that experience (which he could barely remember) could hardly help him now, could it? Layna was going to

163

know he was useless at getting around and he would look a fool when she would finally say: *Don't you know where you're going? I think that…actually, Alex, we should just stop seeing each other after today. I thought that maybe you could help me, but…you're obviously not right for me to be around right now…*

Outside the window the station had almost vanished, disappearing into the distance behind. At that point he wanted, *really wanted* the friend by his side to talk to him, help take his mind off the train's departure. But she wasn't saying anything, and it didn't seem like she was going to either.

He looked to his right at a middle-aged man in the other aisle, whose blonde hair was losing its battle against the grey, and wondered how he could be so relaxed, just sitting there reading a newspaper. Next, Alex noticed the young couple in front opposite, and watched curiously as their heads rolled loosely from side to side in sleep. *How can they be doing that at a time like this?* he wondered. *How can—*

'Sorry if I'm real quiet,' Layna said. 'Just…haven't been out the house in a while, you know?' She paused. 'So you heard back from the agent yet? Anything else?'

'No,' Alex answered. 'Not yet.'

'I know you're gonna be great. Trust me.'

He watched as she made that same smile again, but just couldn't work out if it was genuine or not. It didn't really matter, though, did it? She was talking and was out of the darkness, now on a train heading to

(*Anxiety!*)

London. She was doing fine.

For an hour and a half Alex watched from his window as the train passed by and stopped at many a station. With every one it reached, he felt even closer not only to London, but also to his eventual failure to cope with the big city.

***

A cold wind cut through him as he stepped out at Waterloo. Below the pigeon-infested roof, the chatter and conversations of numerous exiting passengers filled the platform. A suited man by his side lit a cigarette and impatiently began to navigate an obscure path through the forming crowds.

After Alex fed his ticket into the machine at the turn-style and walked on through, he was overwhelmed by the size of the station. It seemed blindingly white to him as he looked around, seeing many shops and kiosks, and a huge digital departure and arrivals board on a wall high ahead. Below it, a hundred or so people gathered, all watching with anticipating eyes like they were partaking in a ceremony of worship.

There were thousands of people walking in every direction around him, and there seemed to be quite a variety of them too. He'd never seen such a mixture of races and skin tones under one roof, their attires ranging from the casual to suits to sportswear. Their faces were difficult to read, and knowing there were so many people about the place, likely feeling such a range of emotions, made him horribly uncomfortable.

But Alex had to stay focused, didn't he?! So he decided to think about his notes and where to go – but then knew he couldn't get the damn notes and maps out because she would see them and realise how *useless* he was!

What was he going to do, then? What was he going to do without the aids he had brought along?

He didn't know, so just kept on walking, not having a clue where he was going. He closed his eyes, knowing he was fucked.

But suddenly he wasn't – because behind his eyelids, in the dark, he could somehow see what he was looking for. Two words. *NORTHERN LINE*. And soon, also in bold black lettering, the stop *CAMDEN TOWN*.

Alex opened his eyes and let them rush all over the station. Every word on every sign seemed blurred, a haze, and as they searched while his feet kept moving, he prayed he was going in the right direction. In the distance, a *Northern Line* sign did eventually materialise. And when it did, he was so pleased – elated – that something had finally clicked into place.

As he turned to Layna, he noticed she was trailing back a little. *Shit!* he thought. *She thinks I actually know where I'm going! Soon she's going to find out. Soon she's going to know!*

165

Once an opening had been spotted between the many people swarming the brow of the stairs, he started to make his way down. He followed the crowd to a row of turn-styles, fed his card through, and proceeded on to wherever his legs led him. He stayed on course with the signs and his inner compass – in which he held little faith – and before long found himself walking through a long corridor.

And then the platform was there! It could be seen!

As Alex waited with the masses of people at the edge, he figured his chances of getting the right train were slim, and that he'd most probably fucked up. His eyes glanced over the posters at the back wall behind the track, but nothing they advertised managed to sink into his brain. The clanking echoes from an arriving underground train were all around, and soon it came to a standstill at the platform, its passengers eagerly pouring out.

Alex was able to make it on, but was out of luck when it came to finding an empty seat. The carriage was packed, with him and twenty or so others standing. As it jolted forward he grabbed at the looping handle above to save his balance. Everything was happening so damn fast!

But wait – something wasn't right. What was it? What was—

Shit! he thought. *Layna!* He'd forgotten all about her, hadn't he?!

Alex looked around for her in panic. But it didn't last long. It didn't need to – because she was right there. Right there by his side.

Additional relief was to be had as he watched the yellow text scroll by overhead, finally seeing that the train's last stop was Camden Town. Another click of confirmation went off inside him.

At the first stop, he and Layna both attempted to occupy a couple of seats after some of the passengers had left, but were beaten to it by other eager boarding travellers of the tube. They were both surprised at how quickly the two people had brushed past them from out of nowhere to claim the prized resting points.

'Next stop, those seats are ours,' Layna told Alex, that little smile appearing on her face again. It was enough for him to just hear her talk, but to actually see her smiling in a way that looked to be more genuine than not, made something good stir inside. It seemed as if maybe life was creeping back into her again – and knowing this helped, calming his nerves slightly, making him feel not so alone on that train.

When the tannoy sounded for the next station of Warren Street, they both glanced at each other, and then, as the exiting passengers soon huddled together and began leaving the carriage, they readied for their move onto a couple of newly vacant seats not far away. As soon as the area was clear they briskly walked over, and when they sat, Layna shot a momentary childish smirk at him before looking back ahead.

Alex loved that smirk. That smirk was fantastic. Just wonderful. It was a smirk that meant she was coming *back*.

He then looked at the window opposite, its surface of course appearing dark, showing the reflections of the passengers either side of him. They looked like ghosts. He could make out his own features, recognising that it was him on the train, and could also make out the features of Layna next to him. She was there too. It was a fact: he *was* travelling on the underground, and he *was* with her.

Eusten and Mornington Crescent soon passed, and the train would shortly be arriving at Camden Town. Alex now thought briefly about what form of transportation would be the best to pick up outside the station to take them to the zoo. But he decided to still go with what he had planned on taking last night: a taxi. It would surely be the easiest, simplest way. It would take them straight there. He would just say to the driver: *Zoo*. That would be it. If he'd gone with the bus option, he could have misread or been unable to decipher the timetable and could've therefore looked stupid. If they'd walked, even with the map he'd printed off, there was the chance he could've gotten them lost, also making himself look stupid. But if the taxi went the wrong way, it wouldn't matter – it would just be the driver who'd end up looking stupid.

After climbing the stairs and leaving the station, Alex's eyes quickly picked up on a row of five black London cabs parked along the street. Embarrassment arrived when he messed up by trying to get into the front passenger's seat, only to see the silent driver's finger point behind. He quickly got into the back, finding Layna already inside.

Fifteen minutes later, after making it through the city's slow lunchtime traffic, he felt disbelief as he finally walked with Layna toward the big ZSL LONDON ZOO sign. It was of the pleasant kind, a pleasant disbelief that he'd actually managed to get them there at all – and, in a pretty decent time.

It was then that he also felt something else, and it made him stop in his tracks. It was the heat of the sun warming his body. He looked up into the sky, and saw there was hardly a cloud inside all that blue. It was peaceful up there. So wonderfully peaceful. He didn't know if it had been like that all day, or whether he'd just never noticed it until this moment. Maybe he'd just never—

'Shall we go in?' Layna asked him.

'Yes,' he said adjusting his attention back. 'Sure.'

As they walked towards the entrance, the voice inside attacked. *You're only* half way *fucking there! You've got to get back home yet! You're going to screw up! – you* know *you are! Think of the pain you're going through just to please this girl! This whole trip is…*look! *– it's making you* sweat! *Just tell her we have to go. You're not well – tell her that! Yeah tell her that! Now* that *she will believe won't she?!*

But as Alex looked over at her, into her eyes, he knew he had to go on. He *didn't* want to leave, to run away or escape. He was helping her. And something seemed right inside – almost like *he* was now feeling good as well.

What was going on, though? Seeing *her* happy was making *him* feel happy? He didn't feel invisible at that point; this person could actually see him, had depended on him, put her trust in him that day. Was this really what she had done? – put her trust in him? Had she trusted him to make her happy? And was he succeeding? Was *he* making her happy? Yes – yes, he was. And for some strange reason that he couldn't understand, it *really* did make him feel good.

***

'I love the zoo,' Layna said, looking over to a group of three penguins about to dive into the water one by one.

'Yes, I realised that when we were at the theme park,' Alex said.

'Animals are just…'

'Just what?' he asked.

'Don't laugh when I tell you, okay?'

'I won't,' he promised.

'Animals are good listeners.' Her face then filled with surprise. 'Why didn't you?'

'Why didn't I what?'

'*Laugh...*'

'I – was I supposed to?'

'No,' she said. 'But most people always laugh at my silly ways, you know?'

'I don't think you're silly.'

'That's because you're crazy too.'

'*Crazy?*'

'Yeah,' she said, the smile on her face growing slightly more before dropping again.

'What's your favourite animal, then?' Alex asked, wanting to keep her talking.

'These,' she said nodding in front.

'Penguins?'

'Yeah.'

'Why the penguins?'

'Well...there is something special about all animals. They're all different I think.'

'And so what's special about these?'

'The penguins are...well, you know they look like a bird. Sound like a bird. But they can't do the one thing all birds can. They can't *fly*. They have wings, but...they're not the same as the others. They'll never be in the sky like them. But they're unique. They don't spend their days trying to fly, because they know they're best in the water, you see? They *know* that. And when you see them dive in and glide through the water, it's...*it's beautiful.*'

Alex didn't say anything back for a few seconds, mesmerized by her words. But then he saw something was wrong. Something was wrong with Layna. She was saying 'Alex, I don't know if I should be *out* – I don't know if I should *be here*! I...' She stopped talking and looked around the zoo, and he could hear the panic in her breath and see it in her eyes. He grabbed her shoulders hard enough to bring her attention back, and looked deep into her tortured eyes and said '*Layna, it's all right.* You *should* be here.' Ahead, a couple stared, then walked by.

Alex saw them. And it angered him.

It *really* did.

169

But he didn't allow himself to get drawn into that roaring fire, choosing instead to distract himself by talking to Layna more. 'Come on,' he said. 'Let's go for a walk.'

And soon, following a moment of looking only at each other, they did.

After ten minutes passed, a more together Layna said: 'So…I want you to tell me something.'

Alex waited for her to go on.

'A while back, you said something to me. You said that the best photos of people…were the ones they didn't know had been taken. What did you mean by that?'

'It's nothing,' Alex shrugged off, looking down to the animal-shape cobbled pathway.

'You should share things, you know.'

'No, really…I don't know why I said it.'

'If you want me to carry on with those shoots of mine…then you'll have to tell me.'

He didn't say anything straight away, even though he knew he'd eventually have to once she used her powers of persuasion.

'So why is it?' she asked, her tone lightly prodding.

'It's…well, it's…' He stopped, not knowing how to explain, wishing he'd never mentioned it before at the pub. Why the hell had he ever said it?! 'Um. It's…'

Shit! he thought. *What am I saying?* He took a deep breath and was about to speak again. But this time, he chose not to think. 'You see all these people around us?'

'Yeah,' she said, glancing around briefly.

'All the people having their pictures taken?'

'Yeah,' she confirmed again, suddenly noticing just how many couples and groups there were posing in front of cameras.

'Well, they all seem to be happy. Right?'

'Of course, yeah.'

'This is happening throughout the entire zoo, in every shot of every couple. Family. Friends. All of them will be smiling.'

'Yeah, but…what are you trying to say, Alex?'

He took a moment before he said it. 'They can't all be happy.'

Layna didn't say anything, mainly because of the bafflement she was experiencing. But intrigue was also there, and her eyes soon signalled for him to continue.

'Not everyone can be happy,' he went on. 'There *must* be some unhappy people in this place, yet there…is nobody honest enough to show how they…*really* feel. The camera…it forces them to smile.'

'But that's what everyone does. It kinda makes the photos better to look at…'

'But *not real*. In fact…all people, wherever they are, will smile when their photo is taken. And if you look at any photo album, or collection of photos of a…family…or friends or whatever…then you needn't bother. They're filled with a big smile. They aren't real. They are…*dishonest*. If you want to get to know people, then most photo albums are a bad place to start.'

'What's wrong with seeing people happy – or at least appearing to be?'

'Nothing. But…what's wrong with seeing them sad, upset, angry, confused…*hurt*? What's wrong with…*really* seeing someone? What's wrong with showing how people *really feel*?'

'So what do you propose – that all pictures be taken *secretly* without the other person knowing?'

'I don't know any of the answers…'

'Do you have a photo album of *real* photos, then? Family perhaps?'

Alex was quiet for a moment before he answered, gazing at the ground. 'No. I don't.'

Layna removed the camera from her neck and offered it to him. 'Let's take a break for a sec,' she said. 'Take my picture, will you?'

'…Why?'

They both stopped walking.

'*Take it*,' she insisted, her expression serious. 'I won't let my face lie. I promise.'

He took the camera, held it to his eye, and after a few seconds said: 'Ready?'

'You don't need to ask me that, though, right? This is a *real* photo. Of me.'

'Right.'

Alex pushed the button, capturing her in the moment. He then looked back at the photo on the screen, seeing there was indeed no

171

smile – but no frown or sadness either. He didn't know what the emotion was. But it was certainly *real*. It was not serious or amused, or that of a familiar expression he'd seen on the faces of other people. The look was just...*pure*.

Layna stepped towards him, not taking her eyes away from his, and said 'Alex...I just want to say thanks. Thank you for everything you've done today. Seriously. I think that you make me...*happy*.' When she noticed his silence her face shied away. '*Shit, um...*' she said awkwardly. 'Listen, you...don't have to say anything, okay?'

Alex looked at her, wanting to say something back. No words could be found, though.

But then he stopped caring. He stopped caring because they were *just words* – and he was tired of talking now.

With his heart beating out of control, and his hairs on end, Alex Merton slowly moved forward, and moments later experienced his first kiss.

20

He sat on the bed, listening to her talk about the shoots she'd done successfully that week, her eyes filled with promise and excitement. She told how one woman, a Mrs Fuller, had been so pleased with the photos that she'd recommended her to do a friend's wedding next month – with the friend literally calling up a couple of days later. It had been completely out the blue for Layna who hadn't been overly confident of hearing back. But she *had* got the call regardless, and of course, agreed instantly. It was to be only a small wedding, but the experience alone would be worth more than what she would earn. Her photography career was starting to walk at last, and the wedding shoot itself, which she would've missed if Alex hadn't persistently tried to help her, had brought a nice little piece of work – something she knew she would love and enjoy doing.

When questioned, Alex spoke of his art and the progress made so far, though he spoke in shorter sentences than Layna, usually looking away when mentioning the subject. His most important news was that he had received a call from Richard Dowsteene confirming he'd booked a private gallery in London, which in fact he owned himself, where Alex's work would be showcased in a month's time. After taking that call, Alex hadn't believed it and so had gone straight to the mirror to look at himself, thinking hard, and then finally confirmed reality by speaking the words 'Exhibition' and 'London', followed by 'June the first.' On top of the good news from Richard, work at Sestern had also gotten better – or *easier* was maybe more accurate – because another kitchen porter had been taken on. Alex's workload was now realistic, because he and his colleague had alternating weekly shifts of 8:00am to 3:00pm and 11:00am to 5:00pm. And the work *did* seem easier. It was more manageable. More normal. More *right*.

Since the trip to the zoo, they'd carried on seeing each other a few times a week. They'd gone out with her friends a couple of times, once to the cinema, and once for a meal. Alex had felt unsettled in their company, and though he'd sensed it was wrong, knew he felt best understood and calmest when it was just him and Layna – just the two of them. Stacey had probed her while they were alone, on a couple of separate occasions, about why she hadn't initially gone to her for help with her problems. Layna had explained it wasn't personal, and that for some reason Alex had just seemed like the right person to have around to drag the pain out of her, and so had placed all faith in him. An apology had then been given to Stacey, though, for not giving her a chance to begin with.

At 7:30pm, Layna now rummaged around in her bag as it began to buzz. 'Hey, you outside?' she asked as the mobile met her ear, getting up to look out the window. 'Okay, I'm just coming down.' She grabbed a thin fleece jacket and said to Alex: 'Sorry, I forgot to tell you I've got to go out with my brother tonight. He's having a few problems at the moment. I don't know what exactly, but I need to go out for a drink with him. Sorry, I just *really* forgot...'

'That's all right,' Alex told her getting to his feet. 'I should...probably get going, anyway.'

They both headed out the room and toward the stairs, but she suddenly cut in front of him and stopped. 'Alex, look. I forgot to tell you – no...that's a lie. *Shit, sorry...*' Her hands were tense as they tried to help explain along with her words. 'I don't wanna' deceive you anymore.'

He didn't know what she was about to say, but could sense she clearly wasn't looking forward to telling him. And *he* wasn't exactly looking forward to it, either...

'It's my brother,' she went on. 'He's...' Her mouth remained open, her tongue poised while her thoughts tried to construct a sentence. 'I lied to you about my surname when I first met you. It's *not* Davis.'

The sound of a knock at the front door made its way up the stairs.

'I lied because...well, I didn't want you to worry. I was going to tell you, but...to be honest, it was easier not to. I know I should've, I just...didn't want to *worry you.*'

'About what?' Alex asked, a frenzy of panic building as he wondered who the hell was waiting outside.

174

'My *real* name. Who I'm related to. But listen – he should be fine when you see him, so don't worry about it. Especially *tonight*...because of the way he is. Look...I've gotta' go now, but I'll call you later on, okay?'

Alex followed her down the stairs and through into the lounge, and as she unlocked the front door, opening it to her brother's voice, he suddenly knew who it was. His chest went cold, tight, stopping him dead in his tracks, and for a few seconds he couldn't breathe. He would have to leave and walk right out through that door, wouldn't he? He would have to—

But he didn't want to think about it. There was no point. There was only one thing that could be done, and that was to leave – *get out*. And the sooner it happened, the better.

His legs felt alien as they started to move. 'I'll see you later Layna,' he forced out quickly, glancing up from the floor high enough to see who the man was standing in the doorway.

The confirmation then came: it was *him*, all right.

And before Alex walked past, their eyes met. The man slurred the word '*Hey...*' to him, his breath stinking of booze, his pupils dilating as they tried to focus.

Alex kept on walking, walking right on and not looking back. That man, Layna's brother, was *him*! – the very same man who'd always tried his damndest to make his life a living hell since day one.

The man hadn't said anything just now, though, had he? But then again, the man couldn't. Not with his sister there. It was against the rules. Because it was a private thing that happened at work, wasn't it? – the private bullying, the verbal abuse. The man had looked different now, though; drunk, wasted, ill almost. Had the man even noticed it was him, *Alex Merton*, who'd walked right by him? *He must've done, right?*

As Alex continued to walk back home, he couldn't help but feel a sickening unease in his gut from knowing that Layna's brother was Sam Henderson.

21

'Mr Merton?' Richard Dowsteene said on the other end of the line.

'Yes, it's me,' Alex replied from his desk, the mobile pressed closely to his ear.

'This exhibition, June the first. I'll be frank with you – and I don't normally run things like this. I've pushed everything else to one side for now. Someone else from the agency can look after that pile for the time being, because right now, *I* want to concentrate on *your* work, Alex. And what I really need back in return, is your time. The exhibition's not far away, you understand? Two weeks is what I want. Two weeks to sit and talk to you. Ideas and...just discussion about this whole project – this exhibition.'

Alex was silent.

'You there...?' Richard asked. 'What do you think? *Two weeks?* Can you get the time? – make it happen?'

'Well, I don't know. I don't know if I...can take that amount of time off. I'll have to—'

'Alex, *please*... Listen. This job you do at the moment – I wouldn't worry about it. If you trust me and believe in this thing, then I assure you, this washing up position...*it ain't gonna be yours much longer.* I'm sure of it. And I think it's time you started believing in yourself. *Don't you?* So what do you say?'

Alex was moved, even somewhat motivated from the agent's words.

'Worst case scenario,' Richard went on, 'your employer lets you go. And that's not gonna happen – but let's say it did. What then? If it *did*...well, you could just find more work washing someone else's dishes, right? But *this* – your art career – *this* is worth taking a risk for. *A leap of faith.* I know – I make it sound simpler than you may feel it is.

I understand that, Alex, believe me. And I'm guessing you haven't taken many of those before, have you?'

'Haven't taken...many what?'

'*Leaps of faith, Alex.* So come on, let's do this! Get the ball rolling already. *I* know you can do it. And *I* know you want this. And guess what? I'm going to help you out a little...because I'm guessing you're probably a bit tight for cash at the moment, right? I'm going to invest in the exhibition. I want to invest in *you*, Alex. In fact, I've already started doing it. I say let's take this thing all the way, and that means saying fuck you to that job of yours – at least for two weeks, anyway. You won't regret it, I promise. *I* say you go in there tomorrow and tell them you're taking two weeks' leave. And if they ask why, then tell them it's because you'd be crazy to waste any more of your time in a position like that when you're a phenomenal artist. Just think: *Fuck' em!* Right? What do you think?'

Alex hesitated, but knew what he wanted to say. 'All right. All right, *I'll do it.*' And as he did, he felt excited, looking to the future and the exhibition with what seemed like hope. And hope, if that was indeed what it was, was a great feeling – purposeful, meaningful.

'You won't regret this,' Richard assured. 'Neither of us will. I'm just glad you called in the first place.'

Alex smiled.

'Listen,' Richard continued, 'I've got to get on. Call me tomorrow – no wait, I'll call *you* tomorrow evening. Then you can tell me the dates you got off work, can't you?'

'All right,' Alex confirmed, though he knew being granted the leave wouldn't come easily.

'This thing's gonna be big, I can feel it. I *know* it is. And *you* should start believing, too.'

Alex didn't say anything, but nodded his head.

'Goodbye for now, Mr Merton.'

And then before Alex could even reply, the line went dead. He was left sitting there thinking, thinking about how he was going to get two weeks off straight away without any notice. Could he do it? Could he just *do that*? But the buzz from the excitement of thinking about his future as an artist captivated his mind, sending it off in another direction, making him think of words inspired by those Richard had just used. *I know you can do it! Fuck' em! Fuck' em all! This is* your *time,* your *moment!*

Was it wrong to just *fuck' em all*, though? And to just fuck over the new guy at work, his kitchen porter colleague who hadn't even been there that long?

But he countered the thought with: *He'll be fine, he'll get help from someone else anyway – and for god's sake, just* fuck' em all! *This is* your *moment you stupid shit! Just do it! Do it already!*

Alex knew what he was going to do. He was going to *do it.* Tomorrow he was going to tell work he wanted two weeks off, and if they didn't like it, then tough shit.

God he felt different! What was he thinking?! Where the hell had *that strength* come from?

He would tell them the reason if they really wanted to know, and then that would be the end of it. He wasn't going to miss the opportunity with Richard, that one chance, just because of *them.*

As Alex was about to get up, he found himself unable to move from the chair. What kept him there was the strange feeling being experienced. It felt like *light.* And he imagined it to look like light too. He could almost see it.

Things were just changing so suddenly, and he didn't know how it had all happened so fast. He was actually doing *good.* He was actually doing something – *going somewhere.* And it was crazy to have people, both Layna and Richard, believing in and seeing him, *really* seeing him with their eyes. He spoke to them regularly, and things were happening. And he had even helped Layna too.

What was going on?!

He began to wonder just who Alex Merton really was. Who the hell was he...?

It was like he was coming out of something – breaking out – and things were just going on and he didn't know whether he had any control over anything anymore. And it was scary to be out of control, wasn't it? But...he was far from dead. He didn't feel dead anymore. And it had to be better than feeling like that, didn't it?

Things were improving. A lot. A heck of a lot.

Alex went over all the recent events a few times more in his head, and soon accepted them, having faith in them enough to smile and believe that maybe – just maybe – he had a chance of finding happiness.

22

Thursday, 29 April 2010

Sam had planned on taking the day off, and had been about to go through with it until he now realised at 09:15am, while sat on the end of the bed, that there was no way in hell he could do it. There'd been a small, yet naive and stupid part of him which had believed that somehow it could have been all right if he stayed at home. But that part of him didn't know jack shit. That was a part of him that tried to pretend The Beast could be dealt with – like it could be simply pushed aside. The Beast meant business, though, didn't it? It wasn't fucking around anymore. If he were to stay at home and give it the fuel it needed, then he'd be eaten alive. If he gave it room to breathe, just that little bit too much air, it would get even worse, spreading like a terminal disease. And it was spreading now, right at this moment. Spreading. Spreading.

He'd already phoned work earlier at 6:00am and informed Joseph of his absence. Only three hours had passed since, but it felt like he'd been sat there for a day already. The Beast was coming for him, and his mind was its playground. It was a horrible...horrible...torturous game of chase. Relentless. And the hiding places, the obstacles he could use to gain distance, were beginning to become sparse. The ground was almost open. And recently, The Beast had been getting close to him – terrifyingly close, indeed – with its claw-like fingers reaching behind, just inches away. And Sam Henderson was in trouble. Because Sam Henderson's legs were now starting to tire...

He rose to his feet and went into the bathroom to start his routine. But as he entered, his hands fell to the sink, his head leaning forward till it pressed against the mirror. Exhaustion was there already.

No sleep had been granted last night, even with the addition of the sleeping pills which he'd had to start taking again lately. And this was the worst time to feel The Beast – during the nights, when he'd want nothing more than to lose consciousness to sleep, desperately trying to ignore the whispers in his ear. He'd started drinking more, but even that didn't seem to be helping, because every time he put the bottle to his lips he was reminded of the very reason he was drinking in the first place. The alcohol now chose when he would sleep (usually after work in the afternoons), and though that must have played its part toward his insomnia at night, he wasn't about to give it up.

Other things had had to be given up also. All distractions that simply couldn't be afforded any longer had to be cancelled. The gym, cable TV, everything – all gone. He still spoke to Will on the phone just as much, but his outings and trips hardly took place anymore. Most nights were spent at home, with nothing to distract him. Not a thing. Even watching porn was useless. The money just wasn't there anymore; all those years of trying to keep up with Will's lifestyle had finally caught up with him. Savings were gone, and so was everything else which had laid in his accounts.

All Sam could do these days was suffer inside the house – inside himself. But how was he supposed to cope? How was he supposed to cope with his mind, his thoughts, his demon, *his Beast?*

***

It was 10:00am, and to everyone's disbelief in the kitchen, Sam Henderson really hadn't turned up.

Apparently, from what Alex had overheard from the management, who'd come into the kitchen earlier to talk to Joseph, it had only been the third or fourth day the man had ever taken off sick in the history of his employment. He felt disappointed – and it was for an odd reason. It was because Sam *wasn't* at work. And without him there, it would surely be harder to get the time off, since if he went straight to the management asking for leave, they would most certainly want to know it had been cleared with Sam first.

Alex continued to put the frozen food delivery away into the portable freezer parked outside on the grass by the Goods In back door. The caravan-sized freezer had arrived a few days ago, shortly after the main walk-in's temperature had been seen playing up, creeping from -19 to 7°C.

181

After ten minutes, he'd finished clearing all the boxes from the curb where the delivery driver had left them. As he headed back inside the Goods In and started to sign the paperwork into the log book, he then saw in the corner of his eye the man he'd been wanting to see walk right past him. How long he had been there already, he didn't know.

Alex instantly dropped the pen and turned to approach Sam who was about to enter the walk-in fridge. How was he going to speak to him, though? – the man he hated to the fucking bone? He'd never even really approached and spoken to him on his own terms before.

But that wasn't the way to be thinking, was it? Instead he should be just going for it – *going for it* – asking the man, and then taking the fucking leave and starting his new life. *Fuck' em all!*

'Sam...?' he forced out.

The head chef stopped, not moving for a moment before turning to face him. And when it happened, Alex thought he looked terrible, possibly emaciated even – almost like a different person entirely.

'What?' Sam's lifeless voice asked, his eyes in no rush to meet.

'Well...' Alex began with hesitation. 'I need some time off.'

'How long?'

'...Two weeks.'

'When?'

'As soon as...possible, really. I was thinking...from Monday the third to the sixteenth of May.'

Sam didn't say anything for a couple of seconds, but then uttered the word 'Fine.'

And that was it. That was all he had to say on the subject. He then turned away and went back to his business, walking inside the fridge, leaving Alex wondering whether the man had even properly understood the request.

Fine? Was that really all he'd wanted to say?

Alex had expected and prepared himself for a lot more, having that morning rehearsed in his head how he would argue out that he was going to have to take the time off no matter what. But there hadn't been any need now, had there? Because it was just *fine*. That was just...it, somehow.

He stood there in disbelief, but also happy he'd got the leave – or at least, so far, the all clear from Sam.

Later after clocking out at 3:00pm, he handed the holiday form in to the management office. But once it was passed over, problems started to surface. They didn't want to grant him the holiday, arguing that the new kitchen porter, Bill, had not been working there long enough, and that Alex was taking liberties by requesting that amount of leave at such short notice. Alex told them again how he'd cleared it with both Bill and Sam and that there were no problems, but the managers both seemed to still not believe him. '*Sam* said yes to this, did he?' Gordon asked with slit, sceptical eyes, repeating himself once more.

After Alex then told them he had no choice but to take the time off due to his art exhibition in London, Gordon was stunned to hear of his achievement, while his assistant manager, Matthew, supposed the kitchen porter was simply a good liar. In the end, they authorised the leave, though unwillingly, knowing they had no real alternative.

As Alex was about to leave, Gordon quickly said: 'Wait one minute.' Alex turned back. 'Before you leave – and this stays between *us*, all right? – I want to ask you something.' Alex nodded, and then shut the door when the pointing finger behind the desk prompted him.

'You can take the leave. No problem. Good luck with the art and...all that. But just tell me one thing – and this conversation really *doesn't* leave this room, okay? I mean that.'

Alex nodded again.

'We've noticed some...*differences*...in Sam's behaviour,' Gordon went on, speaking with slow, carefully selected words. 'His *appearance*, his...' He took a moment to think of how to explain what he wanted to say, casting his mind through *The Big Book of Managerial Tongue*. But it wasn't as easy as initially thought, so he tried a different angle. 'We're worried about Sam. Have you noticed anything strange about him lately?'

Alex could think of a few things, but the most clear and notable was from earlier that morning. He thought it better to keep his answer simple, though. 'His appearance,' he said. 'I'd say it was different.'

Gordon started with 'What about...' but stopped himself again, feeling frustrated with his unusual inability to ask the question in the most professional way. But then he decided to just say the damn thing, not wanting to waste any more time and bruise his ego further.

'We think Sam has a drinking problem. Have you been *smelling* or *seeing* anything lately? Anything from his locker? His breath? That kind of thing?'

'Um…maybe. I couldn't say.' Alex was beginning to already feel like he himself had done something wrong, and that he should've known more in order to answer the questions.

'Okay,' Gordon said, his vigilant eyes still on him, his head nodding slightly. 'Thanks, anyway.' He turned back to his desk, and suddenly the enquiry came to an abrupt halt. 'See you tomorrow.'

As Alex left and headed out toward reception, Joseph stuck his head in through the office door and said his goodbyes for the day. 'Have you got a moment?' Gordon asked him.

'Sure.'

'Thanks, Joseph, take a seat. I've got something I want to ask you. And I'd like it if everything that's said in here doesn't go beyond these walls, if that's okay?'

***

'Sam, look,' Joseph said, trying to make eye contact with the head chef in the Goods In corridor. 'Mate…listen to me.'

'What do you want?' Sam asked, his own eyes anywhere else but with his colleague.

'Look at me for a second, would ya? This is important. *I'm serious.*'

Sam looked.

'They were gonna fire you,' Joseph said.

Sam didn't react until the part of him which cared finally made itself known. 'What do you mean…?'

Joseph put his hand on the man's shoulder, checked behind to make sure they were both still alone, and then carried on. 'I've just been in there. In the office. But I persuaded them otherwise. I told them to give you another chance.'

'Another…*chance?*' Sam sniggered, his whisky breath filling the air between them.

'*Jesus Christ, Sam!*' Joseph hissed, grabbing his colleague by both shoulders and shaking him for a moment. 'Everyone knows! *Everyone!*'

Sam said nothing, his eyes gone again.

184

'Everyone knows about your drinking,' Joseph went on, his voice no longer hissing but unmistakably stern. 'And you look like shit all the time, you know that?! *Jesus*...just look at yourself, would ya? Look at yourself...!' When he received no response, he shook him again. '*What's happening, mate??*'

As Sam's mouth began to open, Joseph thought he was about to finally say something. But only a long breath escaped.

'Take a couple of weeks off.'

'I can't,' Sam let out weakly.

Joseph removed his hands. 'And why not?'

'I just...can't...'

'If you don't – they're-going-to-fire-you. Do you *understand* what I'm saying?' He waited for a reaction but got nothing. 'Don't be a dick here, okay? Do you know how *hard* it was to persuade them in there? *Do you know what they said?* They said you're a good chef, and they said they didn't wanna have to do it, and they said they would've decided against it for a while longer if it wasn't for the customers having already seen you like this.' He waited again for Sam to respond, but it seemed all the man could do at that moment was listen. 'You *have* to take it off. *Do you understand?* Do whatever you can to straighten yourself out. Get counselling, see a shrink – *whatever*! But for God's sake, sort yourself *the fuck-out*! Do you hear me? *Sort yourself the fuck-out.*'

'I'll appeal...' Sam uttered.

'*Against what??*' Joseph fired out. 'Can you wake up, please? Can you do that for me?!' He took him by the shoulders once more. '*You've been drinking on the job, Sam!* There's nothing to fight here. Everyone...*every-one-knows*! Even the customers know – and that's what's *really* gettin up Gordon's arse! He's worried that soon it's gonna start circulating around the offices. Around Safe Insurance. And then things are gonna start turning to shit *big time*. You might be puttin all our jobs on the line here – not just *your own*, Sam.' He paused for a moment, checking they were still alone in the corridor. 'Look, just...take a couple off,' he went on, his voice calming. 'I can handle it. I'll get help in from another site. One of the usual suspects. Agency. *Whatever*.'

'I can't...' Sam repeated, his words even thinner.

'You haven't got a choice. I'm gonna tell them now that you're taking it.' Joseph walked away.

'But I can't…' Sam said again, looking to the back of his colleague. 'I'm sorry. But it's for the best. *For everyone.*'

As Joseph left the corridor, Sam slowly fell back against the lockers, his eyes closing, a forearm soon covering them. He wished it would all just end. That he could fade away. He wanted the pain to be gone now. He wanted to be able to remove his arm and then see he was in another place. Just someplace else.

But when he did, he saw that nothing had changed.

He was still there. Still alone.

Alone with The Beast.

23

'It's next weekend though and I'm scared, Alex!' Layna told him again.

They were both sat on his bed, a sea of photographs from her recent shoots scattered over the duvet.

'Don't worry,' he said. 'You'll do fine. Photography is what you do.'

'It's just a big step for me, I...' and then she cut herself off. 'I'm sorry – I haven't even asked today about *your* progress, have I, Artist?'

'Er...' He looked away. 'I don't know if I am *that* yet. But it's going all right, I guess.'

'He's coming down Monday, right?'

'Monday, tomorrow...yes. I've got to go up to London to see one of his galleries on the twelfth of this month. He says the exhibition might be there.'

'Wow, *Alex-Merton*...' she said impressed smiling. 'I think I'm getting jealous of you now, *you know that*?'

Alex knew it was just a bit of humour, but decided to change the subject. Since it was possible the whole thing could still fall through, it made him feel uncomfortable talking about it. 'So...do you start your new job at the petrol station next week?'

'Yeah, my new *mandatory day-job job*, that is. But never mind that. So Richard's coming down tomorrow, then? To do what exactly?'

'I don't know,' Alex said, knowing her interest in the subject wasn't going to go away that easily. 'Just to talk about the exhibition and my work basically I think.'

'He sounds like he knows what he's doing.'

'Yes, he...he seems to.'

'*Cool.*' She prodded him playfully in the arm with her finger. 'This time next year I think you're gonna be somebody great, you know that, Mr Merton?'

'I don't know about…*that.*'

'Maybe we both will? We'll get out of this place and…' She searched for her next words. '…And start the beginning of our future – of *whatever's* next!'

Alex held onto the word *our*, seeing it clearly in his head. It started to fade, though, once he realised just how ridiculous it was to even think there could've really been anything attached to it.

He then became aware of Layna's prolonged gaze over him, and searched for something to say. But before any words could come out, her eyes broke away as she reached into her bag and pulled out her ringing mobile. The tiredness from all the stress and worry he'd been experiencing about his agent coming over tomorrow night then caught up with him. And throughout the length of Layna's phone call, his mind almost became a blank, though he was too drained to be surprised by it.

'That was my brother,' she soon told him.

'Was it?' Alex asked, his attention returning.

'He's just…' she brought her hand up to the top of her forehead, '…he's just not doing well at the moment.'

Alex didn't comment.

'I don't know what's wrong with him, to be honest. He won't tell me anything and I don't…*really* know what to do, either. But I think he does wanna tell me something, cos he wants us to go out for a drink again. Last time we went out – you know, when he picked me up before? – he just sat there hardly saying anything, and when he did talk, it made no sense. His words were just – well, I don't know what they were! And it wasn't because he'd been drinking, either. I didn't even know he'd *been* drinking until he was driving us there and then suddenly I caught his breath. *And he never drinks, you know?!* Not like *that.* It's just so strange. He actually drove us there – *drunk!* I got a taxi back at the end of the night, but…he drove back – *still pissed.*' She took a moment, her perplexed mind needing it. 'I hadn't actually seen him in years up until that night. Well, I had seen him at Sestern, of course – but that wasn't *seeing* him, exactly, was it? He'd never wanted to even talk to me there when I'd tried to spark a conversation between us. It's...' She took another moment. '...I don't know *what* it is.'

Alex still kept quiet.

'I know he's not a nice man. Especially with...' She stopped herself, but Alex knew what she'd been about to say. 'But, did he ever say anything to you about – *I don't know* – what he's going through?'

'No,' Alex answered. 'He didn't ever say anything...to *me*.'

'It's strange how he's been so ruthlessly...*Sam*. So up together for all this time. And now, he's just caving, falling apart over something. And I don't know what that *something* is. But whatever it is, it's done damage. Real damage. I mean, he's been forced to take two weeks off work!' She paused for a second, letting her mind reach its decision. 'I think I have to see him tonight. I at least owe him that as his sister. But if he's drunk then I'll drive off. I'm *not* picking him up if he's been drinking.'

Alex didn't know if he could pull out any pity from the black whirlwind of hatred he harboured for Sam Henderson. He wondered whether or not he did in fact wish the man any pain, but couldn't make his mind up. But from the downward spiral he'd seen him in lately at work, it *did* make it harder for him to wish hurt, even though it wasn't so long ago, he knew, that he'd been very, very close to wanting to kill the man himself. *Very close.*

'It will be okay,' he said. 'He'll be fine.' And as the words came out, just speaking about the man made him feel nervous, giving him a heightened sense throughout his body, like Sam's presence was in the room.

'Yeah,' Layna said. 'I hope so. I really do.' She then looked at her mobile and said: 'I'd better get going, actually. And go pick him up.'

Alex enjoyed the sensation when she gave him a hug; her breasts, the warmth of her arms, her body, was something he desired.

After she left, he relaxed back on the bed, thinking, thinking, thinking about what had just happened. Maybe nothing had. But maybe *something*. Maybe it had been more than just a hug, and had been an *our future* when she'd said the words? But maybe it had just been a *friendly* hug and a meaningless *our future*? His mind then strayed over to his agent and all things art, and he was wondering, worrying about it all again. And then the questions about himself and Layna were coming back. What had happened? What was happening

189

between them? It went back to the art again. What was he going to have to do with his agent? Where was he going to have to go? Could it be soon when Richard came over that the man was going to tell him he'd made a mistake and that his art was a fucking waste of time? Was *that* what was going to happen? And then it was back again to Layna and then back again to the art and then to Layna and then to the art and back again and back and back and back again and—

Alex needed a distraction. So he got up and headed for the kitchen. He needed to get out of that room, move his feet – do *something*. He downed a glass of water and tried to control his breathing.

Soon he was fine, breathing in and out, in and out, in and out. When he got into the bathroom, he immediately wanted to start telling the mirror he was all right and not to panic, but instead decided to just think the words. When they came, appearing in a white silvery lettering, it felt surprisingly satisfying.

Later that evening, he removed the protective plastic from one of his paintings and held it in front of his eyes. As he looked at it, he somehow gradually began to build what felt like hope and a positive outlook, telling himself that everything – *if he could just keep it the fuck together* – would be all right.

***

Layna hadn't been particularly glad when she'd picked Sam up at 8:00pm, but had at least been relieved he wasn't drunk. At the most, she'd supposed maybe two pints could have been consumed (or whatever the equivalent was in whisky).

There'd been little conversation in the car, apart from Sam saying he was grateful for her coming out to get him. But that was all he'd said. They ended up in The Rabbit's Tail, the same place as last time, sat in the same darkened corner at the back. The pub itself was quiet, which of course wasn't unusual for a Monday night.

Sam took his eyes off the orange juice and lemonade and was about to speak. His mouth opened a little but then closed. It happened a few times, with Layna watching more so with concern than anticipation, but never impatience. She didn't feel like she knew her brother at all – this man, this person, this stranger who'd never

190

once attempted to get to know her – but knew she did want to help him.

Finally words left him: 'Thanks for coming out again tonight.'

Layna felt disappointed with what she'd waited for, but still smiled. 'You're my brother, it's no problem.'

'Thanks,' he said, his eyes lost, travelling through the jagged lines which had been scratched into the wooden table over many years.

She took a deep breath, and then started the ball rolling. 'So I know it's hard, but…can you tell me anything?'

'I want to.'

'That's good. It's good that you *want* to talk, and…well, I'm glad that you feel all right to do it with *me*.' She looked at him for a response, but got nothing. She could, however, tell from his half-contorted face he was probably trying to think of how to express his next words.

'I…' he started. '…I thought I was great. I really…*really* thought I was. But it's got real bad this time. *It's fucking-bad.* And I don't think I can make it out. I'm not even allowed to think about it. I can't look it in the eye and—'

'Look what in the eye?'

He took a gulp from his drink, biding his time.

'Sam…' she pressed lightly, seeing he was afraid to even say the word that must've been on the tip of his tongue.

His glass hit back down on the table with clumsy control. '*It*…'

'I'm sorry, I…don't understand. What's—'

'*IT!*' he suddenly let out, his voice raised, hands up at his temples. '*The fucking thing!* It's like – it's like it wants to…' He couldn't speak for a moment. '*Shit*, I just…'

'If you can just tell me, or describe what it is.'

'*No*…'

'Sam, you have to—'

'*NO!* I can't! I…can't tell anyone. I shouldn't even be thinking about this right now. *Please* – can we just…change the subject? For a while? Or just talk about—'

'*Okay…!*' she agreed trying to calm him, noticing the pub had either gone even more deathly quiet because it was simply a Monday night, or because they'd both caused a stir in the place. 'It's *okay*, don't worry.' She studied him, the once supposedly strong statue now crumbling before her very eyes. 'What shall we talk about, then?'

'*You!* – let's talk about you for a while. Yeah, just – *just you.*'

'Okay you got it. What do you wanna know?'

'What do you do? What do you...like and stuff?'

'Well I like photography. I'm a photographer – an amateur rising, you could say. And I have a few gigs lined up now. Which is good. A wedding and some other shoots. It's what I love doing.'

'Great,' Sam said, his expression exhausted, with beads of sweat appearing at his forehead. 'And...boyfriend? Love life? Stuff like that?'

'Well I don't have anyone, really.'

'What about thingy, er...whatsis' face? *Alex* – what about him?'

Layna now noticed the slurring and mumbling in his voice. It was obvious something was in his system, but whether it was alcohol or medication – or a mixture of both – she didn't know. 'Me and Alex. We're friends.'

'*What...?*' he said with disbelief.

'Yeah. It's true.'

'You *sure* about that?'

'Yes, Sam. I'm sure.'

'You see him a lot?'

'Sometimes.'

'*Come ooooon...*' he provoked, pointing at her.

Layna began to question not just whether he'd been drinking or had taken a few too many pills, but also his state of mind. What was happening to her brother? He was getting more aggressive now, almost like he was turning on her.

'*Come ooooon....!* Why you hang out with that guy, anyway?' His nails scratched at what was becoming a short beard, and then he grinned. '*He's a loser!*'

'He's not a loser,' she said with a sigh, looking to the ceiling – anywhere but him.

'That what you want? *A pot washer?* A pot washer with *no balls? A faggot-fuckin-homo...pot washer?* That it?'

'So I guess you *have* been drinking, then? You have, haven't you, Sam?'

'Just tell me. *Come on....!* What is it?'

192

'I don't think we should continue talking.'

He grinned again, blowing air out his nose.

'And if you *must* know...' she said, '...he's an artist. It's what he does *outside* of work. Been doing it his whole life.'

'*WOW-WEE!*' he spluttered out as he laughed to himself, saliva escaping over his lips. 'So what have we got here? – the next...fuckin Warhol...*fuckin Picasso* or something?!'

'Maybe his agent thinks so.'

Sam paused, needing a second to digest the information. His eyes then lit up and he leaned forward, his face no longer amused, and said: 'What do you mean...*agent?* What are you talkin about?'

'He has an agent representing him. Guy says he's the best thing he's seen in a long time. Has an exhibition in June.'

'*Bullshit!* – that fag's not goin anywhere with his life...!' he laughed.

Layna said nothing, showing only contempt.

'And if he has one...' Sam went on, '...then he's fooling himself, the *stoopid fuck!*'

'It's Dowsteene,' she told him.

'Oh, *Dowsteene?!* – the Vulnham-bred hotshot you went to Uni with? *Of course it is!* I guess Alex is just surrounded by millionaires these days, isn't he, right?' He necked the rest of his drink. 'You're full of shit, the both of you. Richard-fucking-Dowsteene in vile-fucking-*Vulnham*. Now that *is* good! *Funny even!*'

'You better believe it. Alex is going up there to check out his gallery on the twelfth.'

Sam's grin fell as he saw how serious her eyes remained.

'It's the truth,' she said. 'Not that it matters what *you* think.' Her hand reached for her bag. 'I don't know why I even bothered trying to help you, you know? Don't call me anymore, okay? Whatever this is...*it's over.*'

But before she could get up Sam said 'Wait! – wait a minute, I know you! I *know you!*'

'You don't know me. You never did.'

'Tell me what's really going on here – what you *really* want from him...'

'What do you care?'

'There-*is*-something, *isn't there*? What is it? Why are you *so interested* in Alex? Why do you see him all the time? What do you want with a—'

'Fine,' Layna said. 'I'll tell you.'

And as she did, telling him everything, Sam sat back and listened. When she'd finished, he didn't know what to say, but was thinking. Thinking many things. He then looked into her eyes...but they didn't belong to a liar. What she'd said was the truth. And he was shocked. Shocked by what he'd just heard – and especially having come from her.

***

Sam lay on the bed, eyes closed, facing the ceiling. The time since leaving work last Friday seemed to have lasted an eternity. Never ending.

Everything was just over now. Fucked. Blown to jagged pieces. And there was nothing he could do about it. Debt was everywhere, banks were starting to ask questions, and he, Sam Henderson, *The Man of Control*, finally knew he was losing it; everything he owned, his life – himself. The job was still there, though. That was one thing. *But for how long?* How long would they really keep someone like him on – someone who'd drank regularly from his locker – after he went back to work? And how many candidates were they already putting through interview after interview in an effort to replace him? Soon he would surely lose the house, and eventually his mind, once The Beast inside took over. It was only a matter of time. And the darkness behind his eyelids could not save him. It couldn't take him away to a better place, could it? It couldn't hide him, give him shelter, or a hiding place even for temporary refuge.

Something then entered his mind. Something dark. A sharp lethal thought. But where had it come from? That didn't matter, though, did it? Because he had thought of something that had made him sit up from the bed. And so this thought was worth examining, for sure. But what was it? An idea of something which could be done, maybe? Something which could—

And there it was. He could see it. *Feel it.*

Images were in his head, and details were being added at a rapid rate. It was like they wanted to be seen, yearning for a spotlight to be cast upon them.

And he obliged. Boy, did he.

Sam wanted to see them, hear them – measure the possible polluted pleasures which could come from executing the emergent plan.

And soon he could think of nothing else, only able to think about how right it was for it to happen – and how he might feel if he *didn't* act upon the impulse. It was the only thing he cared to make an effort for in his life now.

He would do it. And enjoy it. He would see to that.

Oh he would see to that all right...

His arm reached across to the bedside chest of drawers, gracelessly searching for his mobile, knocking over the bottle of whisky in the process.

Sam Henderson then grinned and began to talk to himself.

'This is gonna be good,' he said. 'This is gonna be *real good...*'

PART 3

From Josephine Lexington's *Merton: Discovering the Invisible Man*:

Despite many reported sightings of them meeting together in London, along with telephone records which confirmed that the prestigious London-based art agent had exchanged a number of long calls with Alex Merton over a period of weeks, Richard Dowsteene defended his actions, and after a short investigation, the police dropped their inquiry. In a statement released to the press, he said:

"Neither I, Richard Dowsteene, or any member of the Dowsteene & Goadman agency have ever approached, met, or entered into any form of personal or business relationship with Alex Merton. On those occasions upon which I directly contacted him, it was in hope of deterring him from harassing me further, and to warn that I would inform the authorities should he continue to persist. This was a man who could not handle rejection. He could not accept the fact that I was unprepared to see his work. However, I've known troubled artists, and could tell – though I knew nothing of the depths of his psychosis at the time – that he was indeed a troubled individual. This was partly why I started to contact him. Probably more than I should have. I sympathised with his desperation to become an artist and disbursed advice. Back then, I felt that – despite the headlines you now read about him on a daily basis – he was simply a ghost who wanted to be seen. And for his work to be seen. The same people who write these headlines have in the past labelled me as a kind of monster also. And if my attempts to compassionately console Mr Merton are too shocking – or even unbelievable – then so be it. All I can say

is that the doors of my agency have been wide open for the police and their investigation, and that my staff, business partners and associates have been questioned, and still, nothing has surfaced. As a company, we now wish to return to business as usual. We ask that the press act accordingly in light of these facts, and also have the decency to think before inciting any further wild goose chases which might damage the stellar reputations of marquee names such as Dowsteene & Goadman."

24

Wednesday, 5 May 2010

At 4:00pm, Richard Dowsteene was standing in Alex's doorway. 'I'll level with you,' he said. 'I'm a business man first, end of day. I gotta make money, right? So have you. So have the rest of the world. What I'm saying is this. I don't represent people because I think they have talent, skill, creativity – *it* – or brilliance in their head...and the ability to put it on a surface. Of course, they have to be in possession of those virtues too. But no – I represent them because I think they can generate sales. I'm a *business man*. I own two highly successful galleries in London, and I don't play games. I don't take risks if I can't see rewards before me. But – and there is a big *but* coming, Alex...' He paused for a second, his eyes narrowing. '*But*...something here has changed me. I haven't felt it since my younger days.' His eyes looked up to the ceiling and down to the floor, and in that moment he felt the memories of old, the electricity, a charge so natural surging back through him. 'What I'm saying is this. I don't know if I've seen anything like this – *your* work, Alex – in a long time. Believe me when I say *I would know*. Anyway, I love it. Want to show it to the world.' His hands clasped together, generating a soft clap. '*And yes* – I want to sell it. But for the first time in a long, *long* time, Alex, I'm willing to take the risk with this kind of work you've created. Like I said, it *is* unusual, un-commercial, un...*everything*. But hell I think it's going to blow the art world to *shit*. And I *don't*-usually-swear...' A pause came, but his palms remained together at chest level like in prayer. 'I want to take the chance. And I want to let you know that I'm with you all the way on this. What I want to say as well is: *Don't* show anyone else your work. Any of it. *I* want to represent you, and I'm willing to pay for the exhibition, and, the rest...the details, things you can't afford right now. And don't worry – I'm just giving you a little boost to reach what would take most artists years. And you should grab this thing by the balls the way *I'm* grabbing *you* by the balls. So don't feel bad or awkward about the money, or anything else. Just remember my commitment is there, and that I look forward to a long working relationship with you.' A short breath of laughter escaped him. 'Hell...*yes* – this is crazy, I know. I know that, Alex. You've never sold a damn thing and yet...well, maybe *I am* just crazy! But I think not. I'll tell you what *is* crazy, though, Alex: you keeping years and years worth of *this* calibre of work under your bed and in your wardrobe for all this time; you working washing pots; you not realising your talent. *That's* crazy. I think that maybe I was meant to come here, you know? And I never get personal like this – but I'm excited. *It's true!* He stopped talking for a few seconds, but kept eyes on his new client. 'But I'm *not* going to get carried away anymore, today – because now, I'm leaving.' Before pulling the mobile from his jacket and turning away, he said: 'Goodbye for now, Alex. I can't make it over tomorrow, but I'll call you.'

'I'll see you soon,' Alex said. 'Thanks a lot Richard.' As he was about to shut the door, the agent called back from somewhere on the stairs: 'And start smiling! People *do* in London, you know? Even *artists*...!'

Alex closed the door, amused by the comment, a light smile forming on his lips. He went back to the desk and let his mind inspect the aspects of a day which had gone by so quickly. Although he'd felt confused by Richard's well-spoken words earlier (and had done since his first visit on Monday), one thing that was comforting about the agent was that, though he seemed to be educated in the highest degree, he *was* unusual, and Alex therefore felt able to communicate with him candidly. He trusted him, and something just seemed right about the whole thing. Alex had been honest since Monday up until now, and had felt able to tell him everything about his art, and had thus probably revealed a lot about his own self in the process. It was indeed still *odd* how he'd related to such a man as this of course, and how Richard had also been so interested and understood his work with such an open mind, heart, and

(*He just wants the money! He doesn't give a shit about* you, *you fucking stupid boy! You shouldn't have ever opened the door inviting him in! It's going to end* bad *again!*)

199

desire to understand what was behind it; his inspirations, influences, reason – though when Alex had been asked for things such as *reason* and *inspiration*, he'd answered there wasn't any. At least he'd not been able to think of another artist or specific art movement, anyway. Nobody who'd influenced his work to consist of its particular visual identity. The only person he'd been able to think of was himself. But it hadn't felt right to have said that. There'd been no urge to tell the man his own head had been of that size. It would've sounded so pretentious, wouldn't it!

Alex had thought Richard had seemed to believe him when he'd explained that his hand just drew, painted, and somehow created the very things on the surface beneath it, and that he didn't really understand or know how they got there, knowing only that he made them with emotion – *deep* emotion – usually ranging from the most violently raw all the way to the darkest most unsalvageable pits of his soul; where tears, shame, guilt, and feelings of his own damnation existed.

Richard, as a person, though his towering lanky frame, expensive designer suits and glasses were imposing (their value seemingly possessing invisible judgemental eyes), was not all that bad. But Alex had still felt confused about some of the things he'd said. The agent had merely talked, but his words had been in the language of business. The phrases, terms, and the rest of the jargon, had been mostly incoherent. But as Alex thought about it now, he supposed it had probably made more sense to him than he'd first realised. No – he definitely had understood the basics, the general idea of the concepts, the timeline, the plan of what was about to unfold from up to and on the exhibition. So

(*You don't know shit Alex! He'll take take take take! Then you'll be invisible again and you won't even know what hit you! I bet you weren't even listening, you were too scared, afraid, weren't you? You know it's a waste of fucking time anyway! I bet he was laughing after he left wasn't he?*)

maybe it was all right, after all?

And then it hit him. Hit in a good way. There was something inside that wanted to come out. *To burst out.* It was a compressed joy, happiness, ecstatic hope – all rolled into one. And he didn't want to keep it tied down. He wanted it free! He wanted to *feel* it!

And soon he did.

He went into the bathroom and looked in the mirror, thinking he looked completely different, seeing a big smile on his face. Even the destructive voice inside couldn't remove it, and when it tried to, he said calmly with a gorgeous pleasure: '*Fuck-off*. I'm doing something here. I'm *actually* going to *do something* here for the first time in my life. So you can *fuck-off*.'

But obviously it didn't. And he'd not expected it to either. But at least in that moment, as it carried on yelling at him about how everything was all going to be a waste of time and that he was worthless, it began to get quieter slightly, being pushed into the back row of a more secluded section of his mind while feelings of positivity shone through and dominated the front.

Alex stood there for another ten minutes looking at his reflection. He couldn't stop smiling. He felt unbelievable, incredible – like a *Somebody*. Someone who was *doing something*, was *worth something*. It was surreal. Bizarre. It almost felt wrong to be feeling *this right*. His physical being, whole body, felt different. Everything was just…*changing*. Everything was moving forward, in all directions, a mess really – but a *good mess*! He was improving, developing, realising his dream! He was becoming what he'd always wanted to be, and this – *this* was his time!

Alex then thought about Layna, the destructive part of his mind trying it on with her also, telling him how wrong he was about her. But the voice was more of an interference than anything stronger, still only background noise. He smiled again, thinking: *No. I don't want to hear it.* He knew he and Layna had something together. There was something there. Something unmistakable. He liked her, and she liked him. And it felt great! It felt just…*amazing*! Fireworks and explosions of happiness (and it *was* happiness) were going off in huge blazes, lighting up his dark skies with beautiful lustrous clarity.

Alex felt like he'd been given a second chance, a second life, like he was a new man, a new person – a new human being.

25

Thursday, 6 May 2010

Ed Dorne sat in the lounge, flicking through the nonsense of TV sitcoms and music channels. He didn't like music, and he didn't like sitcoms. They were wasted on him, and they were a waste of time in general. And that night, through his procrastination, he'd figured out why garbage like this was so popular in modern-day society. Sitcoms were successful for one main reason. It wasn't because they were funny. It was merely a trick, was all. It was the fakery, the *canned laughter*. When a person sat down to watch an episode, it was a thoughtless, apathetic task for the brain. Once they heard the uncontrollable overtures of laughter from the invisible audience, they felt compelled to laugh, feeling that otherwise they lacked a sense of humour or were boring if they did not join in and crack a rib themselves. But it was all bullshit of course. Why add laughter to something that's supposed to already be funny? Answer: to remind many a vacant brain that it is. Now that's faith in your product, all right.

Music was also a trick. And yes – he hated it just as much. Always had done. But he had to admit, he did like some songs. They were usually the ones he didn't like. At least not to begin with. But *this* was it, though. *This* was what he'd realised during that night about the strange sounding stuff – the senseless noise which was in fact labelled and sold as *Music*. The only thing that made people eventually buy it was simply media hype, and thanks to the radio and television, repetition. *Repetition, repetition, repetition.* These music channels, and especially the radio, played the same songs over and over, again and again, constantly. When a listener was exposed to hearing a series of certain rhythmic patterns and melody (a so-called song) a thousand times, they would eventually start to enjoy and even become entertained by it. But this was just because they'd been forced to hear it a *thousand times* already! Would they really *love it so* if they'd heard it just the once? Would they then be rushing to buy tickets and go online to research the band they knew nothing about, kidding themselves naively into thinking they could actually relate to and possibly have something in common with them? Ed didn't think so.

He looked through the glass-panelled double doors to his left and into the dining room where his wife (future *ex*-wife) sat eating what looked like a microwave meal. The expression on her face was awkward, different...*unpleasantly* different. She seemed to have changed.

He often wondered lately whether she was experiencing the greatest difficulty in their current situation, and whether that difficulty was coming from more areas than simply dealing with selling up and having to get her own place. Yes – estate agents, solicitors, and receiving call after call after call from them could get even the vast majority of optimists down. There was something else he'd seen in her eyes, though. Just like now. It was more than likely sheer discomfort. Sheer discomfort with a pinch of contempt (and regret maybe).

But it was strange because he didn't think he felt the same emotions even half as strongly as she did. Of course there was the discomfort and awkwardness. But it was only a small amount, and was only ever really there when they crossed each other in the hallway, making eye contact for a split second. Even the knowledge, the knowing that he still lived with her (for the moment), had not changed much about his feelings. And why should it? Things hadn't changed at all – they still didn't kiss each other goodbye in the morning or before going to sleep, still didn't hold each other, still didn't exchange kind words of endearment, still didn't have fun in each other's company, and *still* didn't engage in intercourse.

The only thing which *had* changed was that they spoke less. Even less than they'd done before. And though it made him feel not too great at the thought of it, he wondered if it really even bothered him. He wondered whether the fact they were separated, were going to be divorced, and were soon not going to see each other anymore, was actually affecting him at all.

The way he saw it was that humans were creatures of habit. And this had encouraged him to contemplate whether or not love existed. Maybe it was just convenience which kept people together – a fear of going it alone or without the other person? It certainly made sense to live with another person, didn't it? Joint income was helpful in all economics of relationships, incorporating sensible spending, money appreciation, and trust. And of course, it helped with the upkeep and all aspects of maintaining and financing a property – which was something he could *truly* appreciate now that he was going to be moving out of his own into a real *shithole*. A creature of habit he had become indeed, one who liked living in a half-decent area with a driveway, and one who would surely soon find himself missing that *stupid-over-friendly* neighbour of his who always waved with an overdose of cheerfulness in the mornings as they both left for work. In his new place, this friendly neighbour would probably be replaced with someone who'd yell indecipherable profanities at him. And that person would be a real uneducated moron, someone who was angry at his life's misfortune, unable to realise that: *He, the individual, is to blame, and that it is those who are without the understanding of the importance of structure, productivity and contribution which must be made toward society, who will suffer.*

But that was all to come in the near future. For now, he was trying to figure out more about what was going through that woman's head in the dining room. Something else must've been up with her also, surely because of the low quality meal she was having. She'd never eaten microwave meals before, had she? In fact, it was one thing she'd never allowed in the house. She must've been feeling shit. Real shit.

But actually, Ed didn't want to think about it too much to be honest, did he? Because he'd rather be feeling sorry for himself right now.

Next, he thought about the kind of things he would miss, and tried to list his favourite things about her on a mental notepad. But he was soon struggling, only able to recall the fact that he just liked the way she was. He couldn't think of anything deep or personal. He didn't even really know what she liked or was interested in – only that it was the opposite of what *he* did. He just knew she was productive in society, was well-spoken like him – though not as intelligent – and had a good way of making people laugh.

204

And there it was!

He'd come up with something for the list: She was good with people, good at making them laugh.

Ed felt good about himself for a short moment, like he'd achieved something...but soon realised it had meant nothing, and that it was too late to feel happy about anything learned about the woman.

At the end of the day, he had to admit (and that was all that mattered: *at the end of the day*) he just didn't really care that much about her. He didn't love her, if he was being honest, did he? And what was love?

Answer: a chemical reaction, science, a temporary blip, a malfunction in your brain which would send you into many years of a dysfunctional relationship. And what was the end result of love...once it had dissolved? Answer: the day after day monotony of making someone, who you once adored, entirely unhappy and willing to kill you if they knew they could get away with it, with only consequence – the fear of the justice system – holding them back. Love was a trick, a year of your life where you would bet your very existence it would never go away and leave either one of you. But the truth was that it would go. It *would* leave.

And so he theorised that if love *did* really exist, then it must've affected a person for a temporary period of time only. It was surely just a drug the brain released to lure a man and woman into procreating, ensuring they served their physical contribution to the further existence of the human race. That was all it was – a chemical trick created by the *devious brain*.

Ed had worked it all out now, and was satisfied with his conclusion.

He then felt even better about the love drug, though – because it hadn't won, had it? It hadn't got its wicked way with him. No. He had *not* got his ex-female pregnant. They hadn't had any kids. Not one. And so they were both leaving the relationship as *individuals*, the same way they'd originally entered into the thing. There was no offspring, and that meant *no complications*, nothing which could cause further financial struggle.

He was a simple *odd number*. He was number one. *Number bloody One!* And as he thought it, he smiled smugly, feeling good that he'd managed to dodge the marriage and baby bullet.

But there were other things that didn't make him feel quite as good. In summary, his life, in many ways, was falling to pieces. His convenient home life would soon be no more, with him having to move out and into a new property, moving from the poorer side of Hilbrook all the way down to Shitville – more commonly known as *Vulnham City*. He would have to get and start a new everything. And yes – he was angry. Angry with the stage he was at; his job, his car, his money, his sex life. *Everything.* His whole goddamn situation – all the things he knew he couldn't change. But it was *his* things he worried about, not hers – and he certainly didn't worry about *her.* Not much, anyway. Her problems were *her own* now. He was more concerned about how a certain middle-aged man was still working in that damn call centre, was friendless, and was still without the finances he craved, and, deserved. And at this moment in time, money was all he wanted. He thought harder about it now, about what it could give him, grant him – the doors it could open. If love didn't exist forever, surely money did. It could grow and you could *see it* with your own eyes.

It existed. And as long as you kept making the stuff, it would never give you half as much grief as love was capable of giving.

And people – they were to be trusted just as much as love. People were selfish. They didn't care for one another. Civilisation was there to fool you. It made you think that when you saw your cheerful neighbour with his hand waving in a friendly fashion in the air, that people had the ability to feel and want to give. But it was bullshit! All of it. People had one agenda, and all civilisation did was allow for people to lie to themselves, hoping they were living in a world not filled with greed, but instead with compassionate, considerate people. *Civilized* people. But it was all lies. And he saw through it clearly. It was time to break down the smokescreen – all the way this time – and see people for who they really were. The men with the money screwed over the little – *civilized* – guy. That was it. And so you had to be like those with the money. If you wanted success, you had to say *fuck you* to the world. You had to trample the little people who still foolishly thought God was up there judging them, and who worried about a hell and thought they should respect their neighbours because of karma or whatever crap they believed in. And there were lots of them, all clinging to the hopeless belief that there was a God, a purpose, a desperate reason to let them know their existence – their participation in the rat race as a slave to money and climber of the giant green mountain – hadn't been a total waste of time. And so if you wanted that money, and wanted to reach that summit, then you had to go for it, go get it – kill for it – and not look back at the man you'd just knocked over the edge; *let him be, let him perish in the lower class flames below; don't worry about him one bit; let that man fuel his own fire of defeat with booze and drugs; let his pain that was meant to be flourish.* And the other people who kept on climbing, at the end of the day (and that was all that mattered: *at the end of the day*), were the animals – the predators. Trust was something they showed for show – but none of them cared for one another. Not *truly*. It was but an illusion. They only cared if your hand reached to shake theirs with a green palm.

No green palm? *Then fuck off.*

That was it. That was life as Ed saw it. And he had to get out of his *own*. He had to lose whatever feelings he had for his supposedly fellow man. He had to drain those feelings like a paralysing disease. He had to start pushing forward, incorporating change, making that *money* – becoming who he'd always wanted to be.

And all he had to do now, was find an opening, a route, an avenue, a way to make his life green.

26

Tuesday, 11 May 2010

That morning, Richard Dowsteene hadn't been best pleased when he'd heard the story from Alex about the break-ins which had happened to a number of his neighbours earlier that year. Richard had quickly told him, with a bony hand placed firmly on his shoulder, that they were going to waste no time at all in moving his artwork up to London. And after he'd made a few calls, he'd come back into the lounge and told him that on Friday all of it would be moved to his gallery or into storage – even though Alex had voiced his dislike toward the idea of other people touching and moving his work without his supervision. But within five minutes, he'd been talked into it, coming to realise just how much of a risk it could've been to have left all the work in his flat. It was, after all, a lifetime's worth. *Irreplaceable.* He'd known that he would simply have to start trusting the man and have to change some of his stubborn ways if he were to get out of that place and become the person he knew he was born to be.

After his agent had left at lunch time, he couldn't believe the buzz he was feeling. He tried to call Layna, but again couldn't get hold of her. He'd rung her the day before too, but didn't worry about her still not having answered or returned his calls, because he knew that recently she'd had her own photography work to deal with – including a wedding. And for this reason, he didn't want to keep on pestering her with calls and texts, did he? Plus, he had his own things to do, like making more notes, organising his work, and preparing it all for its removal to London on Friday. He also had to prepare himself, mentally more than anything, for the trip he had to make up there tomorrow to visit one of Richard's galleries. Earlier, the agent had said he would've travelled up with him, but had had to go back to London that very night, so would instead have to just meet him there.

And it did fill Alex with anxiety from knowing he had to travel to London – again. But this time, as his mind began to conjure thoughts of angst for the journey, it didn't feel quite the way it had done before. This time it was different, because the journey itself would be for a real purpose. Something more concrete. He also knew that now, he was feeling more confident. It was strange to be feeling like this, but he had to admit it was true. And yes – he knew he was capable enough of finding the gallery, and, would get there on time. Everything *would* be OK. Everything *would* be all right. And it felt good to be thinking like that, to be *actually* experiencing positivity inside.

It was a definite first for him, he knew.

It was the first time he'd felt like that in his entire life.

27

Wednesday, 12 May 2010

He woke to the sound of his mobile's alarm ringing at 6:00am. The night previous, he'd thought that maybe he was allowing too much time to arrive at the gallery. But then again, maybe he wasn't. So he'd decided to just be out the flat by 6:20am, and to make a ten minute walk to the station where he would catch the same train as last time – a train with nothing but a direct route. Easy.

Throughout the journey, he experienced similar feelings to those of the first trip. But they were at least only similar. *Not* the same. That was because a part of him was relaxed – now that he'd already experienced a piece of London before – and was managing to somewhat soften the effect on his nerves for what was to come.

At 9:00am, just as he stepped down onto Waterloo Station, his mobile vibrated. He shuffled along to the side, removing himself from the platform's central walkway which soon filled with clustering crowds of people. As they walked by, he pulled out his mobile from his front jean pocket and began to read the text from Richard:

Alex I can't make it for ten so meet me later at twelve. Get a suit. You'll need one for the exhibition. There's one already paid for in L.E Sternling. Just mention my name. All you have to do is pick it.

He couldn't believe it. On the one hand, this could allow him to worry less about being late to the gallery now the meeting time had changed, but on the other, he had to fill that time getting a suit. OK – it *was* already paid for. And he appreciated it. But he still didn't know a damn thing about suits, did he? He didn't even know where any suit shops were in his *home* town. He wasn't a shopper, and never had been. Clothes were just clothes to him. He didn't know nice clothes from...well, not nice clothes. He always just wore what he thought looked half-decent, felt comfortable, and was practical. But as far as suits were concerned, he'd never worn one. Ever.

He imagined a suit, but all he could think of was a grey item of clothing. He started walking along, sliding his mobile back into his jeans, then touching over both front pockets, checking his wallet, keys, and the two folded pieces of paper which had notes and a map printed on them. What else could he see? A tie and smart shoes. *Damn it!* – would he need shoes as well? And a tie? A nice tie? How would he know if it was *nice*? How would he know if *any of it* was nice? Maybe he would buy something awful today – something which would ruin his exhibition? Maybe he would let his agent down? Maybe Richard would look at him with shame later on, saying: *Alex, I think that actually, perhaps...I made a mistake. Perhaps it's for the best if we just...forget the whole thing. It's—*

But he broke his thoughts off quickly.

He was going to be positive about everything, he decided, smiling to himself, straightening his whole posture before starting to walk on.

Today was going to be good. *No, no, no* – today was going to be *excellent*! He then thought of a way to manage what he was worrying about. Today, he would buy a suit, shoes, a tie...and a shirt as well, he supposed – and it would all be *fine*. He would be selective, but time efficient, shopping in that place Richard had instructed him to visit. And then he would travel to the gallery, and arrive *on time*.

It felt good to organise his thoughts and control his emotions like that. '*Everything will be fine,*' his lips mouthed. '*Everything-will-be-fine.*'

***

At 10:30am, Sam lay on the bed, his head throbbing with what he knew must've been some kind of hangover from beyond even hell. Among other things, it included a piercing migraine which throbbed on and off incessantly, pulsing behind his left eye. He wondered, with the little energy he had left to spare, whether perhaps it was actually in fact The Beast trying to literally force its way out, trying to crack his head open.

The bottle rolled out of his hand and slowly off the duvet. His ears waited for the inevitable smashing sound, his mind already picturing the broken shards in the carpet. But it never came. There was just a thud and nothing more.

He sat up, this time not burying his head in whisky-scented hands. He was past that now, though his self-pity still filled the walls of his mind, numbing his body.

So what are you going to do Sam? he thought. *Today's the day. You gonna do it?*

His lips softly uttered: 'I don't know. What do you think?'

I think you should get out the house. A drive maybe? A drive over to you-know-whose. Give me one good reason you shouldn't do it...

'I could do. What's to lose? Maybe a walk? Go to the off-licence?'

Whatever. The booze comes after you take care of business though. It comes after...

He stood up, his hand grabbing at his keys like it was possessed. After making his way down the stairs and past the lounge, he failed to notice Merissa on the sofa watching TV. He didn't hear the laughter coming from the two presenters interviewing the latest contestant, Joanna Celeste, to be voted off Celebrity Scuba Diving. 'Well, you know...I got a lot of stick for being honest,' Joanna was explaining. 'But that's who I am – and yeah, I'm in this thing for one reason. Anyone else – like *them* – who says otherwise, is full of it. *I* have an agenda, and so do they. Don't believe Maury when he says he's just here for the experience. It's like, bull, you know? Look at me – I'm hot and people are gonna notice me. I was born to be glam, guys, what can I say? If you can't be a star...*then what's the point?*'

After Sam fell down, his right knee cutting against the pavement, he looked up at the heavy shower of rain. He tried to recall the day so far, but found it was no easy task. He even had to remind himself of what day it was. And that was strange, wasn't it? – to not know those kinds of things? But there was also something else strange. Something was off. He didn't know whether he was drunk or not. Maybe he was sobering up, then? Or maybe he was just...*malnourished* in some way? When was the last time he ate? Drank some water?

He gazed up at the grey clouds above, wondering for a moment what it was like up there, before clambering into the four-by-four. As he stuck the keys in the ignition he thought: *I haven't cleaned the car this week...* But then a burst of uncontrollable laughter came, his head leaning back hard into the headrest while his tongue repeated the same sentence out loud. He just laughed and laughed. And it was all he could handle at this moment – simple things like that. Simple thoughts. Simple actions. Simple thinking. Because nowadays he just felt lost, hazy, consumed in darkness, shackled and deserted in the midst of a choking fog.

His mobile then started to ring, its screen lighting up and displaying the word *Will*. Before throwing it out the window he said: 'I don't really feel like chattin right now, bud.' And it was the truth. He didn't. He just wanted to drive. Just wanted to feel movement, the visual aspect of moving through the world, to see things rushing by, and to be able to kid himself, for an hour at least, that he had a chance of escaping.

He drove out of the Maple Forest estate and soon journeyed toward his planned destination, arriving there fifteen minutes later. Once parked, he easily gained access to the building after a departing resident had courteously let him in. As he approached the stairs, his left hand pulled the hood over his head, while his right hand remained where it was, tightly gripping the tip of the crowbar inside his sleeve.

***

Alex stopped and put down the large brown bag onto the pavement between his legs while he checked his mobile for the time. He couldn't believe it was 11:30am already! Panic tried to surface and bubble over – but he wasn't going to panic anymore, was he? And not *today*. Besides, the gallery wasn't far from where he was – maybe just under a quarter of a mile away. So as long as he kept walking in the right direction (which he was sure he was) then everything would be fine. He just had to cool it, keep it together, keep everything under control. And he would have to start getting into the habit of doing this if he seriously wanted to launch his new art career – and life – successfully.

He picked up the bag, which he again thought was surprisingly heavy for one that only contained a suit, new shoes, a tie, a shirt, and because the shop assistant had pretty much forced him into getting them, cufflinks too. The man – who'd in fact helped him pick out everything – had been so friendly. He'd seemed to be genuinely interested in his exhibition. And this had made Alex feel *real* good about himself. Back then, when he'd actually told the store assistant, another human being – a stranger at that – about something he was actually doing, it had felt great. The assistant had asked questions about everything, and spoken to him as if he was different, as if he had...*what?* Meant something? Was *that* it? Had he gotten respect from that man? *Yes* – he had done, hadn't he? It was *true*.

Now came the voice, cutting in again with: *He didn't give a fuck – Richard had just thrown a wad of money at him to get him to talk real nice to you that's all!*

But he averted his attention from it in an instant. Because he didn't *want* it! Things had to change. He didn't want that voice! He didn't want the interference. He wanted it out. Gone for *good*.

He focused his attention on whatever was of interest directly in front, trying to calm himself. And soon he was all right.

All he had to do now was just get to the gallery.

***

Sam floored it – but it wasn't because he was fleeing the scene of the crime exactly. He hadn't been seen by anyone, in fact. There'd been no curious eyes or fingers ready to call the police. There'd been nothing. He'd simply just done it. And then he'd simply just left.

As he drove, adrenaline coursed through his veins. It was coursing because of the speed he was travelling at. A speed that could mean death if he were to lose control. But he liked it. Adrenaline helped push back The Beast. And he suspected if he were to crash, and even die, that it would surely be from a head-on collision with another vehicle.

One minute later, he would be unconscious, with the four-by-four rolling many a time before eventually resting on one side. He would be wrong about the crash; there would be no head-on collision with another vehicle. Instead, it would be because of the ceaseless rain which had been pouring down, causing the tyres to lose their grip on a sharp corner. From the country road, nobody would be able to spot his car down the hill, half-covered by the surrounding brush's foliage.

He would lie there motionless, with not even the hard-beating rain able to wake him for hours.

***

'I don't even want to sell any of your work,' Richard said. 'Well...not at *this* stage, anyway.' They continued to walk further around the high-ceilinged gallery. Alex listened with intrigue while his eyes gazed at the art hanging upon the walls. 'That's the good thing about being in my position,' Richard went on. 'It wasn't easy to get here, and sometimes I wonder *how* I did. Really, I do. I feel like I'm a hundred sometimes. But success has given me these two venues – this one being the most suitable to show your kind of work. I have freedom, the money to be able to put a show on for you. For all your work. And all of this for one day, of course – *one day* I hope will be big. One I hope I won't regret.

'I've just done so much in my career that even the risks I take don't seem like *risks* anymore. I make my money too easily. I have too much of it, and until recently when I came knocking on your door, I'd lost my heart I think. And I didn't think I'd ever feel it again. I'd lost myself, Alex. I had ditched that organ a long time ago, and had since been living from a different beat. *Something else.* Forgive me...I sound like a stuck record, yes? But then again, I like boring people...' There was a moment of silence while he drew in a large breath and looked around at the world he'd created; the magnificent room and paintings the walls displayed for his current clients. 'And that's what I'd lost,' he continued. 'I've been selling shit for many years. Not *shit* shit – but nothing new. I always stayed clear of anything that didn't fit my criteria. My *business* criteria. Maybe I died a little while my world was turning green. But after a while, it stopped mattering. And now...*I want* this risk, Alex. I want June the first to start a new chapter for *you* – and *me*.' He looked to his client whose face was full of concentration. 'Look at me opening up to you. It's the first time I've opened up to anyone in years. I don't even open up to *my own fiancée*...!' He put both hands out in front into the air, signalling to the gallery. 'And here we are! It's going to open doors for you, this place. Trust me. I was on the phone to my old rival, an adversary – also in the business – last night, and to a few others also. And they all said. *You're crazy. I* said:

215

Fuck you. And I *don't*-usually-swear. Then, being the man I am, I sent them invites to the exhibition. I like to prove people wrong, you see? It's what I do. It's *even better*...when you can actually see it for yourself on their faces. Which is what I intend to do.' He carried on talking, mainly about how he was going to relish causing an upset.

As Alex looked around the room, Richard's words began to fade out. The young artist took it all in again, the place where his debut exhibition was going to happen, the realness, the reality, the actuality of it all. It was *literally* going to happen, wasn't it? *His* work was going to be here on June 1st. It was *crazy*! But he didn't need his bathroom mirror to prove that it was all real. Not now. Not anymore.

And then he knew. Knew for sure what was going on inside him. It was him, Alex Merton, feeling optimistic.

It was him feeling *good.*

***

Sam didn't know where he was. At that moment he couldn't feel reality, consciousness – but nor could he feel he was dreaming. His eyelids flickered for a while before fully opening. And once they had, all he could see was darkness. His thoughts were dead, he could feel nothing. He wasn't able to wonder where he was, what was happening, or whether he was in danger. He just saw black.

But his senses gradually started to return. The first, which got his attention most of all, was the high-pitched sound of something that was quiet to begin with, but then got louder and quieter on and off. His fingers instinctively touched at his ears, but it didn't go away. The sound suddenly became clear, levelling off at a set volume. What was it? Was it...*birds*? What was—

As alertness returned, one thought crashed into his mind: *WHERE AM I?!*

He tried to move, but realised something was wrong. There was resistance in his neck and his legs felt heavy. His whole body felt heavy, in fact, like everything was leaning to the right. And there was pain, as if something was cutting into his ribs. *What the hell was going on?!*

Once all senses had completely rebooted, his fingers touched his eyes. But all he could see was still darkness. He couldn't tell if he was blind or not, though he thought it unlikely to be true. But he still didn't know where he was – and why he couldn't move.

It was then Sam realised, while trying to move his legs again, that one of them, his left calf – ankle maybe – was trapped. The panic started to build as he tried to pull it, trying to wriggle it free, leaning right back, his arms flaying frantically.

Soon after, he stopped, though. He stopped because he'd felt something. His left hand slowly moved over the cold surface, his fingers coursing over it, acting as his eyes, sensing and discovering the jagged edges, loose shards, and the—

It's...it's my car isn't it? shot into his mind. *I'M IN THE CAR!*

There was something else also. *Grass?* Yes – that was it! And once he thought about the thin green blades – the outdoors – he could smell it, feel it. He breathed in sharply again as the panic grew some more, and could almost taste the moist air which was bleeding its way inside.

It was no dream.

It was too real. Too vivid. He was *there*. There in that situation. And he didn't know how it had happened or why or when. He just knew one thing: he was in danger, and had to act *immediately*.

A fiery jolt of survival instinct surged, shocking his system. His hands grabbed at anything they could, desperately seeking a way out, his eyes wide open yet blind in the darkness. But soon he would know for sure that he wasn't blind. Because as his waist twisted and contracted, making him wince with short breaths, he caught sight of the light to his left. It was barely noticeable. But it *was* light.

And he had to get towards it!

Sam unbuckled his seatbelt and tried to yank himself up in order to get toward the thin glowing hole above. But he couldn't get very far. He'd forgotten. Forgotten all about his *leg*. He looked back at it, but of course couldn't make out a thing; the darkness creating its own prison, its own problems. He grabbed back at his leg, fumbling at whatever it was stopping the escape. He panted, breathing erratically, as he forced all his energy into freeing himself. Soon his muscles burned as he tried, tried, tried, his fingers searching, pulling at the limb every which way, trying every position, trying to free himself, trying to get it out, trying to extend his survival. Beads of sweat ran across his forehead and dripped onto the shattered glass by his side, and still he kept trying, trying, trying, over and over and over again. But nothing was happening, with the misshapen foot well offering hardly any movement or hope of release from its vicious grip.

Sam stopped. He had to. His clothes were wet, sticking to his body, his breathing rapid from exhaustion, his arms throbbing, heart pounding. His body lost tension and slumped off to the side for rest. His face could feel the cold shattered pieces of glass again, as could the cuts in the side of his ribs.

His energy was drained. Every limb limp.

***

That night as Alex stepped down onto Vulnham station, he was still experiencing feelings he hadn't known he was even capable of having. And wearing the suit made a difference too. To be in the suit he would be literally wearing to his exhibition in under a month's time was just surreal. It made him feel smart for the first time in his life. And another first also was that he actually felt like a *Somebody*, someone important, someone with a future, a life – a life to *really* live.

He was alone as he walked along Moulden Road, with only a few cars occasionally passing. He was left with his own thoughts. His intrusive destructive thoughts. But it was different, because now they were tied to a chair in a far corner of his mind, screaming at him still, but with a reduced volume that had been overpowered by better things, better feelings, *positive* feelings.

It was the first day of his life where he thought God must've existed. God had made him, Alex Merton, and chosen him to be an Artist. And he believed it. That was who he was. That was what he'd been meant to be. And everything in his life so far – every single detail – had led up to this moment.

***

The fear and alarm had nearly died out. The dark seemed to be engulfing him, swallowing him. Sam felt himself slipping away, like he was beginning to exist in another form, ceasing to live as a physical being, instead now as just a trail of visions and thoughts captured and incarcerated in a black world.

Something was suddenly sensed. He was aware of it – something lurking in the darkness behind. But it wasn't long before he realised what it was.

It was The Beast!

It had found him. Of course it had! And it was where it always had been – hiding, lurking in the shadows, following, reaching for him with an open-clawed hand ready to grab at his shoulder so it could lean in and let those whispering words spew into his ear.

Sam sprang forward in a violent burst, grabbing at his calf, trying again and again. He couldn't be there with it! He had nothing to distract his mind. *Nothing this time!* He had to escape! It had spoken to him throughout the week, but he'd managed to fight it off, making its words distorted, keeping it away with drink. But now he had nothing! No drink. No distractions. *Not a damn thing!* It was just the two of them now. And The Beast was stronger than he was. He knew it, and had never tried to pretend he'd been the stronger one. He'd just always known that keeping his mind and time busy would keep it away, not allowing it to get close enough to his ear.

What was he going to do?!

Sam could sense The Beast was right behind him, and though he knew he would not make it out and would be consumed in that car wreck, he still carried on pulling at his trapped appendage, fighting the losing battle.

But soon it became too obvious he'd lost. And so he began to gradually slow his efforts.

Slower.

Slower.

Slower...

He was defeated.

He couldn't win and escape this time. Today The Beast would get its way. And maybe it had waited for this moment *all along?*

Sam fell back to his side against the glass and waited for The Beast. And this time he would do nothing to stop it. He had given up. He could fight no more. He would just lie there and take it, he decided. He would let The Beast have its way. He wouldn't move a single muscle.

And Sam didn't have to wait long before he could hear the voice in his ear as it leaned over his shoulder. It was horrible to be giving in, letting go, letting it inside, leaving the door wide open for it to enter. And it didn't waste any time. It was in and it was talking. But not *just* talking – it was showing pictures; pictures which seemed to be of photos or memories of some kind. Both the sounds and visuals overcrowded his mind. They were a mess – too much to hold.

But *that* was it, wasn't it? – he hadn't *completely* let go yet.

And he then knew it was because he *just didn't want to*.

He had to, though, didn't he? He wouldn't be able to hold The Beast off for long. The words were breathing into his ear: *Just let go. Just let go...*

He didn't know whether it was him or The Beast. But either way it didn't matter. Because letting go was inevitable now.

And so he fought no more, finally giving in.

His mind and body felt lighter, like most of his weight had suddenly depleted. And then The Beast was there. Sam took a deep breath before he suddenly started to see what it wanted. Images and words flowed all around in the darkness. He couldn't tell whether they existed in reality or just in his head. But they *were* there. He could see them, real or not. It was all happening, and there was no turning back. Not now. Not till it was over.

Sam Henderson was no longer in control.

Emotions of sadness entered their way in, feelings he'd blocked out for many, many years. He saw childhood memories, all of himself to start with. When he saw the little boy smiling and splashing in the water, he could feel a warmth of colours all around him. He found it upsetting, however, to see such a happy child, a child who was innocent, unhurt, unaware, undamaged; a child not capable of doing anything bad, not yet possessing the knowledge of how to harm any living thing; a child who knew only that the world seemed like a bright, friendly, happy place...

Sam could see it, feel it. The happiness was there, and for that moment, he couldn't see the darkness at all.

Though the images then sped up, he could still feel every detail of every year that passed before his eyes. It was him growing up, right there in front of him. And every second of it was plucking away at the strings of his emotions.

Next, he could see the little boy as a young man who was walking alone. The scenery around the man constantly changed, flickering as if viewed from a worn out film reel. He could feel the insides of the man, his emotions, his very world. Everything. He could completely recognise himself in that person.

Another scene, another time was there. The warmth around him gradually faded away. All he could see in the images was his mother's distraught face telling the young man: 'You have to change. *You have to.* For the sake of the family. Me. Your father. *Everyone.*' His mother's face appeared up close. There was anger behind her eyes as she pleaded for the young man to date a woman – the one she'd found. Her name was Merissa. He could feel what the young man was filling with. It was of something awful. The shame now inside overwhelmed any joy which had ever existed within him.

The images shuffled along, though again he was able to take in everything as it flashed by. Before long, he could see Merissa. She was jubilant, beautiful, so caring and young. She was so uninvolved – with *anything*. And so unprepared for what her life would unfold into. The young man was then taking her out, dating her, making her smile, kissing her, and he was smiling and laughing too, mimicking back her actions of early stage love. Once the date had ended, the young man went back home to his proud mother, in search of her approval. But after, alone in his room, he wept. The sequence repeated itself over and over, revealing many a tearful night.

The young man's time flew by again, and soon he was walking down the aisle with a happy-in-love-face, which had been practiced in the mirror for weeks beforehand. He said his vows, kissed her, and looked back at his parents; his single mother nodded jubilantly, and his father, now sitting next to his third wife, did the same. The next few years of the young man's life came and went. He looked older now, more mature. He was moving into a new house and worked as a chef, making his living from the only profession he'd ever wanted to be in. The man continued to make love to Merissa, still crying secretly after as he lay in bed, except for a shorter time now than he used to.

A close up of his mother's mouth then said: 'Everyone's expecting one. I am, and so is your father. It'll *help*. There's nothing to think about. You need children.' The images fast-forwarded again, bombarding Sam with feelings – *dark* feelings. He could then see the young man as he started to get lost in his job, immersing himself as deep as he could. Next, he was shaking the hand of someone at the gym he'd met for the first time. The young man was fascinated, thinking that this man Will could help; help his life get easier, show him the way, show him how to cope. And from that day, it did get easier. His life became more active, filled with events usually involving Will and his friends. The young man changed, adopting a new lifestyle he pledged to keep alive at any cost. He ate out in restaurants and vacationed more regularly, frequently spending weekends in London. The images consisted of either the young man or Merissa separately – but never in the same frame.

The images suddenly disappeared. It was over now. The show had finished. And the darkness dominated once more.

Tears formed as Sam's eyes closed, and soon he was crying silently.

But when they reopened, he felt aware. He knew about all of it. He knew what had happened to him, why everything was the way it was. Everything seemed to be clearing now. He knew who he was. He knew what he couldn't be honest about before. He knew what he had been forced to do and live as. And he knew what he had pretended to be.

More tears flowed, but they weren't of sadness and pain this time. He felt cleansed, and even the darkness didn't seem like a place to be lost in anymore. He could see his life with absolute clarity. There was nothing else he could've done to become what his mother had wanted, was there? No. He'd tried *everything*. He'd married Merissa and had a child – and he'd done everything to transform himself into a real *straight* man. He'd become a mirror image of Will, the ultimate heterosexual male. He'd copied his traits, his behaviours, and had become ignorant, disrespectful, distant, and disconnected from Merissa and his own son Jake. He'd fabricated stories of adulterous promiscuity which he'd told to Will and others. He'd done all he'd thought necessary to help himself resemble a twenty-first century man. And once he'd become that person, he'd never been able to go back. His work colleagues, and everyone he knew, hated people who were the way he truly was beneath his adopted persona. They joked, laughed, and felt disgusted by that kind of person. They labelled people like that, stamping their disapproval all over them. There was no way he could've told anyone, and been able to change back into the person he really was. The results of his actions would've been fatal for him, wouldn't they? People would've tormented him, tortured him, outcast him. He would've lost his status, the attention he'd received – *everything*. And all he would've been then was one thing, one small word: a *Faggot*.

Sam then realised what else he had done to compensate for the lie he'd been living. He'd taken it all out on everyone else, hadn't he? His *pain*. He'd mainly taken it out on one man, though – his colleague, Alex. He'd taken it out on that poor man, knowing he was an easy, weak target. One without a voice. He'd taunted him, making his life hell for years. And he hadn't cared for one second about what he'd done or what damage his actions may have caused.

It had happened, though. And he hated that it had – that he'd hurt *all* those people.

But at least Sam knew the truth. He could do something now. Change who he was. Start again. Start a new life. Make everything right. Make himself right – *and* his family. Finally mend all of those broken pieces. They could be fixed because now he knew who Sam Henderson was. He knew what he had buried all those years ago. What he had been afraid of. And as for The Beast – it had been no *Beast* at all. It hadn't been trying to savage him, beat him down and destroy him. It had been trying to show him what he'd always wanted – the truth he'd wanted to see for so, so long.

Another set of tears started their journey across his face. But this time they were wiped away quickly. Because now he was thinking about only one thing: *Getting out*. He wanted to break free of the wreck he was trapped in.

He leaned forward, this time using a different tactic, turning his lower leg slowly with thoughtful deliberation while his hands ran over something which felt like a thick sheet of twisted metal. It soon began to loosen, and so he tried to retrieve his foot from underneath. But it wouldn't pass through the opening. He pulled the cold metal up again, trying even harder, straining, moaning through his teeth. Sam's foot still couldn't make it, though. His shoulders burned as he tried, his foot almost coming through – but it just wasn't enough. So he let go and took some time out to breathe.

But then he was leaning forward, trying again, his arms burning again, his muscles telling him again to let it go, but he wouldn't, and he was lifting, lifting, lifting, pouring into it every ounce of raw determination he had left, and then it was lifting, and his foot was nearly there, and his arms wanted to stop, rest, recover, give up, but he gave it more, more, more, lifting, lifting, *lifting,* and then he twisted his waist and pulled his leg and it was out – his foot was *out!*

It was *free!*

He had made it! He had made it!

Sam turned and rotated his body until it was in a crouching position, and then looked up to where the thin ray of light had once been.

He reached up and pushed the passenger door open, which had heavy brush covering it on the outside, and then grabbed the side of the doorway with his free hand as he began to climb out. Soon he was amongst the branches and foliage, sliding along the side of the car on his front before he turned himself over and gasped for the air his lungs demanded. He was exhausted. That was for sure. He couldn't even keep his eyes open.

But Sam was also *free.*

Free from a lot of things.

And now he was back. Alive.

Himself again.

***

Sam slept for fifteen minutes. The air was cool, missing the forecasted chill, the night's sky speckled with stars. He awoke when his ears caught the sound of a car travelling along the road up the hill. And then after half a minute passed, he slowly sat up, realising he would have to start moving.

It wasn't easy climbing out of the ditch and escaping the overgrown brush – but its level of difficulty wasn't exactly something that was about to enter his top ten. Right now, there was only one thing on that list (and it covered every position): escaping a car wreck.

As he began to make his way up the incline toward the hole in the hedge, which his four-by-four had originally created, he immediately found that his legs weren't juiced up enough anymore to manage what felt like a small mountain. So he crawled instead. His hands clutched at the damp grass, with every single blade seeming to help his climb tremendously. He wasn't totalled like his car was behind – he just felt like he needed to sleep for *a week.* In fact, he wasn't even hurt. The skin around his ribs required a few stitches, yes, and his ankle wasn't exactly a picture of health, but nothing was broken. Whatever had happened in that car, he had been lucky.

Damn-ridiculously-lucky.

But some of the pain he'd missed out on then suddenly hit, causing him to throw his hands up. What he saw was blood. And he could see more of it than he could his palms.

That wasn't what had hurt him, though. His eyes noticed that the grass was shining, glistening almost. Then he realised why. It was glass – all the way from where he was up to the roadside. It was scattered everywhere.

Sam carried on moving, placing his hands the best he could. But it wasn't long before he stopped again. He lifted his hands and was hit again. It wasn't from pain, though. It was from his memory; a memory informing him of what the long black object was which he now held in his hands. And shortly after, why he was holding it – and, what he had *done* with it.

His body tensed as his gut was struck with a frozen bullet of shock. He couldn't breathe. Couldn't do anything. All he could do was close his eyes; close his eyes and cry, thinking about what he'd done.

***

Alex was still smiling. He couldn't help it – he just had so much to be happy about right now. Life at the moment was just so...*overwhelmingly good.* No – it was better than that, wasn't it? It was almost *perfect* in a way. He had Layna and Art. And those two things alone meant everything to him. They were his world. They were his—

But as he reached forward with his key, the smile fell from his face in an instant, his feet planting themselves. He looked at the front door of his flat. It was open. And it wasn't just ajar – it was damaged. The proof was there, right on the frame and the edge of the door. Someone had broken in.

He cautiously pushed the door further open and stepped inside, looking straight ahead to the lounge once his finger had pressed the switch to light up the hallway. His senses were concentrated, focused on one thing: Danger. He couldn't see anyone or any kind of movement, though. He couldn't hear anything either. '*Hello...?*' he said. No sound came of an interrupted thief. He said it again and waited for anything that his alert eyes and ears could pick up on.

But nothing came.

Alex then made his way in with a pounding heart, looking into the bedroom and bathroom as he crept past. Nothing was in them. No human life present. He headed onward to the lounge and kitchen, but found the same. The feeling of immediate danger may have left...but that didn't mean relief had arrived.

And then he noticed it, the only thing that was different about the lounge: a white envelope upon the desk. He slowly walked toward it, seeing nothing but the handwritten word *Alex*. He wanted to open it, but decided to firstly shut the front door (the best way it possibly could be) before doing so. When he returned and picked it up, his mind was still a mess. The situation he'd walked into that night was surreal, bewildering. And now all he had that could possibly grant an explanation was in his hands.

Why was this happening?! And more importantly: *What* was happening?!

But the panic couldn't open the envelope. It could only warn and prepare him for what was about to come.

And then he did it. After unfolding the single sheet of paper, he saw it was a typed letter of many words. His heart entered a higher gear as he began to read.

Hey Alex. You don't know who I am. But I'm sure by the end of reading this you'll have an idea. I have some bad news I'm afraid. It's your art. It may

He dropped the letter and ran to the bedroom, his mind racing, praying, and then he was inside looking, looking everywhere, all around, but it wasn't there. Where was it?! *Where the hell was his work?!* He looked under the bed out of desperation, knowing he hadn't even left it there, and then he was in the wardrobe, but there was nothing and he just knew it was gone, but still he ran from room to room searching for it just in case he had moved it, but he knew it wasn't the case, and as he went from one to the next, he felt himself starting to cry, starting to break, and soon he fell to his knees, and for a moment, as the tears started streaming and his face and palms pressed against the wall, he thought everything he had been working toward was over.

But wait! he thought. *Wait! – maybe it's not destroyed?! The letter! Read the letter!*

It may have disappeared. Don't worry, though, it's not far away. It's outside. Go and

He reached with desperation for the feeling of relief, and was glad when he could finally feel even an ounce of it. 'It's going to be all right...' he told himself. 'It's going to be *all-right!*'

His eyes read on.

Go and check the big bin.

Alex raced out the front door, down the stairs and outside to the large communal bins. There was a hopeful smile trying to break through, but the emotions forcing out the tears dominated his expression. He was praying again, praying his work was all right in there. It had to be. *It had to be, didn't it?! It was going to be all right! It was going to be because this was all just a big joke. It had to be a joke, right?!*

He grabbed at the heavy lid and threw it open, but fell backwards to the ground as he choked. Blood appeared from his scraped elbows through his suit jacket, though the pain was not registered as he looked up to the bright light. He slipped and fell again as he tried to clamber to his feet, before steadying his legs and watching as the flames grew with ferocity, sending smoke rising into the air.

'*NOOOOOOOO!*' he cried out, looking around frantically for something – *anything!* – to put the fire out with.

But there was nothing. He was alone. Alone outside in the dark while his dreams perished right in front of him.

'*SOMEBODY HELP ME!*' he yelled spinning around, his eyes flying over the buildings, the street, everywhere.

But nobody did. Nobody even looked out their window as he screamed it over and over into the night air.

Within a minute, Alex had almost lost the ability to shout. He was soon left with his mouth trembling and his eyes pouring, managing just the word '*Please...*' before dropping to the ground. As his head fell between his knees, he then knew what all of this meant. It was all over. Everything he had created. Everything he had done. His work. His entire life. Everything was gone. All lost in the flames.

He looked up at the gigantic blaze, and watched as the debris slowly swirled through the air. It was the snowing remains of his life. And soon it was all around him. Burnt. Destroyed.

Time stopped.

***

When Alex got back to the flat he collapsed on the lounge floor. He shut his eyes, wanting to never open them again, but soon lay staring up at the cracks in the ceiling, the tears continuing to fall. He was in a form of delayed shock. He wanted back everything he'd just lost. He wanted to *wake up*.

But no dream had taken place that night. Only reality. And what his mind told him had happened was true.

His head rolled to one side, allowing his half-closed eyes to catch another glimpse of the thing that was hanging over the side of the desk. His loose fingers reached up and knocked the letter to the floor, and then brought it back for his eyes to read the last remaining words.

It's all in there. Sorry about the condition. It's a rough neighbourhood, after all, Alex. These things happen. But come on, what are you so upset about? Did you really think anything was going to come of it? Did you really think you were going to go places – be famous or something? I knew you were shit from the first moment I saw you, and guess what? It's OK. I've done you a favour. I've saved you! So now you can get on with washing up. It's what you were meant to do. And another thing: have you noticed anything lately with Layna? There's a good possibility that she hasn't been taking any of your calls, I'm guessing? Maybe she has. I don't know. But here's where I'm saving you again. You want the truth? Because I'm sure *she* won't tell you. She's a snake, always has been. I went out with her for a couple of drinks recently, and guess what she said to me? She told me the real reason that she was going out with you, and was your friend, and was fucking you, or whatever it

was. And you know what she said? She said she was just using you. I know – it's horrible right? She said she'd been using you and that it was the only reason she'd ever started seeing you and pretending to like you. She saw you were weak, pathetic, desperate, and so it was easy for her. She looks a little *different* to most people, doesn't she? She's seen shrinks, has been in and out of depression her whole life, and this year had been a bad one for her. And you actually liked her for some reason. You made her feel good. And she took it all from you. You made her feel good, Alex. You made her get back into her photography, gave her confidence, even made her think her ugly scars were pretty. Awwwww. And you did real good. *Really*, you did. But now that she's better and moving on, feeling all goody about everything, she doesn't need you anymore. Now you're just a freak again. But Alex, guess what? That's not so bad. At least you know. At least you know the truth now. I'm being honest with you. I'm trying to help you realise that you are a freak. People will never accept you or like you. So you should just keep your head down, not aim high, wash pots, and just accept it, OK? Face reality. Love is not in the cards for you. You are meant to be alone.

I am sorry.

Best wishes,
The Voice of Reason

That was it. The end of the letter. And though it made tears stream from Alex's eyes again, he didn't believe it. He couldn't believe what the letter had said. He knew it wasn't a lie about the art. But it was a lie about the other thing. It *was* a lie about Layna!

Because he knew her! He knew Layna!

Suddenly he got a burst of energy as he realised he hadn't lost *everything*. His mobile was then in his hand calling her. As the dial tone sounded, he knew he was right. He was so right about her. Because it wasn't true. She wouldn't do that to him. Not her. Not Layna. He was *right!*

The dial tone then stopped, but he couldn't hear her. There was no hello, no answer.

'*Layna?*' he let out, not being able to hold back any longer. '*Layna is that you?*'

He then felt relieved at the very sound of her voice as she started to talk.

'Alex, I'm sorry, I...don't think we should talk anymore.'

The palm of his other hand pressed into the side of his head, and he prayed that he wasn't hearing those words. Not *those* words!

'And I just...I just don't think that we should see each other. Not anymore.'

She *was* saying them, though. It *was* happening. It *was* real. But why?! *Why was it happening?* Why, why, why?! *It isn't true*, he kept telling himself, shaking his head. *The letter isn't true! It's not true it's not true it's not true it's not—*

The line went dead.

And all that was left in his ear was a deathly sound. The flat-lining sound which meant it was all over.

***

Sam sniffed loudly through his cries as he walked along the winding unlit country lane. The self-pity from realising his true identity had been pushed way into the background. All he could feel now was sympathy, regret, and a swamping guilt over what he'd done to Alex. Everything he'd done previously over the years was unacceptable. That was beyond dispute. He could have apologised to him and been forgiven for it. But what he'd done now...that was unforgiveable, contemptible – even *evil*. There was nothing he could say to him now. What *could* he say? What could he possibly say that could make everything all right? He'd made his life hell before – at least at work – but now he'd done something, done something so awful that it killed him to even think about it, to think about what that guy must be going through at this very moment after finding his work destroyed.

And Sam knew why he'd done it, didn't he? Oh yes. It had been out of desperation – a sad, beyond low desperation. He'd been so depressed that he'd not been able to stand the thought of someone else realising who they were and having then gone for gold, something they'd wanted, and expressed themselves without a care of what other people thought. He just hadn't been able to handle it, had he? He just couldn't have let him be. And so he'd ruined Alex's life – done permanent damage.

Being so aware and conscious of his actions was not something Sam was used to. At least he had that now, though. It meant he was changing, truly becoming *himself*. He was regretful, remorseful – but that thing he'd done, that monstrous thing, was something he'd not wanted to be regretting.

God – why had he done it?!

He wished he could change it all. He would do anything to change what he'd done to him. *Anything*. Any pain, any sacrifice, any form of punishment imaginable. But he couldn't. And there was nothing he could do to repay or somehow give Alex back what he'd taken. A life of artwork had been destroyed. He could never give it back to him now. *Ever*.

The rain started to almost feel like hail as it hit his head and shoulders. But he welcomed it, wanting to feel pain, wanting to be punished, wanting to be tortured in any way the invisible forces of nature felt he should.

As Sam noticed the beaming lights from around the blind bend in the distance, he wondered whether it would be a good idea to step out in front of the car at the last moment to get run down. He, and surely even God above, knew he deserved it.

***

Alex remained there, his eyes dry of tears, staring at himself in the bathroom mirror. He wanted to get lost in the reflection and—

But then something was happening. Something was starting up inside. It was getting louder – and quickly. And then he heard the words: *I told you didn't I?*

His eyes looked away from the man in the mirror and fell to the sink.

Didn't I?! Didn't I warn you about all this?

'...Yes,' Alex replied weakly. Though he'd been hesitant to answer, it almost felt like he didn't want rid of the voice that was speaking to him. And that was strange. Throughout his entire life, he had never welcomed the voice. But now, he just let it speak. He didn't feel like fighting it at all.

I told you-what-would-happen. Didn't I?

His eyes glanced back up to the mirror. '…Yes. You did.'

But you wouldn't listen would you? You wouldn't listen to me. *You always think I'm after you, that I'm trying to hurt you…but I'm not! And I think you feel it now…don't you Alex? Yes I know you can feel it.*

'I don't know…' he answered, his voice broken, depleted.

Don't lie to me! You feel it. And now *you're going to listen to me because* I'm *the only one you can trust.*

'I don't…know.'

I told you everything before you even started getting into this. I warned you about her. *I warned you about the* art. *And guess what happened?*

He didn't want to say it.

It all turned out the way I said it would didn't it?

Still he said nothing.

Didn't it?

He couldn't respond. He couldn't say those words.

Didn't it Alex? Didn't it Alex? Didn't it Alex? Didn't it Alex?

He raised his shaking hand to the top of his head. He couldn't take it. His mind was already filled with the voice. It was keeping on at him – echoing on and on and on and on and on!

Didn't it Alex?! DIDN'T IT ALEX?! DIDN'T IT ALEX?! DIDN'T IT ALEX?! DIDN'T…

He wanted it to stop – to stop, stop, stop!

DIDN'T IT ALEX?! DIDN'T IT ALEX?! DIDN'T IT ALEX?! DIDN'T IT…

But it wouldn't – it just wouldn't!

DIDN'T IT ALEX DIDN'T IT ALEX DIDN'T IT ALEX DIDN'T IT ALEX DIDN'T IT ALE—

'*Yes!*' he burst out.

Good. Goooooood! Now I've got your attention haven't I?

He nodded.

Don't you understand? Everything you try to achieve will be stopped. Everything you get will be taken away. They will take everything away from you. They will never let you succeed. Never. They will always pull you back down Alex. Always have done. And they always will. You can't trust anybody, anyone.

'...No, that's not true.'

Oh but it is! Everything you did, everything you wanted, was a waste of time. *They* promised *everything...but left you with* nothing. *You're like a robbed corpse now aren't you? That's what you are. But now you're away from all of them aren't you? You're on your own. You're back, you're—*

His hand clasped hard at his forehead. '*Please...*stop talking to me!'

I kept on telling you so many times! I told you every step of the way about them didn't I? DIDN'T I?!

'...Yes.'

But you thought you could trust them. You thought you could trust her – *your* darling *Layna? Oh she* loves *you, she* loves *you, she* understands *you, she* needs *you, oh you have a* future *together, and oh it was just so fucking perfect wasn't it? Oh...but what happened again? What was it that happened with Layna? What did she* do *to you again Alex? What did she* DO *Alex?*

Both hands were covering his face as he now rocked himself back and forth.

SHE RIPPED YOU TO FUCKING PIECES DIDN'T SHE?! SHIT ALL OVER YOU LIED TO YOU BETRAYED YOU BROKE YOUR FUCKING HEART! SHE FUCKED YOU OVER! FUCKED US OVER! YOU THOUGHT YOU COULD TRUST HER AND THE OTHERS BUT YOU CAN'T! YOU CAN'T ALEX! YOU NEVER COULD AND THIS IS WHAT HAPPENS! THIS IS WHAT THEY DO ISN'T IT ALEX?

'Oh, god...*please stop...*'

They'll always take it away from you. And it's all they've ever done! And right now...they're smiiillliiinnng at you. Sam *is smiiillliiinnng at you. And so is* Layna. *She's smiiillliiinnng about it all right now isn't she? ISN'T SHE?!*

'*Please...*'

She is Alex! She played you! She played you all along! She was selfish! You thought she was the one, like she was some FUCKING SAINT! But she wasn't one of the last ones *was she? You hadn't found* her *had you? You thought you'd found someone* pure *didn't you? Someone* different? *Someone who still thought like* you? *Someone* untouched? *Someone who wasn't* consumed *yet? Someone who still knew what* IT *was? But she wore a mask all along didn't sh—*

'No...'

She did! And then she LEFT YOU! You heard her on the phone and—

'No, no...'

233

*YES YES! – YOU HEARD HER! DON'T LIE! AND SHE
SAID THE EXACT WORDS I WARNED YOU ABOUT! I KNEW
WHAT WOULD HAPPEN AND YOU DIDN'T LISTEN! YOU
THOUGHT IT WAS ALL OVER LIKE THINGS WERE
DIFFERENT, FUCKING PEACHY AND MOVING ON TO
SOMEPLACE NICE BUT NOTHING EVER CHANGES!
NOTHING EVER CHANGES FOR YOU ALEX! NEVER!
NEVER! NEVER! NEVER! NEVER!*

'No...?' his rising voice then let out.

*IT'S TRUE! BELIEVE IT! BELIEVE IT! BELIEVE IT!
BELIEVE IT! BEL—*

'No?'

*NOBODY WILL EVER LOVE YOU! NEVER! THEY'RE
GOING TO WALK OVER YOU FOR THE REST OF YOUR
FUCKING LIFE! THEY'RE GOING TO—*

'No?'

*AND IT'S NEVER GOING TO STOP! NEVER! NEVER!
NEVER! NEVER NEVER NEVER NEVER NEV—*

'NO?' He wanted the yelling inside his head to stop. But it
wouldn't! *It wouldn't!* And he couldn't even move. He couldn't move at
all! He just kept staring at the mirror as the voice screamed at him.

*NOTHING'S GOING TO CHANGE YOU'RE GOING TO BE
STUCK FOREVER AND YOU'LL BE WORTHLESS FOREVER
AND IT'S ALL BECAUSE OF THEM ALL BECAUSE OF
THEM IT'S THEIR FAULT THEIR FAULT!*

And then something was stirring inside, and it felt like he was
trembling all over. Something was bubbling, boiling, and it was
building. Faster. Faster. Faster.

*THEIR FAULT THEIR FAULT THEIR FAULT THEIR
FAULT THEIR...*

His hands clenched and his body went tense, rigid.

*THEIR FAULT THEIR FAULT THEIR FAULT THEIR
FAULT THEIR FAULT...*

He couldn't take it anymore and knew what the feeling was that
was about to overflow.

THEIR FAULT THEIR FAULT THEIR FAULT...

It was going to happen.

THEIR FAULT THEIR FAULT THEIR FAULT THEIR—

Suddenly he screamed into the mirror, punching it with both hands, sending jagged cracks shooting over its surface. Broken shards fell into the sink, leaving behind the reflection of a man that was now distorted, ugly, disproportionate – *inhuman*.

He was then in the lounge grabbing his mobile. He wanted to ring her. Ring her *now*!

While the dial tone sounded, his breath hissed beneath a pair of bulging eyes. And when Layna picked up, before she could say a single word, he screamed '*I DON'T NEED YOU, YOU FUCKING BITCH! I DON'T NEED YOU! I DON'T NEED ANYONE!*'

28

Alex had been in front of the mirror for five hours. The voice had control now. It had stolen his attention completely, shaking him every time he'd tried to look down pitifully at the sink wanting to think about Layna and his ruined life. He hadn't put up much of a fight, though. Because he'd wanted it – to hear its voice. At first, a small part of him *had* wanted to disengage and think about what he'd lost. But too much of him had wanted to listen, to listen to the screams and answers the voice had provided time and time again.

He stared at his reflection, suddenly knowing, realising what he hadn't his whole life. For all those years he'd thought the voice had been out to destroy him, make his life harder. But now he knew the truth. And he felt so cowardly, so wrong for trying to avoid it. He now knew that it wasn't some figment of his imagination, or a kind of mental illness or hallucination or entity which he could not be rid of. No – it was something much more. Something with all the answers. Something that could help him. It *existed*. And he could almost see it living on the outside, on his face, right there in his eyes. It was so real. *Alive*. It had always wanted control, and he'd stupidly fought back, always – *always!* – fighting an impossible, inevitable losing battle. It didn't matter about himself winning anymore. The voice was supposed to win. That thing – that righteous thing that lived and breathed – was *supposed* to rule. It was King. And he had to do whatever it said now.

All your life I tell you Alex! All your fucking life! And for what...?

'I don't know,' he said. 'Why? Why did they do it?'

Because it was SO FUCKING EASY! You're weak Alex. Tell me again *how* weak *you are...*

'I am.'

*You are...*what?

'I am weak.'

Are you actually listening to me?

'Yes! I am – *I am!*'

And why was it so easy for them Alex? Tell me that.

'I made it easy for them. I let them...walk all over me. I—'

No Alex. You're special. *You're* different. *Haven't you been listening to me at all?! They took away everything didn't they? When they knew your art would change the world, they destroyed it. Get it?!*

'...Yes. Yes, I get it – I do!' It was clear to him. So clear. He then waited to hear more of the truths he longed for.

They know. They all do. And it'll never stop. I tried telling you before SO MANY FUCKING TIMES Alex! And now you want to listen right?

'Yes, I'm ready now!'

It doesn't matter what you do – they'll just keep hunting you down like some kind of unwanted fucking animal. They're jealous. *They want what you have. Oh god – what now? Oh no, I know it. I know that feeling inside you Alex. You don't understand again do you? Is that right? Are you confused about something? What is it?*

'Why are they...*jealous?*'

Because Alex, you are more than them. You can do stuff they wanna be able to do. But they can't. And now you need to set it straight. I know you can feel it. Go on, say it...

'I'm not sure.'

Say it Alex.

'I'm not...absolutely.'

Say it!

'How can I be sure it's—'

I SAID SAY IT DAMN IT!

'But how can I—'

SAY IT! SAY IT! SAY IT! YOU KNOW THE ANSWERS, YOU FUCK! I'M YOU! – I AM YOU!

He took a step back, his face contorting as the yelling got louder.

YOU KNOW IT! YOU KNOW IT YOU KNOW IT YOU KNOW IT! DO IT DO IT DO IT! GO BACK TO WHERE YOU LEFT ME! GO BACK BACK BACK BACK BACK BACK BACK BACK BACK BACK BACK...

237

His knuckles tried to bore themselves into his temples, and then he knew he couldn't hang on any longer.

BACK BACK BACK BACK BACK BACK BACK BACK BACK BACK—

'ALL RIGHT!' he screamed into the mirror, his hands slamming down on the sink.

DON'T LOSE ME AGAIN! YOU NEED ME! YOU-NEED-ME!

'I KNOW! I KNOW!'

NOW DO IT DO IT DO IT YOU'RE NOT TIRED NOT ANYMORE NOT ANYMORE DON'T LOSE IT DON'T LOSE WHAT YOU HAVE NOW DO WHAT'S RIGHT GO NOW GO NOW GO NOW START FROM THE BEGINNING START FROM THE—

'I'M DOING IT! I'M DOING IT! I'M GOING!' He was exhausted, his headache growing, pounding harder and harder. He then staggered out the bathroom, still holding his head between his palms and headed for the front door.

DON'T THINK DON'T THINK DON'T NEED TO DON'T NEED TO THERE'S NO WAY ALEX THERE'S NO WAY BACK NOT NOW QUIT LYING TO YOURSELF JUST GO GO GO GO GO GO GO...

As he stumbled into the wall and fell to the floor, something connected inside. Something had become one. *Complete.* The voice was calmer now. And his headache was fading away quickly. He felt relief...but also strength – an *incredible power.*

Once back on his feet, his sunken eyes didn't leave the door. His mind wouldn't let them. It didn't want to wander from the task in hand.

But as he took a step forward, he heard a noise in the background. It was his mobile.

He went into the lounge and put it to his ear, but didn't say a word.

'Mr Merton?' Richard said after a moment. 'You there? How are you doing?'

Alex remained silent.

'I bet you just can't believe it, can you? You're in shock – and it's no surprise! Fifteen odd years of an artist in the making, and here it all is, happening finally. How does it feel?'

Alex placed the mobile down onto the desk slowly, controlling the aggression and desire to detonate right at that moment. He then moved back toward the door, keeping his mind focused on how good he would soon be feeling.

***

Alex had not wasted any time at the rescue centre. He'd gone into the place, got the thing he'd wanted, and came straight out, being back within an hour. It didn't even matter whether the thing was loved or not – just that it was *alive* was enough.

He held it down on the kitchen worktop, and above in the air, he held the knife ready. There were no thoughts inside his head. No contemplation. No apprehension. No second thoughts.

Nothing.

The dog wriggled, its claws scratching and flaying across the slippery surface. The strength in its small body was no match for the man's grip, though. Its wide confused eyes stared up at him, trying to communicate, trying to message its distress. But the empty eyes of the man held no pity, sympathy, or anything of use for the creature before him.

The knife came down hard, ripping through the soft tissue and puncturing its stomach. And then Alex knew, from the high-pitched squealing, that what he saw was really happening.

Reality was happening.

Thick jets of its hot liquid of life flew up, splashing over his face, causing him to blink for a second. When his eyes reopened, he could see it all, blood flying, spurting everywhere, gushing over the worktop and onto the floor, and beneath the mass of red, a crazed animal desperately trying to escape. His knifed hand came down all by itself another time, seemingly without command. And then again, and again, and again, and again. He was out of breath now, drawing in deep lung-fulls of air as the dog became harder to control. But just seconds later, after a convulsive final kick from a back leg, its body went limp. Dead. '*FUCK YOU, YOU FUCKING DISGUSTING*

PIECE OF SHIT!' Alex shouted, saliva falling from his mouth. *'FUCK YOU! NOBODY WILL LOVE YOU NOW! NOBODY! NOBODY WILL WANT YOU! LOOK AT YOU, YOU PIECE OF SHIT! LOOK AT YOU NOW! LOOK WHAT I DID TO YOU!'*

He then stopped and dropped the knife, resting against the side of the worktop without breath. He felt pleased with the thing he saw beside him. It looked nothing like its former self. It was mutilated, covered in its own innards. There was no beauty there. It was ugly. And there was more to be seen than just death and a corpse. It was more than that – *so much more.*

He grabbed it with both hands and stood up, holding the monstrously disfigured body up high. Hot clumps of entrails started to fall to the floor around his feet as he stared at it. For that moment, he was in another place, experiencing a strange unfamiliar high, but one which he also craved and welcomed with an unrelenting lust. When his fingers loosened their grip and let it fall, he felt his veins, his body, his mind – *his everything* – filling with an overwhelming power, a knowing that he had imposed his will unmercifully upon another fellow creature; a knowing that *he* had placed deep, unstoppable, unspeakable pain into something else.

He had done it. And it had felt easy. It wasn't like the last time he had tried. It was different. He was on another level now. It was effortless – natural. It felt right. And now nothing could stop him. Not even himself – because that old weak useless part of him was long gone.

And now there was nothing to stop him from doing the same to people. Nothing to stop him from doing the same to *Them.*

29

All that was inside Alex's dream at that moment was darkness. No beginning, no end. Soon there were white blurry shapes of some kind appearing in the distance. They'd been small at first, but were getting larger. He suddenly realised that he himself was standing there. He could see the white shapes drawing nearer, and as he looked around from all angles, it was clear they were slowly closing in on him. And then he could just about make out what they were. They were human it seemed, but their movements were jerky, mechanical, without a smooth joint in their bodies. New white shapes could also be seen appearing, lighting the darkness. Before long, there were hundreds – maybe even thousands – coming into view. And then he suddenly spun around, seeing them approaching from everywhere, not far away from him now and—

As he awoke, he did not think much about the dream, choosing to not examine the imprint it had left. It was just a dream. And nothing more. He then got ready and left for his first day back at work.

***

'How, though?' Alex asked, looking at his eyes briefly in the rear-view mirror as he reached the end of the road.

You'll think of a way. Don't worry. You will *think of a way. You need time to think, that's all.*

'But how could I even do something like that? How would I do it? How could I do it *right?*'

You can plan today at lunch. Lunch is for planning.

'What about them?'

Them?

'They'll see me. What if they—'

You think they care don't you still? But they don't care what you do – what you scrawl *on some piece of paper. Who gives a fuck? Just do it! You'll be inspired by their disgusting laughs and jokes and chatter all echoing around the food court. And you can watch them, take from them and let it help you Alex. And when one of those fucks looks at you and smiles, you can be smiling on the inside saying: Fuck you...because soon* you'll *be suffering unbearably, begging for your life to end, you and your fuckhead friends! Because then Alex, you will be spitting down their throats, and their screams will flood the food court and every corridor won't they? They'll all GET IT won't they?! It'll be beautiful Alex. Oh, is that an idea you're getting already?*

'Yes...I think you're right.'

Good. That's something to keep your mind busy at work.

'What about him?'

Sam? Nothing to think about. He'll be one of them too. His screams will be amongst the others. You will *get your chance. Just ignore him for now, knowing that he* will *get it soon. His pain will be worth the wait...*

'But how long?'

You have to plan this out. Don't rush it. Plan this thing out. Get it right. Make your mark. Make it count. Make it heard. Make them *pay. Make* everyone *see. Make the* world *see. Make it count, make it count, make it* count *Alex...*

'I want it today, though,' he said, his brow starting to sweat, his face agitated and neck twitching slightly.

Make it count *I said.*

'I don't think I can wait, though...'

Make it count.

'But I want to fucking—'

LISTEN TO ME! You have *to make it count Alex. You kill just one and it won't matter. You want people to know about you,* right?

'...Yes.'

Then relax! Relax your hand on the wheel now. That's it. They all have to pay. Just remember why you are doing this. Remember what they did to you. Make them pay Alex. But...be smart. Be better than them. Nothing can stop you or get in the way of it. This is what you were made to do, remember?

'...I remember.'

So don't fuck it up. Get it right.

***

Ed Dorne sat down with his tray for lunch in the food court. He looked at the contents on the plate, feeling displeased with his decision. He liked fish and chips, but the amount of batter stuck to the thing was criminal. There hadn't been much else back at the hot food counter, though, and he hadn't felt like loading his plate up with a jacket potato or anything from the salad bar – especially with the way he was feeling.

He'd spent days thinking of ways to make his fortune, looking into ventures which involved screwing people over. One way he'd thought of was through the internet. And that was probably going to be his method of choice. Down that avenue, he could effectively scam people without even having to see them – not that he thought seeing their stupid-should-have-known-better faces would have upset him. There were just less risks with that kind of business, and with a good site and trustworthy content, there would always be those who were willing to put cash into anything which promised it could make them rich. And if they did fall for it, then it would be their *own* fucking fault, wouldn't it?

Electronic fraud just sounded like a good idea. Oh yes. And he didn't give a fuck anymore, did he? Not about anyone. And that was why he was willing to do anything. He was an animal, wasn't he? An animal that wanted to finally live big. To live like a King. *And why the fuck not?* He had been the low-key – yet intelligent – guy for too long. And now it was *his* time.

As Ed let ideas fill his head, he noticed a sound, a constant mumbling coming from the table next to him. It was distracting, annoying, and the man, who was producing it, was obviously an imbecile. The man was talking to himself while writing something in a notepad. Ed thought about sticking his head across and saying: *Can you be quiet? – I'm trying to eat my lunch here in peace!* And it would've been all right to say it, he concluded, as the man didn't exactly look like the kind who would turn and swing at him. He looked completely harmless.

Ed leaned over slightly, turning his head in the man's direction, ready to speak out against the repetitious muttering. But before he did, he took a moment to listen to what the words were. At first, it sounded like the man was saying over and over: *Mine own ways loses*. He listened harder, now becoming even more irritated because of the fact that he himself actually seemed oddly interested in finding out what it was. And then it was clear. He could make out the words: 'Time always loses, time always loses, time always loses...' The man was repeating it non-stop, with hardly a pause in between.

Ed looked around, wondering whether anyone else could hear him. But they seemed not to, all either being in conversation or sat too far away.

He looked over at the man again, seeing his mouth reciting the words as if his life depended on it, and then decided against speaking to him, now feeling differently. *Very* differently. He felt apprehensive, like maybe there was a reason why he should not try to make eye contact. The man seemed to be in his own world, and he didn't feel much like interrupting right now...

***

The way Sam had been feeling since getting back to work yesterday was indescribable. One good thing *had* happened during those two weeks he'd had off, though. And maybe without that leave, the events which had led to his rehabilitation and self-realisation of who he really was may not have happened. But during that time he had also committed his worst crime – and that very act had quashed much of the light he'd managed to shed into his own life.

He'd wanted to talk to Alex yesterday at work, and had been thinking all the time, again and again, to just do it, say something, talk to the man, apologise, beg for forgiveness – do whatever it took. But he hadn't been able to. He hadn't had the courage. He'd known he wouldn't have been able to look into his eyes. That would've been the hardest part, for sure. And the worst thing was that Alex himself had said nothing to him either. He'd just ignored Sam like he always had done before. There'd also been something very different in an obvious way about him; the way he'd moved, walked, every little action, the fire behind his eyes that had seemed could ignite at any moment.

A big part of Sam had wanted Alex to hit him, attack him, scream and give him what he deserved, so that then maybe after, he could've felt just the slightest bit better from receiving physical punishment. A cut eyebrow, bloodied mouth and abused ears would have at least gotten him a step closer to repaying his colossal debt.

He stood holding the kitchen phone, ordering new stock from The Stanley Food Company. Though his mouth moved and released words, his mind was in another place, only now able to think of one thing. He hadn't even thought about his position at Sestern, what the management were thinking, or whether they'd seen his wrecked car in the newspaper. They just weren't important enough subjects to him at the moment. He just wanted to fix things. He knew *he* was already fixed enough, at least on the inside in terms of his true identity, and so the physicals, financials, materials and marriage could therefore wait. He just had to fix one thing, one impossible thing.

Alex Merton.

He would have to start by talking to him, apologising – begging on his knees for redemption if he had to – and it would have to happen this week. *No* – it would have to happen today, wouldn't it?! He would speak to him *today*! There was no putting this thing off anymore! He didn't deserve the luxury of deciding when it would happen, did he?!

Sam thought on through into the hours ahead at work, going over in his head repeatedly what he might say, sounding it out in his thoughts. But he would fail again that day, not having what it took to even look the man in the eye.

30

Sam was going to act right now. And from it, there could've been the worst scene ever, the most terrible about to unfold. But he had to do it. *He had to.* If he didn't do it now...*then when*?! When would he do it?

He left the kitchen, forcing his legs to carry him out to find Alex. It had gone 2:00pm, so at least the food court was almost empty now. This would make it possible to talk to Alex alone.

He could see the guy right in the corner, exactly where he'd thought he would be, sitting on his own, facing the wall. *And you're the reason for it aren't you Sam?* he thought. *You are. This is what you've done to him over all these years isn't it?* Every step was hurting Sam, his stomach muscles contracting, his physical being crying out in its own way, demanding constantly not to do it. He was afraid. But there was no way he could go back. He had

(*Don't think! Just do it! Go talk to him!*)

put it off for *too many* days already, hadn't he?

As Sam got halfway there, his head lowered, his eyes not able to even look over to the back of Alex's head. The indignity and guilt was coming on even stronger, getting worse with every step. The gap was closing, with just a few feet to go now, and any second he was going to be right behind him. He could make him out in a painfully clear way as the guy sat there writing into the notepad. And then Sam was there, but suddenly Alex picked up his things, got to his feet, still with his gaze at the table, and turned and hurriedly walked straight into him.

Sam froze. He could not talk, breathe, or hear as he looked into his eyes, not even noticing the sound of the notepad as it hit the floor and released a dozen flying pages. He couldn't do anything. It was like every part of him was locked, under a spell from Alex's stare. He was terrified. There was real intensity. A *living rage* inside them. He could sense the guy breathing heavily onto his face, but still, Alex Merton said nothing. And after what seemed like hours, he then left Sam's vision as he bent down onto his hands and knees and began to pick up the scattered pages, leaving the head chef standing there paralysed, not being able to do anything except watch. As he saw Alex start to walk away, his hand went out and landed on his shoulder. 'I have to talk to—' But Alex grabbed at his hand hard with a violent thrashing speed, clamping it inside his own. Both men's eyes locked together again, and Sam thought this was it – this was the moment he was going to be attacked, beaten half to death.

But nothing would happen. Alex eased his grip, though his hand had been reluctant to let go, and then walked off, leaving Sam behind, able only to watch him walk away.

***

Ed had watched the scene in awe. He'd never seen *such drama*! He'd heard of scuffles and bad words and emotions running high in the building from time to time, but that was usually just scandal, gossip, run-of-the-mill rumours. What the hell had just happened *here*, though? What was going on between *those two*? He wanted to have seen more, possibly a few punches thrown...but, it was real life – not the cinema. And in real life, he knew things usually involved only words. Regular people didn't usually want to hurt each other in the physical sense. It was just the way society had evolved; primitive instincts and violence were expressed inside, behind closed doors – not in public for everyone else to see.

He stood up, deciding to get back to work, also deciding he was going to leave his tray right there on the table, instead of stacking it on the trolley and abiding by the *self-clearing* policy like he usually did. But just as he was about to head back, he saw something under the table: a piece of paper. *So what?* he thought. *What do I care about some piece of paper?* Whoever had been dumb enough to drop it, whether the paper was important or not, deserved to have lost it out of being that dense and forgetful in the first place, didn't they? But something kept him on the spot looking down at it. The words, the black writing. And then it hit him. It was no team action plan or business form belonging to the management, or anything else of that kind – it was from the notepad of that strange man who'd just been in that ruckus (well, silent stare off) with the chef. He'd left it. Dropped it. And somehow it had found his table.

Ed would have left it on the floor if he hadn't been so curious about the title: *Time Always Loses*.

After picking it up, he became annoyed with himself for showing such an interest over three worthless words. He was ready to screw it up immediately and drop it down onto his tray. God he was being silly – stupid even – picking things up off the floor, picking things up that were—

Ed stopped beating himself up as he then read the first sentence again. He couldn't believe it. He couldn't believe what he was seeing. *What the hell had he found?!* He looked about the food court, checking nobody was near, and then looked back to the paper, filling with excitement.

He sat down and carried on reading, amazed by the words and their portent. And as he did, he knew, just knew, that the information he was taking in was private, a secret that surely nobody else knew about...except for its creator, that is.

He glanced around the room, now completely empty of customers. He wanted to keep reading on and on, but the clock on the wall (which owned his arse) had other plans, making him fold up the paper and slide it into his trouser pocket. When he got back to his desk, he found it hard to concentrate. He wanted to read the rest. *He had to!* Surely it was his civil duty to read it all and know what was going to happen – and *when. He had to know! Had to read it!* And as soon as he'd finished assisting the moronic driver on the call, he went into the toilet. What was happening was crazy.

Absolutely crazy!

Ed pulled it from his pocket, and as it was unfolded, he again couldn't believe the thing was there in his hands. He knew for certain the kitchen porter had written it. And not only that...he also knew what was written was real. *Very* real.

After locking the cubicle door, he closed the toilet lid and sat down. As he began reading, his mouth slowly opened, drying quickly.

What Ed saw was a plan. It was vague, with little real detail. But it *was* a plan. It was all there, all written down: how it would happen and

248

the date it would. After every single word had been taken in, he sat there for five minutes thinking about his next move. Who should he inform about it? The police? His boss? Both? *Who else?* He had to concentrate, for the very lives of the people working within every floor of the building were in *his* hands now.

Real people. *Real* lives.

Ed got up, stuffing the paper back into his pocket, and left the toilet, his heartbeat and breathing accelerating. He planned on going straight to security. It was their job to protect the building and welfare of the staff, after all – and so it was only right to give them the responsibility of preventing the very thing described on the paper from becoming a reality, wasn't it?

The journey down in the elevator seemed longer than usual. He wondered whether the whole situation really was as exciting as he thought. Maybe it was just because nothing had ever happened to him like this in his vanilla life?

As the second floor was reached, a thought suddenly came. At that moment, it couldn't be identified – though he could sense it *wanted* to be. He ignored the temptation to think about it and cause distraction from the crucial task in hand, however, instead keeping his concentration fixed on getting to security.

Soon, the security desk at reception could be seen as he made his way around the corner and down the final stretch of the corridor. But as he reached the desk and placed his palms down, ready to speak to the guard, he suddenly realised what the thought had been in the elevator.

He then stood in silence.

'Can I help you, sir?' the guard asked, his face already fed up with waiting.

Ed thought about saying it, telling him about the paper and what was going to happen. He wanted to be a hero. He really did. But he just couldn't do it.

Not now.

Not now that he had a better idea.

He walked away, wondering about the thought which had entered his head and where it had came from. How could it have materialised at such a moment as that? – just as he'd been about to spill the beans on *everything?*

It seemed genius, though, didn't it? And of course, he knew it was only an idea, merely a rough unpolished rock; but still...he *liked it*.

All he had to do now, was figure out whether his *own* plan could work.

***

With each morning Alex awoke, he was beginning to remember more about his dreams. And with each night that passed, it seemed like he was being shown more.

That night would be no different. It started the same, with the blurry white shapes in the distance turning into an army of thousands of human-like yet robotically moving creatures, all making their way into the foreground about to approach him. They started to beam brightly, making holes in the thick darkness. Then they were closer, closer, closer, and he could make out their faces. As he looked around, they all seemed similar. But soon it was beyond clear they were in fact identical, without any sort of variation – all the same, and all bright white, almost glowing. As the creatures drew nearer, he thought they looked to be made of some kind of plastic. They weren't creatures at all, though, he discovered. At least they didn't appear to be. They looked like mannequins. And there were soon noises coming from them which sounded like hisses or whispers, even though their mouths did not move. Blank expressions were stuck on their faces, along with pairs of eyes staring in his direction. It was hard to think about anything else now as the voices echoed throughout the darkness. Then they were all in front of him, and he found himself at the centre of a small circular space which they'd created around him. He was blocked in by hundreds of rows that were still building in number. Once they'd all come to a halt they became motionless, their echoing voices dying out, leaving nothing but silence. Some of them suddenly moved slightly to one side, making an opening as one of the mannequins made its way through the crowd, walking all the way up to Alex. It soon stood motionless, staring into his eyes. It was the only mannequin with an appearance different from the rest; it was taller, its longer legs, arms and torso looking like they had many tiny paned-glass windows attached to them, with its entire body seeming to ignite with a gold-coloured light every few seconds. Its arm then slowly reached toward him, its hand opening, showing an open palm. Alex immediately knew what it wanted, though, and decided to not shake it. But as the length of time grew longer, high-pitched sounds gradually started building, seemingly coming from only the mannequin which stood in front. The other ones were then closer, making an even tighter circle. He began to feel guilty, fearing them as every one of their bland hard faces changed to disgust. They too started to sound like the tall one, filling the air with the strange sounds. But Alex would not do it. He would not touch the hand. He would not shake it. The face of the tall mannequin changed dramatically in an instant. Its mouth was gaping open, screaming and screaming at him and—

Alex awoke as his alarm clock buzzed loudly, bringing him into a brand new day.

A day when he would devote himself to planning.

31

Friday, 21 May 2010

When his eyes opened Ed felt great, even though he'd only had a couple of hours sleep.

He was excited. *No* – he was more than excited. He actually had something going on – *an opportunity to make a fortune*!

He'd stayed up most of the night thinking about it. There'd been no choice. He hadn't been able to shut his eyes, having found himself at the mercy of his hand scribbling away in his own scruffy handwriting, making notes and ideas for the project which lay ahead.

Ed couldn't wait. And he didn't have *time* to wait, because they would all be dead on the 1st of next month. That was just eleven days away. So he had to work his magic – and fast. He had to have it. Bring it. Make it happen. He had to be good – *real* good. And as for ethics, he felt they'd pretty much slipped away now, so they wouldn't be a problem, and *by God*, he wouldn't let that useless part of his genetic makeup interfere: that debilitating controlling disease...also known as a *Conscience*.

No-fucking-way.

As he drove to work, he thought through the plan. As much as he felt the dark twisted excitement within, he was also nervous, fearful, and aware of the potential danger he was getting himself into. If he wanted to pull it off – and he knew it was possible – he would have to go down, down into a dark place which his useless imagination probably couldn't picture even on a vague level. But he knew one thing: that it would be a crazy, deluded place, a hell where he'd be lost, closer to death than ever before.

In the end...it would all be worth it, though.

All Ed had to do today was talk to the man, be believable, and gain access to the inside. He had to seem trustworthy, like an accomplice worth considering. And maybe his trust couldn't be gained in *one* single day – but it was where he had to start.

As he went through the boom gate, he could sense how the morning up until lunch was going to pan out. He was going to be on edge, anxious, with the adrenaline pumping through his veins throughout every second of every minute spent waiting for 2:00pm; waiting for the time when his cash cow would sit down in the corner of the food court.

And then, the games would begin.

***

Ed sat watching the clock on the wall, the second hand ticking away.

1:57pm.

The man would be out any minute now. Any minute.

Ed was waiting in the corner of the room on the same table he'd sat at yesterday, one away from where the future killer would soon be. Ed's own lunch break was just about to finish, but he didn't care. He didn't care about Safe Insurance. He didn't care about that company anymore – and was prepared to be late every day until the 1st in order to secure his lucrative future.

1:59pm.

His finger carried on tapping away on the table, and as he watched the last customer leave, he suddenly felt very vulnerable in the emptied food court.

In the distance, through the opening double doors of The Wash Up, someone could then be seen emerging.

It was him.

As Ed looked, an uncontrollable sense of alarm crashed into his heart, speeding its rhythm in an instant. He felt like he should be doing something – *anything* but looking at the man now approaching the hot food counter. Under the table Ed's heel joined in, starting to tap along with his finger. What should he be doing when the man comes over? Should he be pretending to eat?

(phone! – just go on your phone!)

He followed the command, pulling his mobile out, and started randomly pressing buttons. And then the man was there, pulling out a

253

seat from the table to his side, placing his lunch tray, notepad and pen down before sitting.

(*Holy shit! Holy shit! HOLY SHIT!*)

Ed had previously thought it would be far from impossible to do this. But now that he was in the situation – *now that he was right the fuck in it!* – he could barely get a word out, let alone voice a full sentence. He was simply terrified. He was scared to talk to the man, the animal who was planning to kill everybody, *including* him; because of course, at that moment, he, Ed Dorne, was just another person in the building who didn't mean a thing to the man yet.

(*You have to do it! You don't have time not to! You have to do it now! Come on Edward! Think of the money! Think of the money! Think of your future!*)

Ed realised he would have to do it. He would have to just *somehow* speak to him, wouldn't he? There was no choice.

(*COME ON! Just do it Edward! Do it! Don't think! – just speak! Do it! Do it! Do it! DO IT! DO—*)

'Hey...' he spurted out looking over to the man, his throat dry, a desert. A smile tried to form, but was discouraged by a trembling corner of his mouth. Even now that he'd spoken, he didn't feel any better. Not at all. And it got worse as he watched the man continue to ignore him, not even acknowledging he'd heard a thing.

The silence prevailed, and then Ed knew he would have to come up with something – *the Magic* – to get the man talking. He would have to come up with a way to make the man *believe in him, trust him,* and make the man think he was...*what?* He couldn't think of the answer. How could he make the man trust him? *And why hadn't he thought more about this stuff earlier?!* He should have known this! – *all the answers!*

It wasn't long before it came to him, though.

And then he suddenly knew.

(*Make him think that you are...just like him. Yes! Yes,* that's it! *Make him think you're* the same!)

But how could he do that? How could he act crazy? How could he act like he was prepared to kill all those people? How could he convince this man he wanted in on his operation and wanted to offer his help? He, Edward Dorne, was a straight shooter. He was *vanilla.* And so how could he ever do that, talk like that, make him think tha—

(*Just do it Edward! You're running out of time! Remember the* time! *Just talk! He won't care! He's fucked up* – crazy! *Just talk! NOW! NOW! N*—)

'I want in,' he breathed into the silence.

But still the man said nothing back.

(*Try harder Edward! Come on you can do this!*)

'I…'

(harder! – *just say it!*)

'*I want in on your plan*,' he said, the words flying out

And that was enough, enough to get the attention of the man who slowly turned his head and glared over with his sunken eyes.

(*Don't let him know you're afraid Edward! Don't let him know! Talk again!* Quick!)

'I want in,' he repeated. 'I want to help.' But that was all he could think of.

The man kept his eyes fixed on him, still having not blinked once.

(*Get up! Move over to his table now!*)

Ed felt as if the chair wouldn't let him leave, though.

(*DO IT!*)

He slowly got up and made his way over, soon taking a seat. There was one thing he then found that was more terrifying than having to look into the man's eyes. And it was the fact that, though there *was* something far beyond evil dwelling inside them, it could have gone unseen, unnoticed by a lot of people; a lot of the building's employees who had no idea he was planning to kill as many of them as possible.

(*Act! Make it believable! Say* something! *You hate everyone here as well! Play on it! You don't really give a fuck if they go down anyway* remember?! *So play on it! Play on i*—)

'When I found your plan, I…couldn't believe it.'

(*keep going…*)

'I've wanted to do this for so long and…you have it all figured out. You're going to make them *pay*. But I…*so* want it, too. I want to make them pay for their crimes.'

(*Yes yes yes! Brilliant! Keep going keep going…*)

'You have to let me help…'

There was a long silence during which the man showed nothing on his face to signify he'd had any thoughts or that a decision had been made. And out of sheer desperation to end the unsettling quiet, Ed introduced himself.

Shortly after, the man finally did the same, speaking his first words. 'I'm Alex,' he said. 'Alex Merton.'

***

Ed withdrew his unshaken hand from the air, placing it back under the table where it resumed position tightly grabbing at the top of his thigh.

'You want *in*, you say?' Alex asked.

'Yes...together we will get them all,' Ed tried to assure him. Another lump was swallowed. 'You can trust me.'

'Why?'

'Why...what?'

'*Why* do you want to do it?'

And that was a question Ed didn't know how to answer. *Yes* – he *did* hate everyone in the building, his fellow arsehole colleagues and the rest of the gang, but he'd *never* thought about killing them before, and had never thought about killing *anyone* up until he'd developed his own *get-rich-quick* scheme after finding that piece of paper yesterday.

A way of answering the question came. A way to avoid it completely. 'What *haven't* they done? What *haven't* they done to us, to *so many* others? The important thing, is that they *must pay*.'

He listened as Alex then said with a cold, polluted passion: '*Yes*. Yes, they must. All of them. They will die. *Painfully*.'

'...Yes. They wi—'

'And the world will know it would not have been for nothing. They will know about it. What *I* did.'

'What *we* di—'

'And what it was for. The weak will be put on the map. I will give strength to those who feel but an ounce of my pain, and strike fear into the sharp-clawed hand that thinks *my kind* will always retreat into the dark.'

'...*We* will do it together,' Ed said, forcing his eyes to maintain contact. 'I'm *someone* you can trust.'

Alex leaned in closer. 'Humour me...'

'Let...let me prove it to you.'

'You want to *prove* it?'

256

Ed too leaned in, although to his hand's protest as it squeezed his thigh even tighter. 'Yes.'

'So come round to my place.'

'...When?'

'Mmm, let's see. How about...*tonight?*'

The pain in Ed's thigh then grew deeper.

***

It had taken everything to walk through that door and into the place which housed that monster. Ed had previously psyched himself up, literally forcing himself to go over there, having convinced himself he would've been a coward if he hadn't taken the chance, and that ultimately, it would've been illogical to have walked away from such a lucrative opportunity. But even this reasoning had offered very little toward building his willingness, for he still hadn't known anything about Alex...except that he was insane and was planning a massacre of the Sestern and Safe Insurance workforce.

And those facts alone had been enough to make his heart thump quicker as he'd thought about his decision while driving over there – this and the fact that his devotion to being a part of Alex's operation would surely be tested. Ed knew he would have to be prepared for anything. He would have to be prepared to do something, like maybe cut his arm with a knife or razor. And he even thought about the possibility of having to murder someone or dispose of a body; those were ideas and speculation of the most unlikely, though (certainly the murder part) – and yes, if it did come to that, then he would jump overboard and abort the mission immediately. He wasn't stupid. He wouldn't participate in anything that would see him imprisoned. He would only do and witness enough to enable him to know Alex – to know enough for the aftermath. Because then, *he*, Edward Dorne, would be the name on everyone's lips. *He* would be the guy – the only guy – who knew the answers everyone craved. *He* would be the *Why did Alex do it?* guy, the *What drove him to do it?* guy, because *he* would know *all* the fucking answers! And the press would be all over him, wanting story after story for their public. TV execs would be calling constantly, demanding a revealing never heard before exclusive interview for the morbid interests of their audience. And then would

257

come the book, wouldn't it? He couldn't write for shit – but that wouldn't matter. The publisher would surely find a ghost writer. And it would sell big time! People would want to know *everything*, *every little detail* of the massacre – and, of its perpetrator.

As he'd stepped out the car, Ed had known there was a high possibility he could be facing death that night. His life was in a threatening position. There was no doubt about that. Everything could go wrong, and anything could happen. But as he'd climbed the stairs, the thought of the money and what there was to gain had been far too great. He wanted it more than anything. He wanted the money so badly; and if he had to play with death, support and encourage multiple murder, and have conversations with a madman, then that was what he would have to do.

***

He sat at the desk, his hand firmly holding his right leg down to stop it from shaking. Being in Alex's flat was terrifying. He'd never felt such a sense of vulnerability before, such a sense of his own mortality. Reptiles were everywhere, on the floors in the bedroom, the hall, the lounge, even in the kitchen – *just everywhere*! He hated them. Truly despised them.

But it was just another fear he had to let go of, wasn't it? Another fear he had to control for the moment.

'I bet you're wondering what that smell is?' came from Alex in the kitchen.

'No, I...haven't noticed anything,' Ed lied, the stench having already driven him to the point where he thought he was going to vomit.

'Can't you pick up on that *disgusting smell*?'

'Maybe I have a...blocked, um...bad sinuses,' he managed, resisting the temptation to cover his nose.

Alex stepped out into the doorway of the lounge and said: 'It's a dog. I killed it.'

Though the pain was in Ed's thigh again, the shock itself from what he'd just heard was of a slightly lower impact, since he'd already been certain that something *had* died – whether it had been human or not. In that moment of mounting nausea and fear, however, it didn't exactly fill him with relief to find out it had just been a domestic creature the man had butchered. 'Oh…did you?' he asked, fighting against the temptation to lean forward and clutch his stomach.

'Yes, I held it on the worktop,' Alex began, re-enacting the scene in the air with both hands, 'and then I just stabbed the fucking thing to death.' In the following seconds, he seemed to be lost in the memory. And when he looked back to his guest, he chuckled and said: 'I just…killed the fucking thing, you know?!'

Ed still didn't know what to say, but managed one thing: 'How did it…*feel?*' And as Ed said it, he knew a note of some kind had been hit with the man.

'It felt like…' But then Alex closed his eyes, not finishing the sentence. When they opened again he said: 'Soon you will know what it's like to take one of them. We *both* will. And I don't mean some *damn dog*! I mean the *real stuff. Them.*'

'We *will*,' Ed confirmed. 'We will.'

Alex grinned. 'I'm gonna get some water. You want some?'

'Er…yeah. Yeah, sure.'

As Alex disappeared from sight back into the kitchen, Ed tried to control himself, thinking *Calm down, calm down, calm down! Look at you – you're a mess! He can see it! Calm down Edward, calm down…*

But his thoughts were just words, and in this flat, this place – *this scene* – they were worthless. He knew at any moment he could be dead. He knew that Alex could be getting a knife right now. And it didn't seem too unlikely, did it? Because the man had been in there a while now, hadn't he?

Fuck…!

How long does it take to fill up two glasses with water?

What was he doing in there?! What wa—

Alex walked in and set down the two drinks before taking a seat on the other side of the desk.

Ed was shocked at how normal and civilised it had all seemed as the man with mass murder on his mind had entered the room. It just didn't seem right to see a man such as him holding water, the very symbol of purity itself. And it was deeply disturbing to know he had been walking, working, and breathing in the same place as this man for many years. Everyone had. And the worst thing was that most people didn't have a clue what Alex was really about. They just thought he was troubled, fragile, quiet perhaps. But not *this* – not this of which *he* knew. He'd been in that building – *for all that time!* – with a future killer, hadn't he? And if things hadn't panned out the way they had done yesterday with finding that piece of paper, then there was a good chance that he, Edward Dorne, on Tuesday 1st June, would be dead. And right now he was with his would-be killer, the madman himself...

Ed was *alive*, though. Boy was he alive! He could feel himself – really *feel* himself on a heightened level.

But as he held the glass to his mouth, about to revitalise his throat, he suddenly didn't think this great feeling of awareness was anything to shout about. Maybe some people *did* get a buzz from throwing themselves stupidly out of a plane or off the edge of a bridge attached to a piece of elastic – but the sensation he was experiencing at that moment was *not* the same. In many ways, it was suicide.

He then put the glass down as his arm began to shake.

'What's wrong?' Alex asked, his eyes vigilant.

'I'm fine.'

'Are you sure? You don't seem fine. You don't look *fine*, at all.'

'I just wanna get to business,' Ed said, trying to change the subject in a strengthened tone.

'*Business?*'

'Yes. We need to discuss the plan.'

'Where do you want to start?'

'Well...there's lot's to consider. Little time to do it.'

Alex's head nodded a fraction while his eyes wandered across the room somewhere else.

Ed opened his mouth to speak, but paused, with no words escaping as another creature of some kind (possibly a snake, he imagined with dread) slid under the desk and over his foot. 'Er...so let me get this straight,' he started, but then had to take a moment before actually saying his next words out loud, it being the first time he'd be literally saying *those words* for real. It was harder – so much harder – than he'd thought it would be. 'So...on the first of next month, you're going to poison everybody, all the customers? And while this is happening, you're going to kill Sam Henderson?'

'Yes.'

'All right. For starters...why the first of June?'

'The other kitchen porter who works with me will be on leave, so nobody will get in my way. And everyone in Safe Insurance gets paid the week before. That means the food court will be at its busiest.'

'But, Alex…' Ed said, his mind somehow thinking, bypassing the madness, the sheer horror of the place and situation, '…this is all very abstract.'

'Why?'

'How is this going to possibly happen? There's too much that could go wrong.'

'*Why?*' Alex questioned again.

'For a start – the poison. How are you going to do it? What are you going to poison? What foods?'

'It'll be easy. The menus are printed the day before. All I have to do is see what's for lunch the next day, and that's it. I just put the poison into whatever's going to be served up.'

'It's a bank holiday the day before, though. You'd have to do it on the Friday previous.'

'Yes, I know that.'

'So…are you going to poison the ingredients for just lunch? Or breakfast as well?'

'Just lunch.'

'But the ingredients…some of them may be used for breakfast also. The mushrooms, etcetera. If just one customer gets poisoned, all food will be disposed of. Everybody will then be leaving and will know about the food being contaminated. Then you'll have blown it…'

'No,' Alex said, shaking his head with agitation, his eyes closing for a moment. 'The majority of the breakfast is prepared the day before. In this case, Friday. So it'll be easy to see what would be used for breakfast, and what not to contaminate. I'll only contaminate the main ingredients that'll be used for lunch. And it's going to be a curry day on the first, so all I need to do is just contaminate the pre-made curry, the rice, bhajis – stuff like that.'

'No, that's…that's not going to work. How can you get in tins, bags, boxes and everything, without it looking suspicious? Especially with the rest of the self-service meals, like beans, chips, salad, etcetera? You'll have to do it another way.'

261

Alex leaned back into his seat, his eyes displaying protest in losing absolute control of the plan. '*How then...?*'

Ed thought about it for a few seconds before an idea hit him. And it was to be a good one – which wasn't bad considering the setting. 'You'll have to contaminate the food right there and then, as it's literally being served up – on the *actual day*. That way it's obvious, after breakfast has ended, exactly what's going to be served up for lunch.' He watched as Alex thought about it. 'What do you think?'

'Maybe you're right...' Alex said, his eyes now warming to the idea.

'It's easier, simpler,' Ed went on. 'This way you can do everything. The salad bar, anything you want. You can pour the stuff in. No one will even notice you.'

'*Me?*' Alex asked leaning in.

'...Yes,' Ed said.

'You keep saying *ME*. I'm curious. *Why is that?*'

Ed felt his leg shaking again and looked away for a second, losing control as the man's eyes stared deeper into his. They wanted answers. And *now*. 'What do you mean?'

'What do I *mean?*' Alex said, the anger growing in his voice. 'I thought *you* wanted a part in this?'

'And I will, I...*will* be doing it with you.'

Alex didn't say anything back, letting silence fall between them.

Ed felt like he'd taken a step back in earning his trust, and so then quickly tried to move things along with: 'And another thing. You aren't gonna be able to kill *everyone*. You won't have long. Once maybe ten or so have eaten and it's brought to attention there's something wrong with the food, everyone will stop eating. It isn't enough.'

Alex's head nodded slowly, his breath calming along with his temper.

'We need something that'll work,' Ed carried on. 'Something slow activating that won't kick in for a while. Something that'll go unnoticed for a long period that...*isn't* instant.'

'Agreed.'

'And so what is it, then? What's the poison we're going to use?'

'I haven't thought of that yet. I'll find something.'

Ed suddenly knew what was going to get him back on track to conquer that final mile of trust – and then some. '*I* will do it,' he said.

'Do what?'

'I will sort the poison. *I* will do it.' He soon felt good about the look he received from the man, one which didn't give much away, but still said *maybe this guy is for real, after all...*

'Okay,' Alex said after a few seconds. 'You do that.'

'*Good.* And why this Sam guy? Why get your hands dirty with him? Why kill him yourself? *Personally?*'

'It's the way it has to be. He and the other chefs don't sit down for lunch in the food court.'

'And the other chefs – they'll just stop you, no?'

'That won't happen. They always go outside to smoke on their lunch break. So he'll be the only person in the kitchen at that time of day.'

'At what time?'

'Two o'clock.'

'And he'll be in the kitchen for definite?'

'He always is. Or he'll be doing the stock take in the corridor close by.'

'Why not just poison him?'

'He doesn't eat. I've only ever seen him eat at lunch a few times.'

'Right,' Ed said, taking a few seconds to absorb all the information. 'And what are you...going to do to him?'

'I'm going to cause him more pain than he has ever felt in his entire fucking life. *That's* what I'm going to do to him.'

Ed remained quiet, sensing it was best to just listen.

'I'm going to make his blood flow,' Alex went on. 'And the last thing he will see is *me* standing there, looking right into his eyes. Then he will know what it feels like to have death staring him in the face. Then he will have nightmares about me – *even* in hell. He will feel everything I want him to.'

'What about...' But Ed stopped the sentence from forming, shouting in his head not to be weakened by what felt like his conscience, having nearly been about to question Alex about how Sam's family would feel – with, for some reason, the head chef's loved ones standing out in his mind more so than that of the other hundreds of people who would too be dying.

'*What...?*' Alex asked.

'Nothing. So...and then what?'

263

'I don't want any help with it. I can take him. And only *I* must take his life. *I alone* must show him the pain he has been spared his whole existence. Only *I* must do it.'

Ed realised Alex was stuck, still talking with a sadistic passion about Sam, and so asked him again: 'And what happens after you've done it?'

'Don't you know?' Alex asked, almost laughing through his crazed smile.

'Well...no.'

'Didn't you read it?'

'I don't think it was...on the page I read.'

'*Well can't you guess?!*' Alex fired. 'What do you think we'll do?'

Ed shrugged his shoulders, but soon felt a deep twisting terror when he took a guess. '...Kill ourselves?'

'*Of course, Ed!* How else?! How else would we end it? Do you want to be judged, further abused, in-tolerated by a corrupt society through blind senseless law – not by humans, but by the *inhuman?*'

'...I...understand.'

'We are martyrs, brave warriors,' Alex went on, his eyes' focus stuck on Ed. 'We are sending a message to the world. We are fighting for what is lost. We will be *everywhere*. Everyone will know of us and what we did. Not because of our supposed crimes, but because we took a stand – and fought *back*. You think this is about me and you, Ed? It's not. It's about *more*. It's about the others. There are still others who are pillaged, slaughtered by the stronger new race, but we were sent here to show them what will happen if they try to rise above humanity. We will show *Them* the hell that awaits them if they try to rise above God. That is why we are here, Ed. And *now*, we know our purpose. And that purpose is to make our mark upon the world. That purpose is to show the *lost and the damned* where not to tread. We will show them not just the thorns that are currently scattered about the path close to their feet, but the crushing snares ready to amputate them if they choose to walk over us.'

'You speak...the truth, Alex.'

'We're going to set up an army. *A fucking army*. It's inevitable. It's what my life has been leading towards since the day I was born. It's my purpose – my fate.'

Ed nodded and began to realise nothing was going to stop the events of the 1ˢᵗ from happening. Nothing at all.

'And my parents...' Alex continued.

'What about them?'

'I'm going to kill them as well.'

Ed again needed more time to ingest the new piece of information, and then said: 'Kill your parents? Why-why do you need to do *that*?'

'I'm going to kill them the night before – the night before the first. It starts there.'

'...All right. That's...that's where it starts.' He watched as the man smiled, knowing for sure he was envisioning killing them; his parents, Sam, everyone.

'Aren't you going to ask any questions about what *you're* going to do, Ed?'

'I...don't need to. I already know. You do your part, sorting mum and dad – and Sam – and I'll be there with you, helping spread the poison over the food. I will take my revenge on my colleagues. They *will* pay for their crimes.'

'*Good.*'

And then, while getting up Ed said: 'And leave the poison with me. I'll come up with something. Everything is going to be *perfect.*'

After leaving the flat and making his way down the stairs, he smiled to himself, pleased with his performance, his lies about helping lay the poison, and his new position in the operation. As his fingers fumbled in his pocket and pressed the Stop button on the dictaphone, he thought about the one thing he *had* told the truth about.

It was that he would find a poison.

And boy, he would have to find it fast.

32

Sunday, 23 May 2010

It hadn't taken long to think of what substance to use. In fact, he'd thought of it not long after leaving Alex's flat, while sat watching the *ever* unfunny sitcom which had tried to make relationships (and life in general) actually look funny. Obviously it had been full of shit. But it was this show, during which one of the character's cats had become ill from eating half the chocolates from a Christmas calendar, that had prompted a thought inside Ed's head: the thought of his childhood dog, Jenkins.

He had been the family pet for many years until his demise on what Ed recalled as being January 16th. A Friday. The date had stuck in his head ever since that day, mainly because he'd never been a great lover himself of the so-called *friendly family dog* who'd seemed to get on with everyone except him. He'd received many a snarling threat and enough bites to have given him reason enough to build a growing hatred for the animal over the years.

But Jenkins' life, which had gone on for a fairly good run (probably because of his strong mongrel genes), had come to an end on the 16th. And it was the cause of his death which had given Ed the idea for how to poison a huge sum of people.

He'd remembered that, according to the vet, it was likely that Jenkins had ingested large quantities of a substance which had done irreparable damage to his insides. That substance was antifreeze. At first, his father hadn't understood, and had then rejected the theory completely, stating that any chemicals were *always* kept far out of reach from the children, and that this fact alone was enough to rule out the dog getting his paws on anything that could be deemed hazardous. But the vet had soon made it all clear, explaining that during the winter months many cars which had the fluid in their engines

266

would've leaked the substance onto roads – sometimes in a considerable quantity – and most commonly, driveways while stationary.

And that was exactly how it had happened. Old Jenkins had licked the driveway. A lot. And in the end, it had killed the vicious little bastard.

Ed now drove along in the fading light of the day, thinking, imagining what the interview on TV would sound like. He would be saying (while the whole nation watched in sympathetic awe): *I just...never knew Alex was capable of anything like this. I knew he was going through some hard times and...he* had *talked about doing something like this once. He had. But I thought it was just anger, frustration, not...anything* real. *I just wish he'd come to me. We'd been so close...and suddenly he'd just stopped all contact with me – cut me off. I just wish that...* He would then sigh, showing great pain on his face as the camera zoomed in, and go on with: *I just...wish I could've stopped it.*

***

'It's simple,' he said as he followed Alex into the lounge where they both took a seat at the desk, facing opposite each other once again.

'*Simple?*'

'Yes. The poison problem's sorted.'

'How'll we make it?'

'We won't. No need. I'd originally thought of some more complex ideas, mainly, amongst others, using arsenic or pure liquid nicotine from boiled down cigars, etcetera. But then I realised there's no need to go through all that trouble. And plus, those kinds of substances have strong smells – and the taste would be *awful*. As soon as they touched the first customer's tongue, it would all be over.'

Alex listened with intrigue.

'No...' Ed continued, '...I have found something that requires no preparation, no mixing, no boiling, or anything like that. Something that is odourless and has a *sweet* taste. It's on the shelves. It's available. And it's called antifreeze.'

'*Antifreeze?*'

'Yes. The idea suddenly came to me when...I remembered my dog from when I was a child. I...*poisoned it* with the stuff.'

Alex smiled approvingly. 'So it's fatal? Will they feel it?'

'Pain? It'll be *painful* beyond belief. It contains something called Ethylene Glycol. The stuff's lethal. At first, it'll throw off the body's acidic balance. As time passes, acidity levels will begin to settle again – but then, the Ethylene Glycol steps in. It'll metabolize, causing crystals to form in the kidneys, leading to major organ failure. There'll be widespread tissue damage in all organs, a strong possibility of eventual coma, brain damage, loss of motor skills...etcetera.'

'What about time?'

'It won't be sudden, that's for sure. And that's another thing – they won't even know there's anything wrong for the rest of the day until long after lunch is over. Some may last twenty-four hours, while others may live up to...two, three days perhaps max. *Beautiful*, right?'

'You did good. It's...real good, Ed.'

'It has to be, doesn't it?'

Alex nodded. But then he said '*Wait* – I've seen that stuff. It's green. It's going to stand out. In the kitchen they'll notice it.'

'It's usually green, yes. But look at this.' He turned around the laptop to show Alex the screen. 'Clear,' he said grinning.

'How can it be clear? The colour is added for safety...'

'*Who knows?* It's on this website, though. It's being sold.' He then shrugged his shoulders and said: 'Who gives a shit, right?'

Alex looked again at the image of the clear liquid in the bottle.

'The internet at my place is down,' Ed started to explain. 'So...I'm going to need *you* to order this product. Is that all right?' There was a moment of silence where he wasn't sure what the man was going to say. *Bite, damn it!* he thought hard. *Bite on it! Bite! Bite! Bite!*

'It's fine,' Alex finally said.

'Good. And you know about the menu? How can you be sure?'

'It's been curry every Tuesday since I've been there. It's never changed. Not in over five-fucking-years.'

'And how'll you add it?'

'The curry would've already been made the Friday before. All they'll do is heat it up in one of the steamer ovens. The chefs do a hundred things at once, so they'll never be in one place for too long. They won't notice anything. I'll just open up the oven, pour it in, give it a little stir, and that'll be it.'

'So you'll *just* add it all that morning…before it goes out on the service counter?'

'Yes,' Alex confirmed with all surety.

'And what about *everything else*? The salad bar? Chips? All of those things? Not everyone likes a curry, do they?'

'I'll put the antifreeze in all of that as well. Before the salad and the meat for the wraps go out, I can pour it on. Even into the deep fat fryers. It'll stay in the oil until it's drained out at the end of the week.'

'No…' Ed started, but stopped to let himself think. 'The chips, *yes* – but *not* too much. In fact, we'll have to work out quantities for the curry and everything. It can't be too overpowering – *too sweet*. And it's the same with the salad and diced meat – the little things. You'll have to put a small amount on them to not arouse suspicion. If it's too sweet, the customers will know. There's nothing wrong with them thinking their meal is sweeter than it should be – but it can't be sweet enough for them to mention it to the kitchen. With the salad and small stuff, you'll have to…' He thought for a moment. 'You need to…spray it on, or…' And then he had it. The fingers on his right hand clicked. 'Like a *spray bottle*! Do you have spray bottles there? Of course you do, *right?*'

'There's lots. That can work.'

'And nobody will notice? How do you *know?*'

'Nobody's noticed me there my *whole fucking life*,' Alex said. And then slowly: 'They-won't-see-a-fucking-thing. Not-a-fuck-ing-thing.'

Ed believed him. 'Is there anythi—'

'But soon they will notice me. Because that pain they will feel, that pain twisting their insides, that vomit gushing from their mouths, that agonising wait for death – that will be *me*. That will be *me* inside them. *That* is the poison: *Me*. And they will eat me, just as they have been doing so for all these years. But this time I will be different. They will think they've chewed me, swallowed me, controlled me, keeping me down. But no – then *I* will pollute them. *I* will destroy them. *I* will emerge. *I* will show them pain. And then they will notice something they thought they never would.'

'Yes,' Ed said. 'They will notice *us*.'

But Alex couldn't hear him, already too far gone, too far away, lost in his own world.

33

Monday, 24 May 2010

In Alex's dream, he could see the mannequins stood all around him. The tall leader was in front again, reaching out its hand, the small glass windows on its torso and limbs shining brightly. He knew what was about to happen. But he didn't want to shake the hand and satisfy the creature's needs. As he stood in refusal, he could feel the build up of guilt and shame rising again within himself as the hissing noises of the thousands in the crowd grew, multiplying, getting louder, louder, louder. He knew the leader was about to become enraged, its face about to change, its mouth about to drop open and scream at him. But before it could, Alex was suddenly changing, his body tensing, his fists clenching tighter, tighter, and then *he* himself was yelling with a fury which had exploded, and soon he was grabbing the leader by the throat, yanking it off balance and down to the ground, and he was stamping on its head, cracking it with his foot, crushing it over and over, its face suddenly shattering into jagged chunks that flew across the floor. He was then grabbing at a mannequin from the surrounding crowd and soon ripping its arms off, kicking it after throwing it down, and then he was grabbing at another, punching its saddened shocked face till it caved inwards into its hollow skull, and once he'd destroyed it, he was grabbing at another one, then another, then another, then another, then another...

34

At 9:00pm he pulled up outside. He took the knife from the passenger seat and got out. The large shingled driveway was empty, but he knew the cars were likely to be parked inside the garage as always. His finger soon pressed the doorbell while his other hand held the blade behind his back.

After the door opened, he saw his father, their eyes meeting. Then came the word: '*Son…?*'

'Yes,' Alex said. 'It's me.'

'Jesus Christ, you're not going to believe *this*, honey!' his father called inside over his shoulder. 'Guess who just showed up?'

'*Who?*' called the voice from the lounge.

His father turned back to him and said: 'Well I guess you better come in, son.'

'Yes. Unless I'm interrupting something?'

'No, you're all right,' his father assured him, jogging back to the sofa where his eyes soon lit with the reflection of the TV. 'Come in and take a seat,' he said. 'We're watching the celebrity dancing.'

Alex made his way through the hall and stood in the doorway of the lounge. He watched them as they sat there.

Without breaking her gaze away from the screen, his mother said: 'You all right, Alex? I can't get up, sorry! I can't miss the *semi-final!* But…hey, we haven't seen you in…what? – *years*, have we? It's good to see you, though.' She looked over to her husband as her finger pointed forward, and said bitterly: 'See, that's the guy I was telling you about! He only just managed to make it through last week. One of the lowest scores *ever*, apparently…'

Alex remained standing, watching them.

'So what brings you here, son?' his father asked, his eyes entranced ahead.

'Well, actually,' Alex said. 'I've come to kill you.'

His father broke away from the screen, looking over, laughing to himself humorously.

'I've come to kill you. You and mum.' He brought the knife out and into view.

'*Jesus!*' his father burst out. 'Turn the damn TV off, Anne!'

'*What...?!*' she snapped, her face irritated by his interruption over the judges' comments. '*What is it?*'

'JUST TURN IT OFF! *TURN IT OFF!*'

And then she saw it herself, the very thing her son held tightly in his hand. She grabbed the controller, her fingers fumbling over the buttons as her mind instantly went blank, forgetting its layout. When the standby button was eventually found, the sixty-inch rectangular light went out. Silence hit the room, with only the dimmed bulb at the ceiling keeping it half-lit.

'Take it easy, son,' his father let out slowly. 'What's this about?'

'What's this about?' Alex repeated. 'What's this *about?*'

'...Yes. We can help. We can sort things out. I'm...*listening*. Okay?' He turned to his wife. 'We can *both* listen, and – and...talk about anything. *Can't we?*'

She forced a quivering smile, her head nodding over and over again as she said '*Yes...y-yes of course! We can sor—*'

'YOU WANNA *SORT THINGS OUT*, DO YOU?!' Alex suddenly yelled, erupting in front of them. 'YOU WANNA SORT THINGS OUT *NOW*?! IS *THAT* WHAT YOU WANT?!' He began to pace up and down the lounge, his face screwing, a hand at his sweaty temple.

His father started to say: 'What do you wa—'

But Alex cut him off immediately. 'IT'S ABOUT SOMETHING THAT...THAT DOESN'T EVEN EXIST! IT'S ABOUT...*EXTRACTION!*'

'...I don't think I understand, son.'

Alex got up close to his father, pointing the tip of the knife an inch away from his eye. 'DON'T CALL ME *SON*! YOU DON'T-CALL-ME-*SON*!' He resumed pacing back and forth. 'OF COURSE YOU DON'T UNDERSTAND! *OF COURSE YOU DON'T!*'

'Whatever's happened…we can help. Just put down the knife. We are your paren—'

'*I DON'T NEED HELP!*' Alex screamed, now back with the knife in his father's face. '*I'M* NOT THE ONE! I SEE THINGS *CLEAR AS FUCKING DAY!* I SEE THINGS *CLEAR!* I SEE *EVERYTHING!* IT'S *YOU!* AND *THEM! ALL OF YOU!*'

'*Please, son…don't do anything, please!*' his father pleaded, his face swamped with fear. 'We're *just* mum and dad, *That's all.* And…if you do anything…you *won't* get away with it. You *do* know that? *Don't you…?*'

'*GET AWAY WITH IT?* WHAT MAKES YOU THINK *I CARE*?! *I WANT* PEOPLE TO KNOW! *I WANT* THEM TO FIND YOU!'

'We're *just* two-old-people. You *know* that! We're in our fifties. Come on…you-*don't*-need-to-do-this!'

'I'm sorry,' Alex smiled taking a step back, his voice simmering, yet his eyes remaining stained with ruthless rage. 'But I can't change my mind. Not now.' He took a moment to look into the petrified eyes of his parents. 'I have work to do tomorrow. And I need to be up early, you see? So I'm gonna have to kill you now.'

And then he did.

His father had put up a fight as he'd come at him, trying to wrestle his son to the ground, but his strength had not been what it once was. He'd then lain on the carpet, seconds from death after having felt the knife enter him, watching as his son turned toward his wife.

***

'*It's okay! – I don't care!*' Ed hissed at himself at 10:00pm as he thought about everything he was involved in – mostly about the fact he knew tonight was the night when Alex would be killing his parents. '*They're part of the game! They're old! I don't care about any of it, damn it!*' But he was lying, of course. Because he did care. And the past week had ensured he did. A week without sleep. A week where the face of doubt had surfaced.

His finger flicked the TV channel over again.

He took deep breaths, trying to calm himself, not being able to remove the image of an old couple being butchered by Alex – their *own* son.

(*It's fine! It doesn't matter! Keep* focused!)

And tomorrow he was going to have to be there at work, wasn't he? – knowing that soon all those people were going to die.

(*It doesn't matter! They're* just *people! Don't fall apart like this* now! – *not at the final hurdle Edward! Not at the last second! Think of what you'll have! Everybody'll want a piece of you after* – everyone will! *FOCUS FOCUS FOCUS!*)

He wouldn't even have to do anything, would he? He'd managed to persuade Alex into doing everything, having told him he wouldn't be able to leave his office due to suspicion, and that instead, he would play his part by getting as many people into the food court as possible. So that was it. He would just have to sit there and do nothing while Alex poisoned all the food and then later killed the head chef. And of course, he wouldn't take his own life like he had promised Alex. No – he would just sit in his office, talking to customers on the phone, acting like everything was fine, a normal day...

(*Just be cool! Get through tomorrow and then you* will *be there! Then you'll be at the top of that mountain! Imagine the view Edward...!*)

'I *know*, I *know!*' he hissed again. 'There *are* no problems. There is *nothing* to think about. I *know* there isn't! *I know, I know, I know!*'

274

35

Tuesday, 1 June 2010

That morning nobody even noticed the large lump at the front of Alex's jacket as he walked through reception and all the way up to his locker. He pulled out the bottle of antifreeze and placed it inside, and then carried on with his work like it was any other day. He washed the pots, put them through the dishwasher, emptied the bins, and packed away the deliveries, doing everything he would usually do on a Tuesday. Everything was seemingly normal; the chefs and catering staff were doing their jobs, and so was Alex.

At 10:45am when he noticed that the deep tray of curry had been placed into one of the large steam ovens, he went out to the Goods In corridor, opened his locker, poured some of the antifreeze into a spray bottle, and then hung the bottle by the trigger from his trouser pocket. It wouldn't even matter if anyone noticed it was there, because it looked like it was probably just a cleaning agent, and so he felt no fear in keeping it on his person. If anyone asked to use it to wipe down a worktop, it wouldn't matter. It was odourless. Nothing could give it away. And if they asked why it was a clear chemical, he would say it was water or a cleaning agent which had just been heavily diluted. Who would know? He just knew all those things wouldn't be a problem. They wouldn't be, because nobody would say anything. They wouldn't even see him, would they?

He was invisible to *Them*.

At 11:15am as he was putting some woks onto the shelving unit by the steam ovens, he noticed the ovens themselves were unattended. He went over to the one nearest and turned up the handle, releasing the lock on the large door, immediately feeling the heat escaping into his face. He removed the lid from the deep tray of curry and quietly placed it down, leaning it against the shelving behind. He looked back around the kitchen, seeing it was missing a chef. The others present

275

were either walking around or preparing food, with one of them not too far away from him. And so it was really true, wasn't it? He really was invisible. No one could see him, what he was doing, how he was about to poison the curry.

Alex took the spray bottle from his pocket, unscrewed the trigger, and poured all its contents inside, quickly stirring in the antifreeze with the large metal spoon he'd kept ready on the side of the worktop. He placed the lid back on the tray, closed the oven door, and looked around again in the direction of anyone who occupied the room. But nobody had seen anything – not a *damn* thing. It was just so *easy*, wasn't it? He continued to put away the rest of the clean washing up from the trolley and then went back to his locker to fill the spray bottle again.

Soon he saw the beans cooking on the stove unattended. So, as he walked past, he poured a quarter of the spray bottle in. He looked around the kitchen again, but everyone was still blissfully unaware of his actions. Not a single one of them was looking. They hadn't seen *a thing*, had they? It was just so simple. He was setting up the kitchen for murder. Literally. And not one of the chefs had batted an eyelid.

Before noon arrived, Alex had added the antifreeze to as many foods to be served as he could. He'd poured a quarter of the spray bottle into each of the two deep fat fryers in use, and had treated most of the other foods as he'd stood there washing up, occasionally leaning over to the worktop by the service hole to contaminate any items which had been left for the catering staff on the other side to take out to the counters. The chefs had just left the food for them, forgetting all about it. And nobody had seen him as he'd poured and sprayed the bottle over the many plastic salad trays containing kidney beans and chick peas, cucumber, pesto pasta, mixed leaf lettuce, baby potatoes, red cabbage, and tomatoes and boiled eggs. Nobody had seen him as he'd poured and sprayed over the long shallow tin with peas, the smaller shallow tin with sponge pudding, and the saucepan with custard. He'd looked around after each contamination, still making sure he hadn't been seen. But the chefs had just been too busy. And yes, being invisible had also worked to great advantage. They hadn't noticed any of his actions, and of course, every time they'd looked at the food, there'd been nothing to suggest it had been poisoned. There was no discolouring, no smell – nothing.

When 12:00 noon showed on the clock's face, Alex smiled as he heard the queuing customers chirping away in the food court, about to order their meals one by one any second.

**

Ed could barely hear the customer on the other end of the line now. He was sweating profusely, his face and body dripping. He hung up the call, cutting the man off mid-sentence, and wiped his brow before looking around the now half-empty office.

(*No! Stay* here *Edward! In a couple of hours it'll be done!*)

But his body wouldn't let him sit there any longer, and then he was up, moving, running, and soon getting into the elevator, going all the way down to the ground floor.

(*You're losing it! Keep it together Edward! Why let it all fall apart now after everything you've achieved?! Keep it fucking together!*)

He was nearly there in just over three minutes, and about to enter into the final corridor leading to the food court, feeling every precious second slipping away. As he ran around the corner, he suddenly found himself bumping into someone, knocking them straight down to the floor. The young woman shouted at him immediately. But Ed quickly bent down, grabbed her by the shoulders and interrupted with his hysterical voice: '*Have you eaten yet?!*'

'*What...?*' the woman snapped, trying to pick herself up. '*What business is it of yours? Just get away from me, would y*—'

'*HAVE YOU EATEN YET?!*'

'*NO!*' the woman told him, her eyes bulging with hostility. '*Just leave me ALONE!*'

And then Ed knew he had to run. He had to get to the food court. He *had* to stop it! Because he just couldn't go through with the plan. He just *couldn't* do it! It *wasn't* worth it! He *couldn't* let *anyone else* die! He *couldn't* let his silence kill all those people!

The double doors drew closer and closer as he ran while shouting at the people in the corridor: '*MOVE! MOVE! MOVE! OUT THE WAY! OUT THE WAY!*' He pushed through into the food court, praying, praying, praying that nobody was eating. But then he fell back against the wall as he saw it, sliding down until he hit the floor.

He could see it.

See them all there.

Eating.

Smiling.

Laughing.

It was too late. The place was already half-full – and every one of them would die.

Ed looked up at the fire alarm by his side, and knew then the only thing left to do.

***

As Alex listened to the alarm continue to ring throughout the building, he couldn't *fucking* believe it.

It was no weekly drill. It wasn't going to stop. It just kept going. Going. Going.

He couldn't believe this was happening on today of all days. Why now? Why on such an important day as *this*? And it was only 12:20pm, wasn't it? He could feel his plan and everything he had set in place being fractured, splitting in two, and deteriorating at a relentless rate. Everything was supposed to have gone *perfectly*! It was all supposed to have gone like any other *normal* day! The food was supposed to have been served till *2:00pm*. And the customers were supposed to have eaten right up till *2:00pm*!

He stood alone in front of the sink while the chefs all hurriedly left the kitchen through the fire door. In the food court the catering staff and customers could all be heard leaving also. They were *all* leaving. The *whole* building was being evacuated.

What was he going to do?! His plan had been ruined. He hadn't killed enough of them yet. Not *nearly* enough. He didn't even know how many customers who'd purchased food had had time to eat it. And how was he going to kill Sam now that he'd left? – now that he was outside amongst the crowds of people?!

Alex continued to stare at the blank wall ahead, trying to figure out his next move.

***

Sam was at the back of the car park, surrounded by the masses. Around him, the people were discussing the fire alarm, with some moaning of how they'd been set back with their work, while others warmly welcomed the extra break it had granted them. As he watched and listened, he wanted nothing more than to *be* like them. He wanted to be free, free from his mind's unyielding torment, the burden he carried and could never unload. They had such simple lives, didn't they? They could go to bed without that feeling of never wanting to wake up. He wanted so badly to rectify his mistakes. But he couldn't change what had happened. He couldn't make things right for Alex again. And he would continue to spend every day thinking about what he'd done to him, wouldn't he?

Gordon walked over to him and broke his thoughts as he asked: 'Where's the other KP, then?'

Sam said he didn't know, and then asked the other chefs and catering staff nearby if they'd seen Alex. But they all answered no. He scanned around, trying to spot him, and soon began making his way through the throngs of people, looking back and forth. But the man was nowhere to be seen.

Suddenly his feet stopped as a thought entered his mind, though.

He had thought of a way to help Alex – *maybe*. And maybe it could even help free a miniscule amount of his pain. He was going to go back in there and find him. He was going to go back into that building and get Alex out. He even wished for there to be a real fire taking place inside, and that Alex would be trapped, and that *he* could then save him. He wanted to be able to save Alex, even if it meant burning, experiencing unbearable pain in the process – even dying to save his life.

Sam was off, running down the car park toward the Goods In back door, and before long, swinging it open, shouting '*Alex?! You in here?! Alex!*' He moved past the walk-in fridge, thinking about how good it felt to have been at least attempting to do something to help the man. And then he was praying for a fire, a life-threatening situation to have taken place which had caused the man to have fallen and slipped and broken his ankle or become unconscious somehow, to enable him to pick him up and carry him out. He wanted to save his life so badly. In *whatever way* that might be. He wanted to be able to save *Alex*. He wanted to—

But as he turned the corner of the corridor he wasn't thinking anything anymore. He'd run into something. He could feel something which had gone through him. And then he could see what it was. He could see the knife inside his stomach, the blood flowing out.

As Sam looked up into Alex's sunken wild eyes and tried to speak, the knife suddenly stabbed in and out again, in and out, in and out, again, and again, and again...

***

He let Sam's body slump to the floor, and took a moment to look down at it, the incessant ringing of the fire alarm still sounding. He then opened the walk-in freezer and dragged him inside. Soon after, once closing the door behind him, he stopped to get his breath, having not expected him to have been so heavy. Now all he had to do was go and find Layna. She was the last on the list. Once he had killed her – and *freed* himself after – it would all be over.

And then as if it were fate, as if the plan was being governed by a higher being – of God even – he received a call on his mobile from that very woman, a call in which she told him she needed to meet urgently, and was outside his flat.

Well this is real easy isn't it? he thought. *She's making this real easy isn't she Alex?*

He slid the knife down into his pocket and made his way to reception.

***

Layna waited outside Alex's front door with the envelope in her hand. She knew when he got there, if he would actually come, that he most definitely wouldn't want to talk. But she would try her best to talk to *him*, and if it didn't work, she would make sure he at least got the letter. She pulled it out from the envelope, reading again what she'd written:

Alex,

280

I don't know what has happened. I don't know what was said or what wasn't. Maybe it was all Sam? Maybe it was all him? Maybe it was just his lies? But now I have to find out the truth. I need to know how you really feel. I need to know if you love me. Because I love you. I want to be with you, and I don't think anyone else has ever understood me the way you did. I'm just praying that Sam was lying about all those things he told me you said about me. I know now that they couldn't be true. They just can't be.

Please, just think about things. Let me know how you really feel.

Layna

***

He drove home thinking about everything that woman had done to him, the way she'd lied to him, used him, betrayed him, all the time thinking she could get away with it. But guess what? She wasn't going to get away with it, was she? *Uh, uh.* Not now. That was the dumbest call she'd ever made. And when he got home, she would feel the knife just as Sam had. Soon she would be dead. Soon *he* would kill her.

After he parked and got out the car, slamming the door behind, he could see her through the window up on the second floor waiting. He waved to her, though she could not see him, saying out loud, almost singing to himself: '*You're-gon-na-fuck-ing-die...*'

***

As she started to wonder where he was and if he was actually going to show, she heard footsteps coming up the stairs. But it wasn't him. She watched as the old lady crossed the hall, entering into her flat.

But then she could hear more footsteps coming up, and as they grew louder, she felt nervous. Nervous about seeing him, about that moment where she would look into his eyes. And it seemed like it had been a long, *long* time since that had happened.

He was now there. There he was. It was *him*. And she noticed instantly that a lot had changed. He looked awful as he approached her, cold, emotionless, not saying a word while his hand quickly withdrew something shiny from his pocket.

'Alex, thanks for coming and...leaving work early,' she said, her voice unsettled and awkward, yet desperate to get the words across. 'I *really* needed to speak to you.'

The key in his hand went into the door, turning and unlocking it, his head soon nodding forward, prompting for her to go inside. He followed her in, closing the door behind, and stared at the back of her head as she walked on through to the lounge where she started to say 'I just don't know where to start, Alex, I...'

But as she turned around he was already there, and then he plunged the knife deep inside her stomach. Her body went limp in an instant, crashing down to the floor.

'AH, DON'T FUCKING *CRY*!' Alex screamed. 'DON'T YOU *LIKE* PAIN?! HUH? *HUH?!*' He began to pace up and down the room, his eyes not leaving her. 'WHAT DID YOU THINK? – THAT YOU'D WALK AWAY *SCOT-FREE* AFTER WHAT YOU DID? AFTER WHAT *YOU DID*?! *HUH?!*'

She managed to release the word '*Alex...*' as she reached her hand out to him. But then he started again with 'OH, *P-LEASE*...! WHAT ARE YOU DOING? YOU WANT HELP? IS *THAT* IT? HOW *FUCKING TOUCHING*! *I* WON'T HELP YOU, THOUGH! NOT ME, YOU *DISGUSTING FUCK*!' He stopped pacing and stepped closer, looking down into her eyes. 'YOU'RE GOING TO HELL, *YOU KNOW THAT*? LOOK AT YOU! YOU'RE DYING, LAYNA! YOU'RE FUCKING DYING, AREN'T YOU?! LOOK AT YOU! *LOOK AT YOU NOW!*'

He then stopped talking. He was so tired, panting like an exhausted animal, watching as her arm slowly lowered itself down to the floor. Her breathing continued to diminish, becoming shorter, shorter. Weaker, weaker.

And soon, Alex saw her die.

But as he leaned over the desk, trying to draw air into his lungs, something caught his attention. It was an envelope. It was inside her hand which had seconds ago been reaching up to him. He hadn't noticed it at the time, though.

He moved over to her, bending down, snatching it from her lifeless fingers. He sat down on the floor and looked at it, reading the handwritten word *Alex*. And even though he didn't care about what was inside, he ripped into it, pulled out the piece of paper, unfolded it and began to read the letter.

But then something happened. Something was wrong. As he read through the words he could feel it. Something was *seriously* wrong. It was the letter. It was causing a reaction from within. *Was it true? Was what he was reading true?* Had Layna not really said all those things about him? Had she not deliberately used and abandoned him? Had she in fact *liked him*, understood him – even *loved* him? Was it Sam who had lied? Had it just been Sam's lies *all along*?

Alex was now feeling light-headed, unbalanced, besieged with shock, and extremely aware of reality, where he was, who he was, and of the very letter he held in his bloodied hands. The black fog was draining, leaving his body at a rapid rate. He could feel the hatred, the wrath, fading away fast. It was like the sudden great self-awareness was constricting his throat. And when he could breathe again, he realised what else he was becoming aware of.

For a moment he sat there in the silence of the room, looking down to Layna by his side, her eyes still open. He could feel his lips shaking, trembling, his eyes about to spill out tears. But he knew, knew, *knew* that it was wrong. The letter – what he'd read so far – was *WRONG, wasn't it? It had to be! It had to be, didn't it?! It just had to be!*

He knew he had to finish it, though. Finish the rest of the letter. He *had* to.

***

After reading the last word, Alex dropped the letter to the floor. He knew it was all true now. He knew the truth. But it was all too late.

He began to cry, his head falling into his hands. '*No…oh God, oh God, no…*' he sobbed through quivering lips.

As the raging voice inside his mind tried to return, he fought it off by focusing on one word: *Love*. Because Layna had *loved* him. She had *actually* loved him, hadn't she? She hadn't been like *Them*. She hadn't been like *Them* at all. He had found his *one*, the one who had *understood* him, the one who could *see* him. And *he* had loved her. He had loved her, but now...

But now...

He took hold of her hand, cradling it gently, looking up to the ceiling and smiling while the tears ran down his face.

'You were *real*,' he said. 'You were the one.'

More from the Author

For all the latest information on Sidney Knight and his newest works, please visit his website at www.sidneyknight.com

In addition to his website, he can also be contacted via Facebook and Twitter.

Printed in Great Britain
by Amazon